THESE CROOKED THINGS

Also by Ellen Byerrum

The Art Deco Mysteries

Crook Tales for Two

The Crime of Fashion Mysteries

Killer Hair

Designer Knockoff

Hostile Makeover

Raiders of the Lost Corset

Grave Apparel

Armed and Glamorous

Shot Through Velvet

Death on Heels

Veiled Revenge

Lethal Black Dress

The Masque of the Red Dress

The Brief Luminous Flight of the Firefly (series prequel)

Thrillers

The Woman in the Dollhouse

Plays, writing as Eliot Byerrum

Boom Town Blues

Interviewing Techniques for the Self-Conscious

Red She Said

Ghost Dance

A Christmas Cactus

Gumshoe Rendezvous

Father Jeremy's Christmas Jubilee

The Angel of Death Rises Early

Books for younger readers

The Children Didn't See Anything

Sherlocktopus Holmes: Eight Arms of the Law

The Cassidy James Stories

The Last Goodbye of Harris Turner

The End of Summer

The Portuguese Sailor (to be published 2026)

Praise for Ellen Byerrum

These Crooked Things

"I love this series! The mystery is twisty and puzzling, set against the background of depression-era New York, but the characters are what drew me in and kept me transfixed." *(Goodreads reviewer)*

"Stylish period clothes and banter remind me of classic films. The 1934 mystery is too lively to be considered a 'cozy'... The characters are very well developed and even the 'bad' guys are amusing and have some growth." *(Amazon reviewer)*

"Catchy dialogue. Wonderful caper. Reminds me of the old Thin Man movies." *(Amazon reviewer)*

"This delightful story is full of twists and turns and is not without the occasional comic relief... Very, very satisfying." *(Amazon reviewer)*

"Fast-paced from the word go. Characters were varied and the settings of the theatre and the theatre lifestyle caught my interest." *(Mystica blog)*

Crook Tales for Two
CIPA EVVY Gold Book Award 2024
First place, Mystery/Crime/Detective category

"A romantic murder mystery romp that sets the stage for a fun and entertaining read. A delightful tale with wit, charm and style!" *(Nancy J. Cohen, author of The Bad Hair Day Mysteries)*

"Ellen Byerrum's research is impeccable and the writing style is so immersive, you are transported back in time to join playwright Esme LaForet as she frets about her play's opening night on Broadway, but a series of unfortunate events cause her to become entangled in the darker side of New York with a hero that is not all that he seems!... A really intelligent, well thought-out, entertaining caper and so well put together! I was captivated from start to finish!" *(Ink R. blog)*

"This novel was a joy to read. The writer has a wonderful writing style. Multiple threads are pulled together. The reader is left guessing until the end. I strongly recommend this book for lovers of good mysteries." *(NetGalley reviewer Larry C., media/journalist)*

Killer Hair (also a movie)

"Girlfriends you'd love to have, romance you can't resist, and Beltway-insider insights you've got to read. Adds a crazy twist to the concept of capital murder." *(Agatha Award winner Sarah Strohmeyer)*

Designer Knockoff

"Clever wordplay, snappy patter, and intriguing clues make this politics-meets-high-fashion whodunit a cut above the ordinary." *(Romantic Times)*

"A very talented writer with an offbeat sense of humor." *(The Best Reviews)*

Hostile Makeover (also a movie)

"Byerrum pulls another superlative Crime of Fashion out of her vintage cloche." (*Chick Lit Books*)

"As smooth as fine-grade cashmere." (*Publishers Weekly*)

"Totally delightful...a fun and witty read." (*Fresh Fiction*)

Raiders of the Lost Corset

"I love this series. Lacey is such a wonderful character. The plot has many twists and turns to keep you turning the pages to discover the truth. I highly recommend this book and series." (*Spinetingler Magazine*)

"Wow. I loved it! I could not put it down! I loved everything about the book, from the characters to the plot to the fast-paced and witty writing." (*Roundtable Reviews*)

Grave Apparel

"A truly intriguing mystery." (*Armchair Reader*)

"A likeable, sassy, and savvy heroine, and the Washington, D.C., setting is a plus." (*The Romance Readers Connection*)

Armed and Glamorous

"Whether readers are fashion divas or hopelessly fashion-challenged, there's a lot to like about being *Armed and Glamorous*." (*BookPleasures.com*)

Shot Through Velvet

"First-rate...a serious look at the decline of the U.S. textile and newspaper industries provides much food for thought." (*Publishers Weekly*, starred review)

"Great fun, with lots of interesting tidbits about the history of the U.S. fashion industry." (*Suspense Magazine*)

Death on Heels

"Terrific! A fabulous Crime of Fashion Mystery." (*Genre Go Round Reviews*)

"I loved the touch that Lacey was a reporter trying to track down a murderer, but could always be counted on for her fashion-forward thinking as well. If you haven't yet picked up a Lacey Smithsonian novel, I suggest you do!" (*Chick Lit+*)

"Lacey is a character that I instantly fell in love with." (*Turning the Pages*)

Veiled Revenge

"An intriguing plot, fun but never too insane characters, and a likable and admirable heroine all combine to create a charming and well-crafted mystery." (*Kings River Life Magazine*)

"Like fine wine that gets better with age, *Veiled Revenge* is the best book yet in this fabulous series." (*Dru's Book Musings*)

Lethal Black Dress

"Only a fashion reporter with a nose for vintage dresses could sniff out the clues in this brilliantly conceived murder mystery." *(Nancy J. Cohen, author of the Bad Hair Day Mysteries)*

The Masque of the Red Dress

"It's been too long since the last Crime of Fashion mystery, and fans will delight in seeing their favorite characters return in this eleventh of the series... Author Byerrum makes the scenery come alive not just with descriptions of gorgeous couture of multiple eras, but with the unique personalities populating the struggling-to-survive newsroom. The combination of cynicism and hope is never more apparent than with these jaded reporters, who are accustomed to interns getting blamed by ego-driven politicians... The Fashion Bites articles of tips and the history of D.C. fashion continue to be refreshing and fun, highlighting tips to battle office low-thermostat hypothermia, the need for formal wear rules, and of course, the power of a red dress. This is a welcome return to an enthralling and always entertaining mystery series." *(Cynthia Chow, KRL News & Reviews)*

The Brief Luminous Flight of the Firefly

"Byerrum does a remarkable job of describing what life was like during the 1940s and in presenting an intriguing mystery." *(Grace Topping, author of the Laura Bishop home-staging mysteries)*

"This is an engrossing mystery set in a meticulously researched and fascinating historical context. The filigree of fashion throughout the book amusingly illuminates character and period. Mimi Smith is a worthy precursor to Lacey Smithsonian and *The Brief Luminous Flight of the Firefly* is a worthy precursor to the Crime of Fashion Mystery series." *(Paul Donnelly, award winning playwright)*

"The story is compelling and mysterious and the attention to everyday historical realities brings the era to life." *(Martha Horstman-Evans, award winning director and playwright)*

Sherlocktopus Holmes: Eight Arms of the Law

"The rhymes are so happy, some will make you laugh out loud. If you read it aloud to others you can all enjoy the wordplay. And each verse will help you discover clues to your case, to help find where Sally's missing doll may be hiding." *(Wendy Kendall, MLT News, MyEdmondsNews.com)*

"Great rhymes! Wonderful clues! A first detective novel for young readers. The illustrations are marvelous." *(Beth Schmelzer, BestBooksByBeth.wordpress.com)*

"This clever children's book combines rhymes, education and entertainment, in a charming story that's a tale of mystery accompanied by colorful illustrations." *(Nancy J. Cohen, author of the Bad Hair Day Mysteries)*

The Woman in the Dollhouse

"An ingeniously crafted psychological thriller that bewitches on page one and continues to mesmerize until its shocking conclusion... We can't imagine a better read. Byerrum has deftly structured a compelling narrative that never lets go. You won't either, by the way. This is one book you're practically guaranteed to finish in record time." (*Best Thrillers.com*)

"Reminiscent of the best of gothic suspense fiction, readers will be thoroughly entertained by Tennyson. Her strong will and even sharper wit ensure that readers will be cheering for Tennyson to break free and discover the truth. That the book starts with such a vulnerable beginning only makes the crafty conclusion all the more satisfying." (*Kings River Life Magazine*)

Other praise for Ellen Byerrum's writing

"Devilishly funny. Lacey is intelligent, insightful and spunky... thoroughly likable." (*The Sun, Bremerton, WA*)

"Laced with wicked wit." (*SouthCoastToday.com*)

"Fun and witty...with a great female sleuth." (*Fresh Fiction*)

"A load of stylish fun." (*Scripps Howard News Service*)

"Always well-written, entertaining, and stylish." (*More Than a Review*)

"Skewers Washington with style." (*Agatha award winner Elaine Viets*)

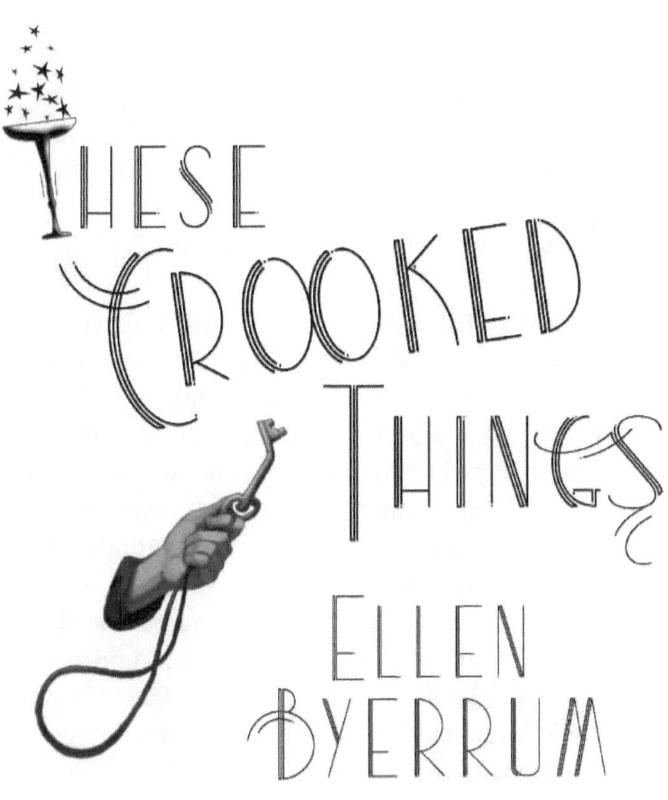

THESE CROOKED THINGS

ELLEN BYERRUM

Lethal Black Dress Press

Visit Ellen Byerrum online at ellenbyerrum.com
facebook.com/EllenByerrum
instagram.com/ellenbyerrumauthor
youtube.com/@ellenbyerrumsfashionbites2378

THESE CROOKED THINGS

ONE

I'D SEEN DEAD things before. But I'd never seen anything as dead as Duncan Balmain, stretched out on the expensive Persian carpet in his lavish Upper East Side apartment.

Once the antic party boy, known for his irrepressible pranks and handsome face, Duncan was now a lifeless shell in a tuxedo and white shirt, his perpetual tan fading to ashes. He lay on his back, jacket open, revealing a bullet hole in his chest, his hands up, eyes half closed. There was minimal blood on the front of his shirt, but much more had seeped through his back onto the expensive rug. Although his position suggested he had been surprised, there was no expression on his face. Whatever he had been thinking he took to his grave.

Many would say Duncan got what he deserved. Others might withhold judgment, but Duncan's reputation came with a lot of baggage. A rich boy who bought his way out of troubles—but not this time.

The scene was disturbed by overturned lamps, a coffee table on its side, a smashed mirror, and a corpse sprinkled with shards of glass.

Graydon and I had arrived a few minutes before at Duncan's swanky uptown apartment. Needless to say, we never expected to see the owner laid out on the floor. Drunk, perhaps, by reputation, but not lifeless.

We were dressed for the party we had just left, not a death scene. Graydon was in his top hat and tails, looking insanely suave, but quite somber. My sky-blue silk gown featured plenty of sparkles and sequins that clung to my figure. The dress was not quite suitable to the November chill, but it was the style and every woman at our gala had worn even skimpier dresses.

A butler opened the apartment door to us, let us into the generous foyer, and collected our overcoats without looking directly at us. I patted my hair in a mirror over a marble console bearing a handsome marble bowl where someone had left a ring of silver and brass keys, one of which was a bent skeleton key that I doubted would open anything. Attached to the ring was a round medallion with initials in a fancy script: D. B.

The butler returned and ushered us into the living room without a word. There was a sharp smell of gunpowder and iron—or blood—in the air. The surroundings were handsome and modern in the Art Deco style, monochromatic in soothing shades of green, but the pictures on the wall were slanted, as if caught in the fracas.

We hadn't been informed that this investigation involved a death. I gasped and held my breath. But I did not scream.

"Have the police been called?" Graydon asked.

"No, sir, Mr. Chaseborn. Only you. I am awaiting instructions from Mr. Balmain Senior."

The man who opened the door brought a sheet to cover the body, but Graydon gestured that he shouldn't touch anything, and we stepped around bloodstains on the floor. There was a spotted trail of dark red from the room where the victim lay to another room down the hall. Whatever had happened before, what scene of mayhem, Duncan Balmain now appeared undisturbed.

"Were there any other staff at home?" Graydon asked.

"No sir. The cook and housekeeper have left. I'm the only one who lives here with the Balmains." The butler was middle-aged with thinning hair, unremarkable save for his English accent. Not quite the same accent as Graydon's; perhaps a little less posh.

A tearful older man with a Scotch in one hand and an unlit cigar in the other stumbled in from a handsome book-lined library. It was as if he were following the crimson stream. His eyes were bloodshot, his hair was wild, and his hands were shaking. The butler lingered in the background, as silent as the bronze statues that flanked the mantel.

"Esmé, are you all right?" I felt Graydon's hand on my shoulder. My fingers reached for his. "Elf?"

Graydon liked to call me "Elf" and I knew he thought I looked like one. My face was heart-shaped and my eyes were blue green, slightly slanted up; however, my ears were not and never have been pointed.

I knew my fiancé was not happy about my presence. We were new at this being-engaged business, and I had talked him into taking me along on this sudden call, away from the gala.

"Thank you for bringing me with you." I gazed up at him and he relented, his eyes crinkling with his own smile. "I know you didn't want me here."

"I still don't. Even more now." Nevertheless, he took my hand and gently squeezed my fingers. Graydon Chase was many things, among them some kind of private investigator, or as he preferred, an *inquiry agent* into all things financial—and now criminal.

He told me earlier, when we were interrupted at the gala, that answering the senior Balmain's call would no doubt be long and tedious, involving boring paperwork and missing money. Now that we'd stumbled (figuratively) onto a corpse, that would require far more than paperwork. It would require police.

"I could leave." Who was I kidding? I wasn't leaving. I wanted to know what happened.

"Sadly, not until the police come."

"Who said anything about the police?" bellowed the angry old man who lingered in the hallway. He was the dead man's father, Edward Balmain. "No police, Chaseborn. I've heard about your work and your discretion. And I didn't know who else to call."

He gulped more Scotch. The fact that he used "Chaseborn" instead of Graydon's business moniker of "Chase" told me Balmain came from the upper echelon of society and knew Graydon from those rarefied circles.

"The police must be called," Graydon said. "If you won't call them, I will."

I bit my lip to keep from shouting, *What the hell is wrong with you, you old fool? Call the police!*

The man seemed to notice me for the first time. "Who is she? Why is she here?"

"My associate, Miss Esmé de LaForet. She can be trusted." I'm not sure Graydon believed that, but it was nice of him to say so. He refrained from saying I came from a part of society the upper class hated. I'd been a reporter and was now a playwright who'd achieved some notoriety. It was a time when many people still believed a decent woman should only be named in the paper at birth, death, or marriage. "Esmé, allow me to present Mr. Edward Balmain."

I recognized "Old Moneybags," as the newspapers sometimes called him. Edward Balmain was the president and owner of Balmain Construction, which supplied labor for some of New York City's biggest projects. His hardened look and callused hands testified that he'd once spent time pounding nails and lifting loads of timber himself, before ascending to his current position.

He also owned a bank; whether for prestige or convenience, I didn't know. By reputation he was a hard, cold businessman, willing to throw women and children out on the streets or onto the railroad tracks, as the melodramas would have it. He famously claimed unions caused the Depression, and his company had been fighting them tooth and nail.

His son, the late Duncan, on the other hand, looked overly refined in a prep school way. I hadn't seen Duncan alive, merely in news photos with a supercilious smile that even in print made you want to slap him. And now there he was on the floor, lying in his own blood. Minus the smile.

"My son." Balmain's voice broke. "My dead son Duncan. That she-devil destroyed him."

"Are you referring to your daughter-in-law, Maura Balmain?"

I had seen the names of all the Balmains in the society pages while seeking information on Rupert Chaseborn, aka Graydon Chase, my fiancé. When I saw the younger Balmains' names, Duncan and Maura, they were inevitably described as one of the "It Couples."

However, the subtext of the news stories revealed that despite being married, Duncan Balmain was a notorious drunkard and skirt chaser. His father was a respected, if cement-hearted businessman, but all Duncan had managed to do was fail upward through a series of jobs.

I learned less about the beautiful Maura. She seemed to fill her time with charity work involving children, but she came from a "less desirable class" of people, which probably meant hard-working, less educated, and most likely Irish.

"She killed him in cold blood," Balmain blurted.

She did? That was a shock.

"Where's the gun?" Graydon asked him.

"She must have it with her."

"Where is she?" I asked.

"Her bedroom. Locked herself in." He gestured toward the hallway and the bloodstains with his glass of Scotch. "She's going to prison. I'll see to it. Put her in the chair, I will."

"I want to see her," I said.

"She won't talk to you. She wouldn't talk to me."

"It's worth a try."

Graydon raised his eyebrow. "Subtly, Esmé. And do stay out of the line of fire."

"That witch just married him for his money! My money," Edward Balmain shouted at Graydon, while I stepped gingerly over the trail of blood to where "the witch" was supposed to be hiding.

I knocked on the witch's door.

Two

"GO AWAY," A tear-choked voice yelled. There was a hiccup.

"Maura, my name is Esmé de LaForet. I'd like to hear your side of the story."

"Who are you?" I heard hard breathing.

"I'm an associate of Rupert Chaseborn, also known as Graydon, Graydon Chase. Your father-in-law called him, but he hasn't called the police yet."

"It doesn't matter, they'll fry me. If I'm not dead already." Sobs grew louder and she gasped for air. "Do you work with—with Rupert?"

I was alarmed at her reference to being *dead already*. And I didn't know I'd be asked for my qualifications.

"Yes. Sometimes. Balmain says you killed your husband." More sobs came from behind the door. "He says it's cold-blooded murder. But there are many reasons that people take a life. I want to hear your story."

"They'll never believe me. Why hasn't Edward called the police yet?"

"He doesn't want this in the papers. He seems very concerned about the papers."

"That damned old bastard. Of course he wants to keep it out of the papers."

I detected a slight Irish accent. I tried again.

"I don't know who else is going to listen to you, Maura. But I will. I promise. And wouldn't you rather talk to a woman?"

The lock clicked and the door cracked open. I put out a hand to warn the men not to storm the room. A swollen blackened eye peered out at me. No gun.

"Graydon," I said over my shoulder. "I need ice and clean towels."

I heard him direct the butler as I opened the door wide enough to slip through. I shut the door and quickly re-locked it. Maura and I studied each other for a moment. Her black eye was the most apparent injury. When her robe slipped off her shoulder there was a patchwork of bruises on her skin. Across her abdomen, blood seeped through her nightgown in a jagged line.

"Something terrible happened to you tonight, Maura."

She swayed on her feet. I rushed to keep her from falling. Her face was wet with tears and her skin blotchy from crying. I helped her back to bed, where more blood stained the covers, blood that now stained my gown. She slumped against the padded blue headboard and piles of matching pillows. The room had a bathroom with a shower. I found a washcloth and wet it to wipe her face.

"Tell me about your husband," I said.

"Duncan was so handsome, such a catch," she said through labored breaths. "I was so lucky he wanted me, everyone told me how lucky I was." It was an effort for her to talk. Tears leaked from her eyes. There was a discreet knock at the door. I opened it a crack.

"Your ice, Miss." The butler handed me the ice and towels. Graydon held back Balmain, and I slammed the door with one hip and relocked it. I covered some ice with a towel.

"Hold this on your eye."

She winced. "It hurts."

"You don't have a maid?"

"A lady's maid? No. I like to do for myself, and the housekeeper, Mrs. Bailey, helps out if I need it. There's a cook half the week. They were here when I married Duncan. I never felt they liked me."

"Did Duncan do this to you? The eye? The rest of it?"

She sighed. "It's not the first time. Everyone in New York thinks I do nothing but walk into walls."

"Did the staff know?"

"Everybody knows. Nobody says anything."

"Not even Mrs. Bailey?" I was surprised. My part time cleaning lady, Amelia Applegate, had an opinion about everything, including her job title. She told everyone she was my 'head housekeeper.'

"She keeps the house stocked with ice bags and aspirin. They all steer clear of Duncan when he's in a mood." Maura was breathing hard.

What was there to say? Prince Charming had turned into the Beast. An old story.

"You should lie back on the bed." I helped her with the pillows.

"He wasn't the same person I met." She sounded as weary as anyone I'd ever known. "It was good at first. Wonderful. He took me dancing, he bought me presents. But there were rules. So many rules. I always had to be perfect, look perfect, do the right things, say the right things, wear the right clothes."

"Are you wounded? Your stomach." I gestured to the blood. For all I knew it could have come from her dead husband.

"I have been wounded since the day I married him. Duncan became so critical," Maura continued. "He started to compare me with other women. Every other woman. The women he could have married."

I handed her a clean towel. She lifted the nightgown, revealing a huge gash, and placed the towel gently on her abdomen. I bit my tongue to keep from screaming at the open slash on her belly. She groaned in pain.

Maura Balmain didn't resemble the gorgeous bride in the silver-framed photograph sitting on the dresser. Her eyes in that tinted picture were dark blue under raven eyebrows. Her hair was glossy and black, longer than the popular styles. But now her skin was deathly white. She'd lost a lot of blood. I'd heard enough stories from enough women to know that if a man hits a woman, he will do it again. Violence was inside him like a devil, written in police reports and newspapers and whispered from woman to woman.

"Tonight. What happened tonight, Maura?"

"Drunk as usual. Or cocaine." She sobbed. "More and more, it was the coke that made him crazy. He called it 'nose candy.' I thought he'd be happy when I told him he was going to be a daddy. But he didn't want the baby. He never did." Blood was seeping through the towel.

"You're pregnant?"

"Three months gone." It came out in a whisper. "I was. I still might be if I live through the night." She reached one hand across her belly, protecting the babe that we both hoped was still there. I stared at the blood on her nightgown. How deep was that wound?

"Good God. Duncan cut you?" I saw a discarded garment on the floor, pink silk, soaked with blood. "We have to get you to a doctor."

"No. I'm not leaving. I'm not going to jail."

I hoped she wouldn't go to the mortuary. "I know a nurse. But you need a doctor—"

"If the police don't get me. If I don't die first."

"You're not going to die. I won't let you." I had no idea if she would die or not. I pressed the towel as gently as I could to her abdomen. She breathed heavily.

"He said I couldn't have it. I'm supposed to stay thin and beautiful. That was our bargain. Women who have babies get fat and ugly. That's what Duncan says. But I was so happy, because I wouldn't be lonely anymore."

"What happened next?"

"He said he was going to cut it out of me. He tried to. He did this. He grabbed a big hunting knife from over the mantel and came after me. But he tripped over that damn expensive rug. I ran to the library, where he keeps his guns."

She closed her eyes.

"The gun?"

"My brother taught me how to shoot. I tried to get the pistol out of the desk drawer, but he slashed me, slashed at my belly. I couldn't let him kill my baby! I threw the ashtray at him, gave me time to get the gun. I thought he would stop when I pointed it at him, but he lunged at me. I squeezed the trigger."

"His body is in the living room, not the library," I said, staring at the tears running down her face.

"I didn't want him dead. I want my baby to live. Baby should have a father. I shot him, but he wouldn't stop. I ran to the living room. Duncan kept coming. I had to stop him, so I kept shooting until he stopped. Murdered a couple of lamps. Assassinated the fancy mirror."

"Where's the gun now?" I asked.

"On the floor." She pointed at a big automatic on the carpet by the door. "I locked myself in here with it. I was afraid he'd break the door down."

Maura's eyes were glassy. I left the gun where it lay and picked up the extension phone on her bedside table. I called Nurse Jesse O'Banyon, and I explained the situation. I begged her to come.

"How far along is she?"

"It's early days," I said, and Maura put up three fingers. "About three months."

"Be there as soon as I can. Try to stop the bleeding. See if there's a doctor in that building. You're near that fancy Doctors Hospital. People with problems and a scandal and money, they go there. Keep the patient quiet."

Jesse had tended both Graydon and me when we were struck by the flu virus that was still raging all over town. Jesse's matter-of-fact competence calmed my nerves. I assured her there was no problem with being paid. I'd guarantee it myself.

"I'll ask the butler if there's a doctor."

"It's a butler kind of building, is it? Let me slip into my fresh uniform. Cops don't bother me when I'm on a case wearing my blue cape and cap."

Maura lay back on the pillows, weeping. I urged her to conserve her strength. I opened the door and called Graydon over. He and Balmain were waiting for me. I slipped into the hall and guarded the door with my body.

"What the hell is going on?" the old man demanded, in my face before Graydon could block him. "Why did she kill my son? My only child?"

Graydon pulled him back. "I've called Jesse O'Banyon," I said to Graydon. "She'll be over here soon. Can you alert the doorman? In the meantime, we need a doctor. It's bad."

I stepped forward and noticed both men looking horrified at my dress. I'd forgotten about the blood. I looked down. It was worse than I thought. Ruined.

"My God, Esmé, what happened to you? Are you all right?"

"It's not my blood. It's Maura's." I turned to the butler. He was instantly at my elbow.

"Sebastian, Miss."

Sebastian turned out to be almost as capable as Robbins, Graydon's valet. He would call for the doctor and alert the front door that a nurse was on her way.

"I don't want a scene! The publicity!" Balmain complained. "We don't need a doctor. My son is dead." He was a man in pain, but my well of sympathy was running pretty low.

"What about the police?" I asked Graydon.

"I called a detective I know at this precinct. He understands how *delicate* this is. He's coming over, but taking his time. As he put it, 'Don't touch nothing, and make sure the stiff ain't going nowhere.'"

I gathered the detective was giving us time to come up with some kind of story. Fine by me. I didn't give a damn about Duncan Balmain or his very important father.

"He's dead, isn't he? Where's he going to go?"

"You're pretty uppity, girlie." Balmain glared at me.

I turned to face him. "Your son tried to cut the baby out of her body. Maura was protecting her unborn child."

His jaw dropped and he staggered back. "Impossible!" he sputtered. "Duncan told me she couldn't have children. Another reason I was against this marriage, to that trash."

"Oh really? There are two sides to every story. Your fabulous Duncan didn't want her to have a baby and ruin her figure."

I looked at Graydon, but he was as shocked as I have ever seen him. He held me back from tearing Balmain's face off.

"It's a lie," Balmain said.

I stared at the corpse of his son, despising a man I'd never even known. We were silent for a moment. Sebastian finished his calls. Like all good butlers, he stored information like a magpie and he knew most of the building's residents.

"Doctor Parkhurst should be here in a jiffy," he said. "She resides on the eighth floor. She works at the clinic for women."

"Are you sure about this, Esmé?" Graydon asked. "About Maura?'

"I'm sure that's her story. She's bleeding badly and I have to get back to her. The doctor will give us a better picture."

"My son." Balmain gulped more Scotch. "He was perfect."

"Your perfect son apparently was two different people," I spat. "Jekyll and Hyde. One face for the public, the other, the darker one, only his wife saw. I'm surprised you didn't know that."

"She's going to pay—"

"I'm concerned that she doesn't lose her baby after this."

"Baby? If there really is a baby." His expression held fear, anguish, and some tiny scrap of hope. If Maura was as much an 'Irish peasant' as Balmain seemed to think, she would have the strength to live, I thought. Then she could lead a rebellion against him.

I returned to Maura, asleep, still breathing. I compressed her wound and watched over her while we all waited. Doctor Wren Parkhurst arrived shortly, and then came the indomitable Jesse. It turned out the two women knew each other and worked well in tandem. Doctor Parkhurst seemed weary, but her dark eyes were lively and kind. Her brown hair, shot with a few strands of gray, was pulled back in a frizzy chignon, her shoes sensible.

"Where is she?" I opened the door for the women. She took in the situation at a glance. "Oh Holy God," was all she said. I left her and Jesse to do what they could.

Sebastian greeted me with a toddy on a silver tray.

"Honey and whisky, hot. Mr. Chaseborn suggested you might like it."

"Thank you." I looked to Graydon and suddenly my eyes were wet. I blinked back tears and lifted the glass. The warm liquid was comforting, but my blood-soaked dress made me shiver.

"You have, darling, from time to time, mentioned something about an Irish cure, and I thought this might help." He clinked his own glass against mine.

"Exactly so." I would have liked to hurl myself at him, take comfort in his arms, but it wasn't the time or the place, and I would bloody his tuxedo. I heard soft voices behind the door, but I couldn't make out the words. The doctor soon opened the door, requested an ambulance, no sirens. They could take the service elevator up.

"Maura?" I feared the worst, but Dr. Parkhurst assured me that Mrs. Balmain was holding her own. She needed to be transferred to the hospital as soon as possible. I later found that ambulances from Doctors Hospital refrained from using sirens so as not to disturb people in their tony Upper East Side residences.

"And she wants to talk to you."

I stepped back in the room. Maura was awake and seemed calmer. "You can't wear that gown, Esmé. Not like that. Take one of mine."

"I couldn't."

"I have too many. Please take it. It's a poor thank-you for saving my life. It's never been worn. It will look fine on you and your red-gold hair. You're Irish, I'd guess."

"Half Irish. And really, I couldn't."

Jesse stepped forward with a dress Maura had selected for me. A lovely royal purple cashmere dress with a wide soft collar, trimmed in pink.

"She picked it out and I think it will fit you. You can clean up in there." Jesse gave me a gentle shove toward the bathroom. "Go on, you look cold. I don't want you getting sick again."

It was a kindness I wouldn't soon forget. I brushed out my hair and wiped spots of blood off my face, arms, and chest. I took off my lovely ruined blue gown and put on the deep purple dress. I didn't realize how chilled I'd been until then.

I took a glance in the mirror and decided I looked somber enough to greet the police.

Three

I COUNTED MAURA Balmain darned lucky that the officers who arrived were a couple of Irish Catholic cops with a total of ten children (or so they claimed) between them. The detective who followed was likewise a Mick named O'Hara, Desmond O'Hara, Graydon's contact, who clearly disliked the ultra-rich who played by their own set of rules.

We all converged in the foyer as the police arrived, the ambulance attendants, Dr. Wren Parkhurst, Nurse Jesse, and Graydon and I. Only Balmain Senior stood rooted where he was in the living room, a furious drunk standing guard over his dead child. He wiped his tears with a wet handkerchief. The blood drained from Officer Clancy's face when he heard what Duncan had done to his pregnant wife, his attempt to murder his own child.

"She has a good chance of making it and keeping the baby," Dr. Parkhurst said, "but she needs quiet and care right now. Is there coffee?"

As if he were psychic, Sebastian emerged from the kitchen with a tray of very hot and black brew. He served the ladies first. Dr. Parkhurst drank hers quickly and Jesse followed suit. I supposed they were used to grabbing whatever they could in their spare minutes.

Deathly pale, Maura was wheeled out on a gurney by the ambulance attendants. She closed her eyes to avoid seeing the devastation that stayed behind. Or perhaps she had fainted. The doctor and Jesse would accompany her to the hospital. I thanked them as they followed Maura down the hall.

"All in a day's work," Jesse said. "Thank God not every day is like this."

Maura Balmain at least was spared more of the tawdry drama in the Park Avenue penthouse. For now, she wasn't dead or in jail, but on her way to a country club hospital that catered to the wealthy. I pressed her hand before they wheeled her into the elevator. She pressed back. Soon, the reporters would be on this story with flashbulbs blazing, and this finally seemed to occur to Balmain Senior.

"As much as I have hated that tart, there can be no scandal. If there really is a child—my grandchild— My God." He shook his head and let the thought linger in the air. The idea of a Balmain heir seemed to steady him. "Do you understand, Detective O'Hara? I know the commissioner."

"Ain't it funny how everybody on the Upper East Side knows the commissioner?" O'Hara said to no one in particular. He let out a sigh of exasperation. "Looks like I got a dead body, one Duncan Balmain. We are familiar with him at the station. A first-class troublemaker. Couple of assault charges hushed up. "

"I resent that," Balmain said. "He's my son and now he's been killed by that witch."

The detective pushed his hat back on his head. "That may be, but I also got a young woman on her way to the hospital, brutalized and bloody. Pretty woman. Pregnant, she says. According to Doc Wren, somebody, presumably the late husband, tried to cut a baby out of Maura Balmain." O'Hara reached for a cup of coffee. "If true, that is one hellacious crime and no one's going to mourn the deceased."

This scandal train was about to leave the station. Maura Fitzgerald Balmain did, after all, shoot her husband, Duncan Balmain. Just wait till the press got ahold of this story.

"She told me that's what happened," I said. "And the black eye. Said everyone on the Upper East Side thinks she walks into a lot of walls."

"Lot of that going around. Right, Riley?" O'Hara said to a uniformed cop.

"A man ain't a man if he hits a woman, Detective," Riley said. "He's a coward weakling son of a bitch. Pardon my language."

"We'll see if she and the baby live. Our investigation may show self-defense." O'Hara was halfway there already. "With any luck. Anybody seen the gun?"

"In the bedroom, on the floor," I said. "I didn't touch it. He attacked her first, she fired in self-defense."

"I can't believe any of this." Balmain was red-eyed with tears and Scotch. "How can this be? Duncan told me she couldn't have children."

"Parents and children lying to each other? Imagine," I said. "Maura says he slashed her with a big hunting knife. Must be here somewhere."

"That's up to our investigation to determine. The medical examiner's on his way." O'Hara scanned the apartment and his eyes landed back on me. I was very glad to be wearing Maura's beautifully cut but conservative purple dress. It covered me up and the cashmere was so warm. I would have made a far tawdrier impression in a blood-stained party gown. "You, Miss. You look familiar." His eyes traveled to Graydon and then back to me. I could see O'Hara's mind at work. His brown eyes were small and shrewd, but not unkind. "Yeah, I seen you in the papers. Photos don't do you justice. And your name?"

"Esmé de LaForet."

"Right. The Scavullo murder. You were right in the middle of that mess. You look Irish."

"Half. Esmé *Rafferty* de LaForet. I was just trying to do a good deed that day. Return a lost watch to Scavullo. It all spiraled out of control." I treated myself to a dramatic sigh.

"That's what they all say. Especially when they're a sassy colleen. If I recall correctly, the two of you brought down two killers."

"It was somewhat sensationalized," Graydon said.

"Of course it was." Detective O'Hara seemed amused. "I got one playboy detective Graydon Chase and one Esmé Rafferty de LaForet. Actress?"

"Playwright."

"Playwright! Theatre people. Right. So what's an Irish mix like you doing with this limey?"

Graydon stepped in, trying not to be bothered. "Esmé and I are going to be married."

"God, I hope it's not for this guy's money." O'Hara stared at me. "You don't strike me as the type."

"I'm not anyone's type!" Well, that didn't come out right.

"Except mine, O'Hara. She didn't know who I was when we met. Dead set against me when she found out I wasn't penniless. Not fond of the English either, but she made an exception in my case. Don't know why."

O'Hara rubbed his head. "Good sense, huh? Okay, for now."

Balmain Senior watched stone-faced. He lifted his empty glass of Scotch for the butler, but O'Hara forbade it.

"You can all get drunk as a skunk after we leave. I want a semblance of rationality here." His attention turned back to us. "How did you two happen to be here?"

"Edward Balmain called my valet, said there was an emergency and I should come right over," Graydon said. "I had no idea what we'd stumble upon."

"I asked to come along," I told O'Hara.

"I'm sure you did."

"It's been a very long day." I started to sway and O'Hara told us to sit down.

"Balmain." He snapped his fingers as if it helped him remember. "Junior and senior." O'Hara lit a cigarette and inhaled deeply. "And Junior's dead. What we got here is a great big problem."

"The problem is my son is dead, and that shanty Irish bitch killed him."

"Excuse me? Which 'shanty Irish bitch' would that be?" O'Hara stared Balmain down. "I'd be a little careful with the language around a bunch of Irish cops, if I were you. And you're the one who don't want any scandal, remember?"

"That's right, and I know the—"

"Yeah, yeah, you know the commissioner. The new one or the old one?" O'Hara checked his notebook. "If Maura *Fitzgerald* Balmain dies, we got a double murder. If she lives, she's gonna go free, I promise you. No one's going to punish a woman for protecting herself and an unborn child. Especially a bunch of Irish cops."

Balmain started to say something, but he sat down instead, shaking his head. "This can't get out." He regarded his empty glass. "What are you going to tell all those dirty newshounds when they come around like a pack of feral dogs?"

"They're not here yet," O'Hara said. "At the moment, there's been a death and a severe assault. An investigation is underway. I feel bad for Mrs. Balmain, poor kid, going through that hell, and with a baby coming. But we gotta let the chips fall where they may."

"It was obviously an intruder," Balmain suddenly declared. We all turned to look at him. "I was wrong. An intruder, I say. Wouldn't you agree, Detective O'Hara?"

"An intruder? Why would an intruder be after your son?" I could see O'Hara was giving Balmain the chance to come up with an acceptable story. I knew as well as anyone that the truth would be too much to take, at least here on the Upper East Side. It would be as bad as announcing that Jack the Ripper was visiting the neighborhood.

"It simply must have been an intruder," Balmain Senior said. "If I'm to have a grandchild, it cannot be the mother who killed the father. I won't have it. You must see that, Detective."

O'Hara shook his head and turned to the butler. "Sebastian, what did you see? Did you see any intruders?"

"Sorry to say, sir, I didn't see anyone or anything." These rich folk had a real mania for butlers and valets who specialized in seeing and hearing nothing. "I was in my quarters down the hall when I heard the shots. To my embarrassment, Detective, I was quite frozen in fear. After the shooting stopped, I got hold of myself and called Mr. Balmain Senior on the telephone. Then I made my way into the living room."

"But you didn't check on Mrs. Balmain?" I blurted out.

"You see, Miss de LaForet," he said. "There had been many loud arguments before."

"And what did you see?" O'Hara rubbed hi chin. "Once you *got ahold* of yourself."

"I saw blood on the floor leading to Mrs. Balmain's room. Her door was locked. Mr. Duncan was lying on the floor in the parlor, and Mr. Balmain Senior was pounding on the door."

"You made it here pretty quickly, Balmain," O'Hara said.

"I live upstairs. In the penthouse," Balmain sniffed.

"Convenient. So there's no witnesses?"

"It was an intruder," Balmain insisted. Under his breath he added, "If she's really pregnant. Are you following me, O'Hara?"

"If people believe it was an intruder," I said, "it could start a scare, and everyone on the Upper East Side will be looking for this guy who's killing the rich and mighty." I said it out loud, though I'm not sure I meant to. I was writing this scenario in my head as I went along. "That could keep the story alive."

"You're saying it would cause a panic?" O'Hara said.

"I can see the headlines from here. Weeks of headlines," I explained. "I was a police reporter."

"Now you tell me."

"Word would get out that a would-be thief broke in and killed Duncan Balmain and attacked his wife. That's what Balmain is planning, right?" The old man in question didn't even have the grace to look ashamed. "The police will have to expend a lot of resources on questioning suspects to make it look good. Suspects that don't exist."

"I'm afraid Balmain's entire class would insist upon it," Graydon said. "And the new commissioner."

O'Hara groaned. "Everything's a can of worms. We'd have to have a big manhunt. Lots of blues out on the street."

"Undoubtedly. And a waste of police resources," Graydon said. "What exactly is your point, Esmé?"

"On the other hand. Say it *was* an intruder. Say some other poor soul dies tonight. Maybe a criminal, a murderer? How many people die in New York City every day, O'Hara? How many poor John Does, how many forgotten men? Men who are guilty of other terrible crimes? I'm just thinking out loud."

I could see this story working on stage, but I couldn't believe what I was suggesting. Stories form in my brain, and sometimes that's where I wish they'd stay.

But Balmain Senior was now paying close attention. I could tell he was a blamer from way back. He wanted a fall guy to pin this rap on. And I wanted to protect Maura, at least for now. Did I care about giving a few cops a little extra work? I did not.

"Are you're saying, Miss de LaForet, that we put the blame on some poor not-so-innocent crook who will just happen to die tonight?" O'Hara wasn't indignant, merely interested. Very interested.

"That is what you're saying, isn't it?" Graydon said.

"I'm only thinking in story terms. Fiction," I said. "And I'm not talking about an innocent man. What if there's some known bad guy? A killer, a thief, who bites the dust tonight, tomorrow. Someone O'Hara's boys in blue fish out of a gutter."

"It could happen," O'Hara said. "Happens all the time."

"Maybe he's homeless, anonymous," I went on. "Maybe he's got a family who wouldn't care about one more charge against him. Someone with a wife who suspects, or knows, all his evil deeds. A wife with many a black eye. And if some money were found on the corpse, maybe she could start over. She might not care what really happened. She knows he's guilty of other terrible things." I looked around to find them all, even Sebastian, staring at me. And nodding. "Hey, it's just a story."

"So we've got this shady dead guy," Graydon prompted me, "maybe a murderer, a gangster, a thug—"

"With a lot of money in his pocket," I said. "That's the way I'd write this. I know the police don't usually find money, but in this case there should be money, plenty of money. That money would have to go to a wife, a survivor, a family."

I stared at Balmain. He nodded. He didn't seem shocked, or even mildly appalled.

"Money," the rich man said. "How much money?" This was clearly a man for whom money had always solved problems. Why not this one?

"Too bad about Smiley dying too soon," Officer Clancy said. "There's this Smiley character, died two days ago in a bar fight. Bad apple. We closed three cases with his death, right, Detective O'Hara? Maybe there's another one like him tonight or tomorrow. Sure would be convenient. For the whole precinct, I mean. And for Mrs. Balmain."

O'Hara smiled. "Easier on the paperwork that way," he acknowledged. "Plenty of John Does die in Hoovervilles and the shantytowns. And nobody wants to see a good Irish lass who was protecting herself and her baby dragged through the mud, maybe end up in prison."

"God knows there are any number of poor devils dead in the gutter by morning," Officer Riley added. "Some may never even have a name."

"This woman tonight," Officer Clancy said. "God willing, she'll keep her babe. The devil who did this to her is dead. But do we dare sully the name of another dead man?" He paused to consider. "Or do we give his widow a chance for a new life? This is the devil's own lottery you're suggesting, Miss de LaForet."

Is that what I'm saying? "Don't listen to me. I'm just imagining how someone might find a fall guy for this dilemma. Maybe for a play."

"Or for real life." O'Hara pointed out what everyone knew. "We all want to save Maura Balmain. Don't we, Mr. Balmain?" Balmain Senior said nothing. He knew I'd turned the tide his way. "We all need to keep our own jobs, and worse things can happen, and have happened."

"Make it happen, O'Hara," Balmain said imperiously. "I'll pay whatever amount you think is fair. A thousand or two, perhaps? Anonymously, of course. Any amount to have this go away. Just do it."

O'Hara ribbed his jaw. "Just might work. All depends on the right scoundrel dying tonight or tomorrow. Let's let Fate decide." He picked up a cup of now-cold coffee. "It's a good story, Miss de LaForet. Perhaps you'd like to join the force?"

He huddled with Balmain Senior and the two officers. I leaned back into one of the soft tan and green sofas flanking the fireplace and just watched them talk. At least this way Maura would have a chance of survival, along with her baby, all because of that Balmain money. Or because of my story?

The medical examiner arrived and studied the corpse. He paid attention to the bloody hole in Duncan, as well as where other blood had spilled and sprayed across the room. He traced it to Maura's bedroom. The police collected my bloodstained dress, the towels, the gun, the bloody hunting knife. The ME didn't say much, but he conferred with O'Hara out of earshot. I was lost in my thoughts when I glanced up to find Graydon looking at me.

"I'd like to go now," I said.

Graydon sat next to me on the sofa, probably closer than O'Hara would like. When we were finally released, Balmain Senior returned to his apartment and Sebastian was allowed to go with him. It seemed the butler's nerves were none too steady. Graydon helped me put on my coat.

Winter was in the air out on the empty street, but it felt calming to breathe in the cold crystal atmosphere without the smell of blood. For a moment, there was no speaking, simply silently taking in each other's presence.

"Esmé, you're crying."

Four

I WIPED MY tears, which had come out of nowhere, and leaned into him, waiting for his arms to encircle me.

"People are horrible, Graydon." My words came out in puffs of steam.

"Not everyone is a Balmain, for which we can be grateful. You were wonderful tonight."

He kissed me gently. I wanted more, but we were out on the public street. We caught a cab in the deep dark night. As usual, he escorted me to my door, then stepped inside to check the premises to make sure I was safe.

"What, no wisecracks about checking for intruders?"

"Not tonight. Stay a moment, Graydon. Please."

"Just for a while." He reached for me.

"Night cap?"

"Brandy and soda, if you please."

I poured two snifters, adding a splash of soda to each. I didn't drink much brandy, but the bottle looked pretty on my liquor cart. I wanted so many things at once, I wanted to wash the evening off me, as well as any residual blood from Duncan and Maura. I wanted to forget the last few hours and most of all, I wanted this man to hold me.

"I'm a mess, Graydon. I want to clean everything off me but you."

"And I want to stay, but I mustn't do anything to hurt our reputations, especially after this night."

"Another murder, you mean?" We had met in a school supply closet when Scavullo was being murdered in an upstairs room.

"As you pointed out, the journalists will be on this, chatting up the doormen, sniffing out gossip. Duncan Balmain was already a notorious character. They will know we were there. And it must be three o'clock in the morning by now."

"Not late for theatre people. My neighbors understand." They were used to my crazy hours. "And it's you who are the roué."

"Hardly. Though I grant you managed to find out a lot about me."

"And all the women you escorted around town. Society news. You broke a lot of hearts."

I claimed the sofa and he sat with me, loosening his silk scarf, checking his watch, sipping his brandy and soda.

"I don't care what they say about me, Esmé, or even write about me, but I will protect your reputation."

"Such as it is. A scribbler, whether I write plays or news stories. Besides, most people don't read the society news."

"No, they prefer bloody murders on the front page. Where we have been linked. We're getting a reputation."

He leaned his head back against the cushions. I put my hand on his delightfully hard chest.

"We *are* engaged. People will understand."

"I want you, Esmé, so very much, and we will find a way to be together soon, away from prying eyes."

"You weren't so particular with your previous lady friends," I complained. I didn't bring up his former hobby—painting nudes of at least two of those lady friends. But we shared a look.

"No, I wasn't. And I have a dismal reputation. But we two are to be married, so I'm cleaning it up."

"Does it matter now?" I'd met three women (including the two nudes) who were after Rupert Graydon Chaseborn. For his money and his status—and his looks. Three who wanted to marry him. After I found out who Graydon was, his real name, and that he was a rich boy, a *very* rich boy. All that money? I was beyond horrified. I had tried to stay away from Graydon Chase. However, Cupid is a contrary little archer and shot us both with his arrows, obviously giggling the whole time.

"I don't want any harm to come to you in any way, even with their idle gossip. I have found the only woman I ever wanted. One who disdains my fortune." He laughed. "But your play should be making a tidy sum by now."

"Mere speculation. We've already made a spectacle in the newspapers. Notorious *playboy* and budding *playwright*."

"Beautiful playwright with red-gold curls. My Elfin Queen." He pulled at an errant strand.

"I do not remotely resemble an elf."

Graydon grabbed my fingers and kissed them. "I do love you so."

I grabbed for him with a faint hope I could change his mind. His hands wandered as if frisking me for weapons. The kisses kept coming.

"Don't stop."

He stopped and forced himself upright. "Sorry. I told the driver to wait." We had to catch our breath.

"I regret that there are so many things we can never reveal. The way we actually met, you holding a gun on me." I closed my eyes against the memory.

"We're building quite a terrible résumé. But that's only on paper. Come here and we'll say good night properly."

He pulled me to my feet and I followed him to my front door. After another lingering kiss, he pulled away, urged me to remain safe, and shut the door. He waited to hear me click the lock, after which I ran to my front window to watch his tall silhouette climb into the taxi that pulled away from the curb.

FIVE

THE EVENING HAD begun on a different note—many different and swinging notes—to a dance band at the theatre gala playing tunes like "In the Still of the Night," "Cocktails for Two," and a brand-new number, not yet published, "These Foolish Things." That tune seemed to be stuck in my head.

Maura Balmain's purple cashmere dress reminded me that I had started out wearing a very different gown, a glamorous and theatrical and rather bare blue silk with a matching bejeweled headband. Now that it was in police custody, I would never see that dress again, though I had retrieved the headpiece.

The azure ensemble was one of my prized purchases from a flop play that producer Salvatore "Sal" Rossi deemed unlucky, precluding that wardrobe from future productions. The play lasted less than a week, and Sal was stuck with numerous extravagant costumes. The actors didn't want them. They would carry the taint of failure. Theatre people can be very superstitious. The clothes I wanted had been fitted for the understudy and never worn, and Sal decided they were perfectly all right for me to purchase—at a steal. I was in need of a wonderful wardrobe to wear about town and to premieres, and those outfits looked like they came straight from the movies. Or Paris.

Because of my amazing new wardrobe, I had a fondness for that terrible play, *Afternoon Tea with Nigel*, but none for its snotty playwright, Julian Davis-Montclair. He had the nerve to insult my play, *Leaving Alamogordo*, a surprise hit, while Montclair's drivel bit the dust in a matter of days.

The evening's fete was hosted by Sal, the bundle of energy who produced shows at the Washington Irving Theatre. He aimed to draw more angels and excitement to *Leaving Alamogordo,* which was moving to the larger Nathaniel Hawthorne Theatre for an extended run. We all wanted to see if the stardust fate had sprinkled upon it would transfer to the new theatre. I tried not to anticipate too much. It turned me into a bundle of nerves.

"Esmé, looking good." Sal Rossi greeted me at the door of the gala with theatre manager May Scott, also known as 'Queen of the May.' Nothing happened at the theatre without May's knowledge or approval.

"You must know everyone in New York," I said, complimenting him on the crowd.

"Not yet, but I'm working on it," Sal said. "There's some serious money here, but we're not overselling it."

He must have sprung for a new tuxedo. This one fit better over his happily bulging tummy. And May was glorious in a slinky silver satin gown. I'd never seen her look so lovely. She'd also abandoned her reading glasses for the evening.

"Nice dress," I said.

"I'm not the only one who recognizes the talent of Wilhelmina Kim." Known as Willie, Miss Kim was our amazing costumer. I looked for her, but I hadn't spotted her yet. May reached for my left hand from behind me. I tried for a Mona Lisa smile, but it turned into a Cheshire Cat grin.

"So the rumors are true then," she said. "Quick work."

Word of my engagement had been printed in the less reputable papers, but of course we read them all. Though we hadn't formally announced our engagement, I was wearing Graydon's ring, a family heirloom with an ostentatiously large diamond and rubies. The groom-to-be, however, was working late and said he couldn't make it.

"By the way," I said, "this room is gorgeous."

"Can I produce, or what?" Sal took all the credit. He and May beamed and moved away to greet others. The Grand Ballroom at the Edison Hotel was close to both theatres, and Sal knew how to score a deal. It was part of his talent of spinning smoke and mirrors into spectacle, and dross into gloss.

The seasonal atmosphere was reflected in chrysanthemums and greenhouse roses, ropes of autumn leaves, gold tablecloths with hurricane lamps and gold candles. Sal had worked out a special deal: The decorations would serve double duty at a wedding reception the following day, the 24th of November. And if the flowers lasted long enough, the Edison could use them for Thanksgiving, only a week away. The thought of the holiday made my head spin. This year was screeching to a close and I missed Graydon's company. I was turning into a sentimental sap.

I had previously arranged for my pal Reggie, Reginald Pendleton III, to be my escort for the evening. That was before my sudden, and recent, engagement to Graydon Chase, now missing in action, trapped between the lines of a ledger. Reggie was merely my friend, but he was there. In a tuxedo, no less. From a wealthy family, this Princeton graduate was masquerading as a reporter until such time as he could claim his fortune. But Reggie always protested that description.

"I landed in the wrong family, Esmé," he would say. "You can't hold that against me."

"I never would. Besides, you don't always act like a rich kid."

He was a born scribbler and he enjoyed the police beat, the edgy, the dirty, the flavorful. Reggie loved a scoop. He stayed with me, dancing to the music until he spied a light-haired lady who looked like a likely conquest. He was off and I called after him, "Be nice."

I switched dance partners several times before I was pulled into the arms of Patrick Dentino, also known as

"Lashes" for his extravagant eyelashes and his too-pretty green eyes. He was handsome in a new black suit, spiffy but not terribly happy. He'd put in time working for the notorious mob boss, Frank Romeo. Pat knew his way around a swing step as well as a boxing ring. However, all that was changing.

"What am I supposed to do, Esmé? Frank tells me I am going to college, and not just any college. *Columbia.* He's calling it the Guido Moretti Scholarship Fund. And it's your fault for figuring out who killed Guido."

Some days you can't win. Frankie the Cat Romeo wanted to reward me for unmasking the murderer of Guido "Ratty" Moretti. Guido was a sweet kid who drove the mob boss's car and for whom Romeo had great affection. There was no way I could take anything from a mob boss. But I had to come up with a plausible way for him to pay me back, or it would be an insult. I thought of Patrick, another one of his protégés, who wanted to be a writer. Attending college would be a way for Pat Dentino to escape the mob. He'd never fit in completely anyway, because he was only half Italian. The other half was Irish. And rumor had it that Romeo was trying to go straight.

"Are you angry, Pat? You said you thought about going to college. Said you'd be good at it."

His shoulders dropped. "I thought I could take a few night classes at City College. You know, with people, real people. Not those phonies in tennis sweaters. Not a full ride to an Ivy League. They don't even let Irish and Italians into Columbia. Or Jews neither. It's not supposed to be possible."

"I imagine Mr. Romeo talked somebody into it." I tried to imagine the conversation for its theatrical possibilities.

"Yeah. Someone says no to Frank Romeo? Not a good idea." Pat actually laughed. "Frankie wants me to go for the class act. He had the nerve to tell them I was a *Protestant.* My mother would die. And she would kill him. Let me tell you, Esmé, those snobs say one word against the Irish—or the Catholics—not to mention the Italians! All I know is I got a list of classes and a new suit. And sweater vests. Imagine! Mr. Romeo says we're all going legit someday soon, and I gotta look the part."

"Sounds like a good plan. I know it might not be easy for you. I'm sorry."

"Don't be. When has it ever been easy? Till then, I see a lot of fights in my future."

"What does your mother think?" Mrs. Dentino was Irish Catholic all the way, but she'd married an Italian boy.

"She's practically nominated you for sainthood. Canonization is imminent. Saint Esmé."

"Oh dear." What else could I say?

"Columbia probably don't even teach the Irish writers. Synge, O'Casey, Joyce."

"Poor Patrick. I'm sorry I laughed, you look so miserable. They might teach Dante."

"Did you know, they make freshmen wear *beanies?* I ain't wearing no beanie. I'm twenty-three years old! I'm too old for a beanie!"

Young Dentino, only two years younger than I, seemed to look at me as if I were his big sister. He was handsome, average height, but muscled like a boxer, and he could probably get away without the standard collegiate headgear. *Beanies* indeed. I saw several women eyeing him.

"What's really bothering you, Pat?"

He looked glum. "What if I can't cut it?"

"You can. Try English and writing courses."

"I'm pretty good with numbers too. Math, you know, and not just horses. Hey, I'm sorry, Esmé, I came here to thank you. I mean it's a heck of an opportunity. I wouldn't tell no one else this, but I guess I'm a little scared."

"You have what it takes. You're smart, you're mature, you've been around. And remember, they'll be scared of *you.*"

"Gee. You think?"

There seemed to be a commotion in the ballroom and I heard some disparaging remarks sent my way.

"She's a mindless hack. It's not a play, it's a newspaper article. I write plays." They were the not-so-dulcet tones of failed playwright Julian Davis-Montclair, author of the notorious flop, *Afternoon Tea with Nigel.* He must have crashed for the free food and the chance to insult me. "Esmé de LaForet is simply a pretty doll, if you go in for that sort of thing." And he was a party crasher, in a borrowed and threadbare tuxedo. Patrick spun on his heel.

"That's the guy, the same guy I warned before. At the theatre."

Pat sped away from me and seemed to grow a few inches taller with every step. He reached the alleged playwright before Sal could get there, grabbed him by the neck, spun him around, and had his arm in a lock. Julian went down without a fight. He was all talk and no action, rather like his stage work.

"You misspoke, my friend." Patrick's fist was poised to strike. "Miss de LaForet is a lady and a playwright of note with a hit play and it's terrific. Apologize. Right now. Or don't you like your nose?"

Terror suffused Julian's pasty face and he had trouble finding his words. A crowd gathered around the two men. Unlike the party, this entertainment was free. Patrick's arm pulled back and his face grew closer to the man on the floor.

"I apologize!" Julian threw a look my way that was pure terror. "I'm sorry, Esmé. I didn't mean it."

He most certainly did, but Patrick "Lashes" Dentino took pity on the coward before he soiled himself. He hauled Julian to his feet and gave him a push.

"Exit is that way. You ain't welcome anywhere near Miss de LaForet. Not ever."

Patrick dusted off his lapels and seemed much refreshed. Happier. Perhaps he should go out for boxing at Columbia.

"You're Pat Dentino, right? Nice work." Sal offered Pat his hand. "I like your form. You got that bum out the door, real efficient, no blood spilled, no decorations messed up. You interested, maybe you could pick up some bouncer work at the theatre, nights, weekends? You watch the door, keep the riffraff out, and you got a couple quiet hours during the show for homework. You interested?"

Sal and Pat's boss, Frank Romeo, were old pals from school days. It was clear that Romeo had talked with him about Pat.

"I might be interested. Yeah," Pat said. Sal and Pat strolled to the refreshment table. I couldn't hear any more. I caught sight of Reggie dancing with the blonde. I wondered if any of those pale-haired women would ever catch him. He was fickle, but he had a definite type. After their dance, he wandered over to me and asked me to trip the light fantastic.

"Are you sure you have the strength?" I asked. "So many blondes, so little time."

"I have time for your particular shade of strawberry blond. Let's dance and you can tell me if the rumors are true."

"What rumors?" He lifted my left hand off his shoulder and confirmed what he'd read in the papers.

"Engagements are made to be broken." Reggie steered me into the center of the dance floor. He had questions.

Six

"MAY I CUT in?" Graydon held out his arms to me and I rushed in, delighted to see him. His English accent sent happy chills down my neck. I found it odd, because at first his voice had irritated me. At least, the Irish and French parts of me. But as I am American, I try to be democratic, and as I gazed up I was lost in his neon blue eyes. Yes, it's a hackneyed phrase, but that's how I felt every time. Lost and happily found. His voice warmed me. We paused. Reggie registered his annoyance.

"I got here first, pal."

"Yet, clearly, I have priority." Graydon swept me away from Reggie, away from the crowd into a lively foxtrot that soon slowed to a waltz, where I could enjoy his nearness and his warmth.

"Reggie doesn't really mind," I said.

"I think he does." His grin made his eyes crinkle.

Graydon's eyes were the first thing I noticed during our first encounter, before he'd even spoken, when he found me hiding from gunshots in a school utility closet. He was holding a gun. On me. I thought he was a gangster. He thought I might be complicit in whatever mayhem was happening on the floor above us. I was insulted. He was amused. And then he kissed me without asking permission. It wasn't a story I would ever share (except here), but I often thought about it and the earthquake of emotions that kiss stirred in me. It was ridiculous to feel so excited at the very thought of him, and yet I hoped I'd always feel that way.

"You said you couldn't make it tonight," I said.

"So I did, but I simply couldn't bear the thought of you here in that enticing gown. And that upstart Pendleton the Third here gawking at you. How could I stay home, staring at paperwork, thinking of my gorgeous fiancée all alone, surrounded by wolves? There was nothing to be done, except to respond to your siren call."

"I'm a siren now? Not an elf? I hope I always have that siren power."

"You would hope that, vixen."

"Elf? Siren? Vixen? I need a program to keep track of all my characters."

He laughed and the band played a slow tune, drawing us closer, yet not close enough. We'd known each other only a short time, but Graydon filled my senses in a way that no one else had. We were engaged, but I couldn't imagine marrying anyone just yet. I needed time simply to enjoy being engaged.

My late fiancé Roger never made me feel as fine or even as noticed. I barely remembered how I could have said yes to Roger's proposal. He was a decent man, good-looking, but after the first rush of infatuation, so very dull. I had planned to break that engagement off, but then he died, a fatal flu that devastated the little town where I grew up. The flu that took both my parents. I fled to New York City, to the newspapers, the theatre, and entanglements with mobsters. And falling hard for Graydon Chase.

Graydon's proposal was unexpected and yet so perfect. We hadn't yet had the moment, or the time to take our relationship to another level. The physical one. Everything in my heart, soul, and body cried out for him. Unfortunately, we seemed to be under a microscope and we had to be clever about finding the place and the time. Perhaps we could simply leave town for a while, a pre-honeymoon?

It may be a radical thought, but I wanted to be sure we were compatible *before* marriage. I'd seen too many women marry the wrong man for the wrong reasons.

Then it turned out the men weren't interested in intimate relations, not with their women anyway. Roger wasn't interested in men, but he never seemed that interested in making love to me, either. I suspected he might have been more interested in the general store I'd inherit. Which happened much sooner than anyone expected. After a near miss with my former fiancé, I wasn't going to make a mistake with Graydon. I breathed in the scent of his delicious cologne, called Hickory Wind.

"I know what you're thinking," he whispered in my ear.

I felt myself grinning. "Do you?" *Bet you don't.*

"Same thing I've been thinking. We simply haven't had the time. Or the opportunity. That ghastly Scavullo affair. Reporters following us around. Mobsters everywhere we turn."

"Can we help it if we make good copy? But it is rude for them to inform the world we're engaged, when we haven't even announced it."

"We could rush the wedding. Maybe they'd back off," Graydon said. It was a terrible suggestion.

"You don't know newspaper reporters. Besides—"

"You want a long engagement." He held me closer.

"A very long engagement." There were so many complications ahead. I was thinking *years*. I noticed people staring at us with interest.

A call came for Graydon during the dance. One of the waiters tapped my dance partner and directed us to a phone. It was Robbins, Graydon's valet, who had received an urgent call from some big shot named Edward Balmain. Graydon cocked the earpiece so I could hear.

"Mr. Balmain said it was very important, sir. He wants you to come to his home most urgently. He wouldn't explain, but he seemed extremely agitated."

"I should go," Graydon said to me. "Balmain is a big money man. Probably some financial crisis."

"I'm coming with you," I said. We grabbed our wraps, and I had to skip to keep up with his long legs. "Do you know this Balmain?"

"Slightly. He owns a construction company. And a bank. Bit of a financier. I assume it's a money crisis. I'll charge him double for interrupting our dance. This meeting will be dull, I'm afraid. Why don't you stay and have a good time?"

"I'd rather be with you."

"It will bore you."

"This place will bore me if I'm not with you." I paused. "I suppose I could let Reggie take me home."

A look of annoyance crossed Graydon's face. "Very well, do come along. We'll try and make it quick."

It wasn't quick and it wasn't boring. But I had no idea the evening would end with blood and death.

SEVEN

THE PHONE WAS ringing in my dreams. Or was it gunshots? In reality it was a knock on my front door the next morning. It dragged me out of my stupor and into a robe to see who it was. The clock told me it was nearly noon, and the sun was pouring through my windows. Thinking it was my housekeeper Amelia, I opened the door.

Reginald Pendleton III himself appeared, looking rather dashing for a reporter, in his khaki slacks, yellow-and-green knitted vest, and brown corduroy jacket, with his Ipana toothpaste smile in place. Yet his eyes were bloodshot.

"Reggie, what are you doing here? It's Saturday morning. And where is Amelia?" I looked around.

"Saw her walking to the market. Said you're getting low on milk or something. Told me to put the coffee on."

"I don't understand."

"You really want me standing here in the doorway where all the neighbors can see us? You in your pink robe? Very nice robe, by the way."

I had a weakness for pretty lingerie. Luckily my neighbors thought I was an upside-down sort of person, sleeping half the day away. I ushered him inside.

"Honestly, Reggie."

"As my future wife—"

"Stop that talk, Reggie. It's not funny and you know I'm engaged to Graydon." I pointed him to the coffee and percolator. "Make yourself useful."

"Have you seen those things called movies, my dear Esmé? Engagements are made to be broken. And you haven't officially announced it yet. I'm sure *The Times* would be interested. Even my paper, *The Post*."

'You're babbling. Besides, *The Post* already printed it."

"You disappeared from that fancy soiree last night, with the British Svengali. Someone has to think of your reputation. Might as well be me." His expression was smug. He knew something.

"By the way, what happened to the lady you were with last night? The cute blonde?"

"Her boyfriend showed up. No matter, I needed a night in. So, what was it with you two? A romantic horse-drawn carriage through Central Park?"

"Not that romantic." The images of Duncan Balmain lying on the blood-soaked living room rug and Maura on the stretcher appeared unbidden in my mind. I wondered what Reggie knew and if he'd heard of the shooting at the Balmain place. He was excellent at putting things together.

"Chaseborn isn't here?" Reggie tried to peer into my bedroom. I blocked him.

"Did someone make you the hall monitor?"

"I can see someone needs her coffee." He retreated to the kitchen, fussed with the coffee, and plugged in the percolator. "Cranky."

I rushed to my bedroom and threw on some slacks and a sweater, my usual Saturday attire. I dragged a comb through my hair and wiped my face. I heard the phone ring, for real this time. As I ran back to the living room, Reggie handed me the phone and sipped coffee, watching me. He certainly had made himself at home. I mimed that he should make himself useful and bring me a cup too.

"Hello?"

"Who was that who answered your phone?" the English-accented voice demanded. Even though he sounded annoyed, I was happy to hear from Graydon. I grinned. If only we could run away for a few days and enjoy the last of this glorious autumn. Reggie returned with a cup of java, heavily laced with milk and sugar, even though I usually took it black.

"Thank you." To the phone, I said, "That's Reggie, Reginald Pendleton the Third. He was knocking at my door. I made him put on the coffee." I yawned and took the cup. My unwanted guest grabbed the receiver and painted a picture for Graydon.

"Everything is perfectly innocent, Chaseborn, though I know it doesn't look that way, and if Esmé would give me half a chance—"

I grabbed the phone away from Reggie and he threw me a wicked grin.

"He was concerned after seeing me leave with you last night, you well-known Chase rake. Or is that rake, Chase? Happy?"

"Not exactly. Where's Amelia?

"At the market."

"She should not leave you alone with him. I will have a word with her."

"No, you won't. She knew him before she knew you. She's a fair judge of character and she can handle him. And so can I."

Amelia took that moment to stroll in with a bag of necessities from the local market. She looked marvelous in a navy skirt and sweater with white collar and cuffs. I didn't insist that she wear a uniform. She said as the 'head housekeeper' (as if I had a staff and not a single part-time cleaner), she needed to look 'professional.' I guess that meant professional like Jean Harlow. She patted her perky platinum curls, which had lightened in recent weeks. Head housekeeper indeed.

"I gotcha some fresh bagels and cream cheese." She glided into the kitchen, followed by Reggie.

"I'm home, Amelia's home, I'm fine, Graydon. Reggie's in the kitchen with Amelia, no doubt stealing bagels."

"If that's all he's stealing."

"Unanswerable questions, my darling. Any news this morning?"

"I wanted to hear your voice. Robbins will be bringing the paper soon. *The Times,* not one of those disreputable scandal sheets."

"Too bad. Those are the ones with the juicy news."

"Don't tell me you think Balmain's death is juicy."

"Not at all. Just commenting on the general tenor of the news these days. Reggie wasn't working last night." The man I mentioned made a face at me over a bagel, freshly slathered with cream cheese. I stood and pulled the phone further away.

"Can you be ready soon, Esmé?"

"Ready for what?"

"Edward Balmain wants to see us, both of us, for lunch at the University Club. Two o'clock."

"One of those clubs that doesn't allow women?"

"Women are allowed in the dining room with an invitation from a member."

"How thrilling." I bristled at the thought of those men and their silly clubs and their silly rules. Obviously, they were up to no good and were afraid of women. "Are you a member of the club?"

"It's a matter of business. One belongs to the right clubs. But Balmain is a member too and this is on his ticket. We're expected. Can you come?"

"What's he up to and why does he want to see me?"

"I imagine we'll find out."

Balmain Senior was used to ordering people around. Although I had planned to spend the afternoon lounging around to repair my equilibrium, it would give me a chance to see the famous University Club, as well as the inner workings of a Graydon Chase inquiry.

"How is Maura?" I asked.

"Holding her own, according to Balmain. She'll be in the hospital a while longer, I gather. You will come?"

Curiosity was always my weakness. "What should I wear?"

"It's a rather tony place. You always know what to wear. Or at least your costumer knows."

He knew all about Willie's magic needles. "A conservative suit then. By the way, Graydon, do you think Balmain would pay for my gown? The one I wore last night to the gala, before Maura very graciously gave me one of her dresses. I know I barged in on your case, but the blue silk is ruined, not to mention, in police custody. I didn't notice at the time because I was trying to stop Maura's bleeding." Inexplicably, I couldn't go on. My voice caught.

"It will be taken care of."

We arranged that he would pick me up. After all, I would need an escort to enter the University Club. I tried to approach this whole meeting as if it were a play and I was playing a part. I was about to find out which part.

"Give me time to wake up and clean up."

I hung up to find Reggie staring at me. He sat on the chair opposite mine, coffee cup in hand, Cheshire Cat smile on his face.

"We can't have any secrets between us, such good friends as we." He had that look, the one reporters get when they're hoarding information. I lifted an imperious eyebrow.

"Cards on the table, Reggie. What's up?" Amelia decided it was a good time to dust, within hearing distance, so she wouldn't miss anything.

"Newspaper's on the table." He picked up the latest edition of *The Post*. The headline:

DUNCAN BALMAIN KILLED IN HOME
COPS NARROW SEARCH FOR SUSPECT

It was prominently placed on the front page, above the fold.

"Don't blame me," Reggie said. "I didn't write it. I'm doing the day-after story."

"So that's why you're here. Fishing expedition."

"That's how I know you weren't canoodling in a romantic carriage ride across the park."

He'd conveniently underlined one paragraph for me, and he smirked. I would have liked to slap that smirk off his face, but I had to read it aloud first.

"Detective O'Hara credited the quick action of playwright Esmé de LaForet and her fiancé Graydon Chase with saving the life of Balmain's wife, Maura Balmain, who was grievously wounded by the unknown intruder. According to Chase, they visited Edward Balmain Senior to discuss some financial matters."

"How did you save her life?"

"I tried to stop the bleeding. I called a nurse I know and told the butler to call a doctor. Luckily there was one in the building. They did the actual lifesaving."

"It's that kind of building? Butlers? Doctors? And maids?"

"Ain't nothing wrong with butlers and maids," Amelia opined and stopped dusting. "So that's why you're looking so rough this morning. You leave her alone, Mr. Reggie. Esmé's got things to do. Finish your coffee and say good-bye."

"Aye, aye, captain." He saluted her with his cup, gulped the last of it, and blew her a kiss. "Keep the paper. We'll talk later."

Not if I could help it.

"And you," Amelia turned to me. "Better drink your coffee and get yourself in a tub of bubbles."

Reggie exited, grin firmly in place. She shut the door behind him.

"He's finally gone. So what happened and why do you have this new purple dress hanging up? Cashmere, no less." Amelia was fingering the item I wore home. "What happened last night?" She scanned the paper Reggie left behind. "You didn't start out wearing this."

"There was a lot of blood, which spilled on my dress when I helped Maura back to bed. She gave this to me."

"Oh no, not your beautiful silk. That pretty robin's-egg color. Where is it?"

"Police custody."

"That's a shame. I mighta been able to get the stains out."

"I don't think so." I pictured the ruined dress. "Too far gone."

"Where'd the blood come from? Did she get shot?"

"It's all in the morning paper."

"You get yourself in the strangest jams."

"Not my fault."

"Didn't say it was your fault. You just got this thing going on. Trouble."

"You thinking about leaving my employ? For something quieter?"

"Are you kidding? I love my work, and I love that you give me endless stories to talk about. So what happened?"

"The paper said it all." That was my story and I was sticking to it. Amelia ordered me to put a wet cloth over my eyes and slather cream all over my face. She was a benevolent tyrant.

"You should look presentable for this meeting, wherever it is. You're a famous playwright and you don't want to shame me, do you? I'll set out your suit like you told Mr. Graydon. Thankfully it ain't pants." Amelia had a grudge against slacks. Or at least women in trousers.

Happily, Act Three of the luckless play from which I pulled most of my wardrobe had the perfect outfit, designed by Willie Kim. I was grateful that character had been a member of the upper crust and not some waif off the street.

Need I say it was a glorious wool crepe suit in forest green? The jacket was close-fitting but flowed over the hips in a deep overskirt. A sewn-in belt was secured by a jeweled pin in front, and the bishop sleeves with eight gold studs, buttoned halfway to the elbows, made it stand out. The skirt fitted closely over my hips but had clever kick pleats so I could take long strides. I wore a green-gold-and-blue patterned silk scarf at the neck like an ascot. I had paid a pretty price for a pair of dark green kid leather shoes and a bag that matched. My hat was fawn-colored with a wide green band around the crown and a matching jeweled pin.

I should always have a costume designer make my clothes. You could find yourself playing any part correctly in clothes like these. They elevated the acting, and I hoped today I could act normal. I took special care with my makeup and hair under Amelia's careful tutelage.

"Not bad," she judged. "Don't step over any dead bodies. You've reached your quota for today."

EIGHT

GRAYDON'S LUXURIOUS PIERCE-ARROW, driven by the reliable Robbins, appeared on the street. I hurried down the stairs to meet Graydon sprinting halfway up. He spared a glance for my third-act suit and held out his arm for me.

"You look perfect, Esmé. Green is always perfect for an elfin queen with red-gold curls. Or perhaps for Robin *Hoodlet*."

In the show, this costume's trim tailoring and subdued forest green telegraphed how much the character had learned and grown. I wondered if I had learned as much. However, I reminded myself that the play, *Afternoon Tea with Nigel*, was a disaster, but today's forthcoming drama was mine to write.

"Robin Hoodlet? And who are you? Friar Tuck? Little John?" Graydon wore a dark suit, white shirt, blue vest, and coordinating tie and pocket square. He looked much more attractive than he ought. I held onto his hand for dear life.

"Anyone you wish. Except the evil Sheriff of Nottingham."

"You have to stop looking at me that way." I could feel heat radiating from him.

"What way?"

"Like you're a starving man and I'm dessert."

"Not dessert. You're the entrée." People in love say stupid things. "We should go. Can't let Balmain get away with any nonsense."

"You read the newspaper?"

"*The Times*. Could have been worse. The story wasn't on the front page."

We were ushered into a private dining room on the ninth floor of the University Club. It was clear Balmain Senior, already awaiting us, intended that our chat remain confidential. The walls were paneled in dark wood that matched the chairs. Red velvet curtains were open, light sifting through sheer panels. The table was set with crisp white linens, china plates, and crystal goblets. People could get used to this kind of living. Our set designers would love a peek at this place.

We were seated and crisp salads were placed in front before us. Balmain had pre-ordered, or more likely his new butler Sebastian had done so. The waiter was not an actor I recognized—so many were—but he was attentive. Because this was a business meeting, I ordered a sedate cup of tea. Once the waiter exited, Balmain addressed us.

"Thank you for coming. I must apologize for last night. I was out of my head. Duncan— Poor Duncan."

"Perfectly understandable," Graydon said.

Balmain turned to me. "The truth is, without you, Miss de LaForet, I would not be anticipating a grandchild today. Last night, I wasn't thinking about that woman."

He certainly had been, when he was shouting that she'd killed his son. Was this the day-after whitewash to make him appear a better man?

"Her. Maura."

"Yes. Maura most certainly would have bled to death, and I wouldn't know the truth, that part of it anyway. My grandchild is the most important thing in the world to me. If the child really happens."

Edward Balmain was not a handsome man, certainly not like his son, but he had a certain attractive intensity. The night before I hadn't had time to study him. Now I did. In his late fifties, he had hawklike features, quick sharp eyes the color of steel that took in everything, and thinning dark hair.

"How is Maura doing?" I asked. "She really is pregnant, isn't she?"

He seemed to flinch at the word *pregnant*, as if it were too indelicate.

"Stable, but not quite out of the woods." Balmain sipped his drink. "Seems to be with child. They're doing the rabbit test to confirm it. But that Doctor Parkhurst—top notch by the way—believes there's a baby. Women know these things, I suppose." He shrugged his shoulders, baffled by the strange powers of women.

"Have you seen her?"

"Not yet. Tomorrow. Today there's a funeral to plan."

"We'd like to visit her." Graydon squeezed my hand.

"By all means. Doctors Hospital will do right by her. Maura Balmain will get all the care she needs with no argument from me."

"Your son told you Maura couldn't have children."

"Such a strange lie. He knew how much I wanted an heir. My son Duncan—" Balmain struggled to find words. "He told me he wanted children, but it was impossible and it was all her fault."

"That's why you resented her?"

"This conversation is entirely between the three of us," Graydon assured him.

"I did resent her, and where she came from," Balmain said. "I thought she entrapped him. As far as I could tell, she was pretty but poor. Hardworking, that's true, but nothing but shanty Irish."

"Esmé is half Irish and half French-American," Graydon said firmly. Balmain merely grunted. What kind of Irish was I? Was there an Irish in between *shanty* and *lace curtain*? Ah yes, some called us the *flannel-mouthed Irish*, those who have a way with words.

"I like your daughter-in-law more and more."

I stared at Balmain and he stared back, then he chuckled unexpectedly.

"I suppose you would," he said. "There's a toughness to Irish women, tough enough to hang on to Duncan through all my disapproval, through all his abuse, tough enough for her to bring this baby to term. At least I hope she can. No frailty there. She stood up to my son and I could see the bruises he gave her. She never said a word against him. I thought it was just because of the money."

"She swore she loved him."

"So did 'Frankie love Johnny.' The song, you know."

Graydon shot me a look. Neither of us knew where this was heading. But reporters know this: Let the subject talk. Keep listening. Things will spill out.

Balmain groaned. "I can't say I'm entirely surprised that Duncan is gone. I am surprised it was his wife who did the deed. He seemed to be afraid of something or someone. There was always something a bit off about Duncan— My late wife named him that. When he was a child, he mistreated animals. Set fires. Stole things. We made excuses for him, she and I, that he'd grow up, grow out of it, mature. But he never did." Balmain rubbed his head as if in pain. "I had to donate a damned building to get him into Yale. My alma mater. I hoped that marriage, even to Maura Fitzgerald, would change him. Seemed to at first, but then his wildness came back."

"His wildness?" Graydon asked.

"Women, alcohol, gambling, drugs— Yes, I knew about the cocaine. Illicit pleasures. Truth is, Duncan had it too easy. I can see that now. He was too good-looking, had too much money, people were always willing to cut slack for him." Balmain seemed smaller for a moment. "You work hard and you try to give your son all the things you never had. Chaseborn, are you amenable to working on retainer? Whatever threats Duncan was afraid of—they're still out there. I want to know."

"My business normally tends toward money crimes, not—crimes of violence."

"Hang it, man, you and she have already made a name for—for finding out these kinds of unsavory things. And I'm told you can be relied upon. I'll make it worth your while."

"Very well. We will do what we can. Remember, this is not our usual scope of investigation." As if Graydon and I had a 'usual scope of investigation.'

"As I said," Balmain said. "Duncan feared something. Exactly what I don't know. There was some trouble with a union, union organizing, agitators, that kind of thing. With Duncan, it could have been anything, personal, social, money troubles."

"What kind of money troubles?"

"The usual. Hanging on to it, losing it, gambling it away."

"The more people know, the bigger the chance of word slipping out," Graydon warned.

"You're telling me not to speak of how Duncan was killed. Why would I tell? No one needs to know."

"I'll have an agreement drawn up," Graydon said. "What happened between you and the police?"

"You saw the papers? They're going with the intruder angle." Balmain paused for the waiter. Our excellently prepared chicken cordon bleu was placed before us. I was starved, but Balmain merely stared at his plate. "Go ahead, the food is good here. Can't say I have an appetite today." He was right, it was delicious. "The police were most amenable to Miss de LaForet's creative suggestion."

"I was merely thinking out loud."

"You came up with a hell of an idea."

"Esmé's big on creative ideas," Graydon remarked, though I was sure he was regretting my idea, as was I.

If I didn't want Maura pilloried in public, neither did I want some innocent man to be blamed. Unless of course, he really was a killer. I knew Balmain's wealthy circles would close ranks after a scandal, but he—and Maura— might be shunned if they knew she had killed her husband.

"To the world, my son Duncan was killed by an intruder. O'Hara said fate was with us. A man was found dead early this morning, he fit the bill, and he had Duncan's gun, thanks to O'Hara. This lowlife was suspected in several murders, and now the world will know that Duncan's beloved wife, Maura, survived the attack and is recovering in the hospital. That story will be in the afternoon papers."

"And the 'intruder'?" Graydon asked. "Who was he?"

"A down-and-outer, killed in a bar fight, after—after Duncan died." Balmain shook his head. "Suspect in a half dozen murders. He was the baddest of bad apples, so we need not have any guilt."

"Did he have a family?" Maybe a little guilt, I thought.

"A wife, three children. They will receive a sum of money to see he's buried, and for the family. I'll see to that. And it seems he was found with a generous amount of cash on him."

Perhaps some good could come out of the whole sordid episode, yet I felt bad about the lies the rich tell. Wouldn't it be more important for women to know that monsters like Duncan existed? That they would go so far as cutting a baby from its mother's womb? Wasn't there some Greek myth about that?

"Have you made funeral arrangements for Duncan?" Graydon asked.

"Not yet. Sebastian will be tending to the details." He shifted in his seat and took a long swallow of beer. Of course he would leave it to the butler.

"What will happen to Sebastian?" I asked.

"He may choose to stay in Maura's employ, though I doubt he will. Bit of a nervous sort. If he wants, he has a job with me. Handy that, lost my butler not long ago. Sebastian is filling in. I'm just glad my wife isn't alive to see this sad day. She adored Duncan. Lived to see him marry. She even came around to Maura."

"You said Duncan was afraid of threats," I cut in. "What kind of threats?"

"He didn't say. Might have been a woman. Or her angry boyfriend. He wasn't the most faithful of husbands. Thought it best not to press him."

Balmain asked Graydon to examine all of Duncan's papers and business dealings. Graydon agreed, and Balmain turned his attention to me.

"Miss de LaForet, I understand that while you assist Chaseborn on occasion, you are also a playwright of some little note."

Little? I glanced at Graydon. "Some. My new play will reopen soon at the Hawthorne Theatre."

"Can I count on your discretion?"

What did he mean? Everyone knew I was involved. My name was in the first-day story. Did he think I would drag this story out on stage? Or blab it around at cocktail parties?

"I shall be discreet," I said, frostily. "I care about Maura."

❧

"Balmain knows more than he's saying," I remarked when we were back in the car.

"Everyone has things they keep hidden," Graydon said. "Things they don't want known."

I gave him a look and he slowly smiled. "Do tell."

"Home, Robbins. You don't mind, do you, darling? It is your home, or will be soon."

He was trying to get me used to the idea, even though he promised we could decide together where we'd live. And I wasn't going to give up my apartment.

"I don't mind, if I can get a good cup of coffee. And what about your secrets, my dear Chaseborn?"

"I can't think of any secrets I might have at the moment. But I wonder—"

"What do you wonder?"

"If there's anything at all you haven't found out about me."

"There are the secret nude portraits of your old girlfriends."

"Not a secret in *my* circle, and well executed too, if I may say so."

A circle in which I would never fit, in that strange stratosphere of wealth and privilege, of exclusion and inclusion. I was an outsider. Like Maura Balmain.

"My circle is more fun."

"I dare say, all those writers and actors, lofty philosophers, and grand ideas that fly around you."

"Don't try to flatter me. Who knows how many women you've squired around town."

I remembered how thoroughly I searched the newspapers' social news when I discovered Graydon Chase was that notorious playboy, Rupert Graydon Chaseborn. How outraged I was. How I needed to know *everything*.

"There must be a statute of limitations on that. No man expects a woman to investigate his every social engagement."

"Public information." I suppressed a giggle. "Besides, darling, I'll never stop wanting to know all about you."

"You and the tax man. The funny thing is, you weren't after my money."

"Not a cent. Simply your heart and soul."

NINE

66 "WHERE IS SHE? Where is that bloody woman?" A tall well-dressed man demanded this information as he burst through the front door of Graydon's penthouse and raced past the dignified Robbins, who trailed behind this angry whirlwind like the tail of a kite.

" 'Bloody'? Isn't that supposed to be a bad word?" I asked. No one answered me.

The tall man stormed past me into the living room with its glorious view of Central Park, but he didn't care. I silently implored Robbins for an answer.

"His lordship," Robbins announced. "Apparently, he is visiting. Unannounced."

"His WHAT-ship?" I stood frozen.

Graydon held out his hands to me. I latched on for dear life.

"His lordship," Robbins intoned, "is the honorable Lord Cyril Corduroy Chaseborn." Robbins remained calm, but I detected a glint of humor in his expression.

"Steady, darling." Graydon held me tight as if I would run. "Forgive me, but he's my father."

"Your father?" I'd had enough trouble when I met his mother.

"It's true," he said. "Contrary to rumor, I was not hatched from an egg."

"Lord Cyril Corduroy Chaseborn," Robbins announced again with a small cough, and Cyril stopped pacing and inclined his head. Majestically. He ceased bellowing for the 'bloody woman' long enough to take my offered hand. Graydon introduced me.

"Father, may I present Miss Esmé de LaForet."

"Corduroy?" I pushed back the urge to laugh. "Seriously?"

"Quite so. My middle name and also our family line and title. A family tradition for our eldest sons. We are the Earls of Corduroy."

Lord Cyril Chaseborn was an *earl?* That meant Lady Jane was a *countess?* Before, in my mind, these two were just ephemeral, theoretical, distant figures of fun. Graydon and I were so dizzy in love (and busy dealing with murders), we hadn't dug into all the gory details of his family. He'd moved across an ocean to get away from them. And wait, corduroy has its very own earl? Why not the Duke of Damask? The Viscount of Velvet? I sent Graydon a baffled look.

"Not the fabric, darling. The French."

"Right," I said. "*Coeur de roi*, in French, would mean 'the heart of the king,' wouldn't it?" Well, if they can have an Earl of Sandwich, why not an Earl of Corduroy?

"And indeed that's what it did mean, back in the beginning," Lord Cyril said. "Eleventh century. The Norman Conquest, 1066 and all that. Our family is quite ancient."

"Oh yes," Graydon smirked. "Our Norman ancestors practically arm-wrestled King John into signing the Magna Carta."

"Normans? So all this time I thought you were English, and you're actually French!"

Graydon laughed, but Cyril was not amused. "We are honorably related to the original barons of the sceptered isle, as Rupert well knows."

"The barons of Runnymede?" I inquired.

"The very ones," Graydon said, "and some of those ancient Chaseborns nearly lost that pile of centuries-old stones of ours back home. The pile we laughingly call Chaseborn Manor."

Oh no, they had a *manor house?* No wonder Lady Jane was writing a gothic romance. Would that Graydon *had* been hatched from an egg.

I felt sheer panic. Until now, Graydon's father was simply a name, and in my mind, short and stout and wearing a top hat. This man stomping down the hall was as tall and trim as Graydon. His blue eyes were similar to Graydon's, though cooler. Hair, salt and pepper. Posture, ramrod straight. I put him somewhere around sixty. Ancient.

His Lordship resumed his striding and shouting around my fiancé's apartment. (I still found that word hard to say. Not apartment—*fiancé*.) The stranger was huffing and puffing and growling in his grumbly English accent. Finally he stopped short.

"Where is she, Rupert?" I was still puzzling over the *his lordship* business. I didn't know the man, never met him, nor did I particularly want to. Especially now. After circling the living room, the dining room, and the study, he returned snorting, "Where is that maddening woman?" His cold blue eyes were blazing.

"Hello, Father. Welcome to New York," Graydon said pleasantly. "You neglected to wire." The elder man ignored him and stomped away, bellowing.

"Insanity?" I whispered.

"Always suspected, never diagnosed," Graydon muttered, moving me out of the line of fire. We made our way back to safety in the living room.

"Your actual father?"

"So Mother says. By the way, it wouldn't go over well to reveal that you and I were at the scene of another crime last night. Therefore, Robbins has hidden the papers. He also removed my painting of you from my bedroom."

That was a relief. I blushed at the very thought of Graydon's racy rendering of me, and that Robbins had touched it. The picture was titled "Fever" and had caught me asleep when I was ill with the flu that ravaged the city. However, it could be interpreted a couple of different ways. And I was in *lingerie*.

"Thank goodness for Robbins, then. And your mother? Where is she?"

"Scribbling in the guest room. Obsessed with the strong-jawed, raven-haired master of the manor house of her literary dreams, or some such rot."

I tried to keep my grin at bay. "She says romance novels are all the rage.'

"I have no idea, but she's thrown herself into it with enthusiasm."

"And where did *he* come from?"

"Jolly old England, I presume."

"But why, and why now?"

"Unknown. He's not the type to chase a wild hare." A moment of doubt seemed to shake him. "No, nothing. You look wonderful, by the way."

"You mentioned that before. I don't know what I'd have worn if I'd known that the aristocracy was on the loose."

Graydon took the opportunity to pull me close and kiss me. I was now glad that I looked so prim and proper, even though Saturdays for me usually called for trousers and a comfortable old sweater. After our meeting with Balmain, I was feeling the need to change into my Saturday clothes. A new idea for a play was fluttering right above my head and I wanted to work with it. A crime drama. However, it would have to leave me alone for a while. There were kisses to be had. "Happy Days Are Here Again" was playing on the radio. Ironically, I might add.

"Jane! Where are you? I know you're here," Lord High-and-Mighty Chaseborn returned shouting, and we pulled apart. "I saw your car and Andrew, your driver, on the street, polishing a fender where the entire world can see him."

Lady Jane Chaseborn emerged from the guest bedroom, looking younger and more relaxed than when I first met her. Her short hair was bouncy and she wore a bit of makeup. Who knew you could be restored to life by writing a gothic romance novel?

"Oh hello, Cyril. You bellowed? How is the lord of the manor?"

He pulled a crumpled tabloid newspaper from his overcoat and waved it theatrically like a prop.

"Have you seen this?"

She was unfazed. "I don't read that kind of paper here in the States. And how are you?"

"Vexed."

"So, the same, then. Good for you." I told myself to take dialogue notes.

He spun from her to Graydon. "And you! It says you are engaged. *Engaged.* To be married?!"

"That's usually what it means." Graydon indicated me. "My fiancée." But his father paid no attention.

I craned my neck to see the newspaper headline.

PEER'S SON TANGLES WITH MOBSTERS WITH
AMERICAN PLAYWRIGHT

News had traveled across the sea, but I would have recast that headline. It made me sound like I was *with* the mobsters, and I wasn't. I had been on my own until Graydon showed up with Frank Romeo. The evening ended with arrests for murder in a crowded restaurant whose patrons had overheard everything. Jane calmly took the paper.

"Yes, indeed. We're going to discuss a formal party for the announcement this afternoon."

"We are?" I asked, but no one seemed to hear me. It was apparent they hadn't seen today's newspapers about the Balmain murder. Thank goodness. The man who I supposed was Graydon's father threw the paper down, and I snatched it up. I'd heard about British newspapers.

"We haven't told anyone yet," I said, to no one in particular. I glanced at the lovely ring Graydon had given me. Our engagement was in its infancy and we hadn't prepared for meeting relatives, other than Lady Jane, who had come at me blazing with indignation. Before we came to terms with each other.

"You?" He finally turned his gaze on me and my ring, a Chaseborn family heirloom. "And who are you?

"This is Esmé, Esmé Rafferty de LaForet. My Esmé. My fiancée." I appreciated that Graydon put his hand around my waist, yet that gesture seemed to offend Lord Cyril Chaseborn.

"Hmph. You don't look like a woman of the theatre," Cyril sneered. "And with a name like that, what are you, French? Irish? What?"

"A 'woman of the theatre'? How dare you?" His sneer made it sound like I was a trollop, a gold digger. "Do I look like a woman of the theatre?"

I knew what his stereotype was, something straight out of *Gold Diggers of 1933*.

"Well, not precisely. Your clothes are quite—acceptable."

"That is a marvelous outfit, Esmé," Jane said. "You must share your secret sometime."

"I have the most clever designer," I said. "Like all the best gold diggers."

"Oh, pay no attention to Cyril, he's terribly old-fashioned."

I was glad Graydon hadn't divulged that particular secret, the origin of my wardrobe. My marvelous suit was a costume from a play, as I am indeed *a woman of the theatre.*

"Esmé is a fine playwright," Jane told her husband. "And *Leaving Alamogordo* is delightful, a boffo hit, as they say here. We shall see it again when it opens in its new theatre."

"Leaving *what*? Alamo *who*?"

"Alamogordo. It's a place. Somewhere in America. It's the title of her play. Do try to keep up, Cyril."

His lordship slapped his forehead. "Robbins, a Scotch, if you please."

Graydon's valet swiftly produced a tray complete with glasses and a decanter of Scotch. His lordship poured himself a stiff one and downed it in one gulp. Mr. High-and-Mighty would be very lucky if he didn't find himself in one of my plays. I caught Lady Jane's look. That look said, *That's simply how we deal with him.*

"I was not consulted," Cyril complained.

"Modern times," Graydon pointed out.

"This London newspaper says, in addition to involving yourself in solving gangland murders, that you're to be married. Married! They had the gall to question me about this! To my face!"

"And what did you tell them?" Graydon asked pleasantly.

"That of course I was quite aware of the romance and I looked forward to meeting your intended in person, and in fact I was on my way to the States." Cyril grimaced as if gargling gasoline. "That we wanted to announce it all together. One big happy family."

"And was that true?"

"Are you quite mad, Rupert? It was a pack of lies! You have kept me apprised of nothing. You have duties! To the family! To Chaseborn Industries!"

"Which has nothing to do with our marriage. The business is well in hand. You know I'm good at that sort of thing."

"And you insist upon this private investigation nonsense. It was fine as long as you kept the subject to money. Embezzlement, larceny, fraud, that sort of thing, that's quite normal, very helpful. But American gangsters? And murders? That's going too far. And involving a woman!" We were all relieved Cyril Chaseborn hadn't seen this morning's New York City newspapers. "I knew nothing about any of this."

Graydon and I shared a look. We didn't plan it that way. Or we might never have met, I thought. What about *my* family? My mother came from Irish stock and my father was French. They'd be horrified I'd become involved with an *Englishman*, Heaven forbid, and even more so that he seemed to be what the British called "aristocracy."

"In my defense, Father, you usually prefer it that way," Graydon said mildly.

His lordship spun hotly on his wife. "And you, Jane—"

"Yes, Cyril?" She seemed quite calm and amused.

"You could have let me know. My own wife." His look of outrage was delightful, almost stage-worthy. I'd have to remember it for my next play. I knew I couldn't take this personally, it would hurt my feelings. But everything is material.

"Well, it all happened very fast, and I've been busy," Jane replied.

"Busy! I can see that. You have practically snatched random women off the street for Graydon to marry in your quest for grandchildren. But to choose *a woman of the theatre!*"

TEN

6 6 PLAYWRIGHT." I STRAIGHTENED my jacket and glared at him.

"A very fine playwright, remember, Cyril?" Lady Jane patted my shoulder. "Esmé's full of rather advanced ideas."

"I can only imagine." Though really he couldn't. He gulped his second Scotch.

"Of course, I still have hopes for my other son to produce an heir." She gestured extravagantly. "Besides, that was before I started writing my novel. I'm not sure I'd have time for nurseries and nappies now."

His lordship grabbed the bottle of Scotch again. I noticed he didn't invite the rest of us to sip Graydon's pricey liquor.

"Novel? What novel?"

"*My* novel, of course," she said haughtily. "You didn't know, did you, Cyril? That I have a brain? I don't think you've asked me anything since 1922. In fact, I was here to discuss it with Esmé. Plot points, you know. As well as the engagement party. Is there any sherry in the house?"

Robbins was ready with her ladyship's sherry on a silver tray. He inclined his head toward me and murmured that my coffee would be out soon.

Cyril peered closely at his wife. "Jane, are you wearing—*trousers?!*" How dare she? Wearing trousers to write? Not riding or playing tennis? Unthinkable!

"Do you like them? I wear pants when I write. Very freeing, don't you know?"

I was afraid he might have a stroke right then and there. "Don't be ridiculous, Jane. What have you got to write about? While wearing trousers!"

"What haven't I got to write about? Gothic romances with gory murders are all the rage, my dear. And I do have ideas of my own." She smiled and sipped her sherry. "There's always that old family scandal of yours from the last century. So amusing."

"What scandal?" He advanced on her.

"Your great-uncle and that dancehall girl. Or was it a boy?"

He snorted. "That doesn't count, the man was barking mad."

"It all counts, Cyril. All stories count. Esmé says *every-thing* is material for a writer. And speaking of barking, wasn't he the one who howled at every full moon? It doesn't really matter, my book is fiction. I have a cauldron full of ideas and I just pull them out."

"This is the most preposterous thing I've ever heard. You wouldn't."

"Why wouldn't I? I have miles to go and I've only just begun." She brushed imaginary dust from her immaculate tweed trousers.

"You've gone mad! Writing novels? Wearing pants? Like some *modern* woman." He looked to Graydon. "Did you know of this?"

Graydon cleared his throat. "It's a recent development."

"Esmé's been so encouraging," Lady Jane said.

I had, in truth, been encouraging her to write a book. It would keep her busy and out of Graydon's way and on my side. Still, I didn't care to be in Lord Cyril's crosshairs. I preferred he'd remained pure fiction in my imagination.

Lord Chaseborn sent a scathing glance my way. He took Jane's arm and guided her to the room where she'd been napping and writing, at Graydon's desk with a fine view of the park. She could have stayed in her townhome, but it seemed she enjoyed a change of scenery. And there had been some mention of an engagement announcement. Lady Jane merely smiled prettily at her husband.

He said with menace, "No one can get under my skin the way you do."

"One must have some accomplishments, mustn't one?"

He shut the door firmly and we heard the lock turn. There was a lot of shouting. I'd always heard the English were supposed to be so subtle. They were not subtle now. Graydon and I crept close to the locked room, but we couldn't make out most of the words, except for a few expletives. "Bloody" seemed to be the most popular.

I should have felt guilty about listening, but I was concerned for Lady Jane, especially after our encounter with Edward Balmain and his daughter-in-law Maura. We stood ready at the door to assist if necessary.

"I love you, Esmé," Graydon suddenly blurted. "You're not thinking of backing out?"

"Constantly," I joked. "I love you too. But your father stared at my ring like he wanted it back in the family vault."

"It was mine to give." He kissed the ring and my fingers. "You have that look. The one that says you're cooking up something in that brain."

"If I am, my brain hasn't let me in on it."

"I've seldom seen Father quite so agitated. But Mother's not quite the same person she was either. And it's all since I met you."

"Don't blame me." I reached for him and he held me. Soon the angry shouts subsided. Sounds of moans and groans replaced them. I was shocked. "They are not—? Are they?"

"No, of course not. They're my parents."

"I think they're having a reunion."

Graydon shuddered. "I don't care to imagine."

Definite sounds of lovemaking were coming from behind the door. I know, because I'm in the theatre. Graydon and I retreated to the study where Robbins had left our coffee with the silver service.

"There's life in the old boy yet," I said.

"That's not funny." He looked terribly English at the moment.

"You're right. It's horrifying." I started laughing and he joined me.

"You understand I'm probably scarred for life."

I took his hand. "You'll get over it."

We laughed, but Lord Chaseborn reminded me a little too much of Balmain and his hatred for his daughter-in-law Maura. Hatred mitigated only by the thought of the baby growing in her belly. Poor child, both of them.

"My father is not a monster, even though he gives a pretty good impression of one." Graydon snorted. "But he likes to be in the know, you know. Upsets him to think anyone might ever do anything on their own."

"Like me? A *woman of the theatre*?"

"We must encourage him to take in more plays. Broaden his horizons."

We sipped our coffee, avoiding the subject of our formal engagement announcement. At least there was one reporter who wouldn't print that story. Reggie for some reason hated to think of me with Graydon. Strangely, I had no trouble thinking of Reggie with all his interchangeable blondes.

The door opened and Lord and Lady Chaseborn seemed much calmer, though she had a definite smirk on her face.

"Your mother and I are going to the townhouse. To *discuss* things," Cyril said.

"We have so much to catch up on," Jane added.

"And Rupert," Cyril continued, "I should very much like to drive that impressive automobile of yours."

"The car? I'm sure Mother will lend you hers. Andrew can chauffeur you about."

"How tedious. I've heard about that fast car of yours. Most intriguing."

"Do you mean the Pierce-Arrow?" I asked.

He ignored me. "Too flashy by half, of course, with that naked archer chrome hood ornament. But no one knows me here, so I can give it a good workout. Excellent for the horsepower, and all that."

"Don't think so. It's a bit of a monster," Graydon said. "And remember the last time? They drive on the wrong side of the road here. Takes a bit of getting used to."

"Nothing I can't handle, my boy."

Robbins, seemingly in fear of disaster, spoke up. "Excuse me, my lord, I'm afraid there's a mechanical issue with the Pierce-Arrow. The, um, carburetor, I believe. The mechanic is awaiting spares. It's not safe until they can—"

"Nonsense, I inspected it in the garage. Just before I came up. Looks fine to me."

"There's always the Ford." Graydon picked up a king from his chessboard and toyed with it. "I suppose you could drive that."

"The Ford? Don't be ridiculous. Earls don't drive Fords."

"Of course not, how silly of me," Graydon said evenly. "Then I'm afraid you're stuck with Mother's car and her driver. How inconvenient." He dropped the king and smiled. Checkmate?

Cyril growled and stomped away down the hall. I took a seat to keep from falling down.

"About the car, Graydon. What is going on?"

"We can't let him drive a car. He suffers from, let's say, overenthusiasm, when he's not being an absolute thunderstorm. He turns into Mr. Toad, the Terror of the Motorway."

"Mr. Toad? From *The Wind in the Willows*?" I vaguely remembered reading it.

"Put him behind the wheel and it's Toad of Toad Hall all over again. He might come back with just a fender in hand, or a bent steering wheel. If he comes back at all." He closed his eyes for a moment. "Or a front seat full of fish, after driving it into a river."

"Your father drove a car into a river? And caught fish? With the top down? I mean, the car, not the fish."

"One time. The talk of every pub in the countryside. For months. Years. No one has ever topped it. Oh, but it wasn't his fault, you see, never his fault. It was the cow's fault, or a sheep or a tree or a rock or the river, and it simply leaped into his path without warning."

"The fish story. Did it make the papers?"

"Memorably. EARL DITCHES POLE, CATCHES FISH WITH CAR. My favorite was EARL DRIVES, FISH FLEE FOR THEIR LIVES. It's humorous now, I suppose."

Lord Cyril and Lady Jane emerged from the guest room and together strode purposefully for the front door.

"Rupert, we shall discuss the matter of your engagement later," Cyril said through clenched teeth.

Robbins was instantly at the door with their wraps. Soon they were gone and peace was restored.

"Except for that close call with the car, I think that went rather well," Graydon said.

I don't know if he intended it to be hilarious, but I was helpless with laughter.

<h1 style="text-align:center">ELEVEN</h1>

G RAYDON FOUND A dark and pricey restaurant, suitable for hiding away from family and the press, and he drove the anonymous little Ford, rather than his lovely Pierce-Arrow, which stuck out in a crowd.

The restaurant was the kind of place I would normally pass by. Too expensive, all mahogany and red leather with prints of quails and ducks on the walls, reminding me of the University Club. Ushered to a quiet table for two with a half-circle banquette, we ordered martinis, though my head was still swimming from the day we'd had.

"I'm sorry you had to be a part of all that," Graydon said. "Balmain. My family."

"You mean it's not always so exciting? Where are we now? Act one, scene three? Or is it four? Listen, I asked you to take me to Balmain's apartment with you. No one could know what we would find." I leaned into him, breathing in his scent.

"A woman is alive because of you, darling. But it was all so bloody and awful."

I closed my eyes, but I couldn't block the image of Duncan Balmain lifeless on the expensive Aubusson rug. I opened them to Graydon, his dark hair slightly mussed. I reached up to smooth his hair.

"You didn't want me there, I know. Like so many other things to which, and to whom, you don't want to expose me, such as your friends and family and your social class." A sudden thought: Was he ashamed of me?

"My beautiful Esmé, my so-called society friends bore me to death."

They bored me too. They never talked about important things, like ideas, or feelings, or the political storm clouds gathering in Europe. They yammered on about money and possessions, yachts and country homes. All lovely things, but not the meaning of life.

My associates and friends, the reporters and playwrights, the designers and actors, and even friends slightly tinged with crime, like Patrick Dentino, they all had stories to tell. We could rattle on all night about all the things we knew and imagined. We could solve the problems of the world in an all-night diner and then retire to a cold water flat.

"You, on the other hand, are a beautiful, magical elf," he said.

"Ha. I am neither elfin nor magical. I'm just—real."

"Says the magical creature. You talk about my shallow friends, yet how many men that you met at that gala last night wanted to take you out?"

"At least three. Dull boys. Nothing to talk about but filthy lucre and did I think an investment in my play was wise? No mention at all of murders or mayhem."

"Esmé, about that man in your apartment who answered the phone. Pendleton."

"You know Reggie, and he was there because of you."

Graydon's expression was puzzled. "Because of me?"

"He was worried about my safety. After I left with that notorious playboy Rupert Chaseborn. I'm not sure he believes we're truly together."

"He knows I go by Chase. And he's still calling you his future wife."

"So do you." I smiled. "Reggie is simply a pal, my first friend in New York. He's teasing."

"I don't like it and I don't like him."

"Something on which you two agree."

"With good reason."

"I didn't expect you to be at the party last night. But I had to go. It was a command performance for me to meet investors in the play. Sal's always looking for backers. I called on Reggie because I knew he had evening wear ready on a moment's notice, and besides, that was before our engagement."

"That's all?"

I almost laughed. "Are you jealous, Graydon?"

"Constantly. I'm concerned about you. About your reputation. Our reputations."

"This is New York. Everybody has a reputation. No one cares."

"Who knows if some Fleet Street flack is skulking about, spying on us. Not because of me, mind you, but because of Father landing here. How did they get that story?"

"How does anyone? Some British correspondent stationed here scanned the local papers and telegraphed the story. And like everybody else, they jumped the gun on our engagement."

"I don't like it."

This was a more conservative side of Graydon, offspring of the aristocracy. When were we going to ever get together, in a more personal way? He wanted me, I wanted him, but it was all so complicated. When I was ill, he stayed all night, making sure that Nurse Jesse was very obviously *present* at my apartment. Reputation, you know. With all the mixed signals Graydon had been giving me, he could be a train conductor.

"If I hadn't gone to the party for your play last night, you wouldn't be involved now."

"Was it last night? It feels like a hundred years ago." Our martinis arrived, small yet expensive. His hand snaked around my back and drew me closer.

"Esmé, I'm afraid I'll have to deal with a dozen Reggie Pendletons vying for you. Scoundrels, every one."

"And what about you? You need a woman who can straddle both your worlds. I'm the one who can mix with your detecting business *and* foxtrot across the dance floor with your society snobs. But what on earth can I do about your *family?*"

"I rarely take them out dancing."

"And were you ever going to tell me about being a *Chaseborn?*"

He sipped his martini. "I'm sure I was. At some point. It got harder when it was clear you had no idea. Such a freeing notion."

"I fault myself. I read the papers, I should have known all about you. What kind of reporter was I? Well, not a society reporter, that's for sure."

Graydon and I were still gazing hopelessly into each other's eyes over martinis when I heard the clicking of shutters and the dazzle and pop of flashbulbs. I blinked and rubbed my eyes as I caught sight of a couple of reporters with big four-by-five cameras sprinting away.

Graydon was already out of his seat giving chase.

TWELVE

THE SUNDAY NEWSPAPERS splashed the Balmain murder follow-up story all over the front pages. Duncan's killer had allegedly been found. As Balmain had predicted. That was remarkably quick work, and I wondered if anyone would believe it.

The police story followed closely—too closely—my suggested scenario from the other night. A ne'er-do-well suspected of other murders was killed in a bar fight, and the cops fingered this Johnny Akers for both the Duncan Balmain murder and the assault on Mrs. Balmain. Thus was the story put to rest by the police, if not the press corps. I'd have to have a word with Detective O'Hara.

I scanned all the headlines at a newsstand, and the Balmain story was everywhere. Reggie's was the most complete. Would the Johnny Akers angle dampen interest in the story? I hoped so.

A small sidebar in Reggie's *New York Post* story featured a picture of Graydon and me, looking into each other's eyes at the restaurant the previous night: GUMSHOE LOVEBIRDS, the cutline read. Just what you want all your friends to see, as well as your future in-laws, but if it weren't Graydon and me, I'd consider the photo pretty dreamy. Except for the jarring invasion of privacy. Graydon had given chase to the unknown cameramen in vain, and any hopes of finding some private time and space evaporated. Graydon drove me back home.

According to the newspapers, Balmain's killer had been found slain in a bar fight hours after the crime. Johnny Akers had a well-known grudge against the Balmains, who had fired him from a construction job. The police also found a watch on him which they said had been taken from Duncan, and a pistol which was still being tested. I hadn't witnessed that particular sleight-of-hand on Friday night. Perhaps it happened after I left. There was no mention of a knife or a stabbing. The police apparently implied both Duncan and Maura had been shot by the same intruder. Very neat.

Akers was the prime suspect in at least three other murders, including one for hire, according to Detective O'Hara. This all made him an excellent suspect, and Edward Balmain himself had blessed the coverup Friday night. The police could have come up with this scenario without my help, but any small thing could easily upset this applecart. How many other official stories were lies? And had it really harmed anyone? I wondered. Johnny Akers was beyond caring.

Every newspaper in the city wrote its own take on the murder, but only Reggie had interviewed the widow Akers. Akers had grown up in a solidly middle-class home, but he'd failed at everything. His widow Enid Akers and their three children now lived in a squat near the river, in the last remaining Hooverville in lower Manhattan. Reggie reported that the shack had tarpaper walls and a roof, sturdier than most, as the dead man had once worked as a carpenter. The photograph showed walls papered with comic strips and a rag rug on a rough wooden floor. Enid was more than willing to talk, even as she waited for the city to clear out the structures and uproot her and her children yet again.

"It's a sad day when you find out the man you married is a brute," Enid said. "He threatened to kill me every time he was disappointed or drunk. Broke my arm one time, he did."

The police had found the perfect patsy in Johnny Akers. I had no trouble believing this man had killed others. But I knew he hadn't killed Duncan Balmain.

Reggie Pendleton duly reported that the widow was 37 years old with brown hair shot through with gray strands.

Her face was lined with worry, her dark eyes brimming with tears, at least at the time of the interview. Her faded calico dress was covered by a baby blue hand-knit sweater, Reggie reported. Enid was a make-do kind of gal. Did she think her husband was capable of murder, Reggie had asked.

"He'd done it before now, hadn't he?" Enid answered. "First time he killed a man it was an accident. After that, he seemed to lose his soul. He got away with it a time or two. We moved away from New Jersey because the cops were getting too close. I guess I don't have to hide that anymore. It's a load off my mind." At this point in the story, she wiped her eyes with a hanky. Did Akers hate Balmain? Enid said he did.

"Had a job with Balmain Construction, Johnny did. But he was a union man and Balmain told him they didn't want no union workers. Threw him out, he did. That was enough for Johnny to hate him and his whole class."

Reggie's story noted that Balmain Construction claimed it was exploring the idea of unions, but had resisted attempts so far. However, Reggie noted, with Roosevelt in office, that day was coming, union officials said. Enid seemed something of a philosopher.

"I've been thinking about the grand irony of life, thinking about the wife of Mr. Duncan Balmain. She, so high and mighty and beautiful, and me, a careworn nobody. Both widowed on the same night, sisters of a sort, you know. I am devastated that she was hurt. I don't know what possessed my Johnny in that moment."

Tears slipped down her face, Reggie wrote, adding, "Enid Akers has learned the art of crying silently."

I tucked the paper in my purse.

❧

I'd heard that Église St-Jean-Baptiste was built for the French-Canadian servants of the wealthy Upper East Side.

It was money well spent, a place of beauty and majesty, much grander than the little church I knew growing up out West. Ornate and joyously decorated in blues and golds with stately marble columns, it offered balm to its parishioners. St-Jean-Baptiste was not as large as St. Patrick's Cathedral, but just as beautiful to my eyes.

The church was a good walk from my apartment, across Central Park and not too far from Graydon's. His family was Protestant in name but country club in attitude, meaning they attended church only on Christmas and Easter. Such an alliance would horrify my mother, but I wasn't marrying his parents, only him. I didn't know whether I'd see him later or not. We hadn't made plans yet and he might be busy with his parents.

As I approached the church, I heard French voices chattering around me, discussions of small domestic details, what they would serve for dinner, a sale at the market, an issue with the landlord. It was comforting. My father spoke the language with my mother, whose American accent remained terrible, though it amused him. I picked up what my mother referred to as "kitchen French" and my father as "outlaw French." Yet my accent was good and I could follow simple conversations. I smiled to myself. I knew the language and yet I didn't know anyone in that church. And that was the comforting thought. Anonymity is often underrated.

Several women smiled and nodded my way. I must have passed inspection in my black crepe suit, actually a dress and fitted jacket. Another outfit from that failed production of *Afternoon Tea with Nigel*. The suit featured interchangeable collars and cuffs. Today I chose the large gold organdy collar that resembled an outrageous bow and matching cuffs with pretty buttons. It made me feel both theatrical and polished. And if I was going to meet up with Graydon's father again, I decided my clothes should be worthy of a woman of the theatre.

Designer extraordinaire Willie Kim had created a hat that I could customize to wear with the suit, whichever collar I chose. It was a lovely black picture hat that dipped down on one side. I wore it with a large gold bow, secured with a jeweled pin. Following the crowd up the steps into the sanctuary, I sat in a pew toward the back. I didn't want to draw attention, although my clothes certainly did.

There were so many options, I didn't know who to pray for. Or should I confess I had a part in the story that would further mar a man's reputation? Already a bad reputation, but still. Was it true that the late Johnny Akers hated Duncan Balmain? What would he say? That he was dead and gone, so it didn't matter? Or that for once in his life, the money "found" in his effects would give Enid and the children a shot at a better future? Did his dead soul mind being the fall guy? Or did he want the story to come out more tangled than ever, starve his family, and harm a woman who was merely protecting her unborn child?

I gave myself a headache and no conclusion. A shiver ran through me when I glimpsed a camel-hair coat behind one of the marble columns. The coat was the kind that the gangster Frankie the Cat Romeo wore, his signature look. Was he keeping tabs on me? Again?

I blinked and looked once more. The coat was gone.

Thirteen

AFTER CHURCH, AFTER another brisk walk on that cool day—perfect to try and work off a guilty conscience—I reached my destination with pink cheeks, exhausted from my mental gymnastics.

Was I in a hotel or a hospital? Doctors Hospital lived up to its reputation as the luxury retreat for the sick and wealthy. There were no wards, only private rooms for private patients and likewise swanky accommodations for patients' families. The lobby looked like that of a fine residence. It figured Balmain would send his daughter-in-law where the usual questions would not be asked. It was all very hush-hush, and very plush-plush.

Any hint of scandal was worse for Edward Balmain than the death of his son. He might have been conflicted, but ever the careful businessman, he was holding fire until he was sure Maura was pregnant. I inquired for Mrs. Balmain at the huge polished wood reception desk.

"Go right up, Miss de LaForet." I was surprised to find I was on The List.

The lobby didn't have that medicinal hospital smell, but it wafted though the air on the floor where Maura Balmain's room was located. Nurse Jesse was coming out of the door as I approached.

"Miss de LaForet! You certainly have brought me work!"

"Sorry."

"Don't be. I'm seeing how the other half lives—and dies. And getting paid for it. Get a load of this place. Swank, pure swank."

"How is Maura?"

"She's awake. Surgery went well. One strong lady." Jesse cracked the door open and peeked inside. "You have a visitor, Mrs. Balmain."

The room was painted a delicate pink. The patient looked equally delicate, snuggled under a fluffy rose-colored satin cover. Her dark hair was an exclamation point against the pink pillows. Her black eye was turning to blue and green bruises. She would be lovely when everything healed and she lost that aura of fear. The small plant of blooming lavender violets I'd purchased on the street entered before me. I had no idea if she would re-member me.

"Hello, Maura. I'm Esmé de LaForet."

"I know you." Her smile was warm.

"How are you doing?" It seemed an idiotic question un-der the circumstances.

"The morning sickness is getting better, I think."

Nurse Jesse handed her a glass of water with a straw. "You need to replenish those fluids."

Maura gazed at me with one open eye. "How did you manage all this?" She waved at the room. "All this finery? And not a jail cell?"

"Wasn't me. I don't deserve any credit."

"I understand it was you who saved my life, and my baby's. At least, so far."

Jesse sent me a questioning look. "You're doing fine, Mrs. Balmain, and that baby is tucked below your heart. Safe and sound. Now, you're not to worry about anything. And that's straight from Old Man Balmain."

"Don't worry, Jesse. I'll stay in bed for the next six months if I have to." She patted her belly. "My own mother birthed seven of her own."

I hoped the little person inside her was a fighter like their mother.

"Come sit by me, Esmé. It's nice to have company." Jesse produced a chair for me.

"Surely you have friends visiting," I said, "and I don't want to take up your time—"

"Friends? Not likely." She looked away. "Duncan didn't want me to see anyone but him. And *his* friends. They had to be high-class, you know. My friends from the old neighborhood never felt comfortable around me after I married. Oh, look, you brought me violets! I love violets."

I noticed a huge bouquet of orchids from Edward Balmain. Keeping up appearances, no doubt, and my violets looked puny in comparison. However, you're expected to carry something when you're visiting someone in the hospital. The room had a lovely view of the East River and the Gracie Mansion, framed by silk drapes that matched the satin bedcover. What a pretty world it could be for the lucky few.

"Thank you for the dress, Maura. It came in handy, and it was lovely and warm. I'll return it."

"No, it's yours. It will look better with your coloring than mine."

"May I ask you about the other night?"

"You're not thinking about writing a play about this?"

So she did know about me. "Oh no. Not about this. Your father-in-law. He lives in the building, but he didn't hear the gunshots?"

"Edward's penthouse is seven stories above us. I'm lucky Sebastian hid in his room like the little mouse he is. Then I got lucky he only called Edward, not the police."

"I still can't believe Balmain Senior didn't call them," I said.

"That simply is *not done* on the Upper East Side. Edward hates bad publicity. Even more than he hates me, I think. And I'm lucky he only called Rupert Chaseborn. Your Graydon Chase. Because Mr. Chase brought you. And you—saved my life."

To keep from tearing up, I asked her, "Why did you lock yourself in the bedroom?"

"When Duncan fell, I was so afraid he would jump right back up and finish the job. He wanted to kill me. That's why I locked myself in, and I would have bled to death in there all alone. And if the cops had come before you got there, if I lived I'd be heading for the electric chair."

Jesse threw me a warning look. I was upsetting her patient. But it was true, murder in New York meant the electric chair. And ever since the Ruth Snyder case and that scandalous photo in the *Daily News* of Ruth strapped into the chair of death, everyone knew that women were no exception.

"Can you stand reading about the other night?" I pulled out the newspaper.

"Don't be rattling her, Esmé." Jesse stood up in her starched white uniform.

"I can take it," Maura said. "I must, sooner or later." She sat up in bed and took a deep breath. I handed her the paper and she squinted at Reggie's story, her forehead wrinkling. It fell from her hands and she stared at me. "I don't understand. Duncan's killer? It says this man Akers killed Duncan."

"It's a coverup. To keep the Balmain name clean."

"That's horrible. I can't let someone else be blamed for this."

"It's not your doing. Johnny Akers died that night. He apparently murdered other people. And he very conveniently hated your husband. It seems Duncan had fired him."

Jesse took Maura's pulse and glared at me. "It's elevated."

"I'm fine, Jesse, really. Esmé, are you saying Edward arranged this? With the police? To protect my child?" Her eyes lit up with realization. "*His* grandchild. That's why." I heard the door open. Maura smiled at someone behind me. "Rupert. I seem to remember you were there too, that night."

"Maura." Graydon took her hand. "Yes, I was with Esmé."

My turn to smile at him. "I didn't expect you here."

"My keen investigating instincts deduced that you were here." He spared me a smoldering look. He turned to Maura and picked up the paper. "Someone dies every day in New York. This man didn't die for your sins. He had plenty of his own."

"But that poor woman, his wife, living in that shack. What about her?"

Maura had grown up, if not in poverty, then next door to it, in Hell's Kitchen. No wonder she didn't have any friends among the Balmains' society set.

"I have it on good authority," Graydon said, "that Mr. Akers was found with a substantial amount of money in his possession, and it will all go to his widow. Enough for a new start for her and her children."

"Is that true?" Maura said. "I've always heard the police keep whatever they find. Common knowledge where I come from— Wait, I bet they were Irish cops, weren't they?"

Graydon inclined his head. "And they figured balancing the scales for an Irish lass was the bigger blessing, not the bigger sin."

"And my father-in-law financed it. What a puppet master he is." She sighed deeply and held on to her belly. "What's the word from the old man?"

"He's very interested in your health."

"Shocked him, didn't it? My getting pregnant. Duncan told everyone I couldn't have children and he did his best to prevent them. But sometimes the rubber breaks." She closed her eyes and tears slid down her cheeks. "I did love Duncan, you know. Once. I had no idea he was Jekyll and Hyde when I married him. Why couldn't he want our baby?"

"He wasn't right," I said. "In the head. And in the heart."

"I wish I'd run away before it came to this. I thought about it many times. You'd never leave the man you love, but when the monster comes out— He wasn't Duncan anymore— What a terrible legacy for this baby of mine."

"It'll be your baby, Maura, not his."

Graydon added, "He or she has a fierce mother who would do anything to protect their child. That impresses Balmain Senior. And all of us."

"And now it's time for you and that baby to rest," Jesse said. "Party's over, you two."

Maura reached for my hand and squeezed it.

"You saved me, you and Jesse and Doctor Parkhurst, and Rupert, you saved me from his father's wrath. And bless those Irish cops! That's some kind of a miracle. I feel like I won the Irish sweepstakes. At a terrible cost. I will never forget what you did."

"Don't worry about anything now, except taking care of yourself and that baby," Graydon assured her. "I've talked with Balmain. You can stay in your apartment. You'll have money. You'll be safe. Don't think about the other night."

"All I want to think about is cradles and lullabies."

I wanted to hug Maura goodbye, but Nurse Jesse was giving me The Look. Graydon and I walked toward the elevator in silence.

Autumn was marching steadily into winter and the falling leaves made the ground a patchwork quilt of colors, orange and yellow, russet and red. We strolled pathways through the park until we reached the railing next to the East River.

"I don't trust Balmain," I said, out of the blue.

"Nor do I." We leaned back together against the iron rail.

"Is Maura really safe?"

"At least until the baby is born."

"I hope it's a girl," I said. "I'm betting Old Man Balmain wants a boy."

"After that, she may need protection."

"We'll keep an eye on her then?"

"If she wants us to," Graydon promised.

"I hate people." A wind kicked up and I shivered and slid closer to him. He laughed.

"No, you don't. You care too much. And I love you."

He put his arm around me even though we were in public. No, I decided, I didn't hate everyone.

FOURTEEN

66 "HERE AGAIN?" GRAYDON seemed dismayed by my choice of restaurant.

"I'm hungry!"

"You really don't want to run into my parents, do you?" Graydon pulled the blue Ford up to the curb at Lafferty's Irish Pub.

"This way, we'll all have a calm Sunday afternoon," I said.

"You're dressed for Delmonico's, not a tavern."

"I'll just have to bear up." I checked my face in my compact and freshened my lipstick. My gold organdy collar and cuffs were holding up better than I was. Graydon of course looked fine in his Harris Tweed jacket and slacks, a light blue shirt and vest.

"Hell of a week, hey, Miss Esmé Rafferty de LaForet?"

Barkeep Devlin Sullivan was wiping down the bar as Graydon and I entered.

"You said it."

"Haven't seen you since you captured that pair of killers."

"I didn't exactly capture them," I protested.

"She merely figured it out and summed it up nicely for the police," Graydon said. "And an entire restaurant. Dinner and a show."

"You wouldn't be planning a performance like that here, would you?"

Devlin pulled out a newspaper from below the bar. It flaunted the photo of us the night before at the bar where the sneaky photographers took our photo. They must have sold it to other newspapers.

PLAYBOY RUPERT CHASEBORN AND PLAYWRIGHT FIANCÉE SHARE INTIMATE MOMENT

I grabbed for it, but Graydon's arms were longer. It was a scandal sheet for English ex-pats who longed for news from the old country.

"Normally, I'd spit on the thing," Devlin said. "But seeing as how I know two of the culprits on the front page, I was honor bound to buy it."

Graydon scanned it and handed it back dismissively. "My mother gets this thing. They don't approve of publicity, you know."

"Unless it's sensational," I muttered.

"You hiding out under that charmin' hat?" Devlin asked.

"I wasn't planning on it." I removed the hat and smoothed my hair and the bow. "Is my being here a problem?" I loved the familiarity of Lafferty's and I'd hate to lose my sanctuary.

"Not if it has enough dramatic potential." The big man laughed. "I'd never shut the door on a playwright who might write a part for me one day. Even if that Irish lass has entangled herself with an English lord. Of all people. Engaged, for the love of God, Rafferty, and I had to read it in the newspapers."

"Even I was surprised to read about it in the papers. They made a big deal where there wasn't one. It's not official."

"Not with you two loudly declaring your love and all in a restaurant full of people." Devlin laughed long and heartily. He tucked the paper back under the bar. "Something for the kiddies to read one day."

"There were guns around. At any rate, it wasn't my plan and he's not an English lord."

"Oh no, that would be your daddy," he said to Graydon. 'My poor child, Rafferty, what have you gotten yourself into?"

I knew Devlin was yanking my chain and Graydon's as well. But I cocked my head at my fiancé and said to him, "I have no idea."

"Too late to back out now." Graydon picked up my hand to show Devlin the ring.

"Well, I guess it's legal then. And what'll it be?"

"Hot buttered rum," I said. "Dark rum. It's a cold cruel world out there. But maybe it's too early?" I checked the big clock above the bar.

"Not on a Sunday."

"Make it two," Graydon said and the bartender nodded.

"The way I see it, Rafferty, is that it isn't all your fault. People are drawn to you, gangsters and such like. You've the gift of it. You and me, lass, we're the flannel-mouthed Irish, am I right? Even the *English* can feel it. And now you're tangling with the rest of the Upper East Side? I've heard tell of the Balmain overlords." Devlin cocked one eyebrow at me. "Personally, I'll take the gangsters. At least they're honest crooks."

Had everyone I knew read the news of Scavullo and now the Duncan Balmain murder? New Yorkers were a very literate bunch. Everyone read the papers on the subway. Rich and poor, they crowded round the newsboys hawking special editions hot off the press. Devlin's wife, Molly, emerged from the kitchen just in time.

"Don't let him bother you, Rafferty, he's been laughing every day at your expense. Very good news about your play moving to a big new theatre. I hear tickets are scarce."

"Involved with the English, she is," Devlin snorted.

"Your Tweed here, your Brit, well, he's not too bad for the breed." Molly set down our hot buttered rums.

I felt Graydon's hand in the small of my back and the corresponding release of tension in my shoulders. We moved to a cozy table near the fireplace where the flames were crackling.

"At least your parents aren't here," I said.

"Are you making a list of all the places my parents won't go?"

"I should. Well, we haven't had a chance to—get away. To have some privacy." Maybe my place, I thought. Amelia was off today.

He smiled at me, making my blood rise. I could feel the blush start at my neck and work its way up, burning my ears. Still, this enforced celibacy was killing me. How were we ever to know if we were, you know—compatible?

A flash of a camel hair coat caught my eye through the stained glass window, followed by a rush of cold air at the door. What on earth was Frank Romeo doing here?

"He's not with us," I said to Devlin as the mob boss entered.

He mock-groaned. "I should have known the whole international crowd would be following you two."

Frankie the Cat Romeo, also known as Handsome Frank, made his way to our table and sat down without ceremony. Devlin was twice Romeo's size, but he approached the mob boss cautiously.

"I don't serve the spaghetti here, Mr. Romeo. Just simple fare."

"Call me Frank. Contrary to popular opinion, Italians don't eat spaghetti all the time. I hear you got some pretty good potato soup here. And a glass of wine."

Devlin looked at me. "Same for me," I said.

"As will I," Graydon said. "And a platter of bread and butter."

"Let me cut to the chase." Frank Romeo lowered his voice. "Both of youse were at the scene of Duncan Balmain's murder."

"We didn't witness the murder," I offered.

"No one ever does." We three had tacitly agreed that we were square after the Scavullo affair. The truth is I didn't dislike the notorious Handsome Frank Romeo. Nor did I fear him. I knew he was still nursing a lifelong broken heart over Scavullo's widow, Juliette. A wound never to be healed. And it gave Frankie the Cat some empathy in matters of the heart. I would forgive a lot for that.

"What do you want to know, Frank?" Graydon asked.

"The papers said the senior Balmain called you over there."

"That's true. We had no idea what we'd find."

"I insisted on going with Graydon," I said. "It was terrible."

"Word is that Duncan Balmain was not long for this world, so I wasn't surprised he got it," Romeo said. We both stared at him. At least I didn't gasp. I can gasp quite theatrically. Frank smiled. "New information?"

"We have heard there were threats," Graydon admitted.

"Don't look at me," I said. "I didn't know them before Friday night."

"Balmain called me out of a party for Esmé's play. I thought it must be one of those financial crises that wealthy people have when midnight nears."

"Financial crisis," Romeo scoffed. "The ones that have millionaires tossing themselves out of high windows? Never could understand that. 'Life is a brief candle,' as they say. Things can always change tomorrow."

"What can you tell us about how Duncan was not long for this world?" I asked, my heart beating faster. "Someone was going to kill him?"

"A hired killer?" Graydon leaned in close. We sounded like something out of a pulp magazine.

"This is my turf, and I don't mess with murder. That's my reputation, and my word," Frank said. "I only heard this from a friend. Who heard it from another friend."

"Was there a particular reason for this?" I asked.

"There's always a particular reason. I have no idea what that reason was. As I said, I wasn't surprised about Duncan, the little weasel. He was deep into gambling, women, maybe drugs. Not my racket. But the woman who's in the hospital?

His wife? She wasn't supposed to be a part of this. So I hear. And that is never how these things are supposed to go. Especially with her being pregnant."

"You know she's pregnant?" I blurted. "That wasn't in the papers."

"Word slips out." Frank cocked his head. Graydon and I shared a look. "I'm not saying that women can't be evil and in for their share of punishment, as you know."

I did know. Bianca Lombardi was jailed, no doubt heading for the electric chair next year for the murder of Romeo's driver, and as an accessory to the Scavullo killing.

"But I hear nothing bad about this woman," Frank continued. "This Maura Balmain. Supposed to be a beauty. I hear she's going to make it. It troubles me that this happened in Balmain's home with his wife on the premises. There are ways these things are done, and that is not the way. This business is a wild card, from out of state."

"Duncan was dead before Balmain called me," Graydon said. "He thought I could keep the police out of it. Impossible, of course. But I found a sympathetic detective."

"Yeah. I'm guessing the old man wouldn't call the cops until he conferred with someone like you."

Molly came out with our soup orders and an order of hot bread and extra butter. Frank dug right in, and though I was starved I took my time. This "wild card" was all news to me. I was sorry that the hired gun hadn't found Duncan first. Maura would not have to tangle with her guilt. Her very justified guilt.

"One more thing about this is funny." Frank paused for a bite of bread. "I never heard of no Johnny Akers. The dead bum the cops fingered? That bothers me. See, I'm not involved with that tough-guy business, but other guys come to me. Maybe to confess their sins, but I ain't no priest. I can't absolve them, but I can listen. I'm a good listener."

Frank seemed to me a little more sad, a little more reflective than usual.

"And how is Juliette Scavullo?" I asked.

"She won't talk to me. You know that guy? That Greek myth guy who gets his liver pecked out every day?"

"Prometheus." Graydon supplied the name. "Stole fire and gave it to mankind."

"That's what it is. My punishment for not choosing love. I got to live with the thought of Juliette every day of my life. I see her at church. I hear her name. I conjure her up in my dreams, and I awake to nothing. I ain't complaining. My cross to bear. At least I ain't no Duncan Balmain."

❧

"Graydon?"

"Yes, love?"

"Don't let go of me."

"Never."

"Good," I said. "My head is spinning."

Back at my apartment, we were reclining on my velvet sofa in a compromising position, though no actual compromising had been accomplished. Nevertheless, compromising was contemplated.

"The fact that there are two would-be killers of Duncan Balmain would make anyone's head spin," he said. "Head-spinning may be Frank Romeo's ultimate power. Frankie the Cat, indeed."

"If someone was after Duncan, what does Balmain Senior know about it? Specifically?"

"Time to ask. Balmain wasn't exactly forthcoming. He doesn't want his dirty laundry aired and he's afraid you'll put it on stage. Or in the papers. And Frankie the Cat is afraid you won't tell *his* story. You are, after all, a notorious woman of the theatre."

I wrapped both his arms around me and kissed him.

"That's better. Now let's concentrate on happier thoughts."

The phone rang. I hated every phone in the world in that moment. It was a monstrous machine. I answered it reluctantly. It was for Graydon.

"Hello, Robbins." His parents, both of them, were on their way to his place and we were expected there.

Both of them? Together? I liked them better when they didn't like each other.

FIFTEEN

66 "THANKSGIVING IS IN three days." Amelia met me at my apartment door Monday morning with a notepad in one hand and a fountain pen in the other. She was making a list. I felt a stab of panic.

"I didn't know it was your day to clean." Since spending time with Graydon's valet Robbins, Amelia had become even more attentive to details. As my head housekeeper, that meant we both needed to come up to standards. Her standards. I was failing her expectations.

"With the holiday so close, I decided to see what we need. It's only three days away and you're hosting the feast."

Me? I vaguely remembered ordering a turkey and a ham from the butcher. Having so many wonderful and also horrifying things happen in such a short period of time was a shock to my system. Especially after plodding along for years. I was twenty-five, but I suddenly felt a whole lot older.

"I completely forgot about Thanksgiving."

"No wonder, what with your play, the whole Scavullo murder mess, and your engagement to Mr. Chase." She took a breath. "And now you've gotten yourself involved in another killing. It's all over the newspapers. I cut out the stories, and I'm thinking—"

"What now?" I braced myself.

"Maybe we need another scrapbook for these types of stories. One for your play notices and reviews, and one for the weird stuff. Murder and such like." There would be no getting her off the subject. Amelia was a voracious reader of the tabloids.

"If you have time, you can take money out of the house-keeping fund." I kept cash on hand for all the emergencies. I was going to have to increase it. Amelia wore her victorious expression.

"Now, how many are we expecting?"

"Uh—" I didn't even remember how many people I'd asked, but most were from the theatre and would be orphans that day. *Leaving Alamogordo* had just closed at the Washington Irving Theatre and would not open at the Nathanial Hawthorne Theatre until the first weekend in December, which was alarmingly soon. My invitation had been one of those casual *If you have nothing else to do, you can come to my place* invitations.

"Um. Ten or twelve."

What made me Lady Bountiful all of a sudden? The play was a success. Now I worried whether people would expect something extravagant. My parents had always hosted a Thanksgiving open house at our general store back home, with a buffet table and at least four large turkeys and side dishes. During the worst years of the Depression, and before, Thanksgiving supper at LaForet's had become a local tradition. The decorations were paper turkeys with accordion feathers. Neighbors and friends and customers, even those who owed us money, were all welcome. Here in New York City, would something that simple suffice? Hungry actors were one thing, but— I simply didn't know.

"It's lucky you got a nice apartment with plenty of room," Amelia reminded me. "Two tables should do. Unless you want to do it at Mr. Chase's apartment. That penthouse and all?"

"Graydon?" I'd planned all this before we became a couple.

"Obviously he's coming, and what about his lordship and Lady Chaseborn? With you two being engaged, it would be unseemly not to invite them. Especially with you making the society news these days."

And the police blotter, I amended silently. Where was Amelia coming up with all this etiquette stuff? Oh. Robbins, no doubt.

"This is an American holiday. I'm sure they wouldn't dream of coming." At least I hoped not. She gave me a look that said *Don't play with me.* "I guess we better get a head count. Prepare for a dozen."

"I alerted the butcher last week and told him you're gonna need another small turkey. Hens are more flavorful."

"Do you think we need all that?"

"Actors eat a lot when they aren't starving. Ham for the hams. And leftovers."

"Leftovers? You can take them home."

"I was counting on that. Ma will really appreciate it." Amelia had a tortured relationship with her family. She was living at home and on better terms with them than in the past. Amelia was their shining success—a part-time job with me, and filling in at the beauty salon.

"The cost. And the oven isn't that big." I envisioned chaos.

She sat down across from me, for all the world looking like the head of a corporation. The CEO of Esmé Inc. Amelia wore a navy dress with a sedate collar. The platinum curls were gathered on top of her head with a matching navy ribbon.

"You look very nice," I said.

"Thanks. Robbins has been telling me how head housekeepers should dress and comport themselves." *Comport?* That was a big word.

"You've put some thought into the logistics."

She jotted down notes on a stenographer's pad. "We cook the ham the day before. One whole turkey will fit in the oven, and we cut the other up into pieces and roast them in a flat pan. Vegetables in the electric cooker."

"I assume you consulted with Robbins."

Her smirk said it all. "He's very keen on seeing a real American Thanksgiving. He's already arranged to spend the day with me." It was unlike her, but Amelia blushed a little bit. "He'll help serve."

"Serve? You're both guests."

"Robbins doesn't like to confuse roles, even though I told him it would be all right on account of this is America. We'll eat in the kitchen. I'll set it up nice. Not to worry."

"Wouldn't you rather be with your family?"

"Are you kidding me? Ma's planning on mock duck and that's just meatloaf. Coming here and having turkey and ham and a chance to serve a lord and lady? My friends are going to be so jealous. Especially Mona."

"Dinner won't be over till about eightish."

"That's okay, my family don't plan on eating till I come home with the leftovers. Dining late is very continental."

I was just glad I wouldn't have to look at a turkey carcass for weeks.

"Do we have some bicarbonate of soda?" I felt queasy. After the previous evening with Graydon's parents, wrangling over how and when and where we should announce our forthcoming nuptials, I was worn out.

"Headache?" She got up and fixed me a glass of the cure. "Good thing that play of yours is a nice big hit. You got cash and I already paid the butcher with the housekeeping fund. By the way, what are we going to drink?"

"Punch? Wine? Champagne? I don't know. Lay in a supply. Reasonable, but not too expensive. Apple cider, in case we have teetotalers. Though I don't think I know any of those."

I sipped the bicarbonate for my headache and stomach, trying to remember who I'd invited. May Scott, of course, as in 'Queen of the May,' who ran the theatre office with such authority and power. Wilhelmina "Willie" Kim, who might or might not show up with her father. She said they never celebrated holidays after her mother died.

"And Mr. Chaseborn?" she prompted.

"He prefers Chase." Had I invited Graydon? Maybe I'd mentioned it in passing. We'd become a couple, a rather too well-known couple, courtesy of the newspapers. And I'd invited Nina Oglesby, who was now a society reporter. I would have panicked, but I was too tired. I'd have to schedule a panic attack for later.

"And what about Mr. Reginald Archibald Pendleton the Third?"

"Reggie? Oh no, he has a command performance with the Pendleton clan in Maine. And he's mad at me."

"He's in love with you."

"He is not."

"I think he is, at least a little, and he does not care for Mr. Chaseborn. A sure sign." I threw myself down on the sofa and put the pillow over my face. "You can't get out of this that easy. I figure you'll need me every day this week, It's Thanksgiving week. I'll do all the work and you do all the worrying."

"I talked to Hank Turnbridge about some fall decorations." Hank was the set designer who'd painted the mural on my bedroom walls and ceiling. He had a firm grasp on the theatrical. "He said he'd rustle a few things up for the mantel. If he shows up, just pay him." I retrieved my purse and put some more dollars in the housekeeping fund. Amelia laughed.

"He wants to do it. You're pretty famous, not just with the plays, but with all the blood and guts. You know?"

"I haven't seen guts. Just blood."

"By the way, I was thinking you need some little turkey plates for dessert. They're all the rage."

I threw another two dollars on the coffee table and ran for the door.

SIXTEEN

66 "TELL ME ABOUT Johnny Akers," I demanded. I'd detoured to the police station before heading to the theatre. I stared imperiously at Detective O'Hara, expecting an answer.

"Miss de LaForet, do come in."

O'Hara shut the door of his cramped office. He leaned back in his squeaky chair and lit a cigarette, tossing the match in a battered brass ashtray. "Swanky, ain't it? I'd offer you coffee, but the stuff we make here might kill you." His office was small and stuffy, painted a depressing green. The files on his desk were piled high. "Johnny Akers. Bad apple, that one."

"I didn't honestly expect you to embrace my ramblings and blame some random mug for a murder." I paced as far as I was able. About three feet.

"We didn't do it on your word alone. Old Man Balmain was pushing hard for it. With guys like Duncan, it would have turned out this way anyway. You did nothing wrong, Esmé. Maybe you gave us an idea on how to tie up this messy case. Turns out Edward Balmain does know the commissioner. The old one, anyway."

"So there's a different standard for the high and mighty?"

"So far, but we got a new commissioner. You hear? Lewis Joseph Valentine. Not the sweetheart you might expect. Supposed to clean up corruption in the police force. Mayor LaGuardia's appointed, or is that anointed one? Sworn in two months ago, September."

"Think he'll make a difference?"

"Maybe." O'Hara breathed out a stream of smoke. "Odd duck. Supposed to be a ball of shiny integrity, but a little too fond of beating up suspects, if you ask me. Likes 'em bloody. Don't know how that will play on the Upper East Side. I'm standing back for now."

"But what about Akers?"

"Akers was stabbed in a bar fight. Legit. Six witnesses. Drunken witnesses, but they all say the same thing. Akers started the fight. Picked on the wrong guy, who acted in self-defense, and it wasn't even a gun. A knife." The detective inhaled deeply. "Akers was so surprised he didn't even have a chance to pull his gun."

"Right. The gun. The one he used to kill Duncan Balmain?"

"The very same. It's locked up in Evidence. Where it can't do any more harm."

"Reggie wrote that Akers had killed other people."

"He slithered out of the charges, but yeah." O'Hara finished his cigarette and stubbed it out. "Lucky break. Things don't usually turn out so neat. And that piece in *The Post* by Pendleton, interviewing the widow?" He held up his own copy of *The Post*. "It's a capper. Akers hated Duncan Balmain. Lost his last good job when Balmain Junior canned him? The guy was a gift that fell in our laps, wrapped up with a bow. We get to close three other murders. Me and my boys might even get a citation."

I slumped into an empty chair.

"It feels all wrong," I said. "But it also feels a little right."

"How does it feel wrong? Criminals aren't smart. We couldn't have an unknown homicidal maniac running around the Upper East Side, scaring the fine denizens, who all know the commissioner *personally*." O'Hara had played this game before.

"Still, I don't like it." I dropped my voice. "Akers didn't do this."

"We couldn't be blaming Balmain's poor wife, could we? A fine Irish lass who made a bad choice of husband. A monster who tried to cut the babe out of her, good God!

Left her bleeding out like that? I'd never seen such a terrible thing. I got four of my own children. Her pregnancy is no lie. Doctor says the rabbit died today. Balmain Senior, he knew his kid was no good. Knew he used Maura as a punching bag."

The detective was such a good talker I had trouble remembering why I came. "The money. Did Balmain make good on the money?"

"Five thousand smackers. It's right here in my office, not in the evidence room with the rest of Akers' effects." He pointed to a small safe in the corner behind his desk. It was covered with files and newspapers. "When Mrs. Akers comes to pick up his things, or I decide to deliver them personally, she'll get the whole amount. Swear to God."

"That money belongs in a bank, O'Hara. I don't want her to receive a small fortune, only to lose it to the first thief that comes along."

"She mentioned moving to Brooklyn or New Jersey and it'll have to happen soon. That Hooverville she's living in is set to be demolished. Why don't we make sure she has a police escort to that bank? Good enough for you, Esmé de LaForet?"

"It'll have to be. I'm trusting you, O'Hara."

❧

There was a hired gun from out of town on the street, not merely in the pages of a paperback novel. But Frank Romeo wouldn't tell us his name. Might be a good thing, yet I turned my collar up and watched every stranger warily.

What does a killer look like? The movies make them ugly, scarred faces and distorted features. In my experience that wasn't the case. Male and female, some were as attractive as if they strolled out of an Arrow Collar Man advertisement. Comely yet deadly. After all, Handsome

Frank Romeo had earned his moniker through his looks, and he always said he wasn't a killer. But rumor suggested otherwise.

What did all these killers have in common? They were human, driven by human emotions, like rage, jealousy, and greed. I'd known a few handsome men without a soul, men who seemed hollow inside. Men left over from the last war. Men used to killing.

In addition to this nameless hired killer sent to dispatch the late Duncan Balmain, there was a dead man named Johnny Akers, who'd been blamed for the killing. According to the widow, Akers hated Duncan. And then there was Maura Balmain, who actually did kill her husband and nearly bled to death protecting her baby.

It was all so tangled. Why was Duncan in the crosshairs of more than one killer?

Seventeen

THE PLAY I was reading kept slipping out of my hands—and my brain. It wasn't a good sign for the playwright, or for my mental state. Though I was grateful for the quiet of the office I shared with May at the theatre.

I thought I sensed Graydon's Hickory Wind cologne. Wishful thinking? I closed my eyes and breathed in deeply, and Graydon materialized right in front of my desk, where I read scripts when I wasn't distracted with life and death and murder. A brown tweed jacket and vest would be stereotypical on any other Brit, but on this one they were attractive and casual. His brown fedora was in his hand. His neon blue eyes focused on me.

"Graydon." I felt my mouth turn up in a smile.

He was out of place at the Washington Irving Theatre, and I was still in a dither from my visit with Detective O'Hara and the calendar closing in on me. Graydon perched casually on the edge of my desk and leaned toward me.

"About Thanksgiving," he said. "Robbins informs me we are having a traditional holiday feast at your place."

"What! 'We'?"

Is this what my life was going to be? Being *informed* what I was up to by everybody else? Weeks ago, I had invited people to a holiday dinner. At the time, I wanted a friendly crowd and I didn't want to be alone on the holiday. Now it was going to be a madhouse and I would, no doubt, long for a little solitude with Graydon.

"I had envisioned something smallish, family style. Casual. Not formal. And I didn't think—"

"That I'd come?"

"I didn't even know you then, and, well, you are British—"

"And naturalized American, don't forget."

"Never. But this was planned before— Before we were a couple."

"But darling, we are a couple. Whither thou goest and all that. I think it sounds charming, wonderful. Robbins has bought all the glossy magazines on the subject of the great American Thanksgiving dinner."

"This is insane."

Graydon had a beautiful, full-throated laugh. "All the better."

"I'm beginning to think you enjoy chaos." Is that why he was an 'inquiry agent,' a private detective, so he could snoop on the other side of life, the side that wasn't wrapped in expensive tweeds?

"You are the queen of chaos and drama, and I enjoy you."

"Flatterer. Your parents will be out of the country, right? Right?"

"Oh, no, they're very excited about coming."

"They're coming? How do they even know about this?" I jumped out of my chair and paced, trying to stop myself from hyperventilating.

"Mother overheard Robbins speaking to Amelia and she interrogated him relentlessly until he gave it up. Perhaps she should be the detective, not me."

"What did you tell her?"

"That a formal invitation would be forthcoming. I'm sorry, Elf. I do have my cowardly moments when it comes to the parents."

As horrified as I was, I knew the invitation must be offered. They already knew about it. It would be an outrageous snub if I didn't. I sat down and pulled out my new and freshly engraved notes, my name in navy blue on immaculate white linen paper.

"What are you doing?" he asked.

I noticed that May was calmly watching us with a grin. She poured herself a freshly brewed cup of coffee from her personal percolator. The air was perfumed with the heavenly aroma. I needed coffee desperately, but you didn't ask May, she had to offer.

"Inviting them. Personally." I jotted off a note and handed it to him.

"Perfect. Don't worry, I know Robbins will assist Amelia and everything will be in hand. Formal attire?"

"No, not quite, a dinner suit, I suppose." I wasn't as well versed in what men wore when. The nuances in attire for them could be subtle.

"No problem, Robbins will tell me. And what will our hostess wear? Mother will want to know."

I had asked Willie to make something for me for the holidays. Together, with some influence from Paris designs, we came up with a plush silk velvet frock in a deep copper color, with pale gold satin trim. The color was good on me. We'd had the last fitting, but I hadn't seen the final gown yet. I'd have to check in with the master costumer. May read my mind, or perhaps my panicked face, and picked up her phone to summon Willie.

"If you really want to marry me, Graydon, you're going to have to accept that I am not well-versed in elegant dinners for the aristocracy. I'm not uncomfortable with people I know, but I don't think I'll ever know your parents."

"Neither will I, and they are acting very suspiciously lately."

"No doubt giggling behind closed doors. Meanwhile, I am in a panic."

He started laughing again. "Dead bodies and gangsters you handle with aplomb, but a simple meal stymies you."

"A simple meal! You're out of your mind. There are expectations. There are rules. This is *Thanksgiving!*"

I thought of the folks who used to attend the feast at my parent's store, LaForet's, a fancy name for a general store that sold everything from Campbell's soup and chicken feed to barbed wire. It was a tradition in our dirt-poor tumbleweed town, even before the Depression. Many of our neighbors couldn't afford a turkey, but they all showed up in their best clothing, whether it was clean overalls or a suit that had seen better days. Women in calico dresses, and their children in outfits sewn from patterned flour sacks they had bought at our store. It was a day of celebration and my parents and I didn't think of the work that went into it. We sang songs all through making the pies and the many side dishes. Yet now, facing dinner for twelve or so, I was a wreck.

"So what if it doesn't meet your expectations?" Graydon said. "It will still be memorable."

"My only expectation is living through this."

"Ah, that reminds me. Duncan Balmain's funeral is tomorrow at ten. Can you make it or do you have work?"

"She wouldn't miss it," May said. She tried to hide a smile with a lift of her eyebrow, but it didn't work. She was finding my whole predicament far too amusing.

"Pick you up at nine-thirty tomorrow, if I don't see you sooner."

He stood to leave as Willie strode in, carrying my new dress, her arms overflowing with the soft pile of velvet. She grinned at him and winked at me.

"Here it is, Graydon, so you can tell your mother."

"It's beautiful, Willie." I held the gown up so he could see it. "Tell Lady Jane it's cocktail length."

"Smashing as always, but I'd expect no less. Goes wonderfully with your hair." Graydon took my hand and I followed him to the stairwell. Watching out for press photographers, he took me into his arms and kissed me. "Maybe Wilhelmina would be interested in creating a wedding gown."

It was my turn to laugh. "I can hardly think ahead to Thursday. If I have to contemplate the wedding, I shall start hyperventilating again."

"May I see you tonight?"

"I'm having a nervous breakdown tonight. It's all the rage."

"Very well. See you in the morning. You are quite bewitching in funeral attire. As I well remember." He reminded me that we were *formally* introduced at another funeral and I felt a rush of something like desire.

❧

Back in the office, May replenished the scripts on my desk. Willie stood with the dress.

"Do you want to try it on?"

"Yes, please, we have to know what the hostess will be wearing," May said. "After all, I need to coordinate with you. And my Jell-O dessert."

"Jell-O? You're joking," I said. She shook her head.

"Red. I'm bringing a cherry-red Jell-O in a fancy mold, on top of pink whipped Jell-O with a whole can of cherries in syrup. A Jell-O double-decker. It's very dramatic."

I slipped off my perfectly acceptable knit dress and belt and Willie helped me on with the gown in its soft copper glory and gold satin piping, a square neckline, bishop sleeves and deep cuffs. It was very autumnal and felt like heaven.

"I'm glad you wanted the velvet. Very refined." Even Willie was excited. "And are Lord and Lady Chaseborn really coming?"

"So it seems." I took a deep breath.

"Why are you so nervous? Don't they like you?"

"Split decision. His mother likes me. His father considers me *a woman of the theatre,* and therefore practically a—"

"Ha! Just wait till he meets a costumer, a producer, and a few disreputable actors. We should put on a show, kids. Let's all dress in autumn shades. You're in copper and May in red, and I'll wear gold."

"Like Anna May Wong?" I asked. Willie was a big fan of the Chinese actress. "Wait, I don't like that gleam in your eyes."

"Go ahead, Willie," May said. "I like that gleam."

"I'll wear something special," Willie said. "Will we be playing games?"

"I hope not. No games, no drama, no complications."

"Likely story. What time is this feast?" May asked.

"That parade at Macy's ends at four. I don't want to interfere with that. Come at five for drinks, dinner at six."

"Do you have enough dishes?" May asked.

"If I didn't before, Amelia will make sure I do." The ring of a cash register went off in my head. I couldn't help it, I'd worked in my parent's store too long. This was going to be a very expensive dinner, I thought.

But I had no idea.

Eighteen

THE FOREST GREEN Pierce-Arrow, a mechanical marvel, pulled up to the curb the next morning with Robbins at the wheel. Onlookers stared. Children pointed. I was ready to fly down the steps, but I waited for Graydon to climb up and retrieve me. He smiled more often these days, and his face lit up when he saw me. I grinned.

"Good morning, Esmé. You're looking magical this morning. Planning any surprises?"

"I'll leave that up to everyone else." I put my arm through his. "For the record, I hope it's a quiet day."

Graydon wore a sober black suit rather than his navy blue, a crisp white shirt and subdued maroon tie. I enjoyed watching him walk, long-legged and sure of himself.

I wore my beautiful and theatrical black crepe dress and jacket set again, but I changed the collar and cuffs from the flamboyant gold to a demure violet set, more acceptable for a funeral. This design by Willie was versatile, to say the least. My chic black hat was a Lily Daché that had been donated to the theatre by a wealthy subscriber. It was close fitting with an asymmetrical brim, decorated with a blue-green ribbon and a small spray of violets. And according to the incomparable Willie, it set off my eyes.

Graydon held the door, I slipped in, and he scooted in beside me. "What exactly are we supposed to be doing there?" I asked. "How well did you know Duncan?"

"Not well. Some of our circles overlapped. Balmain Senior needs moral support, though he didn't put it that way. He has no close family, though his sister-in-law may come. We are to sit with him."

"Where his family should be? Of course he doesn't want Maura there, even if she were able. And have you told him there was another killer gunning for Duncan?"

"It's on the agenda."

"Do you trust Frank Romeo?"

"Oddly, of all the people involved in this, outside of you, I trust Frank the most. He's what we might call an honest criminal."

"My feelings exactly," I said. There was a discreet cough from the driver. "And I trust you, Robbins."

"Goes without saying," Graydon added. He took my hand. I realized how much I'd missed him without even knowing him in those years when there was no hand to hold mine. I wondered if there was a way we could sneak off and do something that would make both of us *thankful* before the official holiday. He knew what I was thinking. "Soon, Esmé, soon."

"When is your father going back to London?"

"Not soon enough."

Duncan Balmain's funeral was held in the chapel at the mortuary. The sixty or so seats were filled with so-called mourners, with an overflow of reporters and photographers lining three walls.

I spotted Reggie Pendleton in his brown corduroy jacket, holding a notebook and pen. He winked at me. I looked away and Graydon and I followed Edward Balmain's lead. We sat with him in the front near the expensive polished casket.

Balmain Senior wore a bespoke black suit and crisp white shirt, sitting as still as a man made of stone. He inclined his head to us but spoke little. Though I'm sure he mourned his son, this was just one more business challenge to be met. An older woman with gray hair sat down on his other side. Ruth Balmain, his late brother's widow, Duncan's aunt.

The officiant's remarks were brisk and nondenominational, designed to offend no one. However, there were a few audible snickers when he said Duncan was, no doubt, where he deserved to be, in a better place. Several of Duncan's friends spoke briefly of his high spirits and love of a good party, but little else. Others were silent and subdued.

One friend of Duncan's seemed saddened. Perry Windover, a well-known member of another wealthy construction family, bore red-rimmed eyes, which might be attributed to a few tears, or a few drinks. I recognized his name from the society pages. He had the grace to speak kindly about his friend.

A pale man whose summer color had faded to the shade of his wheat-colored hair, he looked completely beige, like a department-store mannequin. Windover was slightly taller than average and a fair copy of his other upper-class compatriots.

I glanced at Graydon to reassure myself that he still stood out from these other wealthy men. His hair shone with a dark gleam, lightened by the sun. His features were stronger, his blue eyes brighter, kinder, more amused. This man has a soul, I said to myself.

"Duncan was my boyhood friend. We shared everything, except women," Windover was saying. I heard a few titters. "He was a grand compatriot, a boon companion. We may have been tossed out of a prep school or two together, but we regretted nothing. We lived fast and hard, yet I never expected him to leave us so soon. I'd always thought we'd be old men together, sharing a glass of Scotch in the dimming of the day and lying about our early escapades. So I will drink to Duncan today. I will say a prayer for him and his lovely widow Maura that she may rejoin us soon."

He returned to his seat next to his fiancée, one Katrina Fleiss. Although she had that debutante sameness of the other debs I had met, she stood out for her white-blond hair and skin, almost ghostly in her well-cut navy Bloomingdale's suit. Her lipstick seemed too bright against that skin, a marble statue with blood-red lips. She wiped away a tear and smiled at Perry as he held her hand. Perfect bookends, they shared some secret look.

Windover also exchanged nods with another man. I heard someone say he was one Tom Gates, who'd been at Yale with Windover and Duncan. He seemed to give Windover the brush off. Gates was with a woman, perhaps his wife, both wearing dark brown. A respectful color, but not funereal. Unlike the others, they looked healthy, well-fed, unmoved, observing this funeral as a mere social obligation. Gates seemed to be focused on something else, something slightly out of sight. Did he like Duncan? Despise him? I had no idea. Several other men who looked like fraternity brothers exchanged nods.

Balmain Senior sat stone-faced through these remarks. But to everyone's surprise, including mine and Graydon's, he took to the podium. Everybody snapped to attention. He wasn't expected to say anything and he didn't take long. He expressed his sorrow at losing his son, whose bright future had lain ahead of him. He stunned the crowd by announcing that his sadness was mitigated by the fact that Duncan's child, his own grandchild, was on the way. He reported that Maura was sorry to miss the funeral, but she was recuperating in hospital from her ordeal and regaining her strength for the baby. He thanked the crowd for coming and invited everyone to a small reception following the service, and then later to the graveside. A hymn from a competent soprano ended the service.

Balmain's announcement of the pregnancy ensured that Duncan's name would be remembered, at least for a while. A ripple of surprise rushed through the crowd before we were released to an adjoining room with catered food and drink. Except for the reporters, who bolted for the pay phones.

The mourners, if you could call them that, could be sorted into several distinct camps. Big burly men in ill-fitting jackets and loud ties, from Balmain's construction company, men with callused hands who built bridges. They had been angling for a union, efforts that had been rebuffed so far. Rumors whispered that Duncan's death may have been a retaliation for blocking unionizing efforts. But these men were still there, ignoring the rumors.

The other mourners, in black, sprang from the same prep school and luxury mold as the deceased, businessmen in finely tailored suits and manicured nails, the Balmains' fellow business owners. They said the right things to Balmain Senior. So sorry, Duncan was a grand fellow, what a loss.

Edward Balmain's sister-in-law, Ruth Balmain, was a tiny woman barely five feet tall who seemed very affected by it all. Her black dress was not flattering, yet appropriate to the event. Her lips trembled, but her steel-gray hair must have matched her spine. She stood as tall as a small person could. She had been married to Edward's brother, dead for years, no children. Her nephew Duncan was her substitute. Her presence seemed to keep Edward Balmain on an even keel, though I was simply guessing.

"I'm sorry for your loss." I introduced myself. "Esmé de LaForet."

"Thank you. Such a waste. You're with Rupert Chaseborn." All this class seemed to know him. It wasn't worth explaining that he went by Graydon Chase. She probably knew that too.

"Yes, I am. Duncan had a lot of friends, it seems."

She scanned the crowd. "Duncan was a victim of his own good looks and absolutely no discipline. I hoped he'd grow up some day. He was always in trouble. I expect that's what did him in."

"He'll leave a child."

She allowed herself a small smile. "No one expected that. It's the only good to come out of this."

"Do you like Maura?" An inappropriate question, perhaps, but I really wanted someone to like her.

"I don't think I know her well. Pretty doll of a thing. He seemed crazy about her, but even she couldn't get through to him. The child might have changed things. To think if he had lived and known about his baby—it would have been quite a Thanksgiving this year."

I agreed and moved on. In addition to Balmain's sister-in-law, several other women were in attendance, perhaps far-flung family members and friends. I recognized two of them and my heart sank. The Snow Queen and Prisspot, two postdebs who had posed for Graydon's nude paintings. I'd seen them beautifully rendered in the buff and that was quite enough for me.

The Snow Queen, known to most as Millicent or Millie, gave a fine imitation of a tuberculosis victim, or perhaps the Bride of Dracula. With her raven-black hair and corpse-white skin and black garb, she looked like a leftover Halloween decoration, a dancer in "The Skeleton Rag." I'd once overheard her voicing her intentions to marry one very eligible Rupert Graydon Chaseborn.

In contrast, Prisspot, aka Priscilla Summerdine, was beige through and through, from her beige skin to her beige ponytail. She looked a little healthier than the Snow Queen.

Prisspot liked to pretend she was merely Graydon's friend; however, I once saw her place her hand possessively in my beloved's pocket. It was before he and I became a couple, but still, it annoyed me. Graydon leaned down to listen to something Edward Balmain was saying and the postdeb duo approached me.

"Esmé! How lovely to see you," Prisspot said. "Have you met Millie?"

"Of course we've met." The Snow Queen herself extended a bony hand. Millie had the same debutante drawl as her friend. They must have run in the same circles as Duncan. Were they also "friends" of Maura?

"It's too bad about Duncan," I said, to switch the subject.

"Tragic," Priss said. "So young and so beautiful."

"And so bad! Oh, I mean, in that attractive bad-boy way," Millie caught herself.

"Maura's doing well," I said, to see their reaction. They both reared back a little, like skittish fillies, betraying that they hadn't thought much about the widow.

"Oh yes. Maura. The baby. Such a surprise," Millie said. "Duncan told everyone she couldn't have children."

"He didn't want anyone taking the attention away from him," Priss said. "He could be such a baby himself. He complained when his friends had children and couldn't make plans on holidays."

"Children do so get in the way," Millie agreed.

"That's what nannies and boarding schools are for," Prisspot said. They both laughed.

"Maybe they should simply be raised in laboratories," I said. They laughed again. Sarcasm was lost on these two.

"That would suit Duncan," Priss said. "Maura must have secretly wanted a child. She seems the type."

"After Duncan, there aren't that many eligibles left. But then Graydon isn't married yet, is he?" I fumed silently. Millie the Snow Queen was a nasty piece of work.

"Perry is still available," Priss reminded her.

"So easy to forget about Perry. Congratulations, Esmé, by the way."

They both gave my outfit the up-and-down look, disappointed that there was nothing to criticize. They were dressed in serviceable and expensive black suits. Priss wore a beige hat with a sad black ribbon and Snow Queen Millie went bareheaded.

"For what?" My play? My engagement?"

"For bagging Rupert, of course."

Her smile was a challenge, but to my relief, Graydon showed up.

"Don't be ridiculous, ladies, I'm the lucky one. I wore Esmé down with my relentless wooing, not the other way around." He took my left hand and lifted it ever so slightly so they could admire my dazzling diamond-and-ruby engagement ring. "You see, she really didn't care for men of means, or the English, or private investigators, and many other things. Including me."

"That was then," I said. "This is now."

Millie sniffed. "I understand Lord and Lady Chaseborn are both in town." When outmaneuvered, change the subject.

"They aren't going to the royal wedding?" Priss said. "Why on earth would they be here instead of there?"

The two women were up to date on their upper-class gossip, relayed via special cable to *The New York Times*. The Duke of Kent and Princess Marina of Greece and Denmark would be married at Westminster Abbey on our Thanksgiving Day (which of course meant nothing to British royals). Millie and Priss made it clear that nothing on earth could be more interesting than the stately vows of this fairytale duke and princess. Newspapers were predicting a million people crowding the streets of London, even sleeping in the street before the event.

"They are here to meet Esmé, of course," Graydon said. "Father couldn't wait to fly over."

Now both sets of wide eyes were fixed on me. I smiled as brightly as I could. "Yes, that would be me."

"But missing a *royal* wedding!" Priss blurted.

"You know what they say," Graydon teased. "You've seen one royal wedding, you've seen them all."

"I was unaware they said that," Millie said. "But why on earth would they be here in New York?"

"Esmé is here." He was up to something and I didn't trust his wily smile. "And she is hosting an intimate Thanksgiving feast for family and friends in her charming Upper West Side apartment."

That did it. That tidbit of society gossip would, no doubt, make the papers. I cringed silently.

"And your *parents* will be there?" Millie, I think.

"They are very keen on it."

Reggie took up the rear, listening carefully. I quivered inside as he pulled out his reporter's notebook.

"It's an intimate gathering," I said. "Mostly my fellow theatre people. I understand Lord Chaseborn *adores* theatre people."

"Well, Rupert," Priss said, "we knew your mother was a bit odd." I glared and she quickly tried to make it better. "I mean, you know, *unorthodox*. Progressive."

"Lord Cyril Corduroy Chaseborn is quite interested in the bohemian life of the theatre." Graydon was having too much fun, but we would pay for it later, I thought, if his parents caught wind of it. These postdebs from his past were eating it up with a spoon.

"I'm dying for coffee." I pulled Graydon away and threw them a victorious little smile. "Ladies, lovely to see you."

I practically bumped right into Reggie. He flashed the old school grin. "I assume I'm invited to your Thanksgiving gala? You mentioned it weeks ago." I did. Before I met Graydon Chase. I moaned.

"But you told me weeks ago you'd be at your parents' house."

"Change of plans. They're heading to other relatives in Connecticut."

"Aren't you invited?"

"Complicated. My aunt hates me. Best I don't attend. Mother gave me a list of rules, from what to wear to how I must flatter my aunt's pumpkin pie, and a long list of embarrassing subjects I must not mention. Criminals. Guns.

Dead bodies. I declined her invitation. However, I assume yours is still open?"

"If you think your mother's rules are tough, Reggie, wait till you hear mine. First and foremost, you cannot write about anything that happens. It's off the record."

"About those rules," Graydon began. "I am the enforcer of the rules."

"I'm not a society reporter, Chaseborn, so unless there's a murder, not counting the turkey, you have nothing to worry about. Besides, Nina will be there."

"I'm not kidding, Reggie. No tricks, no story," I warned. "And I'll talk to Nina."

"How can you doubt me? Besides, I've liberated some very old port and possibly some excellent champagne from the family wine cellar. My gift to you."

Graydon loomed over the inches-shorter Reggie. "I know you're old chums with Esmé, but if you step out of line, there may well be a murder. Not counting the turkey."

Reggie grinned and saluted. Prisspot and the Snow Queen descended on Reggie, bombarding him with questions. We made our escape.

"You're bearing up nicely," I said to Graydon.

"I'd rather not have Pendleton at your Thanksgiving soiree." He paused. "And I realize you'd rather not have my parents, soon to be your parents-in-law. So it's a draw. But we'll get through this together."

"Will we? Your father hates me. And what if he doesn't like turkey?"

"Is your American turkey anything like, say, quail? He loves quail."

"Not at all. But I have a plan."

"And what is this plan?"

"If this dinner is a disaster in any way, I will pen a play about it. And I will name names."

Nineteen

"NICEST THING DUNCAN Balmain ever did for me," a hefty man said as he lifted a sweet roll onto his overfilled plate.

The reception was catered and served buffet style, the tables decorated with black linens and white lilies lest we forget it was a funeral. I assumed that people wouldn't feel like eating, but the men in Balmain's company ate quite heartily. They weren't paralyzed by grief.

I accepted a cup of coffee from an attendant. The luncheon buffet was very respectable, small meat pies, sliced prime rib, a variety of cheeses and salads, rolls and desserts. I couldn't eat. Graydon took only a roll, to blend in.

We all knew funerals are for the living. People need the final ceremonies and the last goodbyes, but Duncan's sendoff was exhausting. I wasn't quite sure what we were doing there as Balmain Senior didn't take much note of us, until later.

Following the luncheon, we all trundled back to our cars for the graveside service. The crowd from the funeral home had thinned out. I overheard bits of conversation, less decorous than at the formal service, from burly men who looked like construction workers.

"He had to go, he tried to cheat the devil. The old man was willing, but it was Duncan who kept the union off-site."

"Not the union! No one's that stupid. Besides, the union's coming. Roosevelt is pro-union."

"Whoever did it, no one's going to miss that pretty boy. He couldn't do anything. Caught with his fingers in the till many a time. A time or two Daddy had to cover the payroll."

"Someone's spreading rumors that the union did it. Now why would a union trying to gain a foothold in the company kill the golden goose?"

"You don't think they did?"

"Union doesn't work that way. Old Man Balmain was coming around."

"But not Duncan."

"I wanted to kill him plenty of times, but someone else did me the favor."

They all laughed.

Under the autumn sky, flamboyant with fluffy clouds in the vast turquoise firmament with trees still holding red and orange leaves, the final goodbye to Duncan Balmain was more affecting than I expected. It's hard to have a funeral on a beautiful day.

We walked to the graveside, to the flower-covered casket. Balmain Senior moved slowly, holding his sister-in-law's arm. Though Ruth Balmain was tiny, she steadied him. He seemed a smaller man as he touched the casket and choked back a sob. Ruth wiped a tear away and touched the gravestone next to his grave. It was Duncan's mother's.

"She was a sweet soul," I heard Ruth say to her brother-in-law. "And Duncan's in a better place. We all know that."

Balmain looked away and said nothing.

It was cool and the crisp air prickled my skin. I gathered my wool shawl around me. A portion of the mourners had dropped out of the final services, including the Snow Queen and Prisspot. Perry Windover stayed and brought up the rear, wiping his eyes.

"I'm so sorry, buddy," he whispered to the casket.

What was he sorry about? Some secret? Or simply the guilt of being a survivor, when his old friend was dead?

"Ashes to ashes, dust to dust." The officiant intoned the traditional words, but the mourners seemed lost in their own thoughts. There were extra lilies to throw before the coffin was lowered and the gravedigger started tossing the dirt.

Graydon nudged my elbow. I looked up at him and stared in the direction he was looking. There was a flash of a camel hair coat in the distance. But I didn't have time to wonder why Frank Romeo was there in the cemetery.

Following the services, Graydon and I had one more stop. But not before I lifted a few lilies off the casket.

"For Maura," I said.

"You're going to see her?" Balmain Senior asked.

"I think it's appropriate," I said.

"A brief visit," Graydon said.

The older man nodded. "I've been thinking about her and Duncan and the child to come. I don't want the kid to hate me. For that matter, I don't want him or her to hate any of us."

"Maura doesn't want to fan those flames either." I fiddled with the lilies.

"I'll visit her in time." He turned and headed to the car that was waiting for him.

"Robbins is waiting." Graydon nudged me. "But we could walk for a few minutes."

"Does it have anything to do with the camel hair coat?"

"I think those tombstones over there might be interesting."

We walked toward our last view of the bright coat. Frankie the Cat stepped out from behind a mausoleum.

"I see you're here for the whole nine yards, for the late lamented Duncan Balmain."

"What are you doing here, Frank?" Graydon asked.

"Paying my respects. As one does. For Guido." His former driver who had been killed in Frank's car. The three of us strolled in unison down a grassy lane. I noticed Patrick Dentino at the wheel of a new car parked on the cemetery road.

"He's still driving for you?" Graydon asked.

"Till he goes to school. He's gonna make us all proud. Always with a book, that one."

I could see Pat reading in the car, a big, brand-new, dark purple Packard Twelve. He noticed us and smiled.

"And a new car?" I said.

"The old one had too many memories." The car in which Guido Moretti was killed. "Guido's tombstone." We stopped at a freshly carved marker: 'Beloved Son,' Guido Moretti, with his birth and death dates. "For his ma, you know."

"I know."

"Stay safe." Frank Romeo slipped away. He was there not merely to admire the tombstone, but to check on us. The infamous mob boss was fiercely loyal to those friends he treasured. It was a little unsettling to find myself in that group.

The sun was warm, I don't know why I shivered. I spun around, but I couldn't see anything out of place. I dropped one of the lilies on Guido Moretti's grave.

<h1 align="center">TWENTY</h1>

"WERE THOSE FOR Duncan?" Maura asked when I handed her the lilies. She held them gently, and she looked up with tears in her eyes. "I'm so glad. He always liked to keep up appearances. He loved to wear a small lily in his lapel. How did it go?"

"Beautiful and appropriate," Graydon said.

Her black eye had subsided, just a bit of green now, which made her look younger and less like a punching bag. Her blue silk peignoir was not what most people would wear in the hospital. Nurse Jesse was there keeping Maura and the baby company. She took the flowers and went to find a vase.

"I didn't know if you'd want them," I said to the patient.

"I hoped someone would tell me about the funeral. I'll press one lily and put it in with my box of memories of Duncan. Thank you." Her eyes shimmered. "My thoughts have been full of him and how we first met. And what a terrible pass this life has come to. Duncan's out of it now. It's so like him to cause a big mess and then disappear. He made me feel so lonely sometimes."

Jesse brought the lilies in a vase and a silver tray and tea set for us, Maura's guests. Just one more luxury afforded at Doctors Hospital.

"Thank you, Jesse. I can take it from here." Maura poured and handed out cups of Earl Grey.

"You both look a bit peaked." Jesse addressed Graydon and me. "Days like this can be vexing."

We gratefully took the tea and recited the highlights of the funeral and reception. Maura cradled her stomach and cooed to the babe from time to time. She looked up and said, "There's no way I can know this, but I think there are two of them. Inside me."

I looked to Jesse with a question, and she answered, "Sometimes mothers know these things before we do."

"That would be wonderful." That would lay to rest any rumors that her pregnancy couldn't be true.

"I don't think I'll be lonely anymore. I hope they don't grow up to hate me."

"How could they? You're taking such good care of them."

"How was Edward? He can be a terrible old man, but I saw how disappointed he was in his son. He truly has no one else."

"His sister-in-law Ruth was there. And now he has you. And your babies."

"Ah yes, Ruth the Ruthless, he called her." Maura smiled sadly. "She always powers through. Ruth was always nice to me and not because she had to be. She understood how things were with us."

"Edward was stoic. He asked us to be there for moral support."

"And to keep our ears open," I added.

Edward Balmain knew that Duncan had been threatened. Frank Romeo knew there was a hired killer who missed his assignment. Was someone intent on killing the senior Balmain as well?

"Did you know Perry Windover?" Graydon inquired. "He was one of the few who spoke at the service."

"Duncan's friend." She contemplated her cup as if reading the leaves.

"He seemed quite broken up," I said.

"Yes, he would be. They were two bad boys who never grew up. Now who will Windover raise hell with?"

"Bad boys?" Graydon prodded.

"He peddled drugs to Duncan. The cocaine. Said it was medicinal, but it made Duncan crazy. It's illegal. They didn't care."

"There was another man," Graydon said. "Tom Gates and his wife."

"I've met them. Nice of them to go to his funeral." She had trouble with the word *funeral*. She took a deep breath. "As hard as it all is, I'm thinking I can go back to church now."

"She was confessing all morning," Jesse broke in. "Feeling better, I suppose."

"Father Donnelly has been visiting," Maura said. "Duncan didn't want me to go to church, but I have the need of it. The need of prayers and forgiveness, and the need to go on living."

Graydon shot me a look. I was far from a good Catholic, but being of Irish and French blood, I had the need of it too.

"Did it make you feel better?" I asked.

"Better is not a word I'm using these days. But the good priest says I had no other choice. I told him it was Duncan or the baby and me, and my soul. Duncan was out of his head. He'd gotten so much worse since our marriage." I knew Father Donnelly was bound by the confessional not to reveal what he'd heard. "If I'd known Duncan longer before we married, I might have opened my eyes. I was dazzled by him. I wonder if that's how Mrs. Johnny Akers felt about her man."

'There's always love in the beginning," I said, wondering if it were true.

❧

"Graydon, you said, Once you've seen one royal wedding, you've seen them all. Explain, please."

We were famished, though a bit overdressed for a diner. To be fair, we didn't eat much at the funeral luncheon and the tea only made me hungry. We ordered two blue plate Specials: fried chicken, potatoes, and gravy.

"You look very elegant, Elf."

I was beginning to get used to his nickname for me, though I grew up with people who were called by their given names. I lifted my eyebrow.

"Royal wedding. Have you seen one?"

"Had to say something, didn't I? With those predatory crows hovering over us. And no, I've never been to a royal wedding. No interest."

"But your father?"

"Taking a leave of absence from his duties, ostensibly to visit his wayward son and meet you. And he gets to skip the royal folderol. He hates all that."

"Why? Are there so many?"

"Enough. This latest one makes six since 1921, according to the old man. As if he's personally aggrieved. All Queen Victoria's progeny, grandchildren and so forth. Dukes and princesses, protocol and rules, marching by rank, sitting and waiting, waiting some more. And there is this extra bonus. Father can now place the blame on us for his having to miss it."

"He doesn't even know me yet. Wait till Thanksgiving and he can hate me forever."

"Never worry about that, darling. He will love you, at least secretly."

"Why do you say that?"

"You'll give him so much to talk about."

Twenty-One

HE DAY BEFORE Thanksgiving came, and so did the newspapers, full of blood-soaked stories. Amelia arrived early to help prepare the feast, and she unceremoniously dumped the morning papers in my lap.

"I'll put on coffee while you put on your face."

"Good morning to you, too." I leaned back and opened *The Post*.

I knew the press had attended the Balmain funeral, no doubt thinking it was a fine ending to the strange overindulgent life and bizarre death of Duncan Balmain. The murder of an heir to a fortune merited their interest, and as a bonus, they could juxtapose their gruesome stories against the warmth of the Thanksgiving holiday.

However, the pictures of Graydon and me—featured prominently with a hackneyed headline—were a surprise. Since when had I become a *detective?* And with my fiancé, when our engagement hadn't even technically been announced yet? But there it was. In big headline type.

GLAMOROUS DETECTING DUO SEEKS CLUES AT DUNCAN BALMAIN'S FINAL GOODBYE

What clues? I would throttle *Post* newsboy Reginald Pendleton III if he dared show up to Thanksgiving dinner. I prayed he wouldn't have the nerve.

The phone rang. Now what catastrophe could it herald? Ah yes, Lady Jane Chaseborn, Graydon's mother.

"Esmé, Jane here. Just reading the morning news. With you two so busy, I had to take a subscription to *The Post*. Dreadful rag. So interesting."

"I'm so sorry." I hunted for the coffee as Amelia appeared with a fresh cup. She looked happy and competent, not to mention judgmental.

"This way I at least can keep tabs on you two," Jane said, "where you are, what you're up to."

"It's not exactly a social calendar, which I don't keep."

"Another murder wasn't enough?! And you two involved, once more? Investigating? Detectives in love. I am annoyed, though I do love that you both look so happy together."

I wanted to sink into the floor. "Is there something I can do for you, Lady Jane?"

"I know you're busy, what with this Thanksgiving event thing."

"It's simply dinner." And I was losing my mind over it. "A festive traditional dinner."

"Cyril and I are so looking forward to it. But just a word. Perhaps best to lay in a good supply of Scotch. It soothes him when he gets a bit fractious. Toodles."

Fractious? I called Graydon at his office. "Hello, Elf. Esmé, this is a lovely surprise."

"Scotch?"

"Ah. You've talked with Mother. Never worry, there will be Scotch. Chaseborn's Scotch."

"Chaseborn? No relation, right?" I was still not privy to all the industries to which his family was connected.

"Small distillery in Scotland. Yes, it's ours."

"We're going to have a chat someday about all the things you own or run." I was a playwright, that was simple, but Graydon, still in many ways, was a mystery.

"Someday we will."

We kept the conversation short. Graydon was up to his ears digging through Duncan Balmain's tangled financial dealings. I had just enough time to throw on some slacks and a sweater, and my face, before the theatre's resident set designer Hank Turnbridge and his wife Irma arrived with the seasonal decorations I'd asked for.

Wearing dungarees, they came bearing baskets of autumn leaves. They also had a little red wagon full of pumpkins and the largest cornucopia I'd seen outside of a parade or a department store window. And the turkeys. So many turkeys. I tried to direct the action, but Hank was like a man possessed, a man with a vision. I hadn't had time to raid Woolworth's for a few holiday decorations myself—now I was reconsidering that choice.

You would have thought Hank was setting up a stage in the middle of my apartment for a play called *Autumn Madness,* or perhaps *Who's Hidden in the Leaves?* Amelia was buzzing with excitement and caffeine. She produced a pot of coffee in the silver service, a platter of sweet rolls and butter, and sausages from somewhere.

Hank dressed the mirror with charming swags of leaves and even festooned the chandelier with ribbons and roses in shades of apricot and deep red. I was grateful that he hadn't come equipped with cornstalks and scarecrows.

He directed me to put together an arrangement of flowers and leaves for the entryway table. Amelia was ready with a large vase that I'd never seen before. Once again, making sure she was indispensable.

"This is so beautiful I think even Robbins will be impressed," Amelia declared.

I hoped so too, but what kind of mess would it leave? I wondered. Hank read my mind.

"Don't worry, we'll come around after the holiday to strike the set."

The set. My apartment was already very theatrical, to be sure, and Hank had painted the mural on my bedroom walls and ceiling. I knew my theatre people would love this festive excess, but what about the aristocrats? I heard they liked things subtle, to the point of boring. I told myself Graydon needed to see how I lived. Though I had never before hired a set designer to help set up a party.

"Saw your picture in the paper," Irma pointed to *The Post*.

"Some people have a knack for it," Hank said.

"A knack for what?" I said.

"A knack for getting in the papers. Falling over dead bodies. So to speak. And looking smashing doing it."

"I never fell over any of them."

"I'd be curious to see a murder scene like that for our next show, *What Cost Murder?* You know, rich guy gets what he deserves?"

"Can't have a poor guy getting it," Irma cut in. "People don't want to identify with some poor dope. They eat it up when a rich guy dies."

"By the way," Hank said, "how did the killer get in? The night Duncan bought the farm."

Maura had been at home, but I had wondered how someone else would gain entrance. There was a small terrace off their living room. But someone could just as easily knock on the door and be let in by Sebastian the butler.

"Beats me. We arrived after the fact," I said. "Short answer: probably the front door. Balmain and Akers, the killer, knew each other, the police said. But there's other possibilities for your set. The servant's door goes through the kitchen. And there's a door to the terrace."

"I only ask," he said, holding a couple of pumpkins, "because going through the front door would be different than through the servant's entrance. Design-wise. For when I build the set. On the other hand, the terrace has promise."

"How so?"

Hank set down the pumpkins. "Well, if the killer came in through the front door, he must look like he belongs there. Maybe he does belong. But if he came through the servant's entrance, he wants to blend in with the background folks, like a workman or staff. He comes in through the window, or terrace? He's been hiding in the night. I'll have to work on that one. Maybe I should read the script."

"You do that," I said. I had. I hadn't recommended it.

"What do you know about this killer?" Hank asked.

A little too much, I thought. Neither he nor Irma knew what had really happened to Duncan Balmain. But Hank's questions, along with what Romeo had said, raised more questions. Now I wondered if Maura was even supposed to be at home that night, or if the hired killer had been misdirected on purpose. Either way, Duncan was dead.

"I only know what I read in the paper. More coffee?"

Hank stretched and lifted his coffee cup. We all stood to admire his work. There were two tables for twelve guests, my dining table and one hauled up from the storage closet in the basement. My mantel and the buffet were full of pumpkins and glass turkeys. The larger birds were nested in a frothy basket of leaves for the tables' centerpieces.

"I should really help," I said.

"Leave him be." Irma helped herself to a sweet roll. "He's in his element. I'm enjoying this superb coffee and I get to rest before heading to the madhouse, which we lovingly call our home."

I liked Irma, she was so calm and soothing. I had an envelope ready for her with money to cover costs and a little extra for Hank's work. I hoped it would be enough. "Can you take this now, so it doesn't get lost?"

She lifted the envelope, peeked inside, and smiled broadly. "This will be a happy Thanksgiving." She tucked it away. Meanwhile, Amelia took her break with us. She made herself comfortable on the sofa and lifted a cup of coffee.

"It's gorgeous, just gorgeous. All my mom has are a couple of wax pilgrim candles and a battered old wax turkey. They're so old they're half melted."

"What about your home, Irma? Are you like the shoemaker's children without shoes?"

"Are you kidding? Looks like the Pilgrims just landed. Hank's built a kid-size Mayflower ship in the yard for all the grandchildren and the neighborhood kids. And costumes! They all want to be Indians, with bows and arrows and hatchets. No fatalities yet." She paused to consider. "And no scalping. Though there was that one time."

"That sounds very complicated." It did not make me yearn for the pitter-patter of little feet. And little hands with hatchets.

"It's going to be a massacre," Irma said. "But it will keep the children and Hank busy and out of my kitchen. He never really grew up. The theatre was his only plausible career choice. You going to the parade at Macy's?"

"Not this year," I said. "I'll be making pies."

"Apple, pecan, and pumpkin," Amelia put in. "And cranberry sauce and corn pudding as side dishes. You wouldn't think it, but Esmé can cook when she wants to."

"This kind of effort," Irma waved at the apartment, "can mean only one thing. Esmé's in love and his parents are coming."

"It's like you're psychic or something," Amelia said.

After they left, Graydon stepped through the entry and took one look. "Oh my God, I knew it would be festive, but—" He howled with laughter. I threw him a stern look. "I'd expect nothing less from a playwright of your stature with access to all the props."

"Is it too much? I simply asked Hank to dress things up." I leaned back on the sofa and shut my eyes.

"Things are dressed up, all right. However, I'm glad to see this *now*, so—"

"So you can warn your parents?"

"I've told them Americans are enthusiastic about this holiday. However, this says it much better than words."

He had brought two bottles of the best Scotch, or at least the kind Lord Chaseborn favored, from the family distillery. The navy blue label with gold script was tasteful; the slogan, less so.

CHASEBORN'S SCOTCH WHISKY
A TASTE OF THE HIGHLANDS—AND HEAVEN

"You better kiss me, Graydon, before our engagement is torn asunder by Thanksgiving."

"Not possible. There is no turning back now." His blue eyes did something to me, something distracting, and then he kissed me.

"You don't think this is ridiculous?" I indicated the autumn forest that was now my living and dining rooms.

"I do. But in the most interesting way." He joined me on the sofa and thoroughly mussed my hair and my clothes.

"Do you know how to carve a turkey?" I inquired, when we came up for air.

Twenty-Two

THANKSGIVING MORNING DAWNED cool and bright. I opened *The New York Times*, relieved not to see any mention of Graydon and me, together or separately.

The rest of the news ranged from lurid to murderous to fascinating, the kind we were used to in the city. Notorious bank robber Pretty Boy Floyd was dead, shot multiple times by federal agents. *The Times* helpfully noted that a dozen of America's most wanted had been dispatched by the Feds this year, including Baby Face Nelson, John Dillinger, Bonnie Parker and Clyde Barrow, and many others.

In other news, the bodies of three unknown young girls were found deceased in the Pennsylvania woods. And to top it off, another suicide was reported, a man who could not find a job and had run out of hope. I folded up the paper and hid it so my company wouldn't find it. It was hardly the kind of conversation stopper you wanted for a national holiday.

Amelia and Robbins arrived to attend to last-minute details. I greeted them with relief, and the suspicion they were judging me. My apartment looked like opening night of some Broadway musical, full of dancing turkeys and singing Pilgrims, before the critics had their way with it. The tables were set, place cards arranged, and the banquet lace tablecloths dressed everything up. My mother's Staffordshire china accompanied the glistening crystal goblets for wine and water, and the turkey-themed dessert plates.

Still, I wished it was going to be the friendly little madhouse I'd originally planned. This felt way too formal. I took out the still-warm pies, two of each, and arranged them on the buffet among the festive decorations.

The turkey was in the oven, smelling delicious. The potatoes were boiling. The electric fryer was ready for the last-minute vegetables. All but the final touches were ready, as Amelia had promised. She and Robbins would tend to the rest. I had only to finish dressing.

The dinner was to be family style, with Graydon carving the turkey and plates delivered to each diner by Amelia and Robbins. I didn't care what the etiquette was, I had placed myself next to Graydon, his mother was on his right side, and his father was on my left. Hemmed in. Hard to escape. So it goes.

Amelia's cheeks were pink and pretty, her expression full of excitement.

"This looks wonderful, I gotta say. I've never seen a dinner this fancy."

"You helped. Along with Hank and the pumpkins. Is that a new dress?"

"You like it?"

"Of course."

It looked like a heavy black crepe with a few discreet pearls attached to the white collar and cuffs.

"Robbins helped me pick it out. He has such good taste." He looked embarrassed. "We should take pictures."

I popped a new roll of film in my Leica and took photos of them in front of the fireplace. They donned crisp white aprons and Robbins insisted that we take pictures of them serving, which I found weird, but Amelia seemed to be having spasms of delight, so I acquiesced. I left the camera out where we could take pictures of the guests later.

Robbins unbent enough to say, "I've never seen anything quite like it. It's very—welcoming."

"Don't be nervous, Esmé," Amelia said. "I mean, you're only entertaining a few close friends, members of the press, the theatre crowd, your fiancé Mr. Graydon, and an honest-to-God *lord* and *lady*. From England. Who came to see you, instead of a royal wedding. No big deal."

Amelia thought that would calm me down? My stomach lurched.

"Yes," I agreed. "Sounds like a full-blown disaster in the making."

"If I may say, Miss Esmé, there is no need to worry," Robbins said. "Everything is under control."

"Thank you, Robbins. And Amelia." However much they would charge me, it was worth it. "Just one question. Where did all the extra dishes come from?"

"Mr. Rupert said I should provide anything you may need. You are quite well supplied, but with so many guests coming—"

"There's always a chance some random actor will show up," I agreed. Robbins seemed surprised.

"Isn't that rather irregular?"

"They're *actors*."

"They're like cats, Robbins," Amelia chimed in. "Not to worry. We'll just throw another plate on the table, grab a chair from the closet. It's how we do things here in America." Amelia patted his elbow, looking regal. Her hair was a crown of white-blond curls. "You," she pointed at me. "I'll get you a Bromo-Seltzer to calm down your tummy."

Family style or not, over a dozen people at a sit-down dinner was crazy to me. Dessert would be more informal, served buffet style. I fingered the delicate turkey dessert plates that Amelia picked up.

"Thank you for these, they're perfect."

Amelia glowed with pleasure. "I figured these would be the ones you preferred. I put these on your Macy's charge account." She handed me the glass of Bromo.

"I don't have a charge account." The room started to spin.

"You do now. Good thing the guy in customer service had seen your play. Let me look at the turkey." I trailed her to the kitchen where she donned an apron and opened the oven door.

"About that charge card—"

"Don't worry, it was a snap. He said they don't usually give them to women, but there are exceptions. I didn't want to use up the cash in the household account."

"That's what it's there for."

She ignored me. "This bird looks beautiful. Where's the baster?" I pointed and she squirted the bird with juice. "Ham is in the warmer, looking glorious."

I must have stood with my mouth open, because she suggested I get ready. She sent a meaningful look at my casual clothes. She hated seeing me in trousers.

"Why don't you go fix yourself up and I'll do your hair."

First I mixed up the autumn wassail, so called by my parents, a hot harvest punch of apple wine, brandy, fruit juices, and spices. It simmered, perfuming the air with cinnamon and cloves. I poured the concoction into a giant pot on an electric hot plate, stationed just beyond the foyer, set up next to the bar cart, full of pretty liquor bottles, including the special Scotch that Graydon had delivered the night before.

"If I may ask, Miss Esmé. what is this?" Robbins said. He gazed suspiciously at the punch.

"Family tradition. We always had a hot punch to greet people, whet the appetite, and ward off the cold. Teetotalers may sip plain hot cider. If there are any."

"I see. Very appropriate. It has a divine aroma."

Amelia hustled me to the bedroom, where she made quick work of my hair, twisting it into a coil at the back of my neck, entwined with a ribbon that matched my dress. The shorter hair at the front was curly and framed my face.

"You sure you don't want me to cut it? Short and stylish? Maybe like a vamp?"

"I don't feel vampy today. Thanks."

She sighed. Dramatically. Then she left to check on the turkey. By this time, I had become rather proficient with makeup, though I was surprised she trusted me with it. I dabbed on a bit of shadow and liner and plenty of mascara. I thought false lashes would be a bit much for an at-home dinner. The copper-colored velvet cocktail gown Willie had designed was gloriously comforting. I admired the intricate work about the shoulders where she had fashioned velvet leaves in autumn colors. She always included a touch of the theatrical for my enjoyment. I chose my cameo necklace on a velvet ribbon and earrings to match.

Today I would be playing the part of a hostess with everything under control. Acting! I told the butterflies in my stomach to calm down and sipped Amelia's Bromo-Seltzer.

I opened the curtains over the French doors to show off the extravagant mural that Hank had painted. Flowers soared out of the green velvet headboard into lush blossoms, blue sky, and fluffy clouds. I could keep the doors closed, but I knew everyone would like to see it, except perhaps Graydon's parents. There was a rolling rack with hangers for guests' coats in the front hall if the closet was full. Any excess would be piled on the bed.

Things were at the ready and I had only one more hour to worry, amid exhortations from Amelia to calm down. I decided the Bromo wasn't enough and poured myself a bit of the autumn wassail.

To my surprise, Graydon arrived with his parents in tow much earlier than expected. I wanted to answer the door, but Robbins got there first. I managed to grab the Leica just in time to capture their arrival.

As they entered, Graydon winked at me. Robbins collected their coats and stashed them away in the closet. Graydon kissed me on the cheek, which had the surprising effect of further relaxing me. Better than wassail.

"My goodness, Graydon said it would be festive, but this is so much—more," Lady Jane said.

"Looks like the woodland fairies held a drunken orgy in here." Lord Cyril was his usual charming self.

"At least they're happy fairies," I said. "It is exuberant and I look forward to Hank's magic if the Washington Irving ever produces *A Midsummer Night's Dream*."

"I daresay you could hide Oberon and Titania in here," he said. "And Puck and Bottom too."

"Now Cyril, I understand a wonderful set designer is responsible for this holiday décor."

"Was he drunk?"

Jane took him by the elbow, but he moved to the fireplace and picked up a framed eight-by-ten photograph. He studied it for a moment and stared at me.

"Good lord! Is this Jack Dempsey? The boxer? You're there with Jack Dempsey? In the flesh?"

Twenty-Three

66THE MANASSA MAULER himself, with my father and me." I pointed him out. "Exhibition fight, 1929. I covered the fights as a reporter in those days."

"Rather bold, I'd say," Lord Cyril said. "For a woman."

"This was out West. You might say the Wild West. My parents weren't crazy about my job, but when my dad got to meet the Mauler himself, it changed his mind. Mr. Dempsey is a very nice man, by the way. Owns a restaurant here in the city."

Cyril harrumphed at me and then the photo. "Legendary puncher, what?"

"I have copies of the photo if you'd like one."

He spun around, eyeing the rest of my digs. "Rupert tells me this place is yours."

"Yes."

"Good heavens. They let women buy their own flats here in America?"

"Occasionally." And now I seemed to have a charge account at Macy's.

I was proud of my Edwardian Five apartment, which I'd purchased at an incredible price from a desperate owner during the Depression. When it came to a cash sale, he didn't mind that I was a woman. I think he assumed I was a widow.

Cyril wandered out to the small balcony, left the door open, and came back in. He announced that the wind had picked up.

"Perhaps you'd like something to warm up." I led him to where the drinks were waiting.

"What's this? Hot punch?" Cyril asked.

"Autumn wassail." Amelia had materialized with glass mugs on a tray. "Miss Esmé's family recipe."

"We also have Scotch. A very good Scotch. If you prefer," I said.

He sniffed the aroma. "Wassail, you say? Don't mind if I do. Take the chill off."

Under all his tweeds and full of hot air and bluster, I wondered that he could possibly be chilled.

"Your Lordship." Robbins held a cup for him. "Lady Chaseborn?"

"Oh, yes." She sipped and declared it delicious. Graydon ushered his parents to the sofa where they could enjoy the fire and a tray full of appetizers on the coffee table.

"Good idea, this," Cyril said. "Jane hasn't let me eat a bite all day."

"Cyril!"

The doorbell rang. Luckily the bit players, I mean the *actors* and theatre folk, started to arrive. My Leica and I were ready for them all. May Scott produced her improbably tall cherry Jell-O dessert, which was given pride of place on the buffet with the other sweets, to be admired by all. I knew it would be a hit on novelty alone, and I took its picture to prove it actually existed. As promised, the Jell-O matched her crimson-colored crepe dress. Wearing something other than her normal navy or black-and-white attire was startling, and May looked quite pretty. Her cropped black hair was dramatic against the color and she'd left off her glasses.

Libby Sheridan and Hamilton Gardner were next, the understudies who'd impressed audiences of *Leaving Alamogordo* when the flu knocked the leads out of their roles. Apparently, they'd been rehearsing Thanksgiving tunes, with pretty harmonies, with which they greeted us as they walked in the door. It was beginning to feel more and more like that play with the singing Pilgrims.

Were they auditioning for something?

Seth, another backstage wizard at the theatre, followed them. I'd invited him to keep Willie company. He was a pale blond boy who helped Hank out and was handy with a hammer. He was also up on all the current dances. I suspected his dapper dinner suit came from the costume loft. Seth instantly took in the decorations.

"Wow! Hank told me about the autumn décor for your party. Nice work. Say, Esmé, did you figure out how the killer got in the Balmain apartment? We've been trying to puzzle it out."

I stood with mouth agape, trying to signal to him that the subject was not open for discussion. Luckily, a knock sounded at the front door. Robbins answered. It was Willie and her father, Mr. Kim, who was well dressed in a somber suit. But Willie stole the show.

She could have doubled for the actress Anna May Wong, stunning and exotic in her yellow gold cheongsam. Willie's late mother was a white woman who'd married Mr. Kim and moved to Chinatown to help with their restaurant. She died when her daughter was young. Willie was a beautiful mixture of both races. She could play up either her Chinese or Caucasian features, depending on her mood and method. I stared at her dress. I barely remembered to take her picture.

Piping edged the dress in green, and there were embroidered lilies and roses in an asymmetrical pattern. It must have taken her forever, but I knew how quickly she could sew and how she expressed her feelings in fabric. The theatre folk all applauded her dress and she took a bow.

"That's lovely, Willie," I said.

"All the rage in Shanghai," Willie said. Her father just shrugged.

"Telling Willie what to do is like ordering rain not to fall. She is like her late mother." Father and daughter exchanged a look.

"We're grateful she rains her talent at the theatre and for those of us fortunate enough to know her," I said. "I'm wearing one of her designs right now."

If Willie thought she would shock my future in-laws, she was wrong. They were their unflappable English selves, and I made introductions all around. Meanwhile Seth looked like a thirsty man eyeing a glass of water. Willie took Seth's arm.

"You can sit next to me."

Seth gazed at her and just said, "Wow."

Luckily I'd already planned for that and seated them together, again breaking all the etiquette rules. But before she took her place next to Seth, Willie pulled me aside. The other women turned it into a huddle around the wassail. If I thought the Balmain murder story was no longer a topic of dinner conversation, I was wrong.

"What do you think, Esmé?" Willie said, *sotto voce.* "There's something unsatisfying about this Johnny Akers thing. Duncan Balmain was the type of man who deserved to be plugged by a *woman.*"

Mr. Kim touched his daughter's arm. "You said we would keep this polite, daughter."

"I am being polite." She grinned. "I'm merely curious about the whole thing."

May agreed. "The guy clearly cheated on his wife with way too many women."

"I try to remember," Libby said, "that real life is so often like the theatre. I should have known he was a rotter. There's one in every play I ever read. Even Shakespeare. Like Iago."

"That wasn't in the papers," Lady Jane said.

"Between the lines," May said, suddenly a font of information. "The society pages mark all the times he was with women who weren't his wife."

"He was a sleaze," Willie agreed. "What say you, Esmé?"

"As a playwright, I'd say there are a lot of motives going around. Like a carousel. Just pick the horse you like."

Cyril butted into the huddle, sounding positively Victorian. "The man's wife was badly injured. Do you think a woman could have done that?"

"With one hand tied behind her back," Willie said. Seth stared at her with admiration. Or perhaps fear.

"Luckily the culprit has been named," Graydon said. "One Johnny Akers."

"Didn't he live in Hooverville?" Seth asked." Have you seen that place? It would drive anybody around the bend. Specially 'cause he was fired by, guess who, Duncan Balmain." It seemed everybody had read every newspaper story on the subject.

"Hooverville. I must put it on my agenda," Cyril said.

"Not without me," Lady Jane piped up. "Perhaps Rupert and Esmé could give us a tour."

"Hardly talk for a holiday," I said, knowing that people all over America would be digesting the gory news about Baby Face Nelson with their Thanksgiving meal and saying prayers of thanks that it didn't affect them. "Does everyone have wassail? Cheers!"

Despite my warning, Reggie Pendleton, reporter sans discretion, had the nerve to show up, and in a sports coat, not dinner clothes. I hoped he'd get called away by his paper to cover something bloody and boring. He pushed Nina Oglesby ahead of him as a shield, knowing I wouldn't clobber him if she was around. I did, however, send him a look of utter disgust. In response, he produced a bottle of champagne and some fine old port and handed them to Robbins. I wasn't impressed; Reggie had lifted them from his parents.

"Something smells good," he said.

"Everything smells good." Nina rushed into the foyer, rubbing her hands. "Is there hootch in that hot punch? I'll take some."

Robbins served them both. "I know you're irritated by my story, Esmé, and Graydon," Reggie said. "But the pictures were too good."

"So you're responsible for that tabloid story?" Lady Jane said. "Good heavens! And yet you look almost like a gentleman, young man. Can you explain yourself?"

He cast his boy-next-door smile on her. "Dropped on my head when I was a baby."

"I daresay."

"Isn't it a little early for insulting Esmé's guests, Jane?" Lord Cyril smirked.

She smiled. "I have not yet begun to insult, and I shall not. I was merely *inquiring*."

"This is going to be a great party." Nina was a hardened reporter from out West who had come East to write society news (and the Great American novel), but she loved gossip, a great big dish of it. She had taken on a sophisticated polish since arriving in New York, but she couldn't hide her freckles. Her short chestnut curls defied gravity and her green gown made her look like another member of the elfin forest brigade. She sipped the wassail.

"Delicious."

I moved to the foyer to oversee the punch. I needn't have worried. Robbins was on duty. Nina sidled up to me.

"Esmé, what's wrong?"

"Nothing." I took a deep breath.

"You should be flying high. You seem jumpy."

"Jumpy?! His lordship! Her ladyship! How am I supposed to handle this whole future in-law thing? Especially these people. They're— They're *English*."

"Oh that." Nina made a wry face. "Think of Margaret Tobin Brown. Some call her Molly Brown. Unsinkable mining gal who helped row a lifeboat on the Titanic. Denver's so-called high-society crowd snubbed her. She showed them, went to Europe and charmed the locals. She survived Denver *and* Europe *and* the Titanic. You can survive a couple of high-hat Brits."

"Every look from his father, Lord High-and-Mighty, is a sneer. At me." I glanced his way. Lord Cyril seemed quite content with his wassail and Lady Jane at his side. I imagined the stern lecture she must have given him before they arrived.

"Let 'em sneer. How many robber barons did you cover? Outlaws? Gunfights? Snobs are just water off a duck's back for a reporter, and we can swim." She grinned at me. "Hey, after that two-bit dust-choked town you came from, and my town too, New York is a cakewalk. 'Specially when there's cake."

I hugged her. Thank God for Nina. This was what I needed to hear.

"Okay. And what about you and Reggie? You're going to tell me you're not sweet on him? What about all those blondes?"

"I know he loves that Jean Harlow hair. But it's just hair and the gallons of dye those gals use, they're gonna be bald by the time they're thirty. And I know he likes to chatter on about you. But underneath it all, he's crazy about me. He just doesn't know it yet."

"Can you wait that long?"

"Try me."

"Come in by the fire." Graydon arrived and showed the way. Reggie appeared at his elbow and seemed to be dragging the entire party behind him.

"Reggie, you are going to behave, or become firewood," I warned him.

"I'll make sure of it," Nina promised as we crowded around the fire. "Reporters are used to being kicked out of places, but I'm off duty and I'm hungry and I'll have another cup of this delicious witch's brew."

"Capital idea." Cyril reached out his cup for Amelia to refill.

"One question, Lord and Lady Chaseborn, if you don't mind. Why choose to come to the States instead of the royal wedding in London?" Nina was angling for a juicy society page tidbit. I raised my hand in warning, but

Graydon whispered to me that they'd be disappointed if no one wanted to know.

"My dear, royal weddings may sound lovely and romantic," Lord Cyril intoned, "but they are a perfect waste of a perfectly good day. All that pomp and circumstance, protocol and tedium, standing and waiting, and bowing and scraping, it's hard on the back. And the spirit."

"Yes, indeed," Lady Jane agreed. "With so many royals loose on the landscape, these weddings tend to be just one thing after another. The first one is exciting, I suppose. Rather like husbands." Cyril guffawed. "I think my husband may have been bored, and I—his wife—wasn't there with him. I was only vaguely aware of that wedding, what with all the excitement about Esmé and Graydon's engagement."

Graydon offhandedly added, "Don't get his lordship going. He's still upset that the German House of Saxe-Coburg-Gotha pulled off that cheap conjuring trick and turned themselves into the House of Windsor. Interlopers, Johnny-come-latelies. Our family, on the other hand, were around since before the Magna Carta."

"An unbroken line," Cyril rumbled, "since before the Norman Conquest. Unless my sons let the family down."

This was all rot, I thought. A pack of English fairy tales.

"And who knows?" Jane added. "Cyril may actually have missed me, though he would never say so."

"He must have missed you," I agreed.

And evidently he missed interfering in Graydon's life. I invited the company to the dining table before the witticisms got out of hand. We were all just settling into our places when there was a knock at the door.

Twenty-Four

I MADE A move to rise from my seat, but Graydon touched my arm. "Let Robbins see to it," he said *sotto voce*. Thus relieved of my hostess duties, the pre-dinner preparations went on, and soon the tall valet made his way to Graydon's elbow.

"A person named Frank Romeo to see you and Miss Esmé," Robbins announced in a low voice. He seemed distressed. Apparently even he couldn't dissuade Romeo from interrupting our Thanksgiving dinner.

Hamilton, in a stage whisper that everyone heard, said "Frankie the Cat?" There was a hush. The entire table was at attention.

"We'll speak to him." Graydon was already on his feet and helped me up. "Please go on, everyone, we'll be right back."

I directed them to the rolls and butter on their plates, libations were poured, and ten sets of eyes followed us. Before moving on, I leveled a death stare at Reggie to not even think about writing about this.

The gangster waited in the entry. He wore crisp evening clothes, looking as distinguished as a senator and twice as handsome.

"Quite a crowd you got here."

"What's up, Frank?" I asked and Graydon put his restraining hand on my shoulder.

"Sorry to interrupt your dinner, Esmé. I wanted to make sure everything is good with you."

"As you can see. Would you care for some punch? It's a family recipe."

Amelia popped out of the kitchen and poured him a cup of hot wassail. She didn't smile, but her eyes were alight with amusement. I'm sure mine showed panic. Frank sampled the mug.

"Not bad." He looked toward the tables full of my guests and lowered his voice. We pulled away from the crowd. "The reason I'm here— I have some important information for you. The party we discussed? The one who was hired to dispatch Mr. Duncan Balmain? He has flipped his wig. He's determined to off someone to justify his assignment. Which, as you know, he failed to complete."

"Why would he do that?" I asked.

"How do I know? He's a hired gun. From Chicago. Crazy town. They do crazy things out there. Like Capone."

As if mobsters didn't do crazy things in New York.

"He wants to protect his reputation, I suppose," Graydon said.

"Maybe. Your guess is as good as mine. And as far as I know, his name is John Smith. It's as good as John Doe."

"Nobody knows his real name?" I asked.

"Seems he's got a lot of names. Anyways, you should be aware. This ain't in the papers yet. Call this an early edition. This guy might go after Old Man Balmain, or even the widow. In his mind, one Balmain is maybe as good as another and he's got to earn his paycheck. Unless he's been paid already. Maybe half up front. That's the usual."

"Duly noted," Graydon said.

"As I may have already mentioned, my associates say he's got Cupid's Disease, you know? Syphilis? Sorry to bring that up in mixed company."

"I believe you mentioned it," Graydon said.

"He's screwy, and screwy means dangerous."

Frank Romeo and I had attended the same church together. That created a strange sort of familiarity, not to mention our mutual involvement in the whole Scavullo murder. I'd associated him first with Our Lady of Pompeii, not the mob. Then Scavullo got shot and things became complicated. Frank felt the same kind of familiarity with me, I supposed, even though he had agreed we should keep a distance. He said he didn't want to "sully my reputation," yet now he was acting like a protective uncle. This extended now to Graydon.

"I hear this guy is like Capone," he said again. "Another nut job from Chicago who's going squirrely."

Graydon changed the subject. "You're looking very dapper tonight, Frank."

"Checking out a nightclub later with the boys. Supposed to be real classy, and my place has gotta be top drawer. Like this apartment. Nice setup you got here." I didn't ask how he knew my address.

To my absolute surprise Graydon said, "Frank, would you care to join us for Thanksgiving dinner?"

"There is plenty," I said, "and you're very welcome, but please, no talk about the Balmain business." I caught my breath. "There are reporters here craning their necks, and actors who no doubt are doing character studies."

"Dinner? You kiddin' me? I haven't had a real Thanksgiving dinner in a whole lotta years." Frank seemed as surprised as I was. Unless he was acting. "I'd like that. If it's not an inconvenience."

"It's an honor to have you, Frank," I said. I was glad I'd left my Leica on the sideboard. I knew Frank Romeo wouldn't necessarily want his picture taken by surprise.

Frank sipped his wassail and slid smoothly into the dining room, handing his camel hair coat to Robbins, who asked me quietly where we should put him.

"If you please, Robbins, over here by me," Lord Cyril piped up. "We'll make room."

I started making introductions and Robbins brought another chair, from whence I knew not, followed by Amelia with plates and necessities. Willie's dad nodded and said, "Good evening, Mr. Romeo." Frank grinned at him and they shook hands.

"Mr. Kim. Not working tonight?"

Mr. Kim inclined his head and smiled. "My daughter convinced me that Thanksgiving with friends is a more important tradition." Willie beamed at Frank. People stared at Mr. Kim, who explained, "Mr. Romeo has supplied my restaurant with certain liquid necessities over the years. We are old friends."

I had to shut my mouth, which had fallen open again. Even Graydon looked surprised. Who was writing this play? These characters were making up their own story. Frank settled in next to Graydon's dad.

"So, Mr. Romeo," Lord Cyril said. "Tell me. Are you in fact that romantic figure, a real American gangster?" Cyril seemed unusually animated—perhaps it was the wassail—while the rest of the table fell silent, at full attention. "I've read about you in those newspaper stories. You know the stuff, all that sensational murder and mayhem business, involving my son and future daughter-in-law, Miss de LaForet. Lady Jane saves all the clippings."

I felt my face go scarlet. I saw Jane jab her husband in the ribs. He ignored her.

"I've been called a gangster," Frank said, cool as ice. "And a mobster, a bootlegger, a rumrunner. And I've been called worse." All eyes were on Frank. Bootlegger was just the start of his reputation, and here we had a ringside seat. "But that's all over," Frank said. "It's 1934. It's a new day. It's the big Repeal and I'm going legit in a big way. Prohibition is over and done and people are going straight. The time is right to get out of the old business. Sure, there are other rackets besides running rum, but I'm not interested. I want to make a big change, like the whole country is making. I want to run a classy joint full of bright lights and happy people. I always figured people got the right to drink what they want, when they want, and they want to do it in style, out in the open, not down in a dark cellar with the rats. Me, I'm coming up into the light."

Frank smiled at me and I nearly applauded. Practically a Shakespearean soliloquy, delivered off the cuff, and George Raft himself couldn't have done it better.

"Yes, indeed," Lord Cyril said after a pause. "I second that heartily. That whole silly Prohibition thing always seemed completely idiotic to me. We've always been able to drink spirits freely in England. And I understand, Mr. Romeo, you are an accomplished purveyor of spirits?"

"And Lord Chaseborn, I understand you own a distinguished distillery in Scotland? Chaseborn's Scotch? Perhaps we could talk sometime."

"Perhaps we could, over a taste of that very Scotch. Truly the finest in the Highlands."

The two of them clicked their wassail mugs together. There was a wave of slightly nervous laughter around the table, then my guests shouted "Cheers!" all around.

I sent Graydon a look. He gave me the slightest of smiles. We joined in and enjoyed the show, as there was nothing else to do. Robbins and Amelia entered with the turkey and trimmings and suddenly the room went silent again in anticipation.

The beautifully basted, buttered, and browned turkey was placed ceremoniously before Graydon. He lifted the silver carving knife and fork, waited for the company to come to order, and began to carve the bird.

I could have sworn he'd been practicing.

COULD I EVER have a simple dinner party again? One without a butler and maid, or valet and housekeeper? The more smoothly it went, the more inadequate I felt. The silver shone, the crystal gleamed, the food was delivered without a hitch, course after course, and everybody seemed to be getting along.

"Looks just like a magazine." Frankie the Cat Romeo lifted his glass to me. "This is real class, Esmé. I guess you learn how to do this in the theatre."

"Nonsense," Lady Jane said. "It isn't easy. She has a natural talent, that's all."

"My parents and I used to serve a Thanksgiving meal for the community at their general store," I said. "It was always quite a crowd."

I remembered those Thanksgiving meals, how we scrubbed the store for a week, how people waited in line before the doors were opened promptly at two on Thanksgiving afternoon. They included the customers who couldn't pay their bills on time. My mother knew how close to the bone they lived. The shelves and counters were pushed back and our main room was filled with tables and decorated with oak and cottonwood branches, tied with bows from the ribbon counter. The linen was threadbare and it was a week's worth of work, but my parents never complained, and I didn't dare. We were far from wealthy, but my mother said we lived like kings compared to our neighbors, who suffered greatly in the Depression.

My life had since changed dramatically and now I could see how kings lived, or at least earls and countesses. The very wealthy who could skip a royal wedding as *same old, same old.* My father always opened his remarks, "Today we are honored with your presence, and we give thanks for your friendship…"

Now I cribbed from my dad, picked up my glass, and stood. I took a breath.

"Today I am honored with your presence, and I am thankful for your friendship."

"*We* are thankful for your friendship," Graydon added. He and I were partners in everything now. I toasted him.

"Most of us, anyway," Reggie piped up.

"We make an exception for you today, Pendleton," Graydon said, and everyone laughed.

"I'll make sure he behaves," Frank said with a smirk.

"Please enjoy this lovely turkey and trimmings," I went on. "A feast like this is always better when shared with family and friends, especially when so many have so little. Thank you for coming here today. Let us toast the blessings of the coming year."

Everyone lifted their glasses and cheered noisily. Even Lord Cyril.

"Well said, my dear. I concur." Graydon smiled as I sat down. "Now, who wants a leg?" he asked. "White meat or dark? Don't be shy." And I took his picture with the Leica.

Dinner progressed through the courses and the diners happily required a break before dessert. The actors sang and a game of charades erupted impromptu. Not my decision, actors have to act.

It felt warm and overstuffed to me and I stepped out to my small balcony for some air. I heard the door open and thought it was Graydon. I was surprised to see Hamilton Gardner, the able understudy.

"May I speak with you, Esmé? If you don't mind."

"Of course." My first thought was that he wanted a part in my next play, the play I hadn't written yet, the one that hadn't quite announced itself to me.

Hamilton could be fierce looking, though in reality he was as ferocious as a newborn puppy. He ducked his head, as if in apology. I knew he'd come to my Thanksgiving dinner because his family was far away, somewhere in the South.

At the moment, he looked like an actor who'd gone up on his lines and couldn't find any words. I'd seen that look before—slightly nauseous, petrified he'd ruined the show. I noticed he hadn't eaten everything on his plate. Odd, considering his occupation as a starving artist.

"What's wrong, Hamilton? Are you ill? Didn't dinner appeal to you? Amelia is a whiz at whipping up a Bromo-Seltzer."

"Dinner is fantastic and it was swell of you to invite me. However, something is weighing heavy on my mind." He looked both ways, then whispered, "Duncan Balmain."

"Duncan?" How did he even know the man?

He added, "My life might be in danger."

Was he serious? "We need Graydon for this conversation."

"His lordship?"

"No. Graydon Chase, his son." I signaled through the window to Graydon with a toss of my head. It was getting dark and crystalline blue outside, our breath fogging. Amelia appeared with my coat and Graydon settled it on my shoulders like a hug.

"Amelia says you shouldn't catch cold. Nice bit of fresh air out here. What's up?"

"Hamilton believes his life might be in danger." I turned to the actor. "Hamilton, I know you are an actor and tend toward the dramatic. But what has this to do with Duncan Balmain?" I shivered and pulled my coat closer.

"Yes, do tell us, Hamilton." Graydon steadied me. "Anything about Balmain is of interest."

"It's like this. I'm always looking for a good part and—" The young actor rubbed his mouth before speaking. "I had an audition for a part recently, and I aced it, if I do say so myself. But therein lies my problem."

"What was the part?" I asked.

"A man paid to kill someone." He hunkered down into a menacing stance, pointing his fingers like a gun. "All just acting, of course. But it wasn't for a play."

"A killer?" Somehow Frank Romeo had made his way to the terrace as well. He had a snifter of Reggie's good port. "You got paid to kill somebody?"

"No, no, no, it was just a part, as an actor. Just pretend, it wasn't real—"

Frank seemed unconvinced. "Don't hold out on me, kid. Can you explain this to me, Esmé?"

"Actors," I replied. "They act. It's their thing."

Romeo had some nerve dragging his tarnished reputation to my home, then barging into this conversation. Did this gangster's ears prick up whenever someone said the word *kill*?

"It was just an audition for a part, as Esmé said, to *play* a killer. To confront this guy, wave a prop gun in his face, scare him, shake him up, but not do any killing. Gee whiz, I'm an actor! It was just supposed to make him, you know, change his ways. Duncan Balmain."

"Balmain?" Frank's pose stiffened. His dinner jacket didn't show any telltale bulges, but I was sure he was armed.

"Did you get the part?" Graydon asked.

"Yes, sir, I got the part, a personal, one on one, one-time gig. The pay was good—three hundred dollars. I mean, that kind of money doesn't come around every day."

"Did you get paid?" I asked.

"Half up front. Cash. The rest to be paid later, after. But he died first, before my performance could even happen."

"Tell us more about the gig, would you?" Graydon leaned against the door, blocking it.

"You two are a team, right?" Hamilton looked from Graydon to me. He tried to ignore the gangster in the room, or to be exact, on the terrace. "From what I read, playwright and detective. Teamwork?"

"Exactly so, and the assignment?"

The terrace door cracked open and Graydon's father popped his head out. I hoped that was all. My terrace wasn't that large.

"I was simply supposed to scare this Duncan Balmain. Nothing was supposed to go south, and nothing did. I was just supposed to flash a prop gun and tell him he was messing up big time and he had to clean up his act, or else. He was apparently losing too much money for his company. Not much of a manager. Fingers in the till, I gathered. I don't rightly know."

"Anything to do with unions?" I asked.

"Not that I heard."

"I ain't criticizing your acting or nothing like that," Frank said. "I'm sure you could scare a lot of guys. But first of all, killers look like anyone else, not some matinee movie star. Like someone at the bar, someone fixing your car. You, you're a little too big, too good-looking, you stand out. Man whose business is killing has to melt into the background, invisible, a nobody." Frank caught my eye. "So I've heard."

Hamilton was nodding his head in agreement, as if he were in a scene class.

"I say, what's going on here? They want to play more charades in there and I cannot bear the thought," Lord Cyril said through the crack in the terrace door.

"It's complicated," I said.

"Obviously. I gather this has something to do with your detecting business? That murder of the rich man's son?" He shoved his way past Graydon onto the balcony.

"We don't know yet, Father," Graydon said, "and really, you'd be more comfortable inside."

"Ha! I'm staying." Cyril looked inordinately pleased with himself. "I was in intelligence at one time. During the

Great War." He pulled a pipe out of his pocket and lit it, puffing.

I tried to keep my eyes from popping wide open. "You were?"

"A long-ago chapter. That sort of thing runs in the family, I expect. I shall speak with Rupert later."

I glanced sidelong at my beloved. He grimaced. "Count on it."

"If this conversation has something to do with the Balmain murder, Rupert, I've read all the clips," Cyril said. "Your mother saves everything. She's quite thorough."

"And I thought I knew what's what in this town," Frank cracked. "Maybe we should call her ladyship out here."

Graydon laughed. "There's no more room, Frank."

Frankie the Cat scanned the quiet street below. "This gig of yours is screwy, kid. So what happened? "

"I was headed there that night. Last Friday."

"Headed where?" Cyril said.

"To Balmain's place. But I never even got inside the building."

"This mug the cops fingered for the murder," Frank said. "He got there before you did?"

Through the window I saw Reggie going through some elaborate motions in charades. Good thing he and Nina seemed to be a good team, or they would surely have managed to sneak onto the terrace as well. Robbins and Amelia were setting up coffee and dessert.

Hamilton cleared his throat. "Yeah, to the Balmain place. The same night Duncan got it. The same night as the fancy party for Esmé's play. I was on the opposite corner from the back service door where I was supposed to get into the building. I'd bought a paper and pretended like I was reading under the streetlight, like I was waiting for a lady friend. I waited a long time, not knowing what to do. You wait long enough, I figure, someone goes in or out. Nine times out of ten someone will let you in. A maid opened the door. I headed toward her when I heard gun-shots, a real gun, not a prop. I know the difference. I saw the flashes in the Balmain apartment windows, up above. I tell you, I nearly fell over."

"Cut to the chase, kid," Frank said. "What did you do?"

"I didn't wait for the police. I hit the road. Next morning, I read that Balmain got shot and killed. Day after that, turns out a Mr. Akers did the deed and then he got killed. Talk about irony, I mean— What's going to happen to me? Are the cops going to come after me? I don't think what I did was illegal. It was just an acting gig. Will I have to give back the money? Times being what they are, I already spent it. I paid my rent and the grocer and my local bar-keep—"

"This don't make no sense," Frank said.

"Not at the moment, but I imagine we can puzzle it out," Cyril said, signaling to Robbins through the window. Presently the valet brought two snifters of Scotch, one for his lordship and one for Frank.

"Who hired you?" Frank demanded of Hamilton.

"A guy, just a guy through a guy at my local speakeasy, I mean bar, through another guy. I never met the guy who was paying me. I never even got a name."

"You don't know who orchestrated this?" Graydon asked.

"No, I swear. I don't want anyone coming after me, including Old Man Balmain. I hear he's a real terror."

Frank shook his head in pity. "Kid, I guarantee you are not in danger, but you ain't getting any more money. Count yourself lucky."

"Go inside and have some dessert," I said to Hamilton, "or play charades, or do whatever it is they're doing." He wasted no time in going back inside.

"Actors! Actors will do anything you tell them, am I right?" Frank Romeo said, as the door closed behind Hamilton.

"If only that were true. Listen, Frank, that's a crazy story, but he's harmless."

"What I mentioned to you before," Frank said. "About the crazy killer from Chicago on the loose here? Not so harmless. Out of his head from the Cupid's Disease, or from botching his contract, or just 'cause he's from Chicago, who knows? You two be careful, and you tell Old Man Balmain to take good care of that daughter-in-law of his."

"Good lord. Three potential killers?" Cyril said. "One of them a mere actor playing a part? Sounds like diversionary tactics to me. While we're looking one way, the real killer, or would-be killer, gets away. Very tidy."

"The police believe they have the right killer," Graydon said firmly. "We do too."

I'd had enough. "I'm freezing out here, gentlemen."

Graydon ushered me inside, where I was met by Amelia with a cup of steaming wassail.

"Do you have a part in your new play for me?" Libby, the other understudy, asked me.

Frank smirked. "She's working on it, but it ain't ready yet."

Libby breathed deeply and looked at him with large round eyes. "Do tell."

"I understand it's about this handsome gangster. In love. And it's a musical."

I glared at Frank. "No, it's not. If I have a play, it is in it's infancy."

"Someday," Frank said. The man had gall. He turned to Cyril, swirling his drink and admiring the amber color. "This Scotch would be a great addition to my club. And Esmé, you want to share that wassail recipe? Add a little more class to my operation?"

The charades had finally run their course, the table had been cleared, and everyone was invited to partake of the dessert buffet. And even though there were some spectacular pies, everyone had to have a piece of May's strange Jell-O dessert. It was tall and red and it jiggled. Frank stood in line and winked at May.

"Now that's really something," he said. "Looks danger-ous. The most dangerous thing I seen all night."

TWENTY–SIX

66 **G**RAYDON, DEAR. WHY did you invite Frank Romeo to Thanksgiving dinner?"

I was limp and sprawled on the sofa. What had happened to my bones? The guests were gone and most things were put back in order. Except me. Amelia gathered most of the leftovers. She and Robbins were heading to her family's dinner. I assumed this was a pretty big deal. The quiet in my apartment was wonderful. The fire was friendly and warm. I waited for Graydon to answer. He laughed.

"To see what would happen."

"Things weren't strange enough here already?"

"Might as well reach for the heights, as they say."

I laughed too, and he brought me a small snifter of the precious Chaseborn's Scotch.

"It was a setup, you know. Frankie the Cat used our Thanksgiving dinner to get close to your father."

"Who, it must be said, was more than interested. He always thought Prohibition was ridiculous. And inviting Frank to stay was easier than having to explain Frank being sent away. Also, Frank Romeo had something to tell us. The crazy third killer is much more dangerous than he first let on. Or is he the fourth? I've lost count."

"But now everyone will know we dine with famous mob bosses. Count on it making the society news. And you're the one who was so worried about our reputations."

"At least it gives my parents wild stories to tell back in England. And maybe they'll think twice about visiting again. And you and I have already been seen with Romeo. Might as well share."

"We had two reporters at dinner. After Frank's entrance, no one even asked about the royal wedding." I kicked off my shoes. "God. Prohibition! It's very handy that we Americans supplied a ridiculous law for the rest of the world to mock."

"Only fair. You've been mocking us since 1776 and Mad King George."

"Frank was definitely a bootlegger, and God knows what else he's gotten up to. You're right though. Prohibition taught everybody to drink like fish and break the law like mobsters. Everyone I ever knew has been to a speakeasy or two. Or ten."

"Surely not you, Elf?"

"The Twenty-One Club, for one." I remembered that evening with friends, gaining entrance to that very exclusive speakeasy that former Mayor Jimmy Walker had frequented. "Very glamorous and a bit dangerous. By then, Repeal was on its way."

"Twenty-One Club? The fancy room down in the cellar?"

"Yes. It felt deliciously skulky. Stepping through the kitchen and down that narrow staircase to that secret door that looked just like the foundation of the building."

"Ah, you have been there." He drew closer and the scent of Hickory Wind teased me. I snuggled into his shoulder and loosened his tie. "And to think we might have crossed paths so much earlier."

"It was a couple of years ago."

"I'd remember seeing a green-eyed, copper-haired elf cavorting about the place."

"I never cavorted, and if we did cross paths, I still wouldn't have liked you. Rich boy going out with those Snooty Two-Shoes debutantes you were so fond of."

"They were fond of me. Or rather, my money. And you were no doubt escorted by Pendleton."

"Yes, Reggie was the tour guide of the night. He met an alluring blonde there, but he was gentleman enough to escort me home. I wore my best dress, but it was before I discovered the magic of theatre costumes. You wouldn't have paid the slightest attention to me."

"That's where you're wrong."

I wanted to change the subject. "And what exactly did your father do in British intelligence during the last war?"

"Don't really know, but it's something he likes to say. Intelligence types tend to be vague about the details. Just an office job, I suspect. I have the impression it was mostly paperwork. He may have interrogated spies. Or not."

"What did you think of Hamilton's story?"

"It's idiotic enough to be true."

"The big question is, who hired him? Who thought that ruse would work?" I sipped the Scotch.

"Someone inside the company? Someone trying to straighten him out, like an old school friend? Someone in the family? Duncan was such a wastrel, it could be anybody."

"And who hired the man who really was supposed to kill Balmain? The lunatic from Chicago?"

"Good questions, but the world at large believes Johnny Akers killed Duncan Balmain. If we can keep that story intact, it will protect Maura. And her baby."

"It's not a perfect solution."

"It's not a perfect world."

"Something Hank said makes me wonder how that hired killer planned to get inside. We know Hamilton was simply waiting for the service entry door to be opened. Not much of a plan for a real pro. Even a crazy one."

"Hank?"

"The set designer." I waved my hand toward my pumpkin décor extravaganza. "The turkey and pumpkin wrangler."

"I should have known you'd have a personal set designer."

"He wanted to know how the killer could get in, for some play the theatre is looking at. It's a set design problem. It's called— I forget, something with 'murder' in the title."

Suddenly I was very tired of the subject of murder. Graydon seemed to be too, winding one of my errant curls around his finger.

"Let's talk about other things," he said. "Or better yet, let's not talk."

Twenty–Seven

URING MY LUNCH break I sometimes escaped to the theatre itself, where no one thought of finding me. It reminded me of fleeing to the photography darkroom when I was a reporter. There's something sacred about a dark room, and a theatre box.

I sat in the far house-right box above the orchestra, the seats closest to the stage. It was usually reserved for theatre professionals—Sal and May and whichever director was chosen for a show. I had blanket permission from Sal to occupy it when it was empty.

I had an idea for a play that I doubted would see the light of day. I started to write it anyway. Tentative title, *The Audition*. Or maybe *Audition for Murder*. Darn that Hamilton. And Frank Romeo. The play opens in a police station. A detective and an actor sit on opposite sides of a small table under a bright hot light.

> *Actor:* I told you. It was just an audition. I didn't even get to do the performance.
> *Detective:* If that's so, why is he dead?
> *Actor:* I don't know.
> *Detective:* You telling me you were set up to take the fall? It's stupid.
> *Actor:* I'm an actor. I just follow the script. Blame the stupid script!
> *Detective:* So if you didn't kill him, who did?
> *Actor:* I don't know!

And I didn't know either. What was the motive? Simply to scare Duncan? Who hired Hamilton?

And why on the same night that Duncan was killed?

I let the play idea slide but dwelled on Romeo's observation that it was strange that Maura was at home during the shooting. Women weren't supposed to be around during a hired kill. Despite the fact that I knew Maura was in the apartment and she killed her husband in self-defense, was she even supposed to be at home that night? Or away, doing whatever society women do?

I phoned Graydon and let him know where I was going to be.

&

After checking in at Doctors Hospital, I was waved on up to Maura's room, still carrying the pile of scripts I was supposed to read.

Maura was looking healthier and the bruises around her eye were almost gone. A little makeup would go a long way toward restoring her to the beautiful woman she was. She wore a lovely set of hostess pajamas in a heavenly blue silk that emphasized her eyes and provided some room for the baby to grow. I apologized for bothering her.

"You're always welcome here, Esmé. Did you come from work?"

"Yes. I couldn't concentrate." I set the scripts down on the coffee table and straightened my knitted sweater dress. It was royal blue, with generous sleeves and cuffs that were tight at the wrist. Comfortable and warm, it had a matching jacket trimmed in pink and white.

"You have so much to do. I hear your play is moving to a new theatre, and will be opening soon. That's terribly exciting." She pointed out the news in *The Times*.

"It is, but I need to keep a supply of Bromo-Seltzer on hand." I'd had so much going on, I wasn't concentrating on the play. "I have to check in at rehearsals this week, make sure they haven't changed all my lines."

"Occupational hazard, I suppose. But I'm guessing you didn't come here to discuss your play."

"No. How was your holiday? Should I ask?" I was afraid it would make Maura sad and lonely, but she seemed cheerful.

"It was quite lovely. You'd never guess this place was a hospital. My ma and all my sisters and brothers came over here and dined with me. Duncan always made it clear I wasn't to have a bunch of rowdy Irish in the house. They kept me company until Jesse showed up. That woman is a saint."

"The woman is sitting right over here," Jesse said. "And she's no saint. And they weren't rowdy, though they sang a lot."

"They brought me this." Maura showed off a paper fold-out turkey from Woolworth's. She seemed utterly delighted.

"I'm sure you kept everything under control, Jesse," I said.

Maura winked at me. "Like a sergeant, she is. It's been ever so long since our gang sang together. Hymns and folk songs and such. We were all in choirs growing up. Even Jesse joined in."

"They brought pie," Jesse said. "I'll sing for pie."

Maura laughed. "So much pie. I told them, I was eating for two, not ten."

"Did you have plans before, for Thanksgiving with Duncan?"

"Sure, we were supposed to visit Edward and Duncan's Aunt Ruth at his father's penthouse. As we did every year. The meal was prepared by his cook. I don't know why it was so important. It was all very polite and polished. And very quiet."

"No singing, then?"

"They couldn't carry a tune in a bucket. I longed to be with my family, make my own proper meal for once, and sing grace."

I didn't know her well, but it was the first time I'd seen Maura so relaxed. I hated to break the mood. "May I ask something else, about that other night? When Graydon and I showed up."

"Careful." Jesse pointed her knitting needles at me for emphasis.

"She saved my life," Maura said to her. "Of course she can ask me anything. And remember, Jesse, Esmé called you to come to my aid and bring Dr. Wren."

"Were you supposed to be at home that night?" I asked. "And what about Duncan?"

Maura sat up straighter, cradling her stomach. "Strange you should ask that. No, I was supposed to go to some soiree with the society ladies. For charity. Duncan encouraged me to go, which was odd in itself, because normally he wanted me at home."

"Did he give you a reason?"

"I think he wanted me to be more like them, the ones sent to fancy colleges, who'd come out in society. Debutantes."

It sounded very odd to me. Why did he want her away from the apartment that night? So he could meet someone when she wasn't there?

"You didn't like those women? I can't say I'm fond of them myself."

A shadow of a smile played on her face. "No, I didn't like them, always making cow eyes at my husband. Besides, I was feeling a bit queasy from the baby, and I just couldn't stand the thought of being with those people. That horrible Priscilla Summerdine, Prisspot they call her behind her back. And Katrina Fleiss, always looking at me with her superior smile."

"Perry Windover's fiancée?" I'd met her at the funeral.

"The very one, pale as a banshee. I should have known. Banshees foretell a death. But now of course I wish I had gone. Duncan might be alive if I could have put up with those she-devils that night."

That answered one question. Maura wasn't supposed to be home on Friday evening. In any case, it was unlikely that Duncan would be alive. He was on a collision course with death and a hired killer waiting in the dark. Not to mention the nervous actor on the corner hired to scare him.

"But he said he was in danger. It might have happened anyway."

"You're right. Yet either way, I would still be alone today. He was going away for this whole weekend."

Even Jesse looked surprised. "Thanksgiving weekend?"

"Business?" I asked. Why would a man abandon his wife on a holiday weekend?

"It hurt. As usual. He was going away to Stockton, New Jersey, for the weekend. Some popular inn there. Duncan claimed it was for business, but I know he was going to meet the banshee, Miss Fleiss. I saw the truth of it in his calendar, which he left open on his desk. He did that to taunt me. He was having an affair with her. One of many."

I could feel my mouth fall open. I quickly shut it. I knew that people had affairs and cheated on their spouses, but I couldn't understand how they found the time. Not to mention coming up with the lies and the subterfuge to keep it going. As a playwright, I made my plots complicated. People who cheated probably kept it simple. Or they had secretaries scheduling their days. And their infidelities.

"But Katrina's engaged."

"It seemed to be a game Perry and Duncan played. Each trying to score points on the other. Along with a few other frat boys from their clique back at Yale. It's a rich boy's game. Anyway, I'm supposing that's why Perry had been coming around, speaking sweet nothings to me."

"He did? What kind of nothings?"

"Love nonsense. Flirting, calling me out of the blue, always saying 'Don't tell Duncan.' Made me mad. Even called me here at the hospital."

"I never put him through," Jesse said. "He needs to learn a little respect. I don't care if he feels devastated. Who does he think he is?" Jesse stood up and put her knitting away. She took Maura's pulse. "Normal, for now."

Maura's pulse may have been normal, but nothing else about this situation was. Jesse felt her forehead and decided she had no fever, but diagnosed a cup of tea, because she didn't want anyone looking peaked.

"Maybe Perry feels bad about Duncan and thinks he has an obligation to you," I said.

"I've no doubt he has feelings about Duncan, but he should not be trying to make love to me."

"Maura, when I was there that first night, there were keys in a bowl."

"Duncan's. In the blue marble bowl I gave him. Before that, he was forever losing them. Having Sebastian hunt all over for them. He finally got used to putting the keys there."

"One was a skeleton key. But it was bent."

"Wasn't it though. Sentimental, I suppose. From his college days. Duncan belonged to one of those secret societies, one that no one is supposed to know who the members are. But everyone does. Key and Casket, it is. Called themselves Keysmen. As if they weren't all snobby enough without being *secret*. That skeleton key was all about who they let in and who they kept out. It was very showy."

"Perry belonged to this too?"

"Aye, and they were forever going on about the key, arguing whose it was and how it got bent. Duncan wouldn't tell me. I assumed it was one of those embarrassing moments in their past. One of them lost his key, the other key got bent? Who knows? Each Keysman had a personal box with its own skeleton key. The boxes were all supposed to be private. Very hush-hush. Men are such little boys."

"A box? Like a theatre box?"

"No, a *box* box, a wooden box wrapped in leather, the size of a cigar box, one of the big ones. Very special it was.

At least to Duncan. He was like a little boy with a box of shiny rocks."

"You seem to know a lot about this secret society."

Maura laughed, showing off her pretty teeth. "I'd be in the room and they'd be ignoring me. Funny how you can be right there and still be invisible. He seemed to forget I have ears."

"Where's the box now?"

"No idea." She leaned back against the velvet sofa and closed her eyes. "I'd see it appear and disappear. Odd that I never wanted to look inside, poke into their squalid little secrets. Growing up in a big family, like I did, you want your privacy."

I wondered what Graydon would make of this. Did he have a secret club at Harvard? "Can you describe it?"

"Wood and leather, all embossed, very old, very gentlemen's clubby. As I said, big cigar box size." She gestured with her hand. "Perhaps a bit bigger, the ones with a double row. On the lid, a small brass plate with Duncan's initials. He told me it was where members kept their most private secrets. All very ceremonial. Duncan did tell me things, back in the early days. Like a child with a frog in his pocket. They called them their Sin Boxes."

"Sin Boxes? This secret society stuff confuses me."

"Naughty boys playing at secret games," Jesse put in, returning with a silver tray with all the essentials. Maura sat up straighter.

"Ah, tea. Lovely. Thank you, Jesse."

Jesse poured the Earl Grey into china cups from the silver teapot. "You both have too much imagination." She put a plate of small turkey sandwiches on the coffee table.

"You never even peeked inside Duncan's box?" I asked, sipping my tea.

"I saw him take out flasks and shot glasses one time, so I guess they hid their bootleg liquor in them. 'Twas Prohibition, don't you know. He also told me there was a journal with gold embossed initials, in a pocket under the lid. Said it was a place to write down all their sins and then lock them away. I asked him about those sins once, and it seemed most of them were about booze they'd drunk and women they'd done wrong. I wasn't surprised."

I tried to weave a narrative out of all this. Duncan and Perry were chums, from prep school days through college days and beyond. Perry spoke at his funeral. Yet Duncan had no compunction about sleeping with Katrina and leaving his wife all alone on Thanksgiving weekend. And Perry tried to flirt with Maura. What a mess.

"Were you ever at this place in New Jersey?"

"Once, early on, with Duncan. It's lovely and green, right near the river, the Delaware. We had such fun back then."

Sal, my producer, had mentioned that town in New Jersey and the inn. Some called it the Colligan Inn, others the Stockton Inn. He said it had been a notorious watering hole during Prohibition. Perhaps it was a good place to hide secrets. Or discover secrets.

But whose?

Twenty–Eight

DUNCAN'S PLAN TO abandon Maura right after Thanksgiving appalled me. I wanted to know what was so interesting in Stockton, New Jersey. Besides Katrina. On the other hand, I was suddenly intoxicated by the idea of getting away for a day or two. New Jersey would do.

The inn, Sal told me, was now being discovered by writers and the theatre crowd, although it had been in operation for over two centuries. That area, and Bucks County across the river in Pennsylvania, was already a well-known artists' colony. Apparently, the air itself was inspiring, and I felt singularly lacking in inspiration.

I called Graydon's secretary, Mrs. Lydia Carter, from a pay phone and confirmed he was at the office. I told her I was coming over.

"Esmé, this is a surprise." Graydon emerged from his office into the anteroom with his sleeves rolled up. He wore a lavender shirt with his tweed pants and vest. He was normally frugal with his smiles, but he spared a beautiful one for me. I must do something about that catch in my heart every time I see him.

I heard a discreet cough in the background. "Would you like some coffee? I believe the ever-capable Mrs. Carter has just put on a fresh pot."

His secretary poured for us. Should I mention I was relieved that the sturdy, stable Mrs. Carter was no post-debutante? Somewhere close to forty, she was nice looking, though not beautiful and no threat to Graydon's powers of concentration at work. She had a tasteful seasonal bouquet on her desk.

"Thank you." I took the offered coffee and followed him back to his lair. "I'm sorry to interrupt." I sat in the chair opposite him and admired his landscapes on the walls, which he had painted. They were much more serene than his nudes. I set my stack of playscripts on a table.

"So glad you did. What's up? You seem pensive."

"I need to get away from here for a couple days. Away from the city."

"Away? Away where? Why?"

"Everything is going so fast. With killers, and your mother and father, and the engagement party. I need a break. Maybe just overnight."

"A break? From me?"

"No! You're the only one I don't want to flee. You may come with me if you like, but I am going. And I know where."

"Esmé, what's this all about?" He looked alarmed. "I hate it when you mention killers."

"I saw Maura today. Duncan was supposed to meet Katrina Fleiss this weekend, for a fling at a place in New Jersey called the Colligan Inn. Or the Stockton Inn. Same place, apparently."

"How did she know that?"

I shrugged theatrically. "He'd deliberately left his calendar open where Maura could see it. He planned to leave right after Thanksgiving, which was to be at Balmain Senior's."

"And you want to retrace his would-be steps?"

"Did I mention I need a break? And we might learn something. Did Duncan go there often? Did the staff know him? Who else did he bring who wasn't his wife? Did the gunman from Chicago go there? Just a hunch. And a lot of questions."

"You decided to visit Maura today? Without me?"

"I went to work first, but the muse had already taken a powder for the weekend. I merely wanted to see if Maura had a nice holiday, under the circumstances. She did. Her family came and brought pies and sang songs." I moved to the window and he put his arms around me while we watched the light fade. "Graydon, could you find a moment to meet with Perry Windover?"

"That twit? Why?"

"He and Duncan were partners in crime, so to speak. You would understand him. Men like him, with all his duplicities, the lies men tell."

"My specialty? The lies men tell?" Graydon lifted his imperious eyebrow. "Not very flattering, my love."

"You are an investigator. Balmain is paying us. And you went to Harvard, so you understand these people better than I do. Perry has been sniffing around Maura like a hound dog, telling her how much he loves her. She's sick of it."

"And with Duncan barely cold. But Windover's engaged, isn't he? To that Fleiss woman?"

"Theoretically. Maura says Duncan was having an affair with Katrina Fleiss."

"Windover's intended? And the other reason for you to want to gallivant off to— Where is this place again? New Jersey?"

"I'm dying, not to be able to be with you." I ran my fingers over his wrist. His hands were so warm.

"You mean?" He kissed my neck. I should warn him about that and how it makes me feel. On second thought, maybe not. I lifted my hair for him.

"You know what I mean. Hiding out from reporters and your parents and all that nonsense, just so we can be together."

"I do understand." He drew me into an embrace. My breath came quicker. "I can't bear to be away from you. And I don't even know what we've stepped into this time. It's—"

"Ludicrous?" I suggested.

"That's one word for it. Actors, killers from Chicago, a woman who shoots her husband."

"She had to. Law of the jungle, kill or be killed." I paused to consider other possibilities. "I'm glad you didn't wind up with one of your debutantes."

"Perish the thought. I didn't know it, but I was waiting for you, Elf. Esmé, my dearest. And perhaps getting away from here will give us the distance we need to put this case in perspective."

"You understand I won't agree to an engagement announcement until I'm sure we'll be compatible. In every way."

"Two minds with but a single thought."

"And two bodies," I added.

"Let's call this *jaunt* part of the case. Probably a blind alley, but worth exploring in light of Frank Romeo's warning about the hired gun from Chicago. I certainly couldn't let you go alone."

"We'd be far away from prying eyes. Without our staff, yours and mine, snooping around." I smiled at the thought of Amelia and Robbins becoming increasingly chummy.

"Who, I am sure, will welcome time off for themselves. What's this place like?"

"I understand there are silver dollars embedded in the floor of the bar. The area is also an artists' colony and the inn is said to have some murals of interest. Seems to be a writers' mecca."

"I'll make the arrangements," he said. He checked his desk calendar.

"You or your secretary?"

He grinned. "Often when I say *I*, I mean Mrs. Carter. It will count as a business expense. And she understands that in this case you are my associate investigator."

"Does she know we're engaged?"

"She's seen your ring. Happily enough, she approves."

"I was thinking about taking the train."

"If you like. I'll take a car. So we aren't observed sneaking off together."

I had to recomb my hair and touch up my makeup. Graydon picked up the phone. "Do you need to go back to the theatre?" he asked me.

"It seems I'm taking the afternoon off," I said. "And taking a pile of scripts home with me. Who are you calling?"

"Old Man Balmain."

Twenty-Nine

BALMAIN HELD A National Recovery Act poster in one hand and a drink in the other when we arrived. We had interrupted his afternoon brandy.

"This is to calm my nerves," he said, lifting the snifter. "And this just gives me indigestion." He set the poster down on the coffee table. It featured the NRA's blue eagle badge on a red-and-white background.

Balmain's company hadn't yet agreed to the National Recovery Act code, Graydon informed me later. President Roosevelt's aim was to eliminate cutthroat competition, to create fair practices, and set fair prices. Businesses that complied could display the NRA's blue eagle poster to show their support—and forestall boycotts. However, old-style business pirates like Balmain claimed it was a pressure tactic from the government to open the door to unions and regulations. Balmain's strategy was delay, delay, delay.

"What have you found?" Balmain asked. "Please sit down. I believe you know Ruth."

His sister-in-law emerged from the hallway, small, feisty, and colorful. She wore a yellow and blue paisley dress, which stood out against the luxurious but rather bland room. Edward wore a smoking jacket, as if we were in some Hollywood movie. I was unaware that men actually wore those in real life. I made a mental note to ask Graydon if he had one. And if so, why.

We exchanged small pleasantries and Sebastian gathered requests for refreshments. Balmain switched to beer and Graydon followed his lead, while Ruth and I had tea. I had too many things to do to have a fuzzy head. Graydon informed them we might have a lead. We were heading to an inn, he said, in Stockton, New Jersey.

"Stockton?" Balmain's expression softened. "We used to have a fishing cabin thereabouts. We went there often when Duncan was a boy and his mother was alive."

"Duncan planned a weekend at the inn there with a lady friend," Graydon said."

"Not his wife?" Ruth asked, She didn't sound surprised.

Balmain rubbed his forehead. "The boy found it difficult to give up his bad habits. He tried. Sometimes."

"You mentioned that Duncan feared something," I said.

"He seemed to, but I don't know what it could be."

More like he couldn't narrow it down, I thought. Too many options.

"There's more." Graydon tilted his head my way. "I'll let Esmé explain the first one."

"We learned that one of the actors at my theatre had an audition to play a killer to frighten Duncan, to throw the fear of the Lord into him, so to speak. My actor friend was hired to confront Duncan, but he never got the chance to play the part."

"An actor!" Balmain's eyes flashed and he turned toward Ruth. "You didn't! I told you that was a harebrained idea."

"The boy needed something to shake him up." She glared at him, unrepentant. "Something to set him right."

"*You* hired an actor to scare Duncan?" I tried not to look shocked, but I was.

"We'd tried everything else, Edward. Do you have any idea how much Duncan cost this company in waste and errors and stupidity? How much he pilfered?" So she was the company watchdog. She pointed to the NRA poster on the table. "And he was against the company supporting the National Recovery Act, which caused endless trouble with the workers."

"Ruth, you damn meddler." Edward's beer shook in his hand.

"I'm afraid it wouldn't have made a difference," Graydon said. "The actor was supposed to confront Duncan on the very night your son died."

"You know this young actor?" Ruth asked me. "Do you agree that it wouldn't have made a difference?"

"I do, for several reasons." I exchanged a look with Graydon. He picked up the narrative.

"It has also come to our attention that there was a genuine hired gun sent to kill your son."

"What?" Balmain blurted. They both froze.

"We're told this was also supposed to happen the night your son died. We don't know the gunman's identity, but word is he was hired out of Chicago. Perhaps not to leave a trail or implicate anyone in New York."

"You found this out from your underworld connections?" Balmain knocked back his beer.

"We have a reliable informant," Graydon said calmly.

"My foolish boy. But what did he do to deserve that?"

"He was losing his mind, Edward," Ruth said. "He made a lot of enemies at the company, antagonized the men. We could see it. And I know about Maura, that she fired the gun. I don't blame her. I know she loved him, but she feared for her life."

"How did you—?" Balmain Senior began.

"You can't keep anything in this family secret from me. Don't you know that by now? The gun was his, the hunting knife was his. Maura would never have done it if it weren't for the baby. She would have let him kill her."

"Ruth!"

"And it gets worse," Graydon continued. "Our informant says you may be in danger. The gunman from Chicago is said to be upset that he didn't do his job. He may want to make good with a substitute. I'd recommend taking extra precautions, for the two of you and for Maura. He knows this address. And he is said to be—deranged." Balmain's face lost all its color.

"Another question," I said. "I noticed keys in a marble bowl, Duncan's keys. One was a bent skeleton key."

"Yes, I know." Balmain rang for his new butler. "I haven't had the heart to return to his place. Sebastian has been down there, taking care of things."

Duncan's former butler Sebastian had seamlessly transferred his loyalty to Balmain Senior and seemed much calmer. He remembered the keys well.

"I'm afraid the keys are missing," he said. "Mrs. Balmain gave Mr. Duncan the marble bowl and he was diligent in setting his keys there. He had a habit of losing things. And he set great store by the bowl, because she had remembered such a small thing. I was rather in shock that night. I don't recall seeing the keys, and I didn't notice they were gone until a few days later. Perhaps the police took them?"

That was plausible. We would ask Detective O'Hara.

"What can you tell us about the skeleton key?" I asked. "And Key and Casket?" Balmain looked startled.

"We know Duncan was a member," Graydon said. I had filled him in along the way. "We're interested in the key and the members' boxes."

"What were the secrets in Key and Casket?" I asked.

"It seems you've found out quite a lot. I was a member, back in my day. Considered an honor to be invited to join. Keysmen, we called ourselves. I must have made it sound appealing to the boy. Just a lot of adolescent foolishness, if you ask me. As for the box—" He showed us a box on his desk, embellished with a brass plate with his initials. Balmain opened it and pulled out a cigar. "Turned mine into a humidor. All it's good for. I had no use for the journal and all the rest. I'm not a writing man."

"We heard members were expected to use that journal to record their secrets," I said. "Or their sins."

"Schoolboy stuff." Balmain sniffed. "Most were pretty tame, I imagine. Drinking during Prohibition? Who didn't? Course I was a member long before that particular scourge. In my day, I suppose it was our flirtations, high jinks, successful seductions, flirting and cheating, which I would presume were mostly lies. As I said, I wasn't much of a writer. More of a sinner."

"And what about Duncan?" I asked. "Did he write in his journal?" He shrugged.

"What about that girl who went missing?" Ruth said. "It seemed a big deal at the time."

"Shut up, Ruth. That was never connected to Key and Casket." Balmain lit his Cuban cigar. "The daughter of a handyman, the gardener or something, who worked at the house on the campus. She flirted with all the members. Trying to snag herself a rich husband, I expect."

I wanted to slap the cigar right out of his smug face. Graydon sent me a warning look.

"She was practically a child," Ruth interjected. "It was in the papers at the time. Duncan never said much about her."

"What happened?" Graydon asked.

"No one knows," Balmain said. "She went missing one day. The boys, Perry, Tom, and Duncan, were sorry about it. They knew her as a little coquette, nothing serious. They swore they had no idea what happened to her. But bad things do happen, people disappear."

Bad things happen. He said it with a shrug, as if a woman's life meant nothing.

"Did she have a name?" I pursued.

"Olive," Ruth said. "Olive Rivers."

Edward exhaled a stream of cigar smoke. "Yes, that was it. Olive Rivers. Pretty little thing, judging by her picture in the papers. Her father moved away after she disappeared."

"Do you know where Duncan's box is?" I asked.

Balmain gestured vaguely. "Must be somewhere in Duncan's apartment. I'll have Sebastian look for it. I'd like to have it back. Something of my boy's, for sentimental value, you know, nothing more. Now if you'll forgive me, it's been a trying day."

We were dismissed. Old Balmain was obviously lying to us about something.

But where was that box?

THIRTY

ROSE PETALS WERE scattered on the pillows. A large bouquet of flowers, roses and late season blossoms in every color, stood carefully placed on a small table in my room at the inn in Stockton. I took off my hat and coat, and I spied a silver bucket topped up with ice and a fine bottle of champagne. Two flutes flanked it on a silver tray, accompanied by a small box of chocolates. I might have been dreaming.

Our accommodations were on the third floor of Colligan's Inn in Stockton, New Jersey. My bag had been delivered to my room at the end of the hall, and my windows looked out over an expanse of green grass and a flaming red oak, the kind that blazes with color until the end of fall. I could also see a street with small shops, a feast for the eyes, and beyond them the little bridge over the Delaware River. It was just after noon, with hours till dinner. I didn't know when Graydon would arrive in the Pierce-Arrow. Time for a stroll.

I'd worn my smart deep green traveling suit for the pleasant train ride. I knew it was smart because Willie told me so when I purchased all those costumes. I wore it with a collared sweater in light green, rather than a blouse, because it was simply more comfortable. The weather had turned cooler so I had grabbed a warm wool jacket that almost doubled as a blanket on the train.

From my suitcase I pulled out my blue slacks, black turtleneck sweater, and walking shoes, because I had planned to walk the trails down the Delaware. My binoculars and my little Leica camera, just in case. I hung up my crimson velvet cocktail dress, which I'd only worn once to the theatre. It featured a low back and deep V in the front, accented with satin bows and matching round jeweled pins, all costume jewelry of course. The rich color made my skin glow.

Finally, I pulled out my white silk nightgown embroidered with flowers around the neckline.

"May I help you with that?"

Graydon stood in the open door of the connecting room, grinning. I burst out laughing.

"Does it suit you?"

"Oh yes, it does." Now he was at my shoulder.

"When did you get here?"

"Just now. They're bringing my bags up. My room is two doors down." His jacket was off and he wore a sweater over his shirt. "Through the middle room, which is rather like a chaperone."

"But we have all three rooms?"

"Fewer questions that way. It's not the Ritz."

"Not the Ritz? It's better! Look how lovely it all is, and how green and soothing it is outside."

I paused. I felt like a fool waiting for him to scoop me into his arms. And then he did just that.

"I've waited so long for you, Esmé."

"Me too." It hadn't been that long. It just felt like a lifetime. This was a test of our relationship, and I hoped it wouldn't go wrong. "Rose petals?"

His turn to laugh, and he swept up a handful of petals.

"My request. We got the last available rooms, and I just wanted to make it nice for you." He picked up my nightgown and admired it. "This will be beautiful on you. Later."

As he kissed me, Graydon slipped off my jacket, then my sweater. He kissed my shoulder, and I untied his tie and began on his shirt buttons. He lifted me up and onto the bed. I had a moment of panic as desire fought with nerves. Thankfully the bed didn't squeak.

"You're strong," I said.

"You're light as a whisper." He stopped and seemed momentarily unsure. "Perhaps we should talk about protection. It's not romantic, I know—"

"But necessary. You should know that I am an ardent admirer of Mrs. Margaret Sanger and her clinics to help women. Darling, I came fully prepared."

The daunting reality of Maura Balmain's pregnancy hung in the air. I wondered how she would cope as a widowed mother. How arduous that would be, even with the Balmain money. Yet she wanted that child and was willing to fight the devil himself for it.

"So did I. But if anything *unexpected* happened," Graydon said, "we would simply marry immediately."

"I'm sure that would please your parents."

"They would have nothing to say about it."

"And you're going to marry me anyway, you know."

I couldn't keep my hands off him. He was beautifully made, wide shoulders, soft brown curls on his chest. I soon learned what he could do with that body. I tried to match him touch for touch, but obviously he outmatched me in experience.

I'd been chilled before, but now I was on fire. I wasn't thinking, only feeling. A final thought was that I'd missed so much, and I'd been right about my late fiancé, Roger, whose sexual motor had idled much slower. Perhaps like a Model T, compared to a powerful Pierce-Arrow? We would have been miserable together. At least I would. This moment with Graydon was a complete revelation. And there were many more revelations to come, again and again.

Afterwards, I slept for an hour in Graydon's arms. Amazed that I trusted him so completely. Amazed that I could so easily fall asleep.

I awoke to find him watching me. Blessing me with one of his sexy smiles. My fingers danced on his chest. I kissed him, not caring how mussed I looked.

"Was I asleep long?"

"Hours. Again?" he asked.

"Please, Graydon."

"I love how you say *please*. We may have to do this over and over. We need to get this right, don't we? You said it was a test. Any doubts, my Elfin Queen?"

"No doubts. I simply want to be doubly sure."

"We'll make it more than doubly." More kisses and sweet chills. "I adore you, Esmé."

I was thinking marriage could be a fine thing. With the right man.

In the late afternoon the bed was much too comfortable, but the autumnal world outside beckoned. Graydon slipped through the connecting door to the rooms beyond to dress for a walk. I showered and dressed and wandered downstairs, where we were to meet casually, as if just arriving separately. Our little plan was too clever by half, but now I didn't care, I wanted to see the place. I was curious about the inn's notable walls.

The famous murals of country life, I learned from a small plaque in the lobby, were painted in an older style, but they were actually rather new, begun in 1928 and finished earlier this very year of 1934. I stepped into the nearly empty dining room and considered the colorful village scenes.

"Americana. Very interesting." Graydon had materialized behind me.

"I wouldn't think these were your style. Your very painterly style."

"No, they're a bit rustic, but quite nice. I can see the charm of making a quiet getaway out here. And why Duncan would sometimes want to leave the larger world behind."

"Let's leave it behind and take that walk before it gets too dark," I said.

The bellman opened the front door for us. The aroma of woodsmoke and the peppery tang of leaves hung in the air. The shadows grew long through the trees and the seductive blue of near-dusk enveloped us. I adored New York City, but the sheer greenness of the countryside and the last whispers of autumn called me. I was intoxicated with it. I snugged my jacket closer and donned my gloves and hat.

"You know, Esmé, I enjoy your enjoyment of just about anything and everything."

"Even investigations?"

"Well—the jury's out on that one."

We stepped lively down the street toward the river. I may have been guilty of rubbernecking, and I had to stop from time to time to appreciate the autumn leaves or watch the ducks and geese on the dark green water. There was so much to see.

"We're in your territory now, aren't we?"

"What are you talking about?"

"The woods, the forest. Home to elves, I'm told."

"And trolls."

"Are you calling me a troll?"

"Are you calling me an elf?"

We wandered until the darkening sky told us it was time to turn back. On the street leading to the inn, we stopped for coffee at a small café and split a hot pretzel.

"Perfect," I pronounced.

"It's perfect?"

"Perfect." I sent him a naughty smile, which he returned. I pulled apart more of the pretzel.

Graydon found a small art supply store just before it closed. Not the most likely shop for such a small town, except the area was full of artists. He purchased some ink and a pad of drawing paper.

"I might feel the urge to sketch. They say the nudes are lovely out here in the country."

I burst out laughing and practically snorted my pretzel. We had just enough time to stroll the grounds of the inn before dinner. I threw a dime in the inn's petite stone wishing well, as pretty as a set for a Broadway show, and noted the small waterfall behind the place. Everything about the inn seemed adorable and homey, compared to New York. Lifting my trusty Leica I snapped some photos. The twilight held a sense of promise, but we heard angry voices from behind a screen of bushes.

"People," I whispered. The air danced with tension.

"Who needs people? Let's give them some privacy."

"You're so English. Americans love eavesdropping."

A couple was arguing. They were hidden by dense foliage and obviously thought they were alone.

"You're not serious," the woman was saying. "You can't be in love with *her*."

There was something about her voice. I'd heard it before. "Katrina Fleiss," I whispered to Graydon. "The pale blonde from the funeral, remember? Maura called her *the banshee*." It was curious that she had planned to spend this weekend here with the late Duncan Balmain. And here she was with someone else.

"Who said anything about love?" an invisible man replied.

"And that man is Windover. Perry Windover." Graydon drew me back into our shelter of trees and we listened. We heard the shuffling of feet and the snap of a branch.

"So Maura means nothing to you?"

"Maura is none of your business, Katrina. I think it's time for us to call it a day, don't you?"

"Break off our engagement?" Katrina's voice quavered.

"You already did! You slept with Duncan."

I flinched at the name Duncan. How many people had been hurt by that man? It was just as Maura had said.

"You'd been ignoring me for the longest time. Duncan noticed me. It was just a fling, Perry. One last fling before tying the knot. It didn't mean anything."

"He did more than notice you. He stalked you. He never could stand for me to have anything beautiful of my own."

"Is that why you wanted Maura?" she hissed. "To take something beautiful away from Duncan?"

"Leave Maura out of it."

"I came here for you, Perry. Really, I did."

"Tell me, I can't wait to hear your twisted logic." His voice dripped with a sneer. "How what you did was all for *me*."

"He told me about those precious Pandora's boxes of yours, from that infernal Key and Casket Club. He took yours, you know. That's why it's missing."

"My box? Where is it? Tell me. I need it."

Graydon and I shared a look. What was so important about those Key and Casket boxes? Had those randy schoolboys actually tallied their teenage sins in them?

"He said you'd never find it," she said. "But I figured it out. I'm clever. I think your Pandora's box is here, somewhere in Stockton. He told me once he'd show it to me, it was nearby, he said, but then he wouldn't do it. I tried to convince him to give it to me. I tried. For you."

"This is outrageous, Katrina. You were willing to trade your *favors* for it? You're such a little liar. What makes you think I'd believe that story?"

"I didn't sleep with him, you know." That struck my ear as a lie. "We went on—dates. We flirted, we played around, but we never—"

"Oh sure you did. Stop lying to me. You were here with him. And you had to bring me here to throw it all in my face. Duncan loved this place, but it's just another two-bit river town. Fact is, I don't believe you. Not anymore." His voice turned flat, emotionless. Desperation rose in her voice.

"He said it was a big game between you two. Like hide and seek. But now he's dead, and we'll never know where it went."

"I want that box of mine back. I smashed his box, it's gone forever. But I know where to find that key of his."

"Oh, so that makes you the winner? Why are those Pandora's boxes so important? What ancient evils would they unleash?"

"God save us from English majors. We're done, Katrina. I can't let Duncan have everything now, can I?"

"Duncan is dead and it's not like that." There were some mumbled words from the man, sobs from the woman, and then the sound of a hard slap. Through the leaves hiding us I glimpsed the pale woman with red lips and white eyelashes storm off. But was what she said true? Any of it? Some people will go down lying.

Perry moved into the light, rubbing his face where the mark of her hand remained. He straightened his tie, then headed past the wishing well and through the door to the bar. Graydon still held me tight.

"I didn't expect this drama," he murmured. "I thought all the drama this weekend would be our own." He spun me around and commenced kissing me.

"How can you kiss me at a time like this? We just heard Perry has Duncan's key!"

"But is he lying, or is she? I'm just helping us blend into the background, darling. Like any happy couple. Except those two."

I kissed him back, laughing at the absurdity of it all. The sky was fully dark now, with just a glow from the inn's windows to show us the way.

"The unhappy couple may both be lying," I said.

"True. We may have learned something, or nothing. Shall we ponder all this over dinner?"

Thirty-One

GRAYDON WAS MOMENTARILY speechless as I walked down the stairs to meet him in my red velvet dress. At the sight of him immaculately turned out, practically pressed into his clothes, my breath caught.

"You are ravishing in red, my dear."

"It's not too much?"

"Not for you."

"Not for *a woman of the theatre*?"

"That red dress would drive the postdebs mad. Priss is still of the mind that you enjoy shopping sprees in Paris."

"Prisspot may think what she likes. She wouldn't wear a color on a bet. After all that beige, color might kill her."

"Willie outdid herself on the costumes for that flop show," Graydon said. "Or perhaps it's simply you. No one else could wear that dress like you."

I felt tremors all the way down to my toes. "Thank you, but let's talk of something else before we wind up back in our rooms."

A man passing by threw an admiring glance my way, causing Graydon to place his hand protectively on my waist.

We had repaired to our separate rooms to dress for dinner. I appreciated the privacy. If we had changed our clothes in the same room, I don't know if we would have made it to dinner, and I would have starved to death. But happily, I might add.

Among decorations of autumn leaves and pumpkins there was a festive air in the Silver Dollar Bar, and the multitude of silver dollars embedded in the floor by the bar added a touch of carefree prosperity. I wondered if anyone had tried to pry those silver beauties out of the floor. Couples sporting their festive-best clothes were wrapped up in each other, some dancing to soft music played by a trio. No one seemed to be paying any attention to us. We ordered martinis.

"Have you seen the battling lovebirds anywhere?" I quickly scanned the tables, the bar, the small dance floor.

"No. But while I was waiting for you to appear in that amazing crimson dress, I had a chat with the concierge. Charming fellow."

"Did it involve a small bribe?"

"Let's call it a gratuity. Perry Windover took over a reservation made by one Duncan Balmain. He had a room for two for two nights, it seems, but he and the lucky lady only stayed one night. They left soon after we heard their private conversation."

"Together?" I raised an eyebrow in surprise.

"Apparently so, strange to say. And Windover paid for both nights, so the desk man thought he was a fine gent." We paused to sip our drinks and order filets for dinner. "I can tell by that look on your face that you want to toss his room."

"Taking a quiet look is more like it," I said. "But yeah, I'll go with *toss*."

He grinned like he'd stolen home base from the Yankees.

"I told him Windover was a friend, who said he would leave some business papers for me at the front desk. The concierge looked. He even checked the safe. No papers. Not surprising, as I just made them up. Perhaps in a box? A leather box? No box, not anywhere. Windover must have forgotten, I said, and perhaps they were still in his room. The desk man offered to check, but he couldn't leave his station unmanned. I offered to check for him—and he handed me the passkey. I increased that small gratuity."

"And did you find anything?

"No box. I searched every inch. Only this: a lady's hair clip." Graydon handed me a sparkly ornament like a trophy. "Very fancy. What do you make of it?"

The delicate comb was about three inches long, decorated with bright gemstones. Costume or real? They looked real to me.

"Blue stones," I noted. "Possibly real sapphires, which would look nice in Katrina's hair and match her eyes. If this is genuine, she's throwing away a lot of money. It could feed a family for a month. Maybe Perry gave it to her, and she was so angry she left it on purpose. And yet they left together?"

"Perhaps he was her only ride home."

"Or perhaps it was a gift from Duncan, not Perry?"

Our meals arrived. I closed my eyes and breathed deeply. We paused for a few bites of steak and salad. I *ummmed* with satisfaction.

"What happened to the Sin Box? Or boxes?" I finally asked.

"We heard Perry destroyed Duncan's. For all we know, Duncan threw Perry's in the river. Katrina thinks it's here in Stockton. Perry claims he has Duncan's key. Who knows if any of that is true." Graydon paused and his eyes crinkled. "You and I are merely guessing, out on a spree together, for which I'm terribly happy."

We tapped our glasses together. Entirely inappropriate things sprang to my mind. I tried to concentrate on the mystery at hand, not the one upstairs in our room.

"These two once best friends were not on good terms when Duncan died, so why Windover's big show of grief at his funeral?" I wondered. "Also, those college secret societies are *weird*. Were you ever in one of those things?"

"No argument from me. I never indulged in that nonsense."

"I wonder if the Windover-Fleiss engagement is really off."

"I'd say it depends on how much money has already been spent."

"Money? You mean for the wedding?"

"You'd be surprised," he said, "at how many trips down the aisle have gone as planned simply because the invitations have been sent, the papers notified, the caterers paid. Depending on Katrina's anger and money situation, she could always sue for breach of promise. Bad for the groom's reputation."

I knew one of Graydon's would-be paramours had attempted to sue him for breach of promise, though there was never a relationship. She was a sad desperate woman who was trying to pry money out of him.

I had compiled my own newspaper-clipping dossier on Graydon, which included all his known social engagements and proved the woman couldn't have been with him on the dates she alleged. This was right after I found out he was rich, not merely rich but *filthy rich*, and I was outraged at how he had lied to me. He, in turn, was shocked that I had pried into his past. Well, it was all right there in the daily papers, in the society pages. Public information! And I had been a reporter, after all.

"That reminds me, Graydon dear, you haven't returned my papers on you."

"We're well past that, darling."

"I still have my original notes, and they did save your hide. Your very handsome hide," I added.

"Do you always keep score like this?"

"I have that kind of memory. Plus, I think people should be sure about marriage before things get too far, too fast. Or to the breach-of-promise stage."

"Ever practical, Esmé. Please change the subject."

I did. "Did you ask the helpful concierge about Duncan?"

"Matter of fact, Duncan used to show up here three or four times a year. Big tipper, enough to be remembered."

"With or without Maura?"

"Once with, many times without, and twice last month with a blonde. Probably Katrina. Anyway, the man was sorry when he heard of his death."

"So sad. Did Duncan have a favorite room?"

"Third floor, last room in the back. He was apparently a completely different sort when he was here. Remembered fondly. Charming, quiet, polite."

"Doesn't sound like the Duncan Balmain that New York City knew."

We settled into silence, enjoying our filets. and I pondered how a person can be so different depending on the place and time. I was different now from the young woman who traveled East from the dry and unforgiving West. And in a place this beautiful by the river, without any fear of poverty, I might turn into someone very nice indeed. But then, I mused, being suddenly such a *nice* person, how could I possibly write hit plays?

I heard a man at the next table, flirting with a waitress, a little too loudly.

"Did you hear that voice?" I said to Graydon quietly. "That accent? *Chicago.*" I glanced over my shoulder. Graydon followed my look, but the man took no notice of us. Dark haired and husky with a thick neck, he seemed captivated by the pretty young woman in her cap and uniform.

"Chicago?" Graydon's blue eyes were quizzical.

"The way he's stressing his A's. I'm a playwright, ex-reporter, I'm always listening to voices. But it makes no sense for that man from Chicago to be here. Does it?"

"The one Frank mentioned? Here in Stockton, New Jersey? Why would he be here?"

We overheard the waitress saying, "What are you here for?"

"Just a little hunting," the man was saying. He practically purred. "Yeah, just hunting."

"Don't jump to conclusions," Graydon whispered. "No one knows we're here."

"Except your secretary, and Robbins, and Amelia, and the Balmains." I straightened my shoulders. There was no reason to believe this man had anything to do with the killer from Chicago. But I hadn't expected Perry and Katrina here either.

"Where's the little boy's room?" the man inquired, trying to be cute.

She motioned to the hallway and he rose from his seat. As he headed toward the men's room, the waitress shared an eye roll with another. She cleared away dishes before returning with a dessert and another glass of beer for his table.

As he strolled back, I got a better look at the man with the Chicago accent. He glanced at me with a smile that I didn't return. I pretended I hadn't seen his look. Neither attractive nor ugly, he had thick lips and a broad nose, heavy brows. It couldn't be the frustrated killer, I told myself.

"You're absolutely right. That kind of coincidence only happens in the theatre." Graydon grinned at me as if reading my mind. I snorted in response.

"You mean in real life," I said. "Dramatic coincidence only works when it's believable. But is it believable that Perry Windover and Katrina Fleiss would show up here?"

"Not a coincidence, I'd say. Perry knew Duncan had planned to be here, and he took his reservation. He brought Katrina to the scene of the crime, so to speak. Exactly why remains a question."

"Odd to think those two men's relationship continues beyond the grave, especially in light of Perry's infatuation with Maura."

"Old school ties."

We dug into our steaks again. Soon the man from Chicago paid his tab and stood, tossing a five-dollar bill on the table, an alarmingly big tip. "Thanks, doll," he said to his waitress.

"Classy," I muttered under my breath.

"Not as classy as we are. Would you care to dance?"

Graydon took my hand and we glided onto the floor. I loved that Graydon knew his way around any dance floor, even one glittering with silver dollars. The room had a view of the garden and part of the parking lot. The Chicago man trotted out past the windows, where we watched him enter a dark car. He pulled away and the taillights faded in the distance.

There was nothing to indicate the man had anything to do with Duncan Balmain, but I was unsettled. Because of his Chicago accent? Because he leered at me? He had leered at every woman in the place, a wolf on the hunt. I might have dismissed him, except for the hunting comment, which could mean anything. Yet he didn't look like a hunter to me, not one who tromps through the woods. Perhaps East Coast hunters were different from out West? I vaguely wondered how he compared to Hamilton's impersonation of a hired killer. I told myself to relax and let go of my imaginings.

"Graydon?"

"Darling?" He held me close as we danced.

"Could you make a sketch of that man?"

I felt him laughing. "You're priceless. I am not a police artist, you know, but yes, let's give it a try after dinner. Your room has a fireplace."

"And a bucket of champagne."

In my room I slipped off my shoes and loosened my hair, while Graydon retired to his room and returned with the new sketchpad. He'd changed into corduroy slacks and a sweater. He looked delicious.

Graydon's sketch of the man was good, very accurate. Previously I'd only seen the results of his art, not the work that went into it.

"That's very good, if we ever need it." I lifted it up and held it to the light.

"It will do. Chicago Man, drawn from life."

"He looks menacing, a bit like Capone."

"Does he? No scar, though. I could add a scar. And a cigar."

"No, thank you. I hate cigars."

He closed the pad of paper. "I'd rather sketch you, Esmé. Draw you, paint you, capture you."

"You already have, and it's quite shocking."

"You're blushing." He pulled me onto his lap. "You were so ill when I did that, and yet still so alluring. But I can do better. I think we could make it fun this time."

"Don't you want to save something for the honeymoon?"

"Is that a promise?"

"No, it is not. It was simply a question."

"Speaking of honeymoons—"

We had very little to say after that.

THIRTY-TWO

"MORNING, BEAUTIFUL." GRAYDON poked his head through the door of the connecting room. We kissed and looked regretfully at the bed. My bed. Our bed.

We had slept late and missed church (it was Sunday). Another infraction to add to my long list of sins. I debated wearing slacks, but a drive through small towns in the area hunting for breakfast was on the agenda. I didn't know how formal the locals would be on a Sunday. I decided on my traveling outfit, thankful the skirt was knit and comfortable, and I wore low-heeled walking spectators. I had trouble keeping a smile off my face. Graydon wore tweed and corduroy and an air of satisfaction.

"Everything's set and the boy will be up to take your bags. Don't worry, my friend the concierge thinks we're married."

I lifted one eyebrow. "Why does he think that?"

"Because I told him so. Secretly married, you'll recall, jumping the gun a bit. I explained the official ceremony won't be for a year or so. We're saving up for it. It made things easier. And he thinks I'm a very lucky man, by the way."

"You are very lucky. As am I." I grabbed my purse and kissed him out the door. "But don't jump the gun, mate. I want to savor this long engagement of ours."

⌇

The Pierce-Arrow was packed, and I had a hunch. Katrina said she thought Perry's mystery box was *here,* somewhere. But not at the inn, unless it was hidden under the floorboards. Was Katrina lying? Or was my instinct wrong? I was disappointed. And hungry. We decided to search for breakfast first.

The little café was closed, and the restaurant at the inn didn't open till brunch. Soon we found ourselves in Lambertville, New Jersey, a few miles downriver from Stockton. It sat conveniently across the river from New Hope, Pennsylvania, a favorite spot, we were told, for local artists to immortalize on canvas.

Following a brisk walk across the iron bridge, we strolled New Hope's Main Street, looking for a likely spot to breakfast. I wanted something casual and quick so we would have more time to window-shop. Before we found food we found several small art galleries and antique shops, all closed on Sunday, because of Pennsylvania's blue laws.

This wasn't going to stop me from window-shopping, however, and something in one window caught my eye. The shop was called, cleverly, Last Hope Antiques and Collectibles, and it was closed. I peered through the dusty window at a large leather-bound box. A middle-aged face peered back at me. I waved at him. He pointed at the CLOSED sign on the door. I pointed at the box. He shook his head. I smiled. He shrugged, looked both ways down the street, and opened the door.

Inside a dusty smell hit me, with a slight hint of mildew. A graying mustache greeted us, taking pride of place above a smile with slightly crooked teeth. The shopkeeper's cardigan sweater featured elbow patches and his corduroy pants looked comfortably worn, like the goods he sold.

"May I help you? You know it's Sunday, Miss."

"I'm sorry, we're from New York. May I see that box in the window? The nice one."

"Ah, that box." The shopkeeper knew. He pulled it from the front window display, carefully placing it on the counter. As Maura had said, it was about the size of a double-stacked cigar box, covered in mahogany-colored leather. An ornate skeleton key was embossed on the lid. There were a few scrapes on the sides, but it appeared to be in good shape. The brass plate was tarnished, almost black. I rubbed it with my handkerchief until I could make out the initials: P. W. I glanced at Graydon and he nodded, his eyes wide. Perry Windover?

"I have been holding it for the gentleman," the shop-keeper said.

"Holding it?" I asked. "For whom?"

"A Mr. Balmain. Often dropped in here. Visited these parts on the odd weekend. Said he'd be back for it. Paid me to hold it for him. Unfortunately, I hear he won't be coming back for it now." The man took off his wire spectacles and wiped them clean. "Got himself killed, he did. Over in New York City. A terrible, dangerous world we live in. Mr. Balmain thought it was right comical to leave it here. Said someone might come for it, if he didn't. Course I didn't ex-pect you, Miss."

"Mr. Balmain was a friend of ours. Could you be per-suaded to part with it?" Graydon asked, while I pretended to be interested in some crystal goblets. I thought the man might be angling to up the price. "My fiancée here is very fond of antique boxes. She needs a new one for all the love letters she receives."

He and the shopkeeper laughed. "Does she now? I think we can come to terms. It's a very fine old box. Ideal for a lady's jewelry, papers, mementos."

"Darling, does this suit?" Graydon lifted the box for me. "We could replace the brass plate."

I picked it up again, wondering whether it held any se-crets or sins. "Yes, it should do very nicely. As long as you promise to get started on all those overdue love letters. Do you have the key?" I asked the man behind the counter.

"That's the one small problem, Miss," the shopkeeper said. "No key. Afraid it's locked. Originally it would have had a skeleton key, but Mr. Balmain left it here this way. People will have their little jokes, won't they?"

"Do you have any extra skeleton keys around?" I asked. "I realize you don't have the specific key that went with it, but—"

He stared at me straight through his glasses. "You know, skeleton keys are curious things, Miss. Not many different patterns, there are, not like a modern key. Sometimes you can find a mate in the strangest places."

"Oh, I know. My parents had a general store with a hardware department," I said. "My father would never throw away a key. We had a big coffee can full of them, and sometimes he could find a match."

The man scratched his head and toddled off to his back room. He returned with a big glass jar full of wayward keys, some skeleton, some not, a motley mix of shiny fresh-cut keys and older keys, black with tarnish or rust. He poured them out and I tried all the skeleton keys on the box, one by one.

Lucky number seventeen finally fit. This key looked old, but it slid smoothly into the lock, I jiggled it gently, and turned it until it gave a satisfying click. I turned it back into the locked position. I didn't want to open it. Not there. And it would be anticlimactic if the box were empty. I smiled at the shopkeeper.

"I want to save it for later."

Clearly he thought I was a strange one, but it was a decent sale for him. Opening this box, most likely Perry Windover's, called for a private moment.

The man wrapped it in tissue paper for me, put it into a paper sack, and took Graydon's cash, all of $2.50 for the box, plus an extra quarter for the key. We left, our heels clicking on the hardwood floor and out the front door.

"What a find," Graydon said at last. "Hidden in plain sight! Well done, Esmé! And I quite agree. Not the thing, to spill Pandora's big box of secrets inside that little antique store."

"Exactly, and I'll hold onto this box until we're on the road."

"Of course it may reveal nothing, you know. This mysterious P. W. might be some mundane Paul Wilson. Percival Walsingham. Peregrine Wolverhampton—"

"Stop it," I laughed. "I know. But we know Duncan went to a lot of trouble to hide this box. How could it not be from Perry Windover? And now I'm wondering what little game Duncan was playing, taking it from Perry, his supposed best friend. Now Perry wants his box back. What's so important that Katrina gets involved?"

"Questions for breakfast. Or would you prefer to starve?"

"Smart aleck."

Bacon, eggs, and a strong cup of coffee in a milk-green glass cup refreshed me. We skipped the big inn in New Hope and picked a diner full of locals, workmen and truck drivers, who teased the waitresses with familiar banter. For their part, the ladies wielded hot coffee pots above the fray.

"Are you really happy here, in this place?" Graydon asked me. "It's not terribly fancy. Reminds me of a mess hall in the Army."

I leaned back in the booth. "Yet I daresay the food is just as good here as it is at that fancy Logan Inn down the street. Sometimes I love to dress up like we're going out on the town—though we haven't done enough of that—but I also enjoy the unpretentious things. Diners. Little hotels. Shabby little antique stores."

"You, my darling, are a strange mix of practicality and glamour."

"Don't blame me, I grew up in a small town, and I went to a state school, not one of the Seven Sisters." He saluted me with his cup. "I would have paid for the box myself, but I assumed it would be a business expense for you. And this is curious: Balmain Senior wants Duncan's missing box too. But he said nothing about Perry's."

"Rightly so. At any rate, it wasn't expensive. That shopman could have charged me a lot more. I might even have had to—oh the shame of it!—*haggle*. And I would have. Don't tell the family."

"And a box for silly love letters is a noble cause for haggling. I'm pretty sure I wouldn't want to sully *my* love letters with this box." As if I had enough love letters to fill a whole box.

We decided not to open the possible Pandora's Sin Box of Perry Windover's until we returned to New York City. For some reason, in a small town, it felt like there were too many eyes on us. Curious eyes. We strolled back over the iron bridge to Lambertville, where we had parked the Pierce-Arrow. On this side of the Delaware, the art galleries were open, blue laws be damned. In one, I admired a small painting of an old grist mill on the water. Perfect for my front hall. Graydon signaled to the proprietor.

"We'll take that one," he said. I looked at the price. Twenty-five dollars!

"Graydon! You can't just buy me expensive things all the time."

"Why not, if it gives both of us pleasure?" I didn't say *because people were starving,* even though that was the first thing that popped into my head. As if he could read my mind, Graydon pointed out, "That artist could be starving, you know, and we are allowing him—"

"Or her."

"Or her, to lift the brush for a few more precious days or weeks. Besides, it's quite lovely and we can decide later where it goes. On one of *our* walls."

We took another walk through autumn leaves, with their satisfying crunch, down the Delaware towpath along the canal, before returning to Graydon's car for the drive back to the city. With our newfound treasures.

Or were they just another man's trash?

Thirty-Three

66"Y"OU DIDN'T LEAVE the lights on, did you?" Graydon pointed to my window as we parked the Pierce-Arrow outside my apartment building.

"Maybe Amelia let Hank and Irma in to take down the decorations."

"You mean the set? Your apartment is like living inside a play. A very elegant play, probably a comedy. I expect my parents are still talking about it."

"Very funny. I know that's what it looked like, but everything should be back to normal."

We trudged up the stairs with my luggage and our packages. The box, the painting, and Graydon's art supplies. Amelia opened the door with a smile.

"I heard you coming up the stairs," she said. "Let me get your things."

She was suspiciously cheerful. I hung onto the bag with the Sin Box and stepped around her into my foyer. The abundant autumn decorations were gone, replaced by Christmas cheer. However, sitting on my sofa drinking and eating sandwiches and scones were Lady Jane and Lord Chaseborn, who stirred themselves to stare at us. Just when things were going so well...

"There you are," Lord Cyril boomed. "Where have you two been? Caused your mother no end of worry."

"Mother, Father, why are you here? Is something wrong?"

Graydon stepped in front of me as if to protect me from the line of fire. Amelia was saying something about Hank, directing my attention to the mantel.

"Hank wanted to know if you'd like the Christmas garland over the fireplace. He said it was 'on the house' due to you overpaying for the Thanksgiving decorations." I suddenly had a vision of myself running down the street pulling money out of my pockets by the handfuls and tossing bills into the air. "See, it's ivy and holly and berries and those hurricane lamps with candles, interspersed with Christmas balls," she was saying. "Makes a pretty picture."

I managed to squeak out, "Yes, a pretty picture." But that didn't explain the dragons on the sofa.

"We couldn't get either of you on the telephone," Lady Jane said.

"Hiding from us, hey?" Cyril winked at me. He wished. I wished. "We had no intention of staying, but Amelia invited us in and it was tea time. And then she offered to make those delicious scones of yours."

"You've been here since tea time?" I looked at my watch. It was six o'clock and dark outside.

"I made the scones with your special recipe," Amelia said helpfully.

"I didn't believe your scones could be this good," His Imperiousness Lord Cyril said. "Yet I seem to have eaten three of them."

"Four," Jane corrected him.

"I knew you'd want me to make your future in-laws at home," Amelia said, beaming. "Glad to help."

I looked to Graydon for help. I didn't trust myself to speak. I would say something wrong, or simply start screaming. He seemed to be as tongue-tied as I was.

"You look a bit peaked, Esmé," Jane said. "Why don't you join us? Have a scone. You too, Rupert."

This was rich. I was in *my* home, not hers. I put my bag with the Sin Box in my bedroom, in the corner, behind the mirror, returning to the living room only after I shut the door firmly. Amelia gave me a little shove and Graydon followed. We sat down. Amelia bustled around the room like the efficiency expert she was. She brought in a fresh pot of tea, and more sandwiches and scones. I couldn't eat for wondering what the hammer was and when it would drop. It wasn't long.

"Now, let's get down to business. Where have you two been?" Cyril demanded. "I assume it was together, as you just came in the door with packages and luggage."

"Now, Cyril, it's not as if we've given them any time together."

"One does not expect one's daughter-in-law, or soon-to-be daughter-in-law, to up and disappear. And one's son to be complicit in that disappearance."

"Better that, than alone," Jane said.

"I've been terribly busy," I said fiercely, "and I needed to get away. We both did. My play reopens this week and I'll be at the theatre every day. And nights. Besides, we were—working."

"Yes, we had a lead we had to follow. Father, this is unseemly. We are adults, we are engaged to be married. Surely, we are allowed a few hours to ourselves."

I caught Lady Jane looking rather pleased. "Of course you are. But we have so much to discuss."

Eloping for a secret marriage was sounding better and better to me.

"This isn't about Victorian morals," Cyril chimed in. "Though I trust you stayed in separate rooms."

"You needn't ask," Graydon said coolly.

"There is a killer out there who Mr. Frank Romeo says is as crazy as a bedbug, which I assume is a bad thing," Jane said. "And I gather you two may be in the thick of it."

"You and Frank Romeo seem to be getting quite chummy." Graydon looked daggers at his father. There was a loud knock at the door. Even Amelia jumped. She opened the peephole.

"It's Mr. Romeo."

"Of course it is," I said to nobody. Why, God, why?

"Frank? Show him in, by all means."

Cyril strode to the door to greet yet another unexpected guest. I saw the camel hair coat appear first. Frank glared at Graydon and me.

"So you two finally showed up."

"Like a bad penny." I wished we were still far away in the country. There were a lot of things we could have been doing that were more enjoyable. "How'd you know?"

"Dentino's been on the lookout. He was worried. He called me."

"Are you following us around, Frank?" Pat's school couldn't start soon enough for me. His duties to this gangster would end, or at least slow down.

"I wouldn't say following, I might say 'watching out' for you. We got a situation here. We got an unhinged gunman here from Chicago. He's gotta go back home. Those Midwest goons have been very public this year. Sloppy too. Lotta funerals recently. Dillinger, Bonnie and Clyde, Baby Face Nelson, Pretty Boy Floyd, all of them out in the Midwest. Out Chicago way."

Frank shed his coat and handed it to Amelia, signaling that he wasn't leaving anytime soon.

"Care for tea and sandwiches?" I didn't know what else to say.

"Esmé, Graydon, I am not one to cramp your style, and I know you haven't been engaged for long,"

"It's not even official," Graydon said.

The gangster smiled. "Right. Not official, but public, in every paper in the city. But it ain't official yet. You working on that?"

"I have been trying to work on precisely that," Lady Jane cut in. "The formal announcement, the formal party, but as you can see, these two are hard to nail down."

Lady Jane glared at me and Graydon. She smiled at Frank Romeo.

"Jane's been very busy plotting and planning." Cyril seemed positively amused.

"Oh good." It escaped my lips. I couldn't imagine what she had planned. Her famous English restraint seemed to have transformed into unabashed American enthusiasm.

"Perhaps I could talk to your theatre set designer, Mister Hank," Jane said. "Set the stage, so to speak. Something elegant but tasteful, with lovebirds."

Graydon coughed. I hoped he was as horrified as I was.

"That's all fine and good," Frank cut in, "but the loon is on the loose and getting loonier, so I hear. That's what happens with Cupid's Disease, though I ain't got any first-hand knowledge, mind you. He knows he's sick in the head. He wants to blame somebody and because he didn't kill Duncan Balmain, he thinks he's been set up. Maybe he goes after the guy who set up the contract."

"What if it wasn't a 'guy'?" I asked.

"Don't be ridiculous. A woman? Okay, in that one case, say it was a woman. Otherwise, save it for your plays."

"Just asking." You would think I'd slandered all the hired guns in the world.

"We're simply investigating for Balmain Senior," Graydon said. "Trying to determine whether he or anyone is in danger."

"You got the screwiest case here. Actors playing bad guys. That actor is never gonna get inside the head of this guy. Too big, too handsome, too timid. Anyway, my associates have been trying to keep an eye on this Chicago loon, but he's slippery. Some say he should be put down like a rabid dog, but it's not the policy of the local bosses to interfere with each other's jurisdictions." Frank caught himself, as if he had given away too much. "And as you know, I am pulling away from all that."

Amelia was going to say something but thought better of it. She hadn't agreed to stay this late and I could see her mentally debating whether she should go or stay for all this prime gossip. She wouldn't tell the world about anything that went on, but I'm pretty sure she couldn't wait to share it with Robbins.

Cyril seemed restless. "Tea time is over. Is there anything in the house to drink?"

Amelia triumphantly returned with a tray and glasses and a bottle of Chaseborn's Scotch. Graydon grabbed the bottle before his father could, and he poured two fingers in each glass.

"None for me, thanks." I didn't need to feel any more off balance than I was.

"I would prefer something lighter," Jane said.

"Some sherry perhaps?" Amelia suggested and Jane smiled.

"That would be fine," I said, "and then you can keep your evening plans, Amelia. I can manage from here."

My self-titled 'head housekeeper' looked torn, but also relieved. "Gee thanks, Esmé. I pulled my pay from the housekeeping money."

"I'm sure you did."

Amelia cleaned up the dishes, supplied Lady Jane with sherry, and I treated myself to a Coca-Cola. Frank took his Scotch.

"I'm worried about you two," he said. "How you gonna know when this goon is gonna show up? I can't even draw a bead on him."

"Graydon, do you want to show them?" I said, and he opened his sketchbook. "Frank, would you recognize the man from Chicago?"

"I would."

Graydon handed him the sketch he had drawn the night before. It was gratifying to see everyone suddenly at attention. Frank took the picture and held it under a light to see it better.

"Mother of God. That's him. He even looks like Capone. Without the scar. Where'd you get this?"

Graydon and I said nothing. Cyril savored his Scotch, took the picture, then with a bit of pride he said, "That's Rupert's work, or as he would have it, Graydon's. Nice sketch, my boy. Captures a certain sense of menace. Where on earth did you see him?"

"We were following up on something for the Balmain case. It was Esmé who spotted him," Graydon said. "She heard his telltale Chicago accent. And she commissioned the sketch from the artist."

"It was a joint decision," I added.

"What did I tell you?" Frank said. "That one is always thinking. She's the one who figured out who killed my driver, my Guido. Now two people are going to the chair, just like Ruth Snyder. New York State flips the switch on women as fast as for men."

I didn't actually like thinking about that. However, justice could be speedy. It certainly was for Ruth Snyder, who with her lover had killed Ruth's husband in March of 1927, and by January the next year, she was wrapped in the arms of the electric chair. For that last ride home.

"Oh please, gentlemen," Jane said. "That is too sordid for polite society. I don't want to hear about electric chairs for women. Or men, for that matter."

"Sorry, Lady Jane," Frank said. "I was just saying that goons like this belong in Chicago. We got a chance to steer this one back to Illinois, and I got a chance to keep on the straight and narrow with my new nightclub. Can't have mugs like him dirtying up my town."

"Are they in any danger? Graydon and Esmé," she asked.

"I've got my boys watching the streets. But who knows." She hmphed in reply.

"I will do anything I can to help," Cyril said. "In my time in intelligence, in the Great War, I tangled with a spy or two."

Graydon looked like he might be in physical pain. Perhaps it was the spy talk. I suspected he had heard a war story or two (or a hundred) through the years.

"Where did you see this goon?" Frank again.

"New Jersey." I remembered he had winked at me getting up from his table. That in itself was nothing unusual, men often did that, and I had learned to ignore it. "We were having dinner in a lovely place where we didn't know anyone."

"Aha. So this man was on the hunt, you might say," Cyril said.

"Don't be so dramatic, Cyril," Jane said.

"I get that the two of youse are on the same wavelength," Frank said, "and you ain't sharing everything. But now we all know what this guy looks like. You see him once, it's weird. You see him twice, it's no coincidence. It's dangerous."

"What did he drive?" Cyril asked.

"Every day Ford Model A, looked like a dark burgundy, probably a rental," Graydon recalled. "As far as we know, he doesn't know who we are. Based on Frank's info that the killer might be gunning for him, I warned Balmain Senior."

"Rupert, you're sounding like one of those lurid detective movies," his mother said. "Why not take a vacation? Get married and get away. London is lovely this time of year."

"No, it isn't," Cyril replied. "Better to keep to your regular schedules, not to raise any red flags."

"As far as we know, he isn't aware of us," I said. I neglected to say I had worn a striking red dress, and men seemed to remember red. Graydon cocked his eyebrow.

"That's right. And we plan to keep it that way."

"Do try and keep out of the newspapers as well," Cyril said.

"You don't know New York," Frank chuckled. "The press in this town, they like these two and their romance. And Esmé is one of their own, so I'm guessing what we see in the papers is the news jockeys taking it easy on them. Anyway, Esmé, Dentino is going to shadow you. He won't get in your way, he'll be very discreet."

"I don't think that's Pat's best training for college," I said. "And he's still mad at me."

"Nah, he likes you. He's developing the skills he needs to deal with those snobs, beat them at their own game. He's a smart kid."

"Frank, why Columbia? Why not let him go to City College? He says he'd be happier there."

Frank made a face. "You don't know what I had to do to get him into Columbia."

"I can guess. They don't let Catholics in, or Jews, or women."

"I can't do nothing about the women thing, but they said they'd look past the religion thing. This time."

"I heard you told them he was Protestant."

"People say lots of things. Who knows?" He didn't deny it. Poor Pat.

"I'll be at the Hawthorne Theatre all this week," I said. "We're getting the show run in before it reopens on Thursday night."

"Worry not, everyone, it will be business as usual," Graydon said, and I wondered what exactly that meant to him.

"We should go," Lady Jane stood and patted my cheek. "You look tired, dear. The both of you."

Frank grabbed his coat. "Stay in touch. You need anything, see anything, hear anything, you call me."

"And don't disappear on us again," Cyril said, as if we were naughty children who'd forgotten to phone home. "Are you leaving with us, Rupert?"

"Remember, Father, Esmé and I have things to discuss," Graydon said firmly. "Business concerns."

"I hope it's about the engagement party," Lady Jane trilled to us. "Toodle-oo!"

"Make your mother happy, my boy." Cyril helped her on with her coat. "I'll be conferring with Mr. Romeo on his new nightclub, the Scotch deliveries, and other things. We'll talk Chaseborn business soon, you and I."

Finally, they were all out the door. I collapsed onto the sofa.

"What would you say to eloping?" Graydon said. "I hear Paris is lovely this time of year."

"WAKE UP, DARLING, the coast is clear." I felt Graydon sit down beside me. I opened my eyes. It was wonderful. They were gone, Amelia was gone, and it was just the two of us. What luxury.

"Was I asleep?"

"A few minutes."

"I didn't talk in my sleep, did I?"

"Not a peep. Are you prone to talking in your sleep?"

"How would I know? And what about you?"

"I think not. No one's ever complained about it." He held out his hands and pulled me to my feet. "What would you like to do?"

"So many things." I held him tight and kissed him, but duty called. "However, we may have a Pandora of a Sin Box to explore. There are other things we can do—after we take a peek."

"I'm holding you to that." He kissed my neck and his lips traveled downward. After we disentangled ourselves, I retrieved the package we brought from Bucks County and the skeleton key I had stashed in my purse. We sat at the dining table. Graydon brewed coffee and returned with two fragrant cups and a cake.

"I don't remember that cake." I stared at it. Now that our unexpected visitors were gone, I was suddenly hungry.

"Could it be Amelia? It was in the kitchen. This was with it." I opened a small note from Hank and Irma, thanking me for the opportunity to decorate my apartment for the holidays. I gazed at their latest achievement on the mantel, grateful it wasn't as overwhelming as the Thanksgiving decorations. The ivy trailed delicately over the sides, red bows gathered at the corners. Someone had lit the hurricane lamps. The cake smelled of cinnamon and spices and I sliced a couple of pieces, setting them on glass dessert plates. I took a bite and closed my eyes.

"I love watching you enjoy your food," Graydon said.

"Have some, it's delicious." I wondered if my fiancé, who grew up with every advantage, had ever been hungry, really hungry. But that was a conversation for another time. "Cinnamon spice-cake should go well with a Sin Box."

"And the sooner we examine it, the sooner we can— You know." We shared a look.

"Do you think that 'Chicago'—that's what I'm calling him—was in New Jersey to bump off Perry? Or meet with him?"

"Anything is possible," Graydon said. "Frank didn't mention anything involving Perry, and neither did Balmain the senior. We can assume for now that Perry is still in the land of the living."

"In dramatic terms, coincidences shouldn't happen," I said. "Actions on stage should always have purpose, intention, resolution. Things don't just happen."

"And yet in real life, as you say, things do just happen."

"In real life, *crazy* things happen," I said. "Onstage, crazy characters are boring. If their motives don't add up, then the play goes nowhere."

Graydon laughed. "Yet in real life, a crazed killer wanders the streets like a loose cannon, and even the gangsters are nervous? That's anything but boring." He had a point.

"At least *our* life will never be boring," I said. "We're open to the crazy things that happen. We went to Stockton in search of something about Duncan. We found Perry and Katrina. We found Chicago. And on a whim we went walking in New Hope."

"Where we found the oh-so-secret artifact. In a shop window. In plain sight."

We stared at the Sin Box. I was still a little afraid it might be empty. We placed it on the table between us.

The embossed leather box bearing the initials P. W. had a lived-in look. The skeleton key clicked in the lock, and the hinge, though stiff, opened with a creak. As we'd been told by Balmain Senior, it contained the Key and Casket traveling bar: silver flasks wrapped in pebbled leather and small dusty shot glasses. In the depths of Prohibition, this setup must have been a thrilling transgression for the young members of that secret society.

In a leather pocket under the lid we found Perry Windover's leatherbound journal, embossed with the crest of the Keysmen. Behind it we found a second journal. I pulled them out gently. The volumes were thin, perhaps fifty pages each, of onion skin. The cover of each journal also bore each member's name in gold lettering: *Duncan Balmain* and *Perry Windover*.

"I thought the journals would be thicker," I said, slightly disappointed. "Obviously, they weren't expected to write novels. These journals were for sinners, not writers."

"Still, you could write a substantial number of sins in one of these." Graydon hefted them. "If you keep it to very succinct sins."

I chose Duncan's journal. Graydon took Perry's. "If Duncan stole this box, and he had both journals, he would have read Perry's."

"Very likely. Read on. We won't tell Perry we peeked."

Each title page repeated the club crest and left a space for the member's personal motto in Latin. It seemed each member wrote his own. Duncan Balmain had written *"Tempus fugit."*

"Cliché," Graydon remarked, "but appropriate. As he died only months away from the age of thirty, Duncan's *tempus* did indeed *fugit*."

"What's Perry's motto?"

Graydon flipped through the other book. "*Perry Windover. Collige, virgo, rosas.*"

I struggled to marshal my high school Latin. "Virgins gather roses?"

"Close. Something like, *Go and gather roses, you virgin you*. Or perhaps, *Gather ye rosebuds whilst ye may*," Graydon translated expertly. "Also appropriate. An innocent college kid urging himself to *carpe diem*. Come sit next to me, while we read these masterpieces."

We left the box and settled on the sofa with the journals. I leaned into Graydon and he put his arm around me. I wanted to see where Duncan had changed from that untried college boy. I knew that he snorted cocaine, gambled, and drank heavily, all of which could alter a personality. Duncan had beaten Maura and attacked her savagely, and judging from the offhand comments at his funeral, had done badly at his father's company. According to his aunt, he pilfered funds and spent money he didn't have. But when he was young, I told myself, he must have been a better person. Wasn't he?

I read Duncan's first entry aloud, from when he received the box in his junior year. Graydon looked over my shoulder.

"This Sin Box journal is supposed to expiate my sins. God, I wish it would expiate this hangover."

I read on. Pages were filled with heavy drinking and poor study habits.

"Got drunk, made a pass, got slapped. Failed history class. What does it matter anyway? The old man understands. Hangover again today. Couldn't concentrate. Threw up in the men's room after class. Onward and upward."

"Not much of a work ethic," I said.

"Nor much of a poet," Graydon remarked, putting down Perry's journal and reading over my shoulder. "At least he's consistent."

Duncan's entire Yale career was more of the same. The dates of entries continued sporadically beyond his school days—a whole year might have one or two slim thoughts. Then they increased about four years ago.

"I met the most beautiful creature, named Maura Fitzgerald, black hair, blue eyes. She's Irish, not my type, not my class. Far more brilliant, but then, she attended City College, where she aced all her classes. I asked her to tutor me, as a joke. Told me to get lost. Shock that. I suspect she could change my life... But Perry has also started sniffing around Maura. He always wants what I want, what I have. My best friend. The bastard."

I rubbed the back of my neck.

"Care for a drink?" Graydon asked. "To keep us going?"

"A drink and a sandwich. And an aspirin. All of Duncan's drinking is giving me a hangover."

We paused to bring refreshments, two beers and two ham and turkey sandwiches that Amelia had tucked into wax paper for us. I assembled everything on a pretty painted tray and set it on the coffee table in front of us. I flipped to where the notes became longer and closer to the present day. The ink was darker than before. After a long break, in early September of this year Duncan wrote:

"What are friends for? He used to say that, my old friend Perry. Hard to imagine we used to be such good friends. I asked him what happened to Olive. Set him off. He wouldn't tell me. Instead, he broke my box! Smashed it to pieces, stole my silver flasks. I threw the broken pieces in the fire. What he wanted was my sin journal, to find out what I knew. But he didn't get it, because it was in my nightstand. It's all I have left of Key and Casket. And my key, which Perry bent years ago in a fit of temper. No respect. I have no choice but to steal his box in retaliation."

"So that's what happened to the boxes," I said.

"And we know Perry has a temper," Graydon added. "We witnessed it with Katrina. But remind me, who's Olive?"

"Olive Rivers was the gardener's daughter who went missing," I said. "Ruth and Old Man Balmain mentioned her, and Maura too, but not by name. A young girl the boys had argued over. Some scandal from college."

Another entry, a week later. *"I've got Perry's box. More importantly, I've got his journal. Who knew that boy could write? Not many of us kept up our journals, but turns out Perry recounted a great many of his sins. Not merely the vanilla-flavored ones. It's rather sickening to know someone else's secrets. Now I know what Perry did to that poor waif, Olive. I can use this. I can squeeze Perry to cancel my debt for all that beautiful horrible nose-candy that he sells me."*

"We knew Duncan was a cokehead," I said. "Now we know where he got it. We didn't know he was planning to blackmail Perry." I continued reading that same journal entry.

"I only suspected him before, back when she disappeared. Now I know. It's all in his journal. Perry better keep away from Maura. Meantime, I'll go play in his backyard. Katrina's always been looking my way. I've got you now, Perry, and I can do whatever I want."

"Blackmail. Now there's a motive." Graydon sat up straight and spread the journals out side by side. "Let's see how they tally."

Perry's journal had the usual accounting of the college drinking sprees, the attempted and/or successful seductions, but later it changed. Graydon read aloud from one of Perry's entries from the spring of his senior year.

"Olive is my biggest sin. Biggest mistake. She's just turned 17 but seems much older. I didn't know she was just 15 when we started. She should have known better than to fool with a grown man's affections. Now with child, as they say, the bitch. But why should it be mine, it

could be anybody's. I always figured she could be sleeping with Tom Gates too. Everyone knows he was sweet on her. Of course, the little tart denies it."

"Tom Gates." Graydon looked my way. "Why is that name familiar?"

"The other old school tie from Duncan's funeral," I said. "And that bastard Windover! She was just a child, just past sixteen." I hated Perry Windover, possibly more than I hated Duncan. Perry's next entry, a week later.

"Olive insists it's mine and she never slept with Tom," Perry continued. *"No way to tell. Thankfully a solution is at hand. I have a line on a guy who takes care of these problems. Med student. One of my customers."*

A week later Perry wrote, *"I convinced Olive she would have lots of time for babies and she can't ruin both our lives with this one when we're both so young. I gave her money. More than I planned. She blackmailed me into taking her there too. I think I hate her.*

"No one told me she was going to die for god sakes! It happened on a dirty table in a dirty room with a dirty doctor who took care of her dirty business. I was waiting for her across the street at a speakeasy. I don't know why I told her I would take her home. She didn't show up. I went back over there and she was dead. Gone. Lifeless. I didn't kill her! The doc did. I told him it was his problem and he had to take care of it. I threw some bills on her corpse. God, just make it go away. I don't know what hap-pened after that. He may have sold her remains or thrown her into Long Island Sound. I have no idea. What do poor saps without any money do?

"Goodbye Olive. Goodbye my little problem."

I thumbed through the rest of Perry's pages. They were blank.

"That's Perry's last entry." Graydon reached for his beer. I reached for the Bromo-Seltzer. "It's quite enough to hang a man, figuratively speaking."

I opened Duncan's journal again. Toward the end, there were gaps of years. About two months back, I found another long entry, just before the one about Perry breaking his box and bending his key. Lucky thing Duncan had dated this one.

"September 1934. I was at a party of the old chums from Yale and we spoke of old times. Someone mentioned that Bill Rivers had died. Who? The gardener for Key and Casket and a few other clubhouse buildings. Tom Gates said the man never got over his daughter's disappearance. Olive. Good God. I hadn't thought about Olive in years. I'd even forgotten the gardener's name was Rivers.

"I never even thought about Olive, not until she disappeared. She seemed like a constant flirt, but anyone could see she was just a little girl. And you don't play with children. Besides, you could lose a good gardener that way."

"What a prize jackass," I said. "He almost redeemed himself and then he ruined it, with that crack about the gardener. Doesn't the gardener have a name?"

"Class deficiency, I'm afraid." He read on. *"It seems Tom has never forgotten. We got to talking. He might have had her, like Perry always said, but Tom said he never did. And he insisted he would have married Olive when she grew up. Tom said she was pregnant when we were seniors, and he was sure it was Perry's. I never knew. She was just a kid. Perry was a filthy cradle robber back at Yale. Maybe I was so drunk that semester I missed the whole thing. Tom knew she was mad about Perry, and he didn't care. He said life could be worse than marrying someone like Olive, a dark-haired, dark-eyed lass who was always happy to see him. But you know that, don't you Duncan, Tom said to me, you married the prettiest, sweetest one of them all.*

"I admitted I had. And the rat that I am treats Maura so badly. The Devil take me. Anyway, Tom is convinced— has been for years—that Perry had something to do with

Olive going missing. It's easy to believe Tom. He's a straight arrow. Funny. Today, Tom is married to a horse-faced, old-money dame named Hortense.

"I don't want Perry coming around anymore, talking to Maura, flirting with her, trying to get something over on me, the rat. Luckily, Maura is the straightest of straight arrows. But Perry's in my life whether I want him there or not. He's got the best line on my old demon, nose candy. Seems Perry's always been a little more industrious about crime than me. I'm a lazy ass. I wonder if he wrote his sins down, like I have. He's been asking about my journal. I'd like to take a look at his. I bet I could send him up the river."

I threw the journal down. I needed to wash my hands.

"Careful, that's evidence." Grayden picked it up delicately and set it down on the coffee table. "If Perry knew Duncan had his box and his journal, that's a motive for Perry to have him killed. And it starts the clock. September 1934. Two months ago."

"Time enough to hire someone to kill Duncan, his best friend." My mind jumped to our out-of-town visitor. "Is that why Chicago was there, in Stockton? Following Perry?"

"Chicago? Oh, right. Are you finished with that sandwich?" He reached for part of mine.

"If there are no coincidences," I said, "and of course in real life there are, he could have been on the trail of Perry Windover and Katrina 'the Banshee' Fleiss."

"Adds up, doesn't it? Perry's already culpable in Olive's death. Duncan was trying to blackmail him, apparently to forgive his drug debt. We simply don't know why there's a Chicago connection. The man from Chicago is sounding less crazy and more—focused on a goal."

"What are we going to do with this? Give it to O'Hara?" Perry's written confession was an admission of a crime that ended in death. Abortion was still a crime in the

United States, whatever anyone might feel about it. "Who knew what happened to the girl's remains? Her body would be impossible to trace. Unfortunately, Perry never named the *doctor*. Or med student. And now with her father dead, who would even bother looking into it?"

"Maybe O'Hara. It's not impossible to prosecute on this. Not with a confession."

"Poor Olive." I nestled into Graydon's arms and choked back a sob. For a waif I'd never known. "No wonder Perry wanted his Sin Box back. Duncan discovered his big secret. If he read this journal."

"Of course he read it. And Perry knew he knew."

"I wonder if Olive's death was the worst sin of all these sleazy Keysmen."

Graydon laughed. "We only have two journals. We'd need to dig up all their pretty boxes, all in a row."

"You're right. We don't even have Duncan's box," I said. "Duncan burned it after Perry smashed it. Ashes, ashes, all fall down."

Graydon stared at the journals, perplexed. Not a look I'd seen much in him, except of course when I was what was perplexing him.

"Let's set all this aside for now. We know where to find O'Hara."

"Can you stay a while?"

"May I? I've wanted to explore the Elfin Queen's legendary bower ever since I first glimpsed it. I've done nothing but imagine you in it." He turned his blue eyes and his devastating smile on me.

"Tell me again your plan for a secret marriage. Did I hear the word *Paris*?"

"Gladly. I'll carry you over the threshold of the Eiffel Tower itself." He picked me up and I felt as light as a feather. He sat me down on my bed beneath the flower mural. He slowly released the pins from my hair. It fell down my back and swept my shoulders. "Beautiful. It's not red, not blond. It looks like molten copper, all bright and shiny."

"Like a penny?'

"Brand-new. The Copper Queen in her flowered bower."

I laughed. "Now you're the playwright. You weave your words with skill, Graydon Chase."

"As I would my brush, if I could capture you on canvas. Let me try."

"With clothes, or *sans culotte*?"

"You read my mind." He laughed, but I heard a growl in his voice as well. He kissed my neck, trying to confuse me. It was working.

"We can discuss my costume later," I whispered. "For now—"

When he finally left, he left too soon, but not before I knew I wanted this man, now and always. In my bed, and in my bower.

THIRTY-FIVE

"OLIVE RIVERS?" TOM Gates stared somewhere over our heads, as if he hoped, or feared, she might materialize. "Poor Olive. Cute kid. I was crazy about her once. Long, long ago."

Graydon managed to find Gates working in Manhattan on one of his projects. He arranged for us all to meet for a drink the following evening, Monday, at an unassuming pub named Hansard's at the edge of Hell's Kitchen, near Gates's latest project. I knew Hell's Kitchen pretty well, it was near Times Square and the Theatre District, and several of my cast lived there. The name sounded worse (or better) than it was.

Hansard's had all the earmarks of having been a speakeasy until Repeal, when it quickly transformed into a legal joint. It retained the entrance below sidewalk-level and the tiny flap in the door. The wood was scarred and the chairs worn, but the backbar was well stocked. The clear glass in the windows looked new and featured its name in gold letters. We took seats at the bar.

I had come from rehearsals in our new space, grateful that my pants were a refined charcoal gray that didn't show the stage dirt. Hansard's wasn't a place to turn up its nose at a lady in slacks.

Tom Gates was already at the bar, sipping a beer. Graydon ordered a beer and I had a milkshake. We began with some polite chat to feel out Mr. Gates. Call him Tom, he said. Gates was an architect in his family firm, which specialized in commercial buildings. While he liked a modern edifice, he said, they should have some classical inspiration. The Gates family had been constructing buildings in Manhattan for over a century, and attending Yale was a tradition with them.

Tom was a beefy guy with an easy manner, late twenties, like his college chums, more than a college generation older than me. His hair was blond and flopped over his forehead, and his jacket had seen better days, but it was an impeccable label, I could tell. Affable and not at all like the effete snobs with whom he went to Yale, he seemed to find them laughable. But then, his family could probably buy and sell them all. At least according to Graydon.

Tom paused for a sip of beer. "So, Chaseborn, what is it you're looking into and how can I be of interest?"

'Of interest'? Not 'of help'? Interesting choice of words, I thought.

"It all started with Duncan Balmain. His father asked us to look into the circumstances around Duncan's death."

"Right. The old man couldn't believe anyone would want his son dead, I imagine. The golden boy, in all the papers. Gunned down in his own home by some disgruntled ex-employee? Something like that?"

"Something like that. Various names have come up in connection with Duncan. Names like Perry Windover."

A shadow of distaste showed in Tom's face. "So many golden boys come to naught. Have you talked to Windover?"

"Not yet. I wanted your take on things first."

Graydon and I hadn't actually decided how to approach Perry. We wanted to gather more information first, so we could dodge and weave, if necessary, if he became angry at our discovery of his *peccata mea* box.

"And that led you to Olive." Tom lifted his beer and considered the amber liquid. I tasted my milkshake, surprised to find it was full of rum. Hell's Kitchen strikes again. "Windover wouldn't be telling you that sad tale. But somehow you stumbled onto the gardener's beautiful daughter. And now who's left to tell the tale?" He seemed to be a bit of a philosopher. "I thought you investigated financial crimes, embezzlement, that sort of thing. And I hear your family makes fine Scotch."

"You're well informed," Graydon said with a smile. "Balmain Senior simply didn't know who else to call."

"That makes sense," Tom said. "He didn't want some sleazy PI nosing around. Better to go high-hat. I saw you and your fiancée at the funeral. And in the papers. I understand you're engaged. Congrats are in order."

"We haven't announced it yet." I adjusted my ring so I could see it sparkle. "Not formally."

"Why bother, when the press has done it for you? Pretty juicy, you know. Son of a lord." Tom laughed and I had the feeling that laughter came easily to him. "That's life in the fast lane. And you work together too. That's nice. I like that."

"Occasionally." Graydon lifted his beer. "It has worked out rather well."

I smiled at my fiancé. "I happened to be in the right place at the right time. For this case." I straightened my tailored jacket. "I am primarily a playwright."

"With a hit play too. God, that must be fun, working in the theatre."

"It can be. Also a lot of work." Thoughts of today's very rough rehearsal surfaced in my brain. How could so many actors forget so much in so little time?

"Tensy wants to see it. My wife, Hortense. Terrible name, I know, I told her I could never call her that. So Tensy it is."

My turn to laugh. "It reopens Thursday at the Hawthorne."

"I'll let her know. How is Maura doing? Heard she was injured. And the baby?"

"She and the baby are coming along fine." I was impressed that he remembered details from the papers and had the manners to ask.

"That's a relief. Didn't think Duncan wanted kids. Afraid he'd pass down his bad habits with his bad genes."

"How did you meet Olive?"

"Her dad was the gardener for our society house, Key and Casket, if you didn't know, and he handled a few other buildings. He had a real eye for landscaping. I was studying architecture and I enjoyed talking with Bill Rivers. Smart guy. Our firm believes a building should blend in with the land, the surroundings. Bill understood that. Olive would sometimes show up to help him. I can see her in her overalls and pigtails. Always a big smile."

"Wasn't Olive a bit young for you?"

"Some people thought so. I didn't really notice her till she turned seventeen, I was younger than the other guys, I'd skipped a couple of grades. Also, she was from the wrong side of the tracks, a townie, not a real Yalie, not *class-appropriate*. What bunk. Olive had a lot of common sense. Until it came to Windover. He talked a lot of blather to her, same shtick he gave to every female. I was twenty, twenty-one, and willing to wait till she was a little older."

"What do you remember about her?"

Tom seemed to go someplace else in his memories. "Beautiful little thing. Dark-eyed, long dark hair. No flapper cut for Olive. She was always in a good mood, smart, sweet, funny. Her dad set the moon and stars on her. Her mother died when she was thirteen. I fancied I was in love with her, the gardener's daughter. My family thought I was nuts. Not their dream girl, not exactly a debutante, you know. And she could be a bossy little thing." He laughed at the memory.

"You're married now."

"Yes, Tensy's a great gal, organized, practical, keeps track of me. We're talking about having kids. How about you two?"

Graydon laughed again, while I squirmed in my seat.

"We are nowhere near that discussion yet," he said.

It was smart of Graydon to have us meet at Gates's own choice of a bar. The relaxed atmosphere helped loosen tongues. And it seemed to have been a long time since Tom could talk about Olive Rivers.

Before heading to the theatre for rehearsal that morning, I had stopped in the New York Public Library and spent some time going through the New Haven papers from the mid 1920s. For an hour of work, I found only a couple of paragraphs, under the headline:

YALE GARDENER'S DAUGHTER MISSING

There was only one small picture with the story. Olive was young, pretty, and looked to me like a hundred other girls. I was disappointed in my fellow newshounds. This story told me nothing I didn't know. She left home one day and hadn't been seen since. It seemed the police hadn't even contacted anyone from Key and Casket, whose grounds her father managed. No one knew she bled to death on an abortionist's table.

"Did her father know she was pregnant?" I asked.

"Whoa." Tom set his beer down and squinted at me. "Where did you hear that?"

"Sorry for being blunt. I was a reporter."

"I don't know how you worked that out, it was never in the papers, but you're right. She confided in me. It wasn't mine, in case you're wondering, I never touched her. It was Perry's, of course. Her dad didn't know, but I think maybe he suspected. And if he knew Perry had done it, dishonored her, he would have killed him. Planted him under some garden on campus and let the weeds grow over him." He paused. "Listen, if I ever have need of a private eye, I'll hire you two."

Graydon took over. "Did you keep the Sin Box that you received as a Keysman?"

"Sin Box?" He laughed again. "I haven't thought about that thing in years. That was supposed to be a deep dark secret of our little clandestine society, along with some other nonsensical traditions." He shook his head. "I was a member 'cause the old man was a member. Let's just say some of the guys took it more seriously than I did. I never filled out that journal. Got stuck on the Latin motto I was supposed to come up with. I wanted something like *Omnia in sordes veniunt.* 'Everything comes to dirt.' But it wasn't deemed 'appropriate' by the society's elders. I drank the liquor, but I have no idea where that old box went. Tensy might know."

"Do you remember the last time you saw Olive?" I asked.

"Yep. I was talking to her dad. She was helping him, but she said she had some shopping to do. It was a sunny day and she was a silhouette against the sky. Olive left and I never saw her again. Windover claimed he never saw her that day. I never believed that, but I couldn't prove anything."

My milkshake was delicious, but I didn't want to consume all that rum. The men refilled their beers. I could see Tom Gates putting things together. He wasn't some genial simpleton to be played. He slapped the bar with one hand.

"Wait a minute! You have no reason to know any of this, but you know about the Sin Boxes and that Olive was pregnant? This came from someone's secret journal, right? Can't see it being Duncan's. He knew Olive, of course, but he considered her just a kid, just a townie, not worth his time. He was always after more *seasoned* ladies, if you know what I mean. So this all had to be from Perry or his journal. Never pegged him for a journal writer, but he wrote something, didn't he?"

We said nothing, but Tom knew. When someone dies or disappears under sad circumstances, the ones left behind are haunted by their ghost, even if only intermittently. It was a curious effect of the Depression too. So many people went missing. In the little town out West where I grew up, people would buy equipment to pan or prospect for gold, hoping for a better life, and then never be seen again. Often the creeks would claim the missing, and I fancied I'd see their ghosts reflected in the water. It was like that for Tom Gates. He'd be seeing Olive's ghost that night.

"We're looking for people who may have had a reason to want Duncan dead," Graydon said. "Not that I include you in that list, Tom, but we felt you could give us some context."

"Ha. If you're looking for people who wanted Duncan dead, the line forms to the right."

"The police named one Johnny Akers as the killer," I said. "Did you know him?" I was sure he didn't, but it was an important question to ask.

"Never heard of him. You don't believe the police version?"

"Oh, we certainly do," I hastened to say. "But you say more people had a motive for Duncan's murder?"

"Something about Duncan. You ever meet him?" I shook my head. "You'd meet Duncan and somehow you'd know he would leave this world before his time. Reckless. Heartless. A drunk. A braggart. I figured he'd die in a car accident, on a horse, or on a boat. He was too fond of the cocaine and booze. I didn't think it would be at the point of a gun by some random intruder. I had hopes Maura would straighten him out. I only met her once or twice, but it seemed to me she was a rock, like Tensy."

"You attended his funeral. Why?"

"Old friends, I suppose. And Tensy said it was the right thing to do."

Duncan at least had his last rites. Olive was never so lucky, I thought, but I didn't say.

"What about Perry Windover?" Graydon asked. "Do you ever see him?"

"Couple of months ago, at a Keysmen alumni thing. Wasn't exactly a warm reunion. Duncan was there too, the last time I ever saw him. We were talking about Bill Rivers, Olive's dad. He'd just died. I gave Duncan an earful of what I thought about Perry. We were both a little drunk."

"Was Perry there?" I asked.

"He didn't show. Windover is a secretive son of a bitch. Pardon my French." I glanced in the mirror behind the bartender and started slightly. Tom noticed. "Someone walk across your grave?"

"Just a chill. When the door opened." I signaled to Graydon, who glanced back.

Lord Cyril Corduroy Chaseborn was enjoying a Scotch at a table against the back wall. How long had he been there? Had he tailed us? I dug in my purse and came up with some complimentary tickets to the remounted *Leaving Alamogordo.*

"Thanks for all your information, Tom," Graydon said. "You've really helped us put things in perspective."

"If you'd like to see my play, Tom, these are my personal comps, good for two tickets for the run of the show. Just call the box office at the Hawthorne and they'll set you up. Our reopening night is Thursday. It's sold out, but they usually hold back a few good seats." I signed them and handed them to Tom and prayed the cast would be off book—again.

"Much appreciated. Tensy will be pleased." He checked his watch and said he had to go. "If you ever find out what really happened to Olive—" He shook his head and grabbed his overcoat. He pulled out a business card and handed it to me. "You call me. I'll do anything I can for you."

He put on his hat and headed for the door. Tom Gates had spent a long time haunted by the past.

"Did you get what you wanted?" Another English accent was heard in the room. Graydon and I turned to see a smug Lord Cyril taking a seat at the bar with his Scotch.

"I didn't think this part of town would interest you," Graydon said.

"A place called Hell's Kitchen? Good Lord, my boy, however not? And I was here a good twenty minutes before you even noticed me." His father seemed quite pleased with himself. "That man must have been riveting company."

"You were spying on us?" Graydon seemed as fatigued as I was.

"What am I supposed to do? There's a killer out there and my son and heir deliberately puts himself in danger." He failed to mention *me.*

"I'm merely your son, Cedric is your heir. And I can't imagine you stalking *him.* It would be like stalking a marble statue."

"True, Cedric is always safe, predictable, a little boring. But you and she—" He seemed to notice me for the first time. "Scrambling around the city's odd quarters like gutter rats. Tell me more about this so-called Hell's Kitchen. Very intriguing. I am aware of nothing called Hell's *anything* back in the UK."

Graydon ignored that. "We were speaking with a renowned architect from a respected firm which designs major commercial buildings."

"Hmph. And I suppose *she's* wearing pants to outrun the devils of Hell's Kitchen? Or to evade some deranged killer? Or to work on a construction site?"

"I am right here, in the room," I said. "Don't you dare talk over me." I was getting heated and I lifted my milkshake as if ready to throw it. Cyril put up his hands in mock surrender.

"Father, we're learning our Balmain business may have nothing to do with Frank Romeo's insane killer."

"Nonsense. I've been reading the papers, my boy. They are quite sensational over here."

"Does Lady Jane know you're spying on us?" I asked. "Without her?"

Cyril abruptly straightened up in his chair. "Leave Jane out of this. She's also wearing pants today. I suppose *you* taught her that." He waved his glass at the bartender.

"She figured that out on her own. But I applaud her."

"She wants to talk to you about the dark lord of whatever manor house she's writing in that trashy gothic novel of hers. And your engagement party— If you both live that long."

"We will, if only to spite you," I mumbled under my breath.

"Did you learn anything from your little espionage mission?" Graydon asked.

"Only that you seem to be safe for the moment, even in a place called Hell's Kitchen. I suppose the engagement can proceed."

❧

We finally saw Cyril to a cab, then returned to my apartment. I was afraid his parents would ambush us at his place.

"What about dinner?" Graydon asked. "Shall we go out?"

"I'm too exhausted. Just look in the fridge. We could rustle up some sandwiches. Or scrambled eggs."

"It's just as well. I thought you and the old man might come to fisticuffs. Or drinks thrown in faces."

"He's too much of an English gent, I suppose. And he's too big. I shall have to settle for puncturing his ego, if I get the chance."

"I wouldn't recommend puncturing his ego, there's far too much of it. You'd get it all over you. Nasty stuff."

"Don't worry, I shall simply put him in a play. Under a different name. Lord Scuttlebutt, the Earl of Blunderbuss. Funny thing about people. The ones who inspire your characters, they never recognize themselves, while the ones who don't are so egotistical they think everything is about them. Tell me, Graydon, dearest, has he tried to interfere with your romances before?"

"Cyril was seldom around—House of Lords and the war and the business and all that—and then I was shipped off to school. They wanted Eton and Oxford. I wanted Phillips Exeter and Harvard. The States. Freedom. And here I am."

"Why is he here now?" I felt overwhelmed. With my own parents dead, and all my remaining relatives far away, I had gotten very used to living my life on my terms, without interference.

"Ostensibly, he came to escape the royals' wedding hubbub. Says he's bored with all that. Calls the royal family 'a pack of inbred nitwits.' "

"Maybe he missed your mother?"

"I would never have said that before, but now— I think they must have been utterly sick of each other. They each came to the States looking for an adventure, and they have unexpectedly found—each other."

"A change, an adventure, a twist. Makes for good theatre. Most of the time."

I flopped in a chair near the fire while Graydon explored the fridge. Amelia had left just enough for a couple of turkey and dressing sandwiches, which he assembled. He could be remarkably resourceful for a rich boy. I credited his time in the US Army for his domestic skills.

Graydon was a beautiful man. As he worked, I admired his loping gait, his broad shoulders and narrow hips. I wished I could paint him, but I was no artist. He had strange powers over me, intimate powers which I had not explored enough. *Not yet.*

"Darling, I love you. But your parents—" Marriage, unfortunately, involved more than just the bride and groom. It was like marrying a whole other country.

"I know. They are acting rather strange, but they should be returning to England. Eventually. For now, I'm interested in keeping him out of our business."

"Our investigation?"

"More than that. All of our business, professional and personal. But how?"

Thirty-Six

THE SHOW PORTENDED disaster. On Tuesday morning, the lead actors had to chase each other on rolling desk chairs, rather like chariots, but the stage at the Hawthorne Theatre was wider than the one at the Washington Irving, and the added distance was slowing down the action.

Andras Szabo, my director, levered his girth up onto the stage and painstakingly rethought all the choreography and blocking. He barked out each new inspiration to the weary cast until the chairs were flying to his satisfaction, like careening race cars, raising a lot of dust. I sneezed and spied Reggie Pendleton settling down near the stage in his comfortable slacks and inevitable corduroy jacket, No relation, fortunately, to the Earl of Corduroy.

Reggie hadn't shown up since Thanksgiving. However, there was a brief note in *The Post*'s society page about an American Thanksgiving dinner on the Upper West Side, with Lord and Lady Chaseborn in attendance. *The Post* reported that my dinner compared favorably to last year's hit film *Dinner at Eight*, as *my* aristocrats "actually came to dinner." It was Nina's work, fluffy and inoffensive, and I dismissed it from my mind. Even though it mentioned notorious mob boss Frank Romeo had attended, it ranked far lower on actual gossip than the royal nuptials across the Atlantic.

"I'm taking five," I called to Andras on stage. "Reggie, what's up?"

"You tell me, Esmé. Haven't seen you for days."

"Been a little busy. You know. The play?" I sent him a look that said *don't waste my time*. We made our way to the burgundy velvet seats at the back of the theatre where we could talk and I could forget my anxiety about the show. It was replaced by anxiety over what Reggie might say.

"Word on the street is that someone else was gunning for Duncan Balmain the night he was killed. Not the guy the cops fingered."

"What have you heard?"

"You're interested, but you're not surprised."

I was only surprised that Reggie had heard it. "Duncan wasn't a likable guy."

"Is that all you found out in your investigation? Everybody knew that."

"Who said anything about an investigation?" He just raised an eyebrow in response. "How did you hear what you heard?" We were playing reporter games now.

"Around." He ran a hand through his hair. "Word is that someone hired a killer from Chicago to take out Balmain. That doesn't bother me, but I hear this killer is extra loony."

Reggie knew too much. Frank Romeo had warned us this would get out. "How do you know he's a lunatic?"

"Far gone on Cupid's Disease, if you'll pardon the expression." I let him think I hadn't heard it before, and he relaxed. "And get this, he's outraged that someone took his kill away from him. Like someone shot his prize turkey. He's a stick of dynamite waiting for someone to light the match. So I hear."

The leading man stumbled on his lines, but that was Andras's problem. "What is this guy liable to do?"

"Seems he was also shortchanged on his pay. He wants another kill. Listen, Esmé, my darling future wife—"

"Knock that off. I'm engaged."

"So you say. Just stay away from everything related to Balmain."

"You feed me information and then you want me to stay away from the story?"

"Imagine that. It doesn't happen often."

Reggie made his exit, and I took a lunch break at the library. To feed my brain, not my stomach.

⁂

Why Chicago? If Perry hired the guy, what was the connection? Perry was in Stockton and so was the hired gun. Why? And how did one go about employing a killer in the first place? Needless to say, I had no idea. Yesterday I sought information on Olive Rivers. Today it was time to read about Perry Windover.

And there it was, in the giant book of bound newspapers, in his engagement announcement to Katrina Fleiss. Perry had attended something called The Lake Forest Academy, a prestigious prep school about thirty miles north of Chicago. The story noted that he had gone on to Yale, but it omitted that he was a member of Key and Casket, which made sense. It was supposed to be a *secret* society, after all.

Katrina in all her blondness had attended Vassar and was also, I learned, an accomplished aviatrix. That was a fun fact. I now pegged her as a wealthy risk-taker. Why else be attracted to Perry, aside from his family's money and his moderate good looks? And having an affair with Duncan? I was just glad she hadn't been painted into Graydon's club of classical nudes.

The engagement notice also mentioned the Windover family owned a big cement company based in Chicago. Perry ran the New York office. Perhaps that's why he and Duncan bonded originally: old money from construction. I called Graydon from a payphone near the library.

"Glad you called," he said, sounding harried. "I hate to tell you this, darling, but the parents have gotten tickets for your reopening night."

I didn't have time to be upset. "Fine."

" 'Fine'? Are you feeling all right, Esmé?"

"What's one more catastrophe?" I gave him the run-down on Perry Windover.

"Aha. That's where our link is. A Chicago construction company and the Chicago-area prep school. That's very impressive."

"Chicago, and the fact that mobsters are said to appreciate good cement. As in shoes." I peered through the glass of the phone booth to make sure no one was close by. "Also, Reggie Pendleton dropped by the theatre with the news that a crazy Chicago killer is out there and he—Reggie—wants me to stay out of all things Balmain."

"And I've been busy running into dead ends on all things Balmain. How did Reggie know about the killer?"

"Reporters have their ways. Word gets out." I needed to get back to the theatre. "I'm covered in stage dust and the tears of a thousand actors. Would you like to take me out to some dive for a bite of dinner? Where we are completely unknown?"

"Your wish is my command. When and where?"

"I'll be leaving the theatre about six. The front doors are locked, so we're using the stage door in the alley. I'll come round and meet you in front beneath the Hawthorne sign. I'll try to wipe off most of the blood, sweat, and tears from this awful rehearsal."

"Don't you dare, I wouldn't even know you. I'll be looking for *a woman of the theatre*."

I returned to the theatre to see a much more polished run-through. My director, whose fringe of frizzy hair was slick with sweat and his voice hoarse, had cowed the cast and crew into improving their performance, and he wore a big smile on his face. He bore down on me like a freight train.

"Have you recovered yourself, Esmé?" For a man of his girth, he was light on his feet. I raised an eyebrow.

"Andras, what happened? They're so much better."

He lowered his voice. "I told them you were so outraged by their disreputable performance that you were sick to your stomach and had to leave."

"So I'm the bad guy?" I whispered. "That's not fair to use me like that."

He winked. "My dear Esmé de LaForet, playwright extraordinaire, all is fair in love and theatre. Especially when we want a hit play." He kissed my hand.

Andras had a point. But was everything fair in love and life?

Thirty–Seven

IT WAS TOO quiet in the alley. No voices, not a foot-step, not even a siren. And in Manhattan, there was al-ways a siren somewhere.

I escaped from the rehearsal. The stage door shut and locked behind me, and two men stepped out from behind the trash cans. I recognized Perry Windover and his companion—Graydon's sketch brought to life—but I played dumb for as long as I could.

"Hey, you Esmé de LaForet?" The Chicago accent I recognized in Stockton.

"It's her," Perry said.

"Have we been introduced?" I squinted as if trying to remember, and at the same time trying to act normal, whatever that was, as I stepped away from them. I willed my voice not to quaver.

"You and I, we were both at Duncan Balmain's funeral," Perry said.

"I remember. You were the one who said such lovely things about the deceased."

"Ain't that a kick in the can," the other man said. "It's actually kind of funny, praising the dead guy he wanted bumped off. Irony."

"Shut up," Perry growled at the other man. "Duncan and I were chums from way back."

"So you want all your old chums dead?" Chicago said. "Where to start?"

The man from Chicago was not what I expected, though I'd seen him at the restaurant at Colligan's Inn. In the dim light of the alley, he seemed a little unreal, and much closer than I'd like. I could smell his cloying cologne. His hair was black and slicked back from his face from a side part. He was shorter than Perry, smaller than I remembered, and wearing an ordinary gray storm coat with a fur collar, a wool fedora with a black satin band. This guy would look at home behind the counter of a bodega, I thought. But Frank Romeo had warned us that the kind of man who kills for hire is not the guy who stands out. He blends into the background.

"I'm sorry I can't stay and chat," I said. "Graydon is expecting me. He may be here any minute." A bluff. I started to walk away, hoping that would work, at least as far as the street. Perry cut in front of me, blocking my path. "Listen, if you want tickets, we open on Thursday. Was there something else you wanted?" I couldn't help asking the last question. Journalist.

"Answers. I want answers," Perry said. "You and that Rupert Chaseborn are snooping into this. Like you did with that dead gangster Scavullo. The cops already got Duncan's killer. But you two are still involved. Why?"

"Involved? I don't know what you're talking about."

"You and Chaseborn were in Stockton this weekend. Why were you there?"

It would be pointless to deny it. Perry must have seen us, perhaps when we overheard his fight with Katrina.

"Taking a break. It was the holiday weekend. What were you doing up there? It's been a busy fall for us. My play reopens this week."

"I'm supposed to believe that?"

"My name is on the marquee out front. I'll show you." I started to lead him to where I hoped Graydon waited, but he blocked my way.

"Never mind that, everyone knows you have a hit play. Why Stockton, New Jersey? Were you following me?"

"Why would we be following you?" I said. "I only know what I read in the papers. The cops say the killer was a man named Johnny Akers."

"You're telling me Stockton was simply a coincidence? I read that Chaseborn is investigating something for Balmain. Investigating what? I'm worried about Maura, like everybody. I care about her. Why are you following me?"

"I'm not. You seem to be following me." I hoped my face betrayed nothing in the darkened alley. "Listen, I must go. Graydon is waiting for me."

"I like it when dolls play cute, but we're wasting our time with this dame," the other man said to Perry. "You and me, Windover, we got business to transact."

"You're from Chicago?" I asked the man, playing for time. He showed no sign that he recognized me.

"Yeah, South Side. Call me Rudy. No last name."

"Hello, Rudy. I'm Esmé de LaForet."

The alley was an odd place for formal introductions. Graydon was late, and even if he were waiting under the marquee, around the corner, he was too far away to hear me. And what about Pat Dentino? I'd seen him earlier, hanging around the theatre with a book.

Perry shifted impatiently from foot to foot. "It's a simple question. What do you want with me? Or were you following Katrina? Who for? Old Man Balmain?"

"Calm down, Windover," Rudy said. "The lady answered you. She don't know nothing. And manners are important. A man's reputation is everything." He turned to me. "But this jerk, he tries to play me like a fiddle. I prepare myself for this job, I'm careful, I'm quiet, I'm ready to roll, but someone else bags my quarry. Is that fair?" That sounded like a confession. To the murder plot, if not the murder. "I gotta read about it in the papers," he went on. "A bum, no less, a shantytown bum. And I don't get paid, on account of I didn't get to do my job. That's why I'm here. I just want to get paid."

"I don't care who killed Duncan," Perry told Rudy, exasperated. "Now all I want is that key. Just give me the damned key and you'll get your money."

My heart was pounding. *Perry hired this killer. And Rudy's got the skeleton key? And where the hell was Graydon?*

"Rudy, what was this job?" I asked. "The one you didn't get paid for?"

"My job was Duncan Balmain. Same night. Weird coincidence, huh? I get out of the taxi outside the building, I spot the apartment, I pat my roscoe for luck." He patted his coat pocket. "Some guy across the street is reading a paper, waiting for a dame, I guess. He seems a little edgy."

Rudy must have spotted Hamilton Gardner.

"Shut up, Rudy," Perry hissed. "Telling tales is not what we came for."

Rudy ignored him. "Then I hear shots," he continued. "Upstairs in the building. Too many, not like a pro, and I see the flash. Sounds like a real mess. Not professional. And I find out the next day this bum wastes him out of the blue. But the bum got his just deserts right after. What are the odds? Amateurs."

"We're wasting our time, Rudy," Perry said. "Do whatever you want with her."

"She ain't gonna talk. Will you, Miss de LaForet? You won't tell anyone we was here?" He patted his coat pocket again. Rudy assumed a lot. He didn't know writers. He probably figured I was just some society frail. "You afraid I'm going to hurt you? I don't shoot dames. Code of honor. That's another reason I'm taking this personal. I hear the guy's wife is still in the hospital. This Akers mug tried to kill a woman? What a bum."

"Not a professional," I said. "Not like you, Rudy."

"Like me." He turned to Perry, who looked like a man rehearsing his excuses. "Why'd you want him dead, Windover?"

"Does that matter? Besides, it wasn't supposed to happen that way," Perry said. "I didn't know anything about Akers. I wish I had. Would have saved me the trouble of hiring *you.*"

"I thought Duncan was your best friend," I said.

"Until he wasn't." Perry was very cool about it. As cool as he was with Katrina. "And you've got nothing on me."

Something clattered noisily in the dark alley. Rudy pulled a gun from his coat pocket and spun around. Two glowing eyes stared at us from behind a toppled garbage can, and a pair of furry ears twitched.

"It's just a cat," Rudy said. It reminded me of another cat, the cat that had unexpectedly brought Graydon and me together. A saucy tail flicked up as the feline strutted by, then it sat at the gunman's feet and licked its paws. "I'll let you live, kitty," Rudy said to the cat and laughed, a strange high-pitched laugh that sent prickles down my spine.

I felt an almost imperceptible change in the atmosphere. Someone else was in the alley, in the dark, behind the garbage cans. Someone not a cat.

"Take care of her, Rudy," Perry said. "You want to get paid? Do your job. She's just another stupid dame."

Stupid dame? I knew I shouldn't say anything, but my better angels weren't listening.

"You think women are stupid, Perry? Like Katrina, your fiancée? She sounded pretty sharp to me. And what about Maura?"

"Bad show, Perry, old chum. Never call my fiancée a stupid dame." Graydon's voice rang out of the dark, followed by the gleam of his gun. "An apology is in order."

Perry lurched back into another garbage can.

"Chaseborn. What the hell are you doing here?" Graydon edged past the two men to my side. He'd been listening in the dark? Waiting for—what? *Men.*

"Taking care of business, Windover," Graydon said. "Rudy, you should put that gun away now." Rudy raised both hands in the air, reluctant to let go of the gun.

"Who's the Brit?" Rudy demanded.

"Men always blame women, don't you?" I said to Perry. "Duncan was the one who knew your secrets, and he didn't want you hanging around Maura. And you busted up his Sin Box, from your precious secret society."

"A Sin Box?" Rudy asked. "What in purple tarnation is a Sin Box?"

"What do you know about it?" Perry shouted at me. "Women aren't supposed to know anything about that." He took a step toward me—and two pistols turned to point at him.

"We're not supposed to know anything, are we?" I said. "About the Sin Boxes from Key and Casket? About your secret journals? Duncan took your box in retaliation for your taking his, didn't he? Katrina was trying to get it back for you, you jerk."

"Where is it? My box. Do you have it?"

"You stole his box and his secret journal because you wanted to find out what he knew about you," I barked at him.

"Funny thing, Windover," Graydon added, "Duncan's sins were nothing compared to yours. And you were trying to steal his wife. While you were cheating on Katrina."

"You don't know," Perry wailed, "you can't know. And Katrina was cheating on me!"

Perry took a swing at me. I ducked and danced away. Graydon stepped smoothly between us and grabbed Perry's arm, twisting it up hard behind his back. Rudy raised his gun toward Perry.

"You don't touch the lady, jerk," Rudy ordered. This killer was taking my side? I made a mental note for a future play. "My target, Balmain, he's dead. The bum who killed him, he's dead too. Those guys' sins don't matter to me. But you, Windover, you lowlife, what's your sin?"

Perry said nothing, wincing as Graydon twisted his arm.

"It was a girl, wasn't it, Perry?" Graydon said. "A kid, an innocent young girl named Olive Rivers."

It was dark in the alley, but Perry shook visibly. "What do you know about Olive? She was nothing, an invisible nobody. You know nothing."

"She was somebody," I said. "She was a sweet girl and she was pregnant with your child. Seventeen years old and carrying your baby. She told you and you forced her to have an abortion."

"He done that?" Rudy asked. "I don't hold with that sort of thing. I'm a Catholic."

"It was a long time ago," Perry whispered. "In school. I was only twenty-two."

"Olive was just seventeen. She died on a dirty table," I said, remembering how he put it in the journal. "Didn't she? In a dirty room, killed by a dirty doctor, you said. She bled to death and nobody even knows what happened to her body. Olive never had any last rites, not even a funeral."

"If you read my journal, then you know she was a whore. She tried to trap me."

"We know what you wrote," Graydon said. "She thought she was in love with you and you used her."

"I don't like the sound of that, Windover." Rudy stroked his gun, a .32 Colt Pocket Hammerless. I recognized it as the gun of choice of movie gangsters. And Graydon's choice as well. "No funeral? Everybody gets a funeral. How old you say she was?"

"Seventeen," I said, "but she was only fifteen when Perry seduced her. Her mother was dead. Her father was the gardener. But Perry was a Yalie, a Keysman, a big man on campus. He considered Olive far beneath him. Like you and me. Right, Perry?"

"Oh yeah? Above all of us? Way I see it, this clown needs to learn a lesson," Rudy spat.

The noise was explosive, deafening, reverberating from the brick walls in that dark little alley where the man from Chicago shot Perry Windover.

Thirty-Eight

WINDOVER CRUMPLED TO the pavement in utter shock. He screamed and grabbed his thigh, struggling to sit up. The wound was bleeding profusely. It took me a moment to react. My eyes were dazzled by the flash of the gun. My ears were still ringing.

"Forget about it, he's a no-class cheat, a bum," Rudy said. "He should suffer a little, not die quick."

He pulled out a handkerchief and wiped down his gun. Clearly he could have killed Perry if he'd wanted to. Why didn't he? Graydon leveled his gun at Rudy.

"Freeze right there," Graydon ordered. Rudy lifted both hands high and shook his head.

"Take it easy, pal. I don't mean the lady and you no harm."

"Take off your tie," I commanded Perry, but he wasn't listening. "Do it. We have to cinch it tight around your leg to stop the bleeding."

He looked puzzled. I didn't want to touch Perry Windover, but I knelt in the dirty alley and started yanking at his necktie. You don't grow up in the dusty West and not learn the rudiments of caring for a bullet wound or a snake bite. Hunters often sought help from our general store before they went looking for the doctor. Yet I didn't know whether I could save Perry.

Blood was rapidly soaking his trousers and pooling on the dirty concrete. I wrapped the tie around his upper leg and tightened it as hard as I could while Perry squealed. He tried to grab hold of me with slippery bloody hands.

Now I heard footfalls far behind us, down the alley. I stood up and wiped my hands on my now filthy slacks, absentmindedly pushing my hair back with those same bloody hands. I would never wear those clothes again.

"You're real handy with that necktie, pretty lady," Rudy said. "You want to ask Windover any questions, better do it now. And I got something for you, Miss de LaForet. Right here in my left-hand coat pocket." He kept his hands high. "Don't worry, I ain't moving a muscle."

"No tricks," Graydon warned him.

"On my honor, pal. I want the lady to have this. Because Windover wanted it so bad."

I reached into his pocket with bloody fingers. I pulled out a ring of keys, one of them the bent skeleton key I had glimpsed in Duncan's marble bowl the night he died. I held them up for Graydon to see in the dim alley light.

"The fabled skeleton key." To Rudy he said, "Care to tell us how you came by these?"

"Somebody else did that job I got hired to do. But Windover said he'd pay me anyway, and he'd sweeten the pot, if I broke into Balmain's place and stole a leather box and this old bent key. I got in a couple nights later, it was a piece of cake. I didn't find no box, but I found the key. All yours, pal, you and the lady. Who, by the way, looked terrific in *red*."

There were suddenly shadows in the alley, moving our way. I slipped the keys into my trouser pocket.

"Rudy, don't even think about doing anything crazy," Graydon cautioned. "The police are right behind us."

"I know what they say about me, that I'm crazy? That I got Cupid's Disease? But let me tell you, I am as sane as Capone!"

Did Rudy know what they said about Alphonse Capone? I leaned closer to Perry.

"Help me," the bleeding man said. He was breathing hard.

"This goofball don't deserve no help," Rudy said. "He cheated me out of my pay, my job, my reputation, my livelihood."

"Don't leave me here with him," Perry gasped. "He'll kill me!"

"You've done enough, Esmé," Graydon said, pulling me to his side.

"Rudy, help me! I'll pay you anyway." We'd reached the bargaining stage of this transaction, and now Perry Windover was trying to make a deal with the Angel of Death. "I'll pay you double, please, just go and get help."

"Be happy to let you pay," Rudy said. "But I got another idea. You say the cops are coming? This is my moment. My blaze of glory. I hear the clock ticking on my career. I don't want to go down in no dirty alley, but sometimes you just gotta make do. What do you think, Esmé? Should I waste this bum Windover? Go out with a bang?"

"Lay off, mate," Graydon put in. "You've done enough damage. He might lose that leg, you know."

"He called me a stupid dame," I said, "but losing his leg would be punishment enough."

"My leg?!" Perry yelped. "I can't lose my leg!"

Rudy scratched the side of his head with his pistol. "Crybaby. He's gonna be a gimp?"

"He needs a doctor," I said. "Let the police handle it."

"Nobody wants to be a gimp. Let's leave it up to him," Rudy said. "Hey, Windover, you feeling lucky? Should I put you out of your misery? And let the cops put me out of mine?"

Sirens wailed down the street and into the alley, ahead of an ambulance and police cars.

"Put the gun down, Rudolpho," Frank Romeo's voice ordered from behind us. His New York accent seemed thicker, tougher than usual. "It's over."

"Who's that? Who's there?"

Rudy spun around to face a stern Romeo pointing a big Model 1911 .45 Colt.

"The name is Frank Romeo and you are way out of your territory, chump."

"You're Frankie the Cat!" Rudy said. "I heard about you, Handsome Frank Romeo. They say you don't never kill nobody."

"Always a first time. We heard there was a hired killer from Chicago," Frank said. "That would be you, Rudolpho Tortino. This is New York City. We don't have to import no crazy mugs with guns, we got plenty of our own. But I'm going legit, Tortino. You got me? I can't let no loose cannon from Chicago mess things up for me."

"I ain't no loose cannon. I'm a professional."

"Esmé, darling, are you all right?" Graydon whispered into my hair. He pocketed his pistol. Our hearts were hammering together.

"She's all right, pal," Rudy asserted. "The lady is a brick."

"So, these are the kind of hoodlums with whom you consort?" The English accent of Lord Cyril Chaseborn thundered through the alley, in his tweeds and hat, pipe in mouth. He puffed away. I couldn't tell if he was angry or relieved.

"Who's the hoity-toity?" Rudy asked, but no one answered him.

"My God, Father, what on earth are you doing here?" Graydon exclaimed.

"I didn't come to New York to lose a son or a potential daughter-in-law. Your mother would never forgive me. My friend Frank here received a phone call from his man Dentino. Said something was 'going down' tonight. So here we are."

"Who are youse guys?" Rudy asked. "I need a score-card."

I allowed myself to breathe a little easier. At least the police were there, observing before shooting. I caught a glimpse of Detective O'Hara. Perry was still on the ground, sobbing, mumbling, bleeding.

A half dozen police officers marched down the alley, guns drawn. The ambulance careened in from the other side, sending garbage cans clattering across the dark pavement. Rudy tried to run for it, but the cops braced him, threw him to the ground, and handcuffed him, before hauling him to his feet. One of them held up Rudy's prized roscoe.

"No! Not this way!" he shouted. "If I'm going down in this alley, give me my blaze of glory! I want my blaze of glory!"

Frank Romeo shook his head in disgust. "Chicago." His big gun was tucked out of sight now.

"If I might ask, Father, what are you and Frank doing here together?" Graydon asked Lord Cyril. I was temporarily out of words.

"Business. Working out how much Scotch would be an optimum shipment per month. And I have a line on some fine French champagne for him, too."

Graydon groaned and turned back to me. "Oh my God, Esmé, you're covered in blood. You're hurt." He produced an immaculate white handkerchief to wipe my face and tightened his arms around me.

"I'm fine," I said. I was beginning to shake.

"Are you bleeding?"

"It's not my blood. It's Perry's. I must be a sight."

His father chimed in, "Quite. Rather an understatement that. No doubt the wit you express in your plays."

"My wit? Wait until I put *you* on stage!"

Graydon held me back. "Come here. He doesn't mean it."

"You'll get blood all over your clothes."

"I don't care about that." He folded me in his arms. Flashbulbs from cameras lit the alley in a macabre scene. Reporters or cops? I didn't care.

Tears filled my eyes, and I tucked my head into his shoulder. Two men jumped out of the ambulance with a stretcher and took charge of Perry and my makeshift tourniquet. A third attendant approached me. I assured him I was fine. He gazed at my clothes and commented, "Some-one caught a gusher then. Femoral arteries bleed like crazy."

"How is he?" I asked him.

"Breathing. Lost a lot of blood. Lucky he did that neck-tie tourniquet, probably saved his life."

"He didn't do that, I did." The attendant whistled appreciatively.

Detective O'Hara brought up the rear. "What in the holy hell is this all about, de LaForet? You hurt? Or is all this blood the latest fashion on Broadway?"

"Nice to see you too, Detective. Not my blood. And this isn't exactly your territory."

"No, but the police radio said a certain Esmé de LaForet was involved. You sure you don't want to go to the hospi-tal? Or join the force? Offer's still open."

"Hilarious."

"And who's our friend here?" He studied Tortino. "Could this be the loony shooter from Chicago?"

"Don't call me loony!" Rudy pulled his most menacing bulldog expression, his shiny black hair falling in his face. "You ain't getting nothing from me, copper."

"Sounds like a Chicago mug to me. The way he says *cop-per*." He signaled to the NYPD cops, and they dragged Rudolpho Tortino off to the paddy wagon. The detective surveyed the remains of the scene in the dark alley. "Perry Windover from the Upper East Side? Killer from Chicago? The two of them together? This is more of that Balmain mess, isn't it? Who shot Windover?"

"Tortino," I said. "Windover hired Tortino to kill Duncan Balmain. Balmain was blackmailing Windover, who was Balmain's drug dealer. Someone beat Tortino to the kill, so Tortino didn't get paid. Thought he'd been ill used. You saw the result."

"A labor dispute, huh? And who the hell are you?" O'Hara turned to Cyril. "Related?"

"Rupert is my son. Esmé is his intended. Lord Cyril Chaseborn, at your service, sir."

"Detective Desmond O'Hara at yours. And I see we have Mr. Frank Romeo at this party too. What's the story, Frank, you mixed up in this mess?" Frankie the Cat shook his head.

"Just passing through, O'Hara. Lord Cyril and I were in the neighborhood. You might call me—a friend of the family."

"Figures. I bet you know the commissioner too," O'Hara said. "Listen, I need your statements, all of you. Let's say half an hour, at the precinct."

"What do you want to do, Esmé?" Graydon eyed the blood on my slacks and sweater.

"I've got to get out of these clothes."

"First sensible thing you've said," Cyril opined.

Graydon held me back again from slapping his father. "It's his way of showing he's concerned about you."

"Maybe I could write him some fresh dialogue. When I write my next play, about a pompous English aristocrat."

Unaccountably, Lord Cyril began to laugh.

THIRTY–NINE

"OH MY GOD," Willie shrieked. "You're bleeding! What happened to you?!"

"I'm fine. Don't worry," I said, "it's not my blood." I seemed to be saying that a lot these days. Might make a good title for a play: *It's Not My Blood!* A comedy, of course.

"Thank God. In that case, I want to know *everything*."

Graydon and Lord Cyril and I padded our way toward Willie's costume shop at the back of the Washington Irving Theatre, trying not to shed blood on the lobby's carpet. Willie raised both eyebrows at my appalling appearance, while she looked casually elegant in her slacks and beautiful red silk Chinese jacket. I looked like the victim of a knife fight.

"You're working late," I remarked. I didn't expect to run into my friend the costume queen, but I was glad to see her there. She held the wardrobe keys, and I was prepared to buy anything tonight. It would be less embarrassing for everyone if we cleaned up at the Irv, rather than raising alarms at the Hawthorne, where the cast was still rehearsing. Though heaven knows, Andras would probably tell the cast I'd committed murder in a frenzy over their wretched rehearsal.

"What about you? Fighting with the actors again? Don't tell me rehearsals at the Hawthorne are that bloody?"

Cyril spoke up. "As you can see, Miss Kim, they are in need of some wardrobe assistance, before we head to the police station to meet with Detective O'Hara. None of us are hurt, thank you for your concern, and we will depart as soon as possible."

"Police station? Wait, this is not stage blood? It's real blood?" She poked at my ruined sweater. Graydon and I looked as if we had just escaped from a horror film.

"Quite real," Graydon said. "And a little uncomfortable. Not to mention unsightly."

May Scott, who was also working late, let the unbloodied Lord Cyril park himself in my chair and poured him a cup of her freshly percolated coffee. I glowered at them both.

Willie led me and Graydon into the costume shop, her feudal domain.

"Do you want something clean, or in character?" she asked me.

"Not funny."

"After you ruined your beautiful blue gown, I suppose you simply can't help yourself, can you?"

"Are you having fun?" I asked.

"I think so. I can't help but observe that life is hard on your wardrobe."

"I thought you were going home early," I told her.

"And miss whatever this is? Whose blood is that?" She pointed to the bloodstains with her imperious crimson-painted nails.

"Perry Windover's. It's very expensive, Park Avenue, high society blood."

"Windover? I've seen his name in the papers. Is he dead too, like that Balmain character?"

"Not yet. That I know of."

"Your pants are a mess too. I'm taking notes. And making sketches." Willie grabbed a pad and started sketching the many and varied bloodstains I sported. "The way your life is going, Esmé, your next play is bound to be full of blood. I need to be ready." Graydon laughed.

"Esmé saved the blackguard's life," he told her. "She earned those bloodstains in a noble cause. Even if the man is a rotter. Shot in the leg by a mad Chicago mobster."

Willie was unimpressed. "Hmph. Our Manhattan mobsters would have aimed higher, I suppose."

"What will Sal say?" I asked Willie. It was a good thing my producer liked me. And a good thing the play was selling out, especially reopening night.

"I'll tell him it's research," Willie said. "Could you turn slightly? I need to sketch those pretty bloodstains on your throat."

I complied, but I was feeling filthy and sticky. "Do you have anything handy I could just throw on?"

"Of course I do." A few more deft strokes with her pencil and she put the pad down. "How about a harem costume?" She showed it off on its hanger.

"How about no. Just slacks and a sweater, if you please."

"You'd look charming in harem pants," Graydon suggested.

"In your dreams, darling."

"I dare to dream."

Willie unlocked the closets. Graydon's shirt was stained from holding me close, so she found him a navy fisherman's knit sweater, which made him look dangerously sexy. But Graydon grumbled at wearing something *used*.

"It's good for you, darling," I said. "Character building. And it's something a detective might wear."

"In a dime novel," he replied. "Good lord. If Robbins could see me now."

"Relax. This hasn't even been worn," Willie said. "We were going to do some gloomy O'Neill play, set on the docks, I guess, but Sal decided it was too dreary. Sal likes pizzazz, you know. And sequins, something you can see from the back row."

She sponged stains from Graydon's overcoat, while I dodged behind a screen and washed off as best I could. I quietly transferred Duncan's elusive keys to my purse. Willie tossed me a fresh pair of slacks in dark green gabardine and a belted sweater with pine-green stripes on a pale green background.

"I don't know where these came from, but they're washed and in your size. Good colors for you too."

I emerged from behind the screen and Graydon beamed with relief when he saw me. I realized how scary I must have looked.

"You look handsome, so casually dressed." The navy sweater intensified his azure eyes.

"Like a dockside tough. In a bad play." He grinned in the mirror and rubbed his hands through his hair.

"Thanks, Willie. I feel almost human again," I said.

"Instead of a bloodthirsty zombie?" Willie asked. "Give me your comb, let me fix that hair."

She worked a dry shampoo powder into my hair and brushed out the blood. I sat before a mirrored vanity and repaired my makeup. It felt oddly intimate to have Graydon watching. Willie expertly wound my hair into a French twist at the nape of my neck. She also produced a paper bag for me.

"For our friend, Detective O'Hara," she said. I folded my bloodied clothes and threw them in the bag. "Tell O'Hara, sorry, no fortune cookies tonight." I must have looked puzzled. She added, "Everyone eats at our place, because we're nice to them. My father says it's good insurance. Now tell me, was Handsome Frank Romeo involved in whatever this was tonight?"

"He and Graydon saved the day."

"Sadly, a little late for Windover." Graydon took the paper bag.

"You won't mention it, will you?" I asked.

"Who would I tell?" Willie said. "Frank's one of my dad's favorite customers. Big tipper too."

I reached for my purse. "What do I owe you, Willie?"

"For the clothes? Or for my silence?" She grinned wickedly. "Let me think about it. But I want to hear all about this when it's over. Or do I have to read it in the papers?"

"At the restaurant. As soon as I can."

My eyes met Graydon's in the mirror. "You look beautiful, Elf."

"Elf?" I was not amused.

"Elf?" Willie *was* amused. "I have some pointed ears here, if you want to complete the look."

"Not tonight."

Graydon added his bloody shirt to the paper bag as Cyril materialized, tapping his watch. "Your detective friend said half an hour. I assume he meant it."

"We'll catch a cab," Graydon said.

"Just a minute." Willie presented me with a pile of beautiful blue velvet on a hanger.

"What's this?"

"Have you thought about what you're wearing for the reopening night?"

"I've been busy." Not to mention frantic, and I had several gorgeous gowns I'd only worn once.

"And so have I. But this was something never worn, in a great color, in your size. It'll fit, because I already altered it for you. Look how it complements your hair. And Sal wants everyone to look 'prosperous,' he said. Especially people who get photographed a lot for the papers."

I reached for the material like a woman drowning. "But—"

"We'll come to terms. I felt bad that your sky-blue gown was ruined."

I knew this wouldn't be cheap. Willie was a genius costumer, after all.

"You ruined *another* gown? Do you make a habit of destroying your clothes?" Cyril asked, lighting his pipe. "Could be an expensive habit in a wife, Rupert."

"I didn't do it, it was covered in blood," I said, "and not my blood. It's hard to explain."

"This is an even richer blue." Willie stepped between me and Cyril. "Seductive, like twilight time. Perfect for you. Besides, everyone expects you to wear something extraordinary."

"Not to mention theatrical. And expensive?"

She wrote down a number. I reached for my bag, but Graydon grabbed the invoice. "I'll pay for this."

"No, darling, it's my responsibility." I couldn't wait to get my hands on that fabulous blue gown.

Lord Chaseborn snatched the paper out of Graydon's hands and glanced at it. "Quite reasonable, I should say."

"I have my own money," I protested.

"That is not the point," he said. "Consider it an engagement present. And I didn't care to waste any more time watching you two debate." He handed several large bills to Willie, who tucked them away, looking from him to Graydon to me. "Jane would murder me if I didn't do something nice every once in a while." Cyril sighed emphatically. "Now, Miss Wilhelmina, could you send the gown over to her tomorrow? Tonight we have an engagement with the authorities."

CYRIL INSISTED ON coming along with us to the precinct. He was as alert and cheerful as I'd ever seen him.

"Don't forget, I am a witness to that bloody debacle," he said. "Although I don't know why it had to take place in a filthy alley."

"Local color," I said.

It was just past seven o'clock, but it felt like midnight. Graydon handed over the sack of blood-soaked clothes to Detective O'Hara.

"Gee, thanks." O'Hara gave it to a uniformed cop and suggested that Cyril might like to have a tour of the department. Graydon's father took out his pipe and gestured for permission.

"May I?"

"Sure, as long as that's the good stuff. The tobacco, I mean."

Cyril and the uniform went off in search of more local color. I asked about Perry's condition.

"They're not saying yet. Windover might make it, but he won't have a leg to stand on, if you know what I mean." He chuckled at his own joke. "It looked pretty bad. I didn't get much of a statement from him before he passed out."

"And what about Rudy?" I asked, feeling very weird about the killer who seemed to like me.

"Mr. Rudolpho 'Rudy' Tortino, late of Chicago, is being hosted in one of our best cells, barking like a mad dog. We're going to have to move him out of there, he's disturbing the other ruffians. He kept telling me he didn't have Cupid's Disease. You know what? They say it takes years and I'm no doctor, but I'd say the syph is eating his brain already. We'll let the hospital psych ward buy us some time so the district attorney can figure out what to do with him."

"And what will that be?" Graydon asked.

"Not up to me. Hoping we can ship him back to Chicago, where he says he *knows all the coppers*," O'Hara intoned in his best Chicago accent. "Maybe they'll ship him over to Alcatraz to hang with his buddy Capone, who's already a guest there." The detective ran his hand through his hair . "You folks want some bad coffee?"

"Ironic that a simple matter of timing left the task of ridding the world of Duncan Balmain to his widow," Graydon said. "When there were so many others waiting in the wings."

"I hate irony, but you're right," O'Hara said. "The fates had it in for that guy. No matter how you toss the dice, Balmain wasn't going to last the night. Course, every day I see people that I know won't be alive in a week's time, a month, next year."

I rubbed my forehead and Graydon caught my eye. "I know what you're thinking, Esmé, but Maura Balmain is alive because of you. And her child."

I sipped the precinct coffee, which was shockingly strong.

"Yeah, what he said," O'Hara agreed. "And don't forget Johnny Akers' family. They got a chance to change their lives. But it ain't sittin' too well with Enid Akers. Any luck comes her way, she feels guilty, she told me. Crazy thing about this Depression. People been down so long it looks like up."

Cyril strolled back into the office, refilling his pipe. "Shall I take custody of these two ragamuffins?" he asked O'Hara.

"In a minute." O'Hara instructed an officer to bring in a chair for Lord Chaseborn. "Tortino was blabbing about some journal, like a diary, some so-called box of sin? You know anything about that? And some crazy tale about a young kid who died on an abortionist's table."

"A long-ago crime committed by Windover," Graydon said, "and apparently discovered by Duncan. They had a strange relationship, forged at school. Best friends, rivals, enemies."

"Sort of a mutual blackmail pact," I added. "It began in a secret society, Key and Casket, when they were both at Yale."

"Esmé should explain, O'Hara. She followed a path over the weekend to a New Hope antique shop where we discovered Windover's secrets."

I picked up that part of the tale, the long-lost box, the secret journals. O'Hara probably guessed we were working for Balmain, but he didn't prod me on that.

"So Rudy isn't completely off his nut? He said Windover killed a young girl."

"Impregnated a girl named Olive Rivers," I said. "Forced her into an abortion, and she bled out on the table. She was just a kid of seventeen. Perry took advantage of her, starting when she was fifteen."

"Tonight in the alley. What got him so riled up that it ended in gunfire?"

"Me," I said. "Perry wanted to know why we were following him. Actually we weren't, we just ran across him in Stockton, New Jersey. He didn't buy it."

"What were you two doing in Jersey?"

"Following a lead on Duncan. Before he died he'd planned a weekend there, to cheat on his wife with another woman. And there we came across Perry, having a spat with his fiancée, who was the other woman. Tonight I told him it was a coincidence. He called me a 'stupid dame,' and I got mad. And what I said about Perry's many sins got Tortino riled up at Perry. In retrospect, maybe I should have kept my mouth shut."

I heard Cyril laugh in the background, and O'Hara joined in. "I'm surprised it took you so long, Esmé, you being Irish and French and all, Windover's lucky he's got even one leg left. And what was Tortino doing there?"

"Trying to get paid. Turns out Perry hired him to kill Duncan, and you know what happened."

O'Hara whistled. "His best friend? Figures."

"It's complicated. Rudy and Perry were both from Chicago. Perry never paid Rudy for killing Balmain, because he didn't. Because of, well, Johnny Akers."

The detective and I clicked our coffee cups together conspiratorially. "About the dead girl? You got any proof?"

"We do." Graydon took over. "Two journals, found in a Key and Casket Sin Box, wrapped up in secret society lore. One journal was Duncan's, one was Perry's. Now locked up in my office safe."

"That, at least was sensible," Cyril broke in, puffing on his pipe.

"Evidence. You got evidence." O'Hara made a face. "Might be nice to let the nice police detective take a look, don't you think?"

"We were planning on that very thing," Graydon said.

"Windover won't be walking anywhere soon. He might not even make it through the night. If he does, I'd want some charges that will stick. How did you even know about the boxes?"

"For being such deep dark secrets," I said. "lots of people knew about them. Maura Balmain told me first. She thought it was all nonsense. Duncan's father had been a member of Key and Casket too, and he mentioned the so-called Sin Boxes. But I had no idea we could actually find one, until we overheard Katrina Fleiss with Perry. She knew about the boxes too. Katrina suspected Duncan had hidden Perry's in Stockton, but she didn't know about the journals. So I thought—"

"You're not going to tell me this is one of those women's intuition things, are you?" O'Hara made another face.

"Not if you keep making that face at me."

"Two journals, one by the dead man, one by the guy who wanted him dead. I want to see those. Tomorrow morning, on my desk. Agreed?"

"Agreed," Graydon said. I realized we hadn't mentioned Duncan's keys, sleeping peacefully in my purse. Tomorrow would do.

"By the way," I said, "where's Frank Romeo? Don't you need his statement too?"

"Oh, Frankie the Cat and me, we go way back. We had a word at the crime scene after you left. Frank's a straight shooter, you know, no matter what anybody says about him."

O'Hara handed us off to a uniformed cop to give our brief formal statements. Cyril took his time saying goodbye to O'Hara and putting in his two cents on the case. As we were leaving we ran into Reggie Pendleton strutting down the scuffed hallway.

"Well, well, well," Reggie said. "Perry Windover gets shot to bits and who shows up? I understand he's on his death bed."

"Nobody knows that," I snapped. "Stop writing the headline before the story."

"Now you're my editor? Seems Windover and Balmain were buddies. And I hear this hired killer from Chicago is yakking his head off that the late Duncan should have been his? Get this—to kill." Reggie reached for the pencil tucked behind his ear. "Looks like the Grim Reaper stalked Duncan Balmain. Two killers with but a single thought, one of them a pro. And yet one Johnny Akers, an amateur, makes the kill. That'll be my lede. Can I get a quote from the Broadway couple of the hour?"

"Tonight had nothing to do with me," I lied. "I was just in the wrong place, wrong time."

"Or maybe you're just a news magnet, a troublemaker, a—"

"Enough, Pendleton." Grayden stepped in between us. "I'm sure Detective O'Hara will have a statement for you."

"Just one more question," Reggie said. "Why was Windover a target? Was he just a substitute for Balmain? And why are you two involved?"

"That's three questions," Graydon said, "and you already got your answer—wrong place, wrong time. Now if you'll excuse us, I am taking Esmé to dinner."

Reggie glanced at Graydon's fisherman's sweater and grinned. "Where to? A fish fry?"

Cyril cut in. "I know they look like extras in an O'Neill play, Reginald, but they deserve their rest, young man. And their privacy. And their dinner. Understood?"

Reggie poised his pencil. "So Lord Cyril, I understand you were in British intelligence during the war. Can I get an interview? Your take on, say, current events on the streets of New York?"

"Another time, perhaps." Cyril waved Reggie away, staring at something approaching rapidly down the hall of the precinct. "And about dinner, Rupert, I believe Jane has other ideas."

How on earth did Lady Jane know we were at the precinct? But there she was, not wearing trousers, but dolled up in a royal purple dinner dress, her opera coat, and a beaded black dress purse. Her short hair was curled, she wore makeup, and she looked far too happy. This couldn't be good.

"Jane?" Cyril took her by the elbow, looking pleased. "What's the meaning of this?"

"We have dinner reservations at Delmonico's, my dear. The four of us."

My heart sank. "We couldn't possibly. We're not dressed," I said. "And look at the time. And it's been a very trying day."

"We're begging off, Mother, "Graydon said firmly.

"No, you are not, Rupert," Lady Jane said. "Not to worry, Robbins is waiting to whisk Esmé away to dress, and Andrew will drive us to your place so you men can change into your dinner suits. Esmé, I've already consulted with your most efficient Amelia. She'll have you well in hand in no time."

Of that I had no doubt. I was less certain of my ability to keep from screaming. If not for Graydon's hand reaching for mine, I would have.

I'll scream later, I promised myself.

❧

"Delmonico's! We better bustle," Amelia said. "Now, I set out your dress and shoes and purse on your bed."

"Gold lamé? Isn't that a bit much?" I was torn. I loved the dress, but it looked like it came from the Little Shop of Utter Disregard for Propriety.

"I hear it's a very special restaurant. Absolutely everyone goes there."

"So I hear. However, there was an incident tonight that might be in the news tomorrow and gold lamé might seem a bit—insensitive."

"Did someone get killed? Again?" Amelia's eyes were wide with curiosity.

"Shot in the leg. He might live."

"And you were there? Who was the guy? Who shot him? Wasn't you, was it? I know what a hothead you are."

"No! But I was there and I wish I wasn't. It'll be in all the papers."

"So that's why Robbins was picking you up at the police station. Hey, you aren't wearing your own clothes. Let me guess, covered with blood? Again, Esmé? You weren't hit, were you?"

"Nice of you to ask."

She ignored me and opened my armoire.

"Red is out of the question. Because of the blood. How about the green velvet? The one you wore to your opening night? It's low in the front and lower in the back, but at least it's got sleeves."

Those billowing sleeves were decorated with faux pearls and rhinestones. "It's practically demure. No time to waste, Amelia. Let's do it."

A delicate knock at the front door informed me that Robbins was waiting to escort me to the Pierce-Arrow, ensuring that all eyes would be on the car, if not me.

News travels fast though, and photographers were waiting outside Delmonico's for any errant celebrities that might arrive or depart. I was grateful that Graydon and not the doorman greeted me. He took my arm as we passed through the flash of bulbs. To my relief, we were escorted to a secluded table. Jane and Cyril were already seated.

"Am I late?" I said, trying for *demurely*.

"We just arrived," Lady Jane assured me. The waiter pulled out my chair for me.

"You look lovely, Esmé," Graydon said. His father coughed, discreetly.

"That's a charming frock," Jane said. "I remember it from your opening night."

"I half thought you'd beg off from coming," Cyril said. "Having had such a dramatic and harrowing evening. No nerves?"

"Carefully disguised, I hope." I looked to Graydon for help.

"Esmé always rises to the occasion," Graydon said. "Or falls on her knees in an alley to save a dying man. I do wish that hadn't happened."

"Cyril was filling me in on the latest," his mother said. "My goodness, what a night. My dear Esmé, it must have been terrifying for you. Do tell us *everything*."

Graydon and I ordered martinis. Cocktails for two (or more) were blissfully legal now, and if any occasion called for a stiff drink, it was this one.

I was relieved when a noted book publisher, one Bennet Cerf, arrived at our table and changed the subject. He introduced himself, saying he'd heard that Lady Chaseborn, Countess of Corduroy, was in the city and writing a novel. The lady in question positively glowed with pleasure.

"Indeed I am, Mr. Cerf. Simply a little gothic romance. You know, murder, madness, scandal, with a *soupçon* of social commentary," she trilled. She and Mr. Cerf were soon deep in a quiet tête-a-tête. For once, Lord Cyril was content to let her take center stage. Happily, Mr. Cerf hadn't heard about the bloody incident in the alley. Yet.

Lady Jane jolted me out of my peaceful reverie. "And Mr. Cerf, you simply must meet my future daughter in law, Miss Esmé de LaForet."

"Delighted," Mr. Cerf said, taking my hand. "You're the playwright of the hour, I believe. The toast of Broadway. And the noted *detective*."

FORTY-ONE

THE SMELL OF freshly percolated coffee tickled my nose. I peeked over the covers to see my house-keeper looking exceptionally perky.

"Amelia. I didn't think you were coming in today."

"As if I'd leave you in your hour of need." Amelia offered me a cup of her heavenly brew. She was crisp and professional in a brown print dress with pink collar and cuffs.

"Do you know something I don't?"

"Don't worry, I bought another scrapbook for your detecting activities, but sometimes it's hard to tell which is which. I mean, detecting and theatre. They sort of blur together, you know? Also I brought you the morning papers. The boy on the corner saves me extras whenever you or Mr. Graydon are in the news."

As if I needed every single last word on the subject of *me*. One newspaper called the Perry Windover shooting a "business deal gone wrong." All mentioned that Windover was a member of Yale's Key and Casket Society, which hinted, one paper said, at "dark doings." Key and Casket had many prominent alumni, "the Keysmen," and it seemed oddly well-known for being such a "secret society."

I received star billing for jumping in like Florence Nightingale to minister to Perry's gunshot wound. Reggie Pendleton had the nerve to report in *The Post* that, "Playwright de LaForet is always game for adventure," and that Graydon and I were "working on a case together." He did add helpfully that *Leaving Alamogordo* would reopen this Thursday and that show was sold out.

Reporters were speculating on where Tortino might be incarcerated. Alcatraz, current home of his idol, Capone, was a favorite, as well as Old Joliet in Illinois, or Eastern State in Pennsylvania, where Capone had also done time. Because New York nabbed him, some were betting on Sing Sing.

The Post featured lurid photos from the crime scene: Windover being lifted into the ambulance as Graydon and I looked on; "mad-dog killer" Rudolpho Tortino struggling with the cops; and me again, my face and clothes splattered with Windover's blood.

I looked much better in the next photo, dodging the press with Graydon at Delmonico's. The dress photographed well, but the cutline called me a "quick-change artist." I'm sure that would delight the future in-laws. I handed the papers back to Amelia.

"You really don't have to save all the stories, Amelia. Here today, lining birdcages tomorrow."

"I'll start clipping these. Some simply have to go into both scrapbooks. Whenever they mention you're a playwright." Amelia had perfected the art of pretending not to hear me. She held up two front pages. "My favorites."

PLAYBOY AND PLAYWRIGHT ON SCENE AS
WINDOVER PLUGGED
DYNAMIC DETECTING DUO DO IT AGAIN

"That second one," she said, "that was written by *your* Mr. Pendleton."

"He's not my Mr. Pendleton. And he was no doubt perfecting the art of sarcasm."

Amelia answered an insistent knock at the front door, and Willie strode in with a pile of blue velvet in her arms.

"Miss Kim for you," Amelia announced, unnecessarily.

"Amelia, that coffee smells great. Esmé, aren't you up yet?" Willie asked. "I suppose you had a busy day yesterday."

"I was going to have a nervous breakdown today, but— Is that the dress?"

"Take it off my hands, would you?"

Amelia stepped in and took the dress, holding it high, admiring it, while I dashed for the shower.

"I'll get you that coffee, Miss Willie."

Ten minutes later, I stared at my reflection in the mirror. The dress was a heavenly creation of velvet and satin. The twilight-blue velvet looked soft against my complexion. The close-fitting gown featured a deep neckline with a pleated stand-up collar in creamy white satin. The matching cuffs flaunted sequins and faux jewels. It carried an air of authority, suitable for a successful playwright. I only hoped the show would capture the same magic at its new theatre.

"Willie, this is amazing."

"I knew it would look good on you."

"Where did it come from?"

"It was a half-finished costume for that show last season with the leading lady who dropped out before opening."

"I remember that, vaguely. She had a silly name. Parsnips? Spinach? Sage?"

"Sage, that's right," Willie said. "Couldn't learn her lines. No spark with the leading man. She might have pulled it off by opening, but you know Sal. Sal 'encouraged' her to drop out. Sage tried Hollywood next, but turns out she's too fat for the movies. I had to cut the dress down quite a bit for you."

"So the dress is bad luck?"

"No, no, not for you. Besides, she never wore it. I finished it for you, figuring you'd say yes."

"I love it. Has Sal seen the papers?"

Willie laughed. "Everybody's seen the papers. The phones at the box office are ringing off the hook. Everyone wants to see the show and Sal wants everyone to see you." Willie held up one of the papers from Amelia's stack. "This is a good one."

PLAYBOY AND PLAYWRIGHT STAR IN BACK ALLEY GUNPLAY

Amelia brought more coffee and applied herself to the business of documenting all my embarrassments. The dress was perfect. Not so perfect was an appointment later that day with Edward Balmain and Graydon. Our last, I hoped.

I had just enough time to change into my blue business suit for the meeting, another prize outfit from the Irving's favorite flop: an ocean-blue wool crepe with a hip-length belted jacket that sported bright lilac lapels and trim. The matching hat featured a wide lilac velvet band and a bow on the right. It heightened the color of my eyes. In the breast pocket I wore a blue hankie trimmed in lilac lace. I seemed to be on a blue streak, but I didn't have time to think about why that color, or its subtext, was speaking to me.

❧

"At least Balmain Senior is safe from Tortino now," Graydon commented as we rode up in the elevator. "And we can put this business to an end."

I felt like a student on her way to the principal's office. Sebastian greeted us at the door and ushered us into the penthouse. He served coffee in the living room, signaling it was to be a business-like exchange. I took a moment to ask him how he was doing, working for Edward.

"Quite well, Miss de LaForet. It suits me to have a master who enjoys things done well, in a certain way, at a specific time. Very calming, Miss."

"What about Mrs. Maura Balmain?"

"She's a fine lady, to be sure, but I'm afraid my heart clenches terribly at the thought of that last day in her service. And I fear those keys of Mr. Duncan's seem to be lost."

"Oh, they'll turn up," Graydon said. "I'm sure everyone understands how stressful that day was."

"Thank you, sir," Sebastian went on. "You may think me a bit of a timid sort, sir, but I don't care for too much excitement. This new position suits me, indeed it does." He straightened his shoulders. "Mr. Balmain Senior awaits you in the living room."

Edward Balmain looked as if he'd aged ten years since the night we met him, but his clothes were expensive and his tie tightly knotted. Seated in a brown leather wing chair with the newspapers on his lap, he looked anything but casual. We sat opposite him on a divan.

"Couldn't you have kept this quiet?" he said without preamble, looking directly at me.

"It's hard to do when people are shooting people," I said, "and when the police arrive, followed by reporters. And I could have been the next one shot, you know." Not that he cared.

"Reporters! Pack of dogs. And Perry Windover." Edward Balmain shook his head in disgust. "Good family. I never would have thought Perry— You could at least have let the miserable bastard die."

"Goes against the grain," I said. "Catholic school."

He grimaced. The late-edition newspapers contained a lot of Rudy's ravings, and he even spilled the truth, that Windover had paid to have Duncan Balmain killed. Rudy further revealed that Windover was a dope peddler, and Duncan had been a steady client. Sensational stuff. Balmain didn't dispute the veracity of the stories, he was simply angry they had surfaced in black and white.

"Detective O'Hara apparently let the press have a few minutes with the gunman after we left," Graydon said. "It seems Windover was lying in wait for Esmé. He saw us in Stockton, just as we spotted him. But not even he knew what was going to happen. If I had been there in the alley a minute sooner—"

I knew my fiancé was agonized that I had been in danger. I had to look away before my eyes filled with tears. Love can be awkward.

Edward's sister-in-law Ruth floated in, wearing a sort of afternoon dress in russet, as if she were attending a bridge party with friends.

"It's better this way, Edward," she said. "The papers have torn the bandage off. Now they can find some other scandal. And dear Edward—" She softened her tone. "You know Duncan would not have survived that night, one way or another."

"And you even hired some actor to threaten to kill him," Balmain growled.

Ruth looked away. "Seemed like a good idea at the time," she said. "The Windover boy may lose his leg, I hear. And I don't imagine his pale fiancée will stick with him. Plenty of punishment to go around. Let's not punish one another. Our family will get lost in the crowd, I hope."

"You're right," I said. "The press has enough to chew on. There will be another scandal soon." There was a pause.

"Did you find the box?" Balmain finally asked.

"We found Windover's, but not Duncan's." Graydon replied. "Windover destroyed Duncan's Sin Box, but Esmé found Perry's in an antique store in New Hope. She had an intuition, you see. On target, as usual." Graydon sipped his coffee. "We turned it over to Detective O'Hara this morning. No choice. It's evidence."

"Of course." Balmain seemed unimpressed. "Did you find anything inside?"

"Two journals, Perry's and Duncan's. Duncan's included a lot of schoolboy transgressions, but it also showed that Perry was selling drugs all along. In passing, Duncan wrote about Olive Rivers, the girl who disappeared so long ago."

"I wanted that box," the old man grumbled, pulling a fat cigar from his own Sin Box, I knew, though older and less ornate than Perry's. "And I want my boy's journal."

"Talk to Detective O'Hara," Graydon said. "The journal may be evidence in Windover's trial, if there is one. After that, it might be returned to your family. But the box we found was Perry's. If the police release it, it would go to the Windover family."

I realized Graydon was pointedly *not* mentioning Duncan's ring of keys, handed to me by Tortino, especially that bent skeleton key from Key and Casket. The skeleton key that had unlocked so many skeletons. We'd given all that to O'Hara that morning, along with the box and the journals. The box that key opened was gone. And Perry had only wanted the key because it was Duncan's, like Maura.

Where would that key end up? I wondered.

"A trial? More publicity? And more damned rants against my entire class in the press? Good God. What did Perry's journal tell you?"

"He was responsible for the girl's death," I said. "Duncan had no part in that and didn't know about it. Perry got her pregnant, and well, it's quite ugly. O'Hara will turn it all over to the New Haven police. Perhaps they can try to find her remains and press charges."

"That news hasn't come out yet, but it will," Ruth said.

I imagined a headline, something like WINDOVER IMPLICATED IN DEATH OF GARDENER'S DAUGHTER.

"But it will all fall on Windover?" Balmain asked. "And the other one, this Chicago gunman? Not my son?" Graydon nodded gravely. "Very well," the old man said at last.

"This is far more sordid than I expected," Ruth said. "But Maura and the child? Another shock can't be good for her. For them."

Edward Balmain finally lit his cigar and exhaled a cloud of smoke. "I hear she's doing well and the baby is fine. So far. Maura could come back to her home, but she's welcome to stay at the hospital for as long as she needs to." He looked at me. "Will you visit her?"

"Yes, I will," I said. "But I won't be a spy for you, or anyone."

Ruth took my hand. "We're not asking that. I don't want her to feel alone."

"She won't be alone," I said. "Not with her family around her. Duncan never wanted the Fitzgeralds around, she told me, but she has a mother and sisters and brothers who love her. They showed up on Thanksgiving to keep her company. They brought pies and sang songs."

"Sang songs?" Balmain mused. "What a curious family."

"Apparently Maura Fitzgerald's people are quite musical," Graydon said. "Who would have known, in this fortress of affluent silence?" Edward Balmain looked as if he'd been slapped. "I'll send you our bill."

❧

"Now, what do you fancy?" Graydon asked me.

I fancied crawling into a cave where no one could find me, but when we returned to my apartment, I found a message from Amelia. I was to call Maura.

"I should have warned Maura this Windover business would hit the papers," I said. "We've been awfully busy."

Amelia had left the freshly updated scrapbooks on the coffee table, which Graydon leafed through, appalled and fascinated.

"Maura has no doubt read today's papers, darling. She knows all about Windover by now."

"But she hasn't heard it from me." I picked up the receiver and dialed. Maura answered. It was a short call. "I have to go," I said.

"To see Maura? I'll go with you."

"Better you should check in with your office. Maura wants to see me alone."

"Is she all right? Is this something—between women only?"

"We have things to discuss that no one else should hear about. Or ask about."

"So are you protecting her? Or me?" Graydon held me, puzzled but amused.

"Both of you. If I can."

"Will you tell me what this is all about? Later?"

"Maybe. Someday. I'm not even sure at this point. Besides, after we're married, we can't be compelled to testify against each other."

Forty-Two

BEFORE I KNOCKED on the door, I heard her singing an Irish lullaby in a strong clear soprano. Jesse opened the door and I saw Maura setting her knitting down, the picture of content. Maura, with all her bruises healed and a spot of lipstick, was a dazzling beauty.

"Come in, Esmé, but don't rile her up," Jesse said. Nice to get my customary greeting from the trusty nurse.

"And you, don't be upsetting Esmé," Maura said. "I'm alive, my baby is alive, and all because of her."

Jesse threw me a look. "If my patient's blood pressure spikes—"

"That's why I have you, Jesse. And could you bring us some hot tea?" Jesse stepped over to a buffet where the tea service sat.

"How are you, Maura? You look wonderful. You said it was important."

"Yes, and how are you? This picture of you, all this blood, shocking that." She held up *The Post* to show me.

"I'm fine. Not my best angle. Not my blood." There's that play title again. I might have to write it someday.

"Perry's then. If this paper is right, he must be insane. Is it true? He might lose his leg?"

"Looks that way."

"Take a seat before you fall down," Jesse said, bringing us tea. "You look worn out, Esmé. That's what the high life will do for you."

High life? I did what I was told and took a chair opposite the sofa. Maura threw a conspiratorial smile my way. I took off my hat and set my pocketbook down.

"And the banshee? What of her?" Maura asked.

"Apparently after all this, Katrina flew away in her private plane for a solo jaunt upstate. She's an aviatrix, it seems, and a rich one too. It must be true, I read it in the papers." I told Maura about our trip to Stockton and witnessing the lovebirds' spat. "I fear the engagement is off."

"And Perry wanted Duncan out of the way? And he hired this 'mad-dog killer' from Chicago to do the job? Is this story really true?"

"The mad-dog killer told me himself."

Jesse trotted over and checked Maura's pulse. The patient looked troubled but composed. She kept her other hand protectively on her stomach.

"At least the papers got one thing right," Jesse said. "Your Duncan wouldn't have made it through that night alive."

"But it's worse," Maura said. "This poor girl who died. Olive Rivers. I wish she'd had a mother who could have warned her about the wolves, like Perry Windover. Poor loveless girl."

"Her father loved her very much and there was another boy at Yale who loved her. Not Duncan. A nice solid guy named Tom Gates."

"Oh, I met Tom once or twice. I'm glad." She sipped her tea. "All this is so horrible, but I wanted to talk to you about something else. Please read this." Maura thrust a letter into my hands. "It's from Mrs. Akers. Her husband's the one—"

"The man who was blamed for Duncan's death." I still felt conflicted over my part in the matter.

"She wants to meet me."

"Oh dear." Not the most brilliant dialogue, but it was all that sprang to my lips. "That would be complicated."

"She says she's sorry for her husband's actions," Maura said. "I think she deserves the truth. But Esmé, I feel like I'm spinning from all that's happening, all of which came out of my actions. I killed him, not some stranger. Me."

"It seemed like the only story that would save you and the baby. And that might not hurt anyone else."

"And I thank you. Because of you, no police have come to my door. Edward Balmain hasn't tried to kill me or have me locked up. He's provided all this care for me. All because of you."

"And the baby," I said. "And he knows something wasn't right with Duncan. So does Ruth."

"Except for my child, I wouldn't care what the world thinks of me, but I cannot live with thinking of Mrs. Akers and this lie. I don't want it poisoning her life."

It seemed to me that far from poisoning her life, the money—Edward Balmain's money—was improving Enid Akers' lot in life. Maura was set on meeting the woman and I agreed to be there too, in a couple of days' time.

After *Leaving Alamogordo* reopened.

❧

"Everything all right?" Graydon phoned me at home later.

"No one's dead, for a change," I said. "But this has been the longest day." I gave him the scoop as I watched the flames dance in my fireplace. I was settled on my sofa with a cozy throw and a cup of cocoa. "So you see, everything in this house of cards depends on Mrs. Akers."

"Indeed. Would you like to go to dinner? I could pick you up. At your cozy little house of cards."

❧

"I want you desperately, but I can't move," I said, but to whom? I was alone, the world was cockeyed, and the weight of all these crooked things weighed heavily on me. I awoke to someone knocking at the door. My clothes were wrinkled. I'd fallen asleep on the sofa in front of the fire.

"I brought Chinese," Graydon said through the door. "Picked it up at Mr. Kim's restaurant. And frankly, we deserve a night in, without police or bodies or killers or reporters or photographers or other various miscreants."

"What a novel thought. A night in? No family?"

I opened the door and peered around him, afraid that Lady Jane and Lord Cyril might pop out like Jack and Jill in the Box.

"Not tonight." He presented me with a bag filled with pretty containers of savory smelling delights.

"Mmmm. Are there egg rolls?"

"Yes, and fried rice, and many other things recommended by Mr. Kim. Couldn't say what."

Graydon set the boxes down in the kitchen. I pulled out dishes and he retrieved a couple of beers from the refrigerator. I excused myself to change into something more comfortable, or at least not wrinkled. I chose slacks and a deep green sweater. Not quite lounging pajamas, but it would do. I was thinking how grateful I was that Graydon, unlike a lot of men, had learned some handy skills in the Army, like sharing the workload, and coming to a lady's rescue. And bringing Chinese takeout.

When I returned, our meal was on the table. He offered me a beer.

"Or would you prefer champagne?"

"This is perfect."

"We've been through a lot these past few days." He scooped delicious-smelling hot Chinese food onto our plates. "Was it emotional? Your meeting with Maura?"

"A bit. Guilt and anguish are gnawing at her, and now Mrs. Akers wants to meet with her, to apologize for her husband. I agreed to be there."

"Moral support?"

"I'm feeling a little guilty too. This whole thing came from my idea. I handed the police a coverup tied up in a neat little bow like a stage play, and they bought tickets."

"But it's not your fault. O'Hara ran with it, and your motives were pure."

"Were they? Or was I just trying to come up with a clever scenario?"

"You were saving Maura's life. I have an idea. Let's not think about it. I'll stay a little later and we'll do—something to take your mind off your troubles." His smile was most seductive.

"Promise?"

"Why, Esmé, I hope you never look at another man that way."

FORTY–THREE

O PENING NIGHT WAS upon me once again. The same, yet different. I was nervous, but grateful for this rare opportunity. But would this really work? Would the show's chemistry still be there? My reflection in the mirror was leaning toward glamorous. My spirit? Unsettled. After everything that had happened, I didn't know how I felt.

I laughed to keep my spirits up. I knew I was in good hands: Amelia was at the helm of the Good Ship Esmé. She was brushing my hair, having given up on trying to get me to cut it short. Her expertise as a beautician came in handy as she twisted and smoothed it into a fancy style, pinning it so that it gave the illusion of short saucy curls.

"I could manage it myself, you know."

"Sure you could." Was that reassurance or irony? "You know I'm not going to leave you in the lurch," she said, pulling a bit too tight and inserting the last pin. "Now hold still, it's time for the lashes."

False eyelashes always reminded me of that scene in *Dinner at Eight,* when Jean Harlow admonished Wallace Beery, "I've told you a million times not to talk to me when I'm doing my lashes!" I felt mine fluttering beneath Amelia's expert fingers.

"Can I open my eyes now?"

"Sure. That's the ticket."

"I've learned how to do my lashes myself."

"Why bother doing it halfway when you got me? Look at it this way, we all got our jobs. You got a lot to do in this life. Some things are too much for one person. I take care of your place and you write plays." She frowned, which I caught in the mirror. "I'd rather go to jail than try to write a play."

"Good to know. I thought you liked my play."

"Yeah, but I couldn't do it. Spending all that time just sitting and writing? I got things to do."

"Still working at the salon?"

"Couple days a week. I like to keep my hands in the curls." She fluffed her cloud of platinum curls in the mirror and pinched her cheeks. "But I like working for you too. Without you and Mr. Chase, where would I ever meet someone like Robbins?"

"How are things between you and Robbins?"

She blushed. "Pretty good, if I do say so." She applied something to my cheeks. "A little more rouge. You don't want to look pale and sick."

The woman in the mirror was now dazzling, red lips and cheeks, and extra-long lashes. Me. "Don't you think it's a bit much?"

"You gotta look right to meet your public, Esmé de LaForet. After all, you could be photographed."

I was all too aware of that.

"Do you actually read all those clippings that you glue in my scrapbook?"

"Course I do," she said. "What do you take me for? A chump?"

"What will you be doing while I'm at the theatre?" I had a rough idea.

"I might be spending time with someone's valet." She dipped her head. The blush was back.

"Is he as gone on you as you are on him?"

She laughed. "I hope so."

"You could go to the play."

"I already saw your show. Was I relieved, it was actually good. But a second time? Maybe later."

One wouldn't want to disappoint one's *housekeeper*, although there has got to be a better word than that to describe someone who seems to be stage-managing your whole life. "It took you a long time to get to the show."

"Only until all the reviews were in. Anyway, you're sure to have your picture in the papers tomorrow. Lots of pictures. After all, Lord and Lady Chaseborn are going to be there, and they are *news*."

"You are stunning, my blue velvet Elf." Graydon's eyes and voice did something indescribable to me. Luckily, my gown felt like a certain kind of armor, the kind that covers up your fears and your feelings, revealing only what you want to reveal.

We were going to the theatre and I had my part to play, a confident playwright who wasn't a bit worried the actors might forget their lines or fly headlong into the orchestra pit. The dress showcased the genius of Willie Kim. My amethyst earrings dangled, the bracelets on my wrists jangled, my silver shoes felt like wings on my feet. And yes, my eyelashes fluttered. Nevertheless, I didn't feel I was in my element until I saw Graydon and that special look in his eyes.

"Amelia will take all the credit." I could feel my lips curving into a grin. My first of the day. "You're not so bad yourself." Not many men could really pull off a top hat. They drowned in them, but not Graydon. He was majestic in his evening clothes. Was he born in them? He never had to be cajoled into a tuxedo or tails. The aroma of Hickory Wind wafted in the air around him. I inhaled deeply.

Robbins was waiting to chauffeur us to the theatre in Graydon's glorious Pierce-Arrow, mysteriously "restored to health." I noticed a few newshounds hanging around the lobby, waiting to see who might show up. I kept my head high and my hand on Graydon's arm as we strode through the doors of the Nathaniel Hawthorne Theatre.

Andras Szabo greeted us and pulled me aside. He was squished into his tuxedo like an overgrown teenager, not caring how he looked, which was appropriate for a director who cared only about the show. Oddly, his fringe of hair had been combed for the occasion.

"Esmé, what are you doing?" he asked, grabbing me by both shoulders. "So much publicity! Every newspaper, full of murders, mobsters, blood, and always about *you*, not the show! You should string it out a little. This way is too much."

"I had nothing to do with the reporters, and besides, we're sold out. How is the cast?"

"Petrified. Nauseous. Perfect for opening night. Now, if you must make news, make it about the play, the theatre, even the actors. No more about yourself or killers. Unless someone kills a critic. Then I applaud." He checked his watch. "Time to go terrify them. It's going to be a great show."

"Who is that man?" Graydon inquired quietly. I realized they hadn't been introduced before.

"Andras Szabo, the director. That's his style."

"Good. I won't have to punch him for being rude to you."

"Are you trying to make me laugh?"

"No. Really, I was considering it. Is he always that rude?"

"He's a director. It's his job."

Willie danced over in a rustle of glorious red silk and an impressive pearl necklace. She was trailed by a lovesick Seth. He stood aside as she lifted my arms and inspected my gown and jewelry.

"Sublime. This dress is all about conquering the moment. The play it was meant for was terrible, as was the leading lady, but the costumes were exquisite. You are bringing them to life."

"Thank you, Willie. I owe you buckets."

She laughed. "I already got paid, handsomely."

"You know what I mean. I couldn't even think about what to wear, I was so busy."

"Dodging bullets. Soaked in blood. Must be such a bore."

"You should be a comedienne. I'll write a comedy for you."

"I'm busy too. Keeping you in fabulous clothes is challenging."

Sal and May strolled over to us next, looking chipper. May overheard the comment and said, "It's one way to get rid of bad-luck costumes."

"They aren't bad luck for me," I said.

"It's a good thing you're not superstitious, like some people." May eyed Sal.

"Not superstitious, just practical," he replied. "I can't help it if actors won't wear flop-show costumes. They're happy to leave them for a playwright. And Esmé," Sal beamed, "I wanted to tell you, the entire run is almost sold out. Not just tonight."

"If this keeps up, we'll have to extend again," May added.

"Doesn't mean I'm not looking forward to reading your next play," Sal added, "whenever you get around to writing it, in between all your normal excitement, you know, detecting and so forth. But you can't buy publicity like this. And smile, Esmé. People come to see *Leaving Alamogordo,* but they want to see our notorious playwright too." He grinned, thinking he was so clever. "And how *is* that new play coming along?"

"Great. Chugging right along."

What new play? The play was hiding somewhere inside me. I hoped I could find it. What were those tentative play titles again? *Audition for Murder. It's Not My Blood.* I needed to find a different theme.

I turned to see Pat Dentino in earnest conversation with a lovely brunette, no doubt fascinated by his long all-natural lashes. "Patrick's here? You're not making him work to-night, are you?"

"Nah, he just wanted to see the show. He's a little nervous about school. He starts in January. That's something, isn't it, him getting into Columbia?"

"Something." Something called Frank Romeo.

Sal glanced over my head and waved, "Hey, Frank."

"Speak of the devil," Graydon remarked.

I turned to see Handsome Frank Romeo, aka Frankie the Cat, all dressed up and looking very distinguished. He winked at me and made his way over to our group. Flashbulbs lit the space around us.

"You've already seen the show," I said.

"I have. Lashes, I mean Pat, he tells me a writer's work is like a map of their soul. Something like that. I'm going to watch it with that in mind. Anyway, Lady Jane and Lord Cyril are going to be here too."

Things were certainly getting cozy between them and this notorious gangster. Mob bosses and earls and countesses are all at the same level of aristocracy, I suppose. Graydon stifled a laugh.

Everyone scooted off and Graydon and I were alone in a bubble of our own.

"Nervous?" he asked.

"A little. A lot." The reality that the play was going up suddenly hit me with a stabbing pain in the gut. "It will be wonderful if no one falls off the stage, or goes up on their lines, and the cast chemistry holds. And nobody dies."

Graydon looked amused. "Champagne? Now or later? A polite glass or a magnum?"

"I see what you did there. Distraction."

"Is it working?"

"Perhaps. Not sure about the champagne though. I may be sick."

"Maybe some Chaseborn's Scotch. I have a flask, in case of emergency." He patted his coat.

"I'd take you up on that, but I don't want to see a picture of us with a flask in the papers tomorrow. Headline: PLAY-WRIGHT GUZZLES BOOZE WITH SPECIAL BEAU."

The lobby was filling with theatregoers, and I kept a smile glued on my face. Everything stopped, however, when Lady Jane and Lord Cyril showed up. She was in a deep rose-colored gown, replete with a shower of sequins across the bodice, and a diamond and ruby tiara. I didn't know what the protocol was for wearing such a thing, but people were dazzled.

"Family jewels?" I whispered to Graydon.

"I believe so, though I thought she was supposed to leave it in England. She apparently is now deciding these things for herself."

She caught sight of us. "Look, Cyril. They're still alive."

"What are the chances?" Cyril said. "Another successful day in New York with the family." I ignored that.

"Lovely ensemble, Lady Jane. And the tiara."

"Thank you, Esmé. It's actually a copy of the original. It's not exact, a bit more subdued. Suitable for the theatre, you know."

Cyril gave the most elaborate eye roll I've ever seen, but he gathered his titled pedigree and said nothing. Later, Graydon told me there were all kinds of rules in Britain about the wearing of such things as crowns, coronets, and tiaras. But you wouldn't know that from the glamorous late-night crowds in New York, where every third Wall Street wife might be seen sporting a tiara of sparkling gemstones.

Lady Jane Chaseborn was far from the subdued matron I'd first met. The one who was going to eject me instantly from her son's life. Cyril looked very distinguished in his evening clothes. They shared a laugh. She seemed to have quite an effect on him. I wondered how they had ever come to be estranged. Not that I would ever ask.

We were mobbed by well-wishers, and I was happy to note that the photographers were focused on the Chaseborns and not me. However, that reminded me that I had brought my compact Leica. I took photos of Willie and Seth and Sal and his wife Della. I handed off my camera to Seth, who took several snaps of Graydon and me together, and of his parents as well.

At last the long-awaited moment arrived. The lobby lights flickered, the chimes sounded, the theatre doors opened. Butterflies were tap dancing to a jazz rhapsody in my stomach.

"We're in a box, all of us," Graydon's mother informed us.

Graydon took my hand. "Did you know about this?"

"Matter of fact, no. I have our seats." They were my usual, in the back of the theatre, so I could easily flee if the show went badly.

"I'm sure you'd prefer the box, with us," Cyril intoned, assuring there would be no argument. "There are Fleet Street correspondents in the audience, we must put on a united front."

I poked Graydon in the ribs to say, *This is all your fault.* We followed dutifully and I heard Jane saying, "Anyway, Mr. Cerf wants to see my manuscript when it's finished."

Of course he did. She was discussing the publisher we had met. Other writers might spend months trying to get their work submitted through the slush pile or an agent, but slap a fancy title on the writer, "Lady Wellborn, Countess of Whatnot," and you're in.

It didn't guarantee her gothic romance would be published. However, her tale did seem to have narrative drive and some scenes of breathless romance. It just might see the light of day between covers. I amused myself thinking about how Lord Chaseborn might react.

⁊

The first act was rousing. and the first intermission came with laughter and applause. The crowd was upbeat, chattering about the play, laughing as they got to their feet, heading to the lobby, and lining up for legal post-Prohibition drinks. It was very different from nights when the audience seems shell-shocked with horror or boredom. Jane and Cyril were inclined to stay in their box and chat with Frank Romeo. Graydon and I fled to get some air. And champagne cocktails.

Once downstairs, out of the corner of my eye I caught sight of Tom Gates with a woman who had to be his wife, the redoubtable Hortense, or "Tensy." I never imagined he'd jump on those comp tickets so soon. Graydon turned toward the bar to order for us and I stood to the side.

"Esmé. Miss de LaForet."

I turned to see Tom. He in turn presented his wife. Handshakes all around. After reading Duncan's journal and meeting Tom, I was curious about her. Tensy Gates was sturdily built with a friendly face and a no-nonsense attitude. She was not quite pretty, yet tall and handsome and might age well, dressed in that old money way of understatement, a cream-colored gown with an emerald necklace. Her short and practical light brown hair went well with the gown. Graydon returned with two champagne cocktails.

Tom cleared his throat. "You two found out what happened to Olive."

"We'd like to thank you both for settling our minds about that poor girl," Tensy added.

"Windover has slithered out of every punishment all his life," Tom said, "but now they've cut off his leg. That's a small comfort. He's not the kind to endure something like that with grace."

I hadn't heard about that. "They did? Where did you hear that?"

"The afternoon papers have the story." Tom pulled the folded front page of *The Post* from his pocket. "Bone shattered to smithereens, arteries shredded. Couldn't be saved, it seems. I called the hospital and the police, talked with a Detective O'Hara, offered to tell the police anything I know. Now I wish I'd kept that damn journal of mine, such as it was. I'll testify, if they want, here or in New Haven, wherever they need me."

He seemed a man unburdened, and with a new mission. He noticed we had drinks and headed toward the bar. Tensy watched him go.

"I am grateful to you as well," she whispered.

"I'm a bit surprised," I said.

Her face lit up when she smiled. "Don't be. It's impossible to compete with the ghost of a first love, and Tom was so young then. I don't try to erase her memory. I'm always here when he opens his eyes. That's the important part. We decided that whether they find her body or not, he'll put up a stone next to her father's grave. He says Mr. Rivers was a terribly nice man. And I suggested we also arrange for a memorial bench under a tree, on the quad at Yale."

"I think that's a lovely idea."

Tom returned with their cocktails. "I also heard you saved Perry's miserable life. He didn't deserve it. I'm glad he's alive though, now he's got to face the consequences every single day, an amputee with a scandalous past, people staring at him. Every day to think about what he did, and how he got there." He lifted his glass. "To Perry Windover. Long life. It will have to do."

"How did you find out what happened to her?" Tensy asked.

"We found his Sin Box from Key and Casket," Graydon said. "And his journal. Duncan's too. They told enough of the story."

"When I was at Yale I didn't think anyone could take that stuff seriously," Tom said. "But thank God Perry did."

Tensy rested her hand on her husband's arm and they shared a look. Peace, resignation, understanding? I wasn't sure, but it felt good. I gazed at Graydon. His blue eyes reassured me.

The chimes gave us a few minutes to return to our box seats, and I pondered what Tom had revealed. Windover's damaged leg had been removed. O'Hara must have leaked the part about the diary to the press. His boss, the new commissioner, could take this opportunity to pontificate that the law didn't play favorites—it nailed rich guys as well. At least once in a blue moon.

The rest of the show played like gangbusters. No actual legs were broken and the scene with the rolling desk chairs roared on like a runaway train. No one flew into the orchestra pit, as I held my breath. The cast was hot and in sync and I took a chance of breathing deeply. There was wild applause and a standing ovation. All was well at the Nathaniel Hawthorne Theatre.

Sal provided the expected opening-night champagne in the lobby, and Cyril and Jane partook like regulars. They couldn't make the after-party at Sardi's because they were off to preview Frank Romeo's new nightclub, slated to officially open in a week. It was named "Frankie the Cat's Supper Club." At least, *this* week.

Graydon and I sat in a booth at Sardi's, surrounded by Willie and Seth and May and the caricatures of theatre notables on the walls. Everyone was waiting breathlessly for the early reviews to appear, while Andras bustled about, telling everyone what a brilliant job they had done, and no matter the notices, they could be proud. He scooped up hors d'oeuvres with relish and drank with abandon until his face was ruddy and wet with sweat.

It never got old, this excitement, the nerves, the cautious optimism. The show was tighter and brighter and bigger in this new theatre, and I had written some extra lines to cover the larger areas the actors trod. Even our star Clarissa Eldridge didn't complain. Still, the anxiety settled on my shoulders and wouldn't budge until I smelled the newsprint of the early editions, with their judgment in black and white.

Sal burst into Sardi's, a stack of fresh newspapers in his hands.

"Rest easy, kids, it's a hit again, according to *The Post*, and *The Times*, grudgingly. But I hold no grudges," he said. Among the headlines he waved in the air:

LEAVING ALAMOGORDO BETTER SECOND TIME AROUND
DE LAFORET SHOW LOSES NOTHING IN TRANSITION TO
HAWTHORNE

The cast and crew applauded with relief. I heard cheers and whistles. My shoulders felt lighter by a ton. Soon the party moved away from Sardi's. Some of the crowd toddled off home, others to another preplanned celebration.

"Hungry, darling?" Graydon nudged me. "I could take you someplace nice. Or would you care to find that grubby little diner and order a grilled cheese? You know the place, where the cook threatened to throw me out if I bothered you."

Since Amelia made me eat half a bagel with my coffee, I hadn't eaten a thing. And I hadn't indulged in the food Sal provided. I hate caviar and weird finger food.

"Love to. Are you feeling sentimental?"

"Simply remembering where you fled to after your first opening night, running away from some randy boys in the street."

"Occupational hazard. And *you* chased after me too, you randy boy."

"Occupational hazard. My name is *Chase*, after all. And who wouldn't chase after a beautiful woman?"

"Ha. I don't even have a tiara. You mother looked lovely, by the way."

"I thought my father would choke when he noticed that thing on her head."

"Why?"

"Because that tiara isn't supposed to leave the country. Leave it to Mother to have a copy made, or a near copy. As for you, Elfin Queen, would you wear a crown of leaves and flowers to rule your forest kingdom?"

"I think you must mean *queendom*. And I am hungry, but for something simple."

"I was kidding about that diner." He helped me into my coat, holding me close, which made me wonder what I was hungrier for.

"I wasn't. After a sold-out opening night, I can pay for it myself now. It should come to about thirty-five cents."

The little diner featured a row of bright green booths with navy seats across from the counter, where Mick the cook waited for customers. In two of the booths there were stragglers from the after-theatre crowds. I could tell they came from Broadway by their clothes. Spend your money on tickets, but economize after the show. There's a Depression on.

"Hey, look at this, my favorite playwright." Mick took in the sight of Graydon and me together. The original program I'd signed for him was tacked to the wall. "You two certainly have made tracks since that night. I read the newspapers. Playwright and playboy solving crimes, getting yourselves engaged. Congratulations, by the way."

"Not official yet," Graydon said with a smile.

"That ring on her finger begs to differ." Mick didn't miss much. "And I could have told you something was there between you two. Now, what'll it be?"

"Grilled ham and cheese on rye with a side of fries," I said.

"Make that two."

"Make yourselves at home." Mick pointed to the booths.

After all that champagne, I ordered a glass of milk and Graydon a beer. Mick soon delivered our perfectly melted sandwiches.

"So Esmé," he said, "I read today that this Upper East Side Perry Windover guy loses his leg after you went to the trouble of saving his worthless life."

"He might just wish he'd died instead," I said.

"Some people are like that. Won't be easy getting around in a prison cell on one leg."

I imagined Mick would be entertaining his customers with that story, and an idea came to me: a play set in a diner among its regulars.

"You must get all kinds of people here, don't you, Mick?"

"That ain't the half of it. Rich folk," he nodded to Graydon. "And poor folk, and everything in between. Actors, playwrights, reporters, cops, mobsters. For a few minutes at a time, I get to be a part of their lives and they get to be part of mine. You got fights and you got love stories. Sad, happy, tragic. You got it all."

A little diner that's got it all? I wondered how that could fit with my idea of a play about an actor being grilled in a police station for a murder he didn't commit. Maybe just one small story in Mick's day? Graydon looked at the cook with amused eyes.

"And Mick, I suppose the ladies flirt with you all day long?" he asked.

Mick wasn't bad looking. He was well-muscled with chestnut-colored curls and cognac-shaded eyes, his bicep sporting an anchor tattoo from the Navy.

"Ah, they used to, until this one little red-haired pepper pot waltzes in and takes charge of the place. She could knock me over with a feather. We're getting married next summer. Least she tells me so." He started to laugh. "Best thing ever happened to me."

He left us to enjoy our meals and consider his pepper pot of a redhead, his bride to be.

All of a sudden I felt sentimental. And inspired.

"What's that look mean?" Graydon asked.

"Just an idea for a play. And somehow maybe I could put that actor hired to play a killer into it. What do you think of *Mick the Magnificent* as a title?"

"It's a great title," Mick said as he set down two plates of homemade apple pie. "On the house."

Grayden watched him go. "I'm not sure about that title."

"The right title is crucial. I could call it *Pepper Pot*."

"Or maybe *You Got It All.* Something else that's crucial. My parents want to see us tomorrow. Command performance. My flat. About tea time."

"So we can't escape? Graydon, your parents terrify me."

"They're not all *that* formidable. I can usually manage them. Well, sometimes."

"What do they want to talk about?" The sky was falling, or at least it felt that way.

"Our engagement, I presume."

"And the day after that I have to meet Maura Balmain and Enid Akers, and the whole castle of cardboard may tumble down around my ears."

"Esmé, you can't worry about things that haven't happened yet."

"Try me."

FORTY-FOUR

AMELIA DUMPED THE fresh pile of newspapers on my coffee table. The same story Tom Gates had showed us the night before was right on top.

WINDOVER LOSES LEG, LINKED TO HEINOUS CRIME

Reggie Pendleton's *Post* story claimed that Esmé de LaForet—a former *Post* reporter—had saved Windover's life. Who knows? He might have survived without me. Still, I worried that now he might try to hire someone to kill me. It was a relief that he wasn't going to be on the loose anytime soon. Did Perry really fancy himself in love with Maura, or if he only wanted what Duncan Balmain had? And what about Katrina Fleiss? No doubt Windover was sorry he had written his sins down for someone to find. Ah, the power of the pen.

Rudolpho Tortino was a "guest" in Bellevue's psychiatric hospital, at least until the cops decided what to do with him. My guess was that Detective O'Hara would get his wish: they'd wash their hands of him and send him back to the cops in Chicago.

The Post also featured a sidebar story on Yale's infamous Key and Casket Society, but none of the Keysmen would comment on Windover or Duncan Balmain's connection to it. Nor did they confirm that members kept Sin Boxes and Sin Journals. It was a juicy story, nonetheless. I assumed O'Hara had leaked that information. He was your go-to kind of cop.

My apartment was blissfully empty of other people and I made my own coffee, congratulating myself on my ability to plug in the percolator. I wished I had the whole day to myself, with a novel in front of the fireplace.

Alas, Amelia had left a note that the housekeeping fund was low and I should replenish it. And not to worry about my scrapbooks, she would take care of them on her next day of work. I added a wad of bills and change to the old coffee can in the back of the pantry, where I stored the "fund" to keep my ever-so-efficient housekeeper from opening any more charge accounts in my name.

Once she started with Macy's, there was no telling what she might do. Even though women didn't generally acquire charge accounts without a husband, Amelia could sweet-talk anyone. And I suspected she brought newspaper proof with her that I was engaged to a son of a lord.

The clock was ticking, my coffee was cooling, and I had to pull myself together to arrive at Graydon's apartment at four. I would simply inform Lord and Lady Chaseborn that I had a job and couldn't be counted on to jump whenever they snapped their fingers. But I had already spoken to Sal and May and cleared taking time off today to recover from the second "first night" of my play. I gazed at the pile of scripts that I should already have read.

I wore the purple cashmere dress that Maura had given me. It was oh-so top drawer and it served as warm sartorial comfort and armor. I paired the smart frock with pearl earrings and a pearl necklace. And I took care with my makeup, not too much or too little.

Robbins answered the door and took my coat and hat, but Graydon was right behind him to take my hand.

"We're in here." He pointed to the living room and brushed my cheek with a kiss. "You look wonderful."

"And you're still a handsome rake. If only we could be alone." Later, I promised myself. "Have they been beating you?"

"Not yet. They just arrived. The beatings will resume shortly."

Afternoon tea was set up on a silver service in Graydon's carefully appointed living room with its calming azure shades. Robbins entered stage left with sandwiches and sweets. The tea was optional, and I saw that Scotch and sherry were nearby on the sideboard.

This so-called "family meeting" ostensibly was about our engagement announcement. However, there were also complaints about our lack of *decorum*. Jane and Cyril came armed with multiple lurid and sensational newspaper stories. Murders, shootings, scandals, amputations, and a hired killer from Chicago. And there we were, right in the thick of it.

"We're not worried simply about the press here in New York," Lady Jane said.

"The Fleet Street ink slingers can't get enough of this," Lord Cyril said.

"I'm sorry if it embarrasses you," Graydon said. He clearly was not.

"I don't care about me, my boy," Cyril declared, "but your brother is having a hard time of it back home. You taking all the glory and all that."

"Cedric will do as he does," Graydon said. "And I'd hardly say this is about glory."

"Yes, dear, but poor Cedric is not used to being hounded, you know." Jane tried for a moderating tone. "The Fleet Street flacks have been after him relentlessly. We had a cable from him. Here it is: *Whatever are you doing? Stop. This is shocking. Stop. Cedric. Stop.*" Poor Cedric must shock easily.

"You can't tell a reporter what to write, even an English one," I said. "It will merely egg them on."

Graydon's father set his withering gaze on me. "That's right, you were one of them, a *journalist*." He managed to make it sound as bad as being *a woman of the theatre*. Possibly worse. And proud of it, I thought, but did not say. "As distressing as all this is—" he began.

Cyril probably went on at great length, but I stopped listening. Frankly, I didn't think he truly thought it was all that bad. One of their newspapers featured photos of him and Jane at Delmonico's and at the Hawthorne Theatre for my show. They were having a wonderful time, Jane in her ruby tiara and Cyril chatting with the notorious Frank Romeo. Something for the scrapbook. The headlines read:

ENGLISH ARISTOCRATS GO NATIVE IN NEW YORK
LORD AND LADY CHASEBORN KICK UP THEIR HEELS
ON BROADWAY

"Yes, I can see you were positively miserable." I showed the newspaper to Graydon.

"Can't be denied that my fiancée is more photogenic than Cedric's Penelope."

"Let's not get off track," Cyril barked and snatched the paper away.

"What Cyril is trying to say," Jane explained, "is that we don't care about all that, we simply want you *alive*. Your father may rage on about decorum and tradition and how—*unusual* it is that darling Esmé is not—*quite* what we expected in a daughter-in-law—you're so much *more*, my dear—but we are concerned about these dangerous situations in which you two seem to find yourselves."

Jane was speaking very carefully. I knew how much she wanted Graydon to be married, and obviously I wouldn't be their first choice in any event. If only big brother Cedric and his wife would turn out a kid or two and take the pressure off. What the heck is wrong with that simp Cedric, anyway?

"Jane is right," Cyril said. "No matter how much we may differ, the point is, at the end of the day, we do want you alive. Both of you. Not being shot down in a filthy alley like something out of a cheap novel. And tell me why photographers seem to capture every bloodstain in this city?"

I was about to explain that photographers and reporters followed the cops around like bloodhounds and monitored police radio bands obsessively, but Cyril turned to Graydon without a pause. "Rupert, you shouldn't have placed her in danger!"

"Now Father, there were extenuating circumstances," Graydon began.

"Excuses, excuses. Although she is clearly intrepid and resourceful, your fiancée shouldn't have been involved in the first place."

"Graydon did not put me in danger," I said, jumping into the fray. "I demanded to be with him, to be included on his case. We were at a gala for my play when he got the call from Edward Balmain. Graydon assumed it was just a financial issue, and he would have walked into that mess alone." All that blood. "Do you think *I* want Graydon in danger?"

Cyril rocked back in his chair. "No, no, of course not." Jane retreated to the sideboard and poured her husband a Scotch and herself a sherry.

"No matter what you think, Maura Balmain is alive today because of Esmé," Graydon practically shouted. "Maura and the child she carries would be dead, if Esmé hadn't been there."

They opened their mouths to speak, but it was my turn.

"I know I'm not your first choice for a daughter-in-law, Lord Chaseborn, Earl of Corduroy, but I'm not some waif off the street. Graydon and I are going to have a marriage of equals, in intellect if not in dollars and cents, or pounds sterling, or what you will. And I'm making a very nice living with my plays, thank you." At the moment anyway. The next play could be a flop.

"Yes, yes, you're a woman of independent means," Jane hastened to put in. "I quite applaud you for that."

"So you're a suffragette as well as a woman of the—" Cyril asked me.

"My mother was a suffragette, and yes, I would have been there on the front lines."

He turned in exasperation to his son. "Rupert, or Graydon if you will, your duty is to support and protect your future wife."

"He does protect me," I said, "and I will do the same for him, in any way I can. I'm aware you don't want me to marry him."

"When did I ever say that?" Lord Cyril thundered.

"Many times, I'm sure. At least in subtext. Perhaps not to my face."

Jane refreshed her husband's Scotch. She sat with her sherry on the arm of his chair. I had the fleeting thought that this might be the last time I saw them. Graydon had moved across the sea from them, yet he still might break off our engagement in the name of family harmony. Was that really possible? My heart would break.

Lord Cyril chuckled, which of course infuriated me. "Perhaps, before I got to know how delightful you are. What do you say, Esmé? Do you think you could tolerate Lady Jane and me as in-laws? On an occasional basis, of course."

"I think you can be very charming, but mostly you're horrible and just plain mean. Your incessant habit of sarcasm wears me out."

"Indeed, some honesty there." He sipped his Scotch. "Then I shall be honest in return."

"Cyril?" Jane said warningly.

He ignored her. "Esmé de LaForet, you will never be a countess, though you do dress like one. Much better actually, when you're not covered in blood. You dress theatrically, I dare say. And never being a countess I say not as an insult, but as a fact. Cedric is the heir to the title. Being a countess, or an earl, can be a terrible burden. One must be born and bred to it, and Cedric's wife Penelope, for all her, ah, *shortcomings*, is just so."

"You can't possibly imagine I would ever want to be a countess. I am an American! No offense, Jane."

Lord Cyril pressed on regardless. "You are intelligent and clever, though not always wise. You appear in the newspapers far too often for my taste, but then I am old-fashioned. You insist on accompanying Rupert into danger, and you jump to my son's defense like a tigress. I understand you nursed him when he was at the point of death. That is to be admired. You don't faint, even when facing killers. My wife and I admire that quality, and they'll love that in London. Frank Romeo speaks highly of you and I hold him in some regard. In sum, all I can say is that Graydon's life and yours will never be *commonplace*."

"We already have one lovely but boring son," Jane broke in. "We do adore Cedric and Penelope, but they are, well, a trifle *dull*. Penelope doesn't write or paint or play music, or have opinions, or— Well, she does smile nicely, and I have high hopes she'll be a good mother. Someday. Soon."

I realized my mouth was open at this sudden turn. "So, you don't disapprove of our marriage?" I asked.

"Indeed, I do not," Cyril said. "But then, young people today do what they want anyway. And you'll be living in America, I presume?" He sent a meaningful glance at Graydon. What he meant was *as far away as possible*.

"That is the plan." Graydon took my hand and stood behind me. "Our very definite plan. That's the privilege of the second son, isn't it, Father? Cedric gets the infernal title. I get—my freedom."

"Don't get too cocky, my boy." Cyril took a deep breath and downed his Scotch. "That's as may be. Now, I assume you may need to call upon my expertise and advice on various occasions, depending on what ridiculous cases you might choose."

"My investigative cases?" Graydon asked, suspiciously.

"My intelligence background, of course. I might offer the occasional valuable insight. On a consulting basis, of course. And you must realize that your engagement should be announced soon. As soon as possible."

"Absolutely," Jane said. "I'm making a list of people to invite, and I assume it will be a mad mix of charming characters. Of course you must invite all those colorful theatre people and that very interesting publisher friend of yours, Mr. Cerf, and Mr. Romeo, and all those reporters and so on, and I may be in need of some advice from you, Esmé." She beamed in triumph. "I'm almost finished with my first book! Tentatively entitled, *Loving Her Ladyship*."

"Loving *whom*? And your *first* book, you say?" Cyril bellowed. "Oh, good God, Jane, don't tell me you're writing a *second* book?"

❧

"I'd say that was a smashing success," Graydon said. "No breakables were actually smashed, and I told you the old man liked you. He simply didn't know it yet."

"Opinions differ, my darling." I kissed him. "If that is him liking me, I shudder to think what him hating me might be like."

"If that were the case, he would not acknowledge you at all. And here we are in the bower of the Elf Queen. I feel it's quite a signal honor." Graydon lay back on my whimsical yet comfortable bed, gazing at the mural winding its way across the ceiling. "By the way, how is Mother's book?"

I moaned. "I've only read some excerpts. She handed me more of her pages in progress as we left." I sat up and leafed through the pages—the many, many pages—of Lady Jane's gothic romance and tried to recall what she'd told me about it. "It seems to feature a beautiful heroine, a manor house with a forbidding tower, unruly and devious servants, and an inscrutable romantic love interest, as well as shadowy enemies and a mysterious villain. Our heroine is forging ahead into the unknown. As is the reader."

"Sounds very like Mother. Please put that thing away for now, darling. We have better things to do."

I tossed it on the dresser. Why not enjoy the now, before my meeting tomorrow with Maura Balmain and Enid Akers? I fell back onto the bed, or as Graydon would have it, the Elf Queen's bower.

FORTY–FIVE

ENID AKERS WAS not afraid of the truth, as it turned out.

Maura wanted me at their meeting, which made me uncomfortable, but it was my scenario that got the whole ball rolling. My responsibility, in a sense, though a posse of Irish cops had done the dirty work.

I dressed in a mahogany knit dress with rose-colored trim around the sleeves and collar. My matching hat was compact with a pink band and a spray of roses. It felt very businesslike, and on the way to see Maura I tried to examine my conscience in a businesslike way. Would I have done anything differently? Probably not. But then there was that awkward thing, the thing without feathers—the truth.

Although Maura was still ensconced in Doctors Hospital, she was getting back to normal. That is, her new normal: awaiting the birth of the child she desperately wanted. She was no longer subject to Duncan's ups and downs, his ravings and beatings.

"Thank you for coming, Esmé." I was surprised to see Maura wearing a soft pink maternity dress that showed the beginnings of a baby bump. She explained it seemed to show up overnight. "I'll have to buy more clothes. Nothing but this fits quite right." Nevertheless, she was glowing in that way they say expecting women do.

"You look wonderful," I said. "Where's Jesse?"

"Not here. She checks on me every day, but she says I'm no longer in danger. Don't worry, she lectured me thoroughly. I am not to overdo things or get upset," she added with a beatific smile. "I do believe Jesse has a date with a handsome doctor tonight. And I reminded her I can pour coffee all by myself. Let me pour a cup for you." A silver coffee service and coffee cake were ready for her guests.

"First of all," I said over coffee, "I want to explain to Mrs. Akers that it was my fault that her husband was blamed for Duncan's death."

"We'll not be speaking of faults. Life laid out a path for us, and it could have gone many other ways, but it went the way fate led us. Do I blame you for saving my baby? Keeping me from prison or worse? Never. I would lie, cheat, and steal for this child. I killed for this child." There was something new and fierce about Maura. I liked it.

A knock came at the door. I ushered in Mrs. Akers and introduced myself.

"Pleased to meet you," she said. "You must be the detecting playwright I keep reading about."

I was at a loss for words, when Maura came up beside me, extending her hand.

"Do come in, Mrs. Akers. Would you like coffee? There's a fresh pot."

"I'm not one to ever turn down a good brew." The woman's photograph in the paper had made her look older, more haggard. Yet here she was, a handsome woman with a quiet strength.

Enid Akers wore practicality as easily as her attractive new burgundy overcoat with its wide velvet collar, which she stroked as she doffed it. Perhaps for luck, or to remind herself her life had changed. She removed it to reveal a new dress, not flashy but a decent dark blue, suitable for nearly anything.

The two widows faced each other across the coffee table. Maura sat on the sofa and Enid and I took the chairs opposite. The press would have a field day with this picture. I was glad they weren't there to take it.

"I came to apologize for my husband Johnny," Enid Akers said at once, "and to tell you how very sorry I am for it."

"The apology is mine," Maura replied. "Thank you for coming, Mrs. Akers. I couldn't let you think—" What? A momentary doubt crossed her face, but she pressed on. "You're not to blame for Duncan's death, nor is your husband."

"But the police. The newspapers. The money." Enid's cup and saucer rattled. I could see her fear that somehow the money might be taken away. "I thought perhaps in some dark Hell maybe Johnny was paid to do it. What else could possibly explain all that money? And the way he died, stabbed to death in that awful bar— Why did no one pick his pockets and steal the money? Ah, but then, everyone knew he had nothing. His coat was so old, I couldn't keep it in good repair. He'd go out looking like a bum you wouldn't roll for a nickel."

I saw Maura tearing up, and the whole story spilled out of her. "Mrs. Akers, the night it happened my husband Duncan tried to cut the baby out of me with a knife. He tried to kill me and the baby too. That's why I'm here at Doctors Hospital. I had no choice. I shot him. I killed him. Not your husband. It was me."

"He tried to cut—? Oh my dear God." Enid set her cup down shaking. "I have heard terrible things in my life, and Johnny Akers was a terrible man, but I never heard of such wickedness as a husband who would try to kill his own child. And his wife—"

"The police knew," I jumped in, "as everyone knows, that this sort of death on the Upper East Side, in a 'swellegant' Park Avenue apartment, would quickly be covered up. The blame would be cast elsewhere. Even with their tough new police commissioner."

"I suppose that is the way of it." Enid wasn't shocked "But how on earth?"

"That night," I said, "Duncan's father called my fiancée and asked him to come at once. We found Duncan dead and Maura— Well, no one knew if she would make it. I tried to stop the bleeding, and I called for a nurse and a doctor. After the police arrived, it was preordained that this would be covered up. I was simply wondering aloud how they might do it, as if I were writing a play. How convenient it would be if Duncan Balmain's death could be blamed on somebody who was killed the same night or the next. To save Maura from prison, to save her baby, to avoid a panic on the Upper East Side over a killer at large. And the cops took my idea—and they ran with it."

They were both about to speak, but I rushed forward.

"To make it believable, it had to be a man with sins on his record, perhaps someone who had killed before. Men die every day and night here in New York City. Your husband was simply the one the cops came up with, and his bad blood with Duncan Balmain made the story stronger. I'm so sorry. I spin stories for the stage, and I know how reporters think. The police latched onto my idea and pinned it on your husband. He fit the bill." I suddenly felt resentful. "It wouldn't have happened this way if the police had more imagination."

"Well, I'm poleaxed," Mrs. Akers said. "My goodness. I didn't expect this. No, not at all. But then where did the money come from?"

"The money was part of my story. If they found someone to blame, I told the cops, his family *had* to be compensated. It seems your husband was destined to die that night, with or without money in his pockets. And Maura's husband too. At least this way—"

"And that blood money's from my father-in-law," Maura cut in, "to protect his grandchild. You see, Duncan never wanted children. He told him I couldn't have children. The old man held a grudge against me for it. Wanted me to go to the electric chair—until he heard about the baby." Maura paused. "It's up to you now, Mrs. Akers. What are you going to do?"

Enid Akers took a moment to gather her thoughts, sipping the strong coffee. She stared at me.

"Without you, Miss de LaForet, thinking aloud in front of those cops, Johnny would still be dead. And we'd be left with nothing, still living in that shack in Hooverville. And Johnny would still be a killer, I know good and well, just not the one responsible for Mr. Duncan Balmain's death."

"That's about the size of it." I reached for my own coffee, deep, dark, and bracing. I needed it. I told myself not to spin any more stories aloud. Save them for the stage.

"It's true. Esmé brought you a bit of comfort, maybe a chance for a better life, while she saved my life and my baby," Maura said. "The police detective that night and the other cops—all good Irish cops, wouldn't you know—they knew it was self-defense and defense of the babe. They did the right thing. But if you want to put the truth out there, Mrs. Akers, I can't blame you, and I won't stop you."

"Why in the devil would I tell?" Enid asked. "Pardon my language, ladies. And no one on earth would believe me. Johnny *was* a murderer. I lived in fear of him. Him dying when he died, and the way he died, and the money given to us, my good Lord, it's the best thing he ever did for his family. I hate to admit this, but I'd pick his pocket when he was drunk. He never had much, and no memory of it when he woke up. If I hadn't, many's the day the children would have gone hungry." She spread her hands wide and looked at them. "Nickels and dimes. I'd squirrel them away in little hiding places. When he'd accuse me of stealing from him, I'd convince him he got robbed after closing time, and him drunk as a lord."

"I'm sorry for your children," I said.

"I was worried at first how they'd take it. Yet I see a great calmness coming over them. They don't jump with fear at the sound of his voice, always sprinting away from him as if he were the boogeyman. Their own father. In time, perhaps they can forgive him. There's a peace in the house now—our new apartment, not a shack— There's a peace that was never there before. Oh, I should have left Johnny Akers long, long ago."

Maura wiped her eyes. "I didn't know how to leave Duncan. I thought the baby would change everything. I thought he would love his child."

"We always think a man will love his children," Enid said. "Some don't. The truth is, you don't really know a man till you marry him."

I felt a chill run through my bones. I felt I knew my fiancée pretty well, but this was yet another argument for a long engagement. A very long engagement.

"You've talked with Detective O'Hara?" Maura asked Enid.

"Such a nice man. He took me to the bank himself to make sure the money didn't go astray. I wouldn't want him to get in any trouble. No, I'll never tell anyone about the one good fortune that's come to me and my children. What kind of mother would I be?"

"Five thousand dollars is a goodly sum, but it won't last forever," Maura said. She sliced pieces of the coffee cake for each of us. Enid took a bite.

"No, I'll be looking for work as soon as we're settled. Factory work, maybe. I'm a good hand with sewing, and I can cook. Wouldn't mind working in a nice orderly house, cleaner and quieter than a factory."

"I'll be needing a housekeeper soon," Maura said. "If you know of one..."

"Oh, my goodness, Mrs. Balmain, you'll never find a more loyal housekeeper than me, if you're asking. Thank you. My mind is at rest now."

The two women gazed at each other, now sisters of a sort, as Enid had predicted before. Soon they were talking about nothing but babies. I quietly took my leave, thinking that fate did, indeed, work in mysterious ways.

❧

A dark blue Ford was idling outside the Doctors Hospital building on East End Avenue. A reliable anonymous Ford that didn't draw attention to itself. Or the driver. He must have been waiting for a while. I could have walked home to the Upper West Side across the park or hailed a taxi, but my heart leaped at the sight of him. I was glad he wasn't helming the Pierce-Arrow, as lovely as it was. It drew too much attention to itself.

Graydon jumped out and ran around to the side door. His dark hair was lit by sunlight, and his blue eyes that rocked my soul regarded me with curiosity.

"Thanks for the ride, cabbie. I'm suddenly very tired."

He closed the door for me, ever the gentleman. I settled inside and leaned my head against the seat back. He slid into the driver's seat. "How did it go?" he asked.

"As well as could be expected. Actually, much better. Babies make the world go round, did you know?"

"So I hear. Mrs. Akers will keep the secret, then? The more people who know, the more chances the truth could get out."

"She's fully on board with it. Mrs. Enid Akers is a pragmatic woman. Her life is better without the dead weight of Johnny Akers, the innocent killer. She weighed everything carefully. There were a great many tears." I had restored my makeup and hoped I didn't look as wan as I felt.

"Yours too?"

"Mine too."

"Oh, darling. I'm so sorry."

"Don't be. She didn't blame me. She was glad some good came out of Johnny Akers at last. And she wouldn't want that nice Detective O'Hara to get in trouble."

"And here I was half expecting a bit of blackmail." Graydon put the Ford in gear.

"Not everyone is a crook."

"For that I'm grateful. But the story may still get out."

"Maybe, but the truth will lose out to the legend. It's a better story, the mother and child who survived. The mother who then offered a job to another widow."

"You're telling me Maura hired the Akers woman?"

"Her new housekeeper. And both of them are thrilled about it." We drove in companionable silence for a while, but the shadow of two dead men and the women they abused, these crooked things, hovered over me.

"Love is hard, Graydon."

"Life is hard, but harder without love."

"Your life is a lot. A whole lot."

"My life?" He started laughing and pulled the car over where we could look at beautiful Central Park, still glorious as the last leaves were falling. I moved closer and leaned my head on his shoulder. "I daresay yours is even more so, Esmé, what with actors, directors, mobsters, critics, and that very creative brain of yours."

"You are too much, Graydon. Too handsome, too rich, too kind. You're a target. Women hunt you like big game, and your parents are—" I left out the word *crazy*. I felt the weight of it all.

"Yes, my parents are unexpectedly a lot more. They never actually took much interest in me before I met you. They like you. Perhaps in spite of themselves. They are far more interested in you than they are in Cedric and Penelope. And before you, I only dealt with figures, debits, and credits and ledgers, and pursued things like hidden assets and secret embezzlements."

"And the bootlegger who wanted you to extract him from the mob?"

"One time. That would never happen again. It's against all odds."

"And now your father wants to get involved in your business."

"It's odd. I never thought I'd be so anxious for Cedric to start a family and take the heat off me."

"I love you, Graydon. But it's impossible."

"Beyond impossible." He lifted my chin up to kiss me. "Yet if I know anyone who can make the impossible *possible*, it's

 Ellen Byerrum

you. I love you, Esmé. I want to marry you. Shall we set the date for the engagement party? Shall we make it possible?"

"I won't give up my independence. Or my career. Or my apartment."

"As if that were possible." He grinned at me. "And I will never ask it of you. Promise."

"Then yes. As long as we always face the music together."

"Music? I hear wedding bells." He kissed me. I kissed him back. "Ah, hard is the life of the Elf Queen."

"You're a smart aleck, Graydon Chase. Did you inherit that from your father?" We drove off toward that unknown country: matrimony. "By the way, where's the Pierce-Arrow tonight?"

"Parts unknown," Graydon said. "I had to lend it to the old man. We may never see either of them again."

"Oh, I'm sure they'll turn up again, darling. Perhaps in Hell's Kitchen. With a carload of fresh fish."

"I can see the headlines. EARL GOES FISHING IN HUDSON RIVER. Where to, Esmé, my love?"

"Into the future."

AUTHOR'S NOTES

WHO KNOWS WHERE and when an idea takes place, takes hold, and emerges later—into a story?

My fascination with the 1930s may have begun with a visit to New York City some years ago, when we visited friends, saw a Broadway show (or three or four), and had a memorable dinner at the famous 21 Club. I will be forever grateful to Lila and Bromley Steele for taking my husband and me to dinner at 21 and arranging for a tour of the historic speakeasy hidden deep in the cellar.

Down the narrow stairs, behind the camouflaged two-and-a-half-ton secret door, we entered the speakeasy, a beautifully appointed wood-paneled dining room and wine cellar. Thousands of wine bottles once awaited celebrities and special occasions. We admired the cozy private booth (with phone) where New York Mayor Jimmy Walker (in office 1926-1932), a strong opponent of Prohibition, enjoyed illicit drinks with his friends. And we were told a story about Mayor Jimmy.

Sometime during Prohibition, the mayor was partying with his pals down in the speakeasy when federal agents unexpectedly raided the club above. The speakeasy crowd partied on for hours, untroubled. But when the mayor was finally ready to leave, the feds were still upstairs, ransacking the premises for contraband liquor. So Mayor Jimmy Walker used his private line to call out his NYPD boys in blue to tow away all the agents' cars. The feds ran out in a panic to chase their vehicles, and the mayor made his escape.

Though my Art Deco series begins in 1934, just post-Prohibition, I could spin a dozen or more stories from that one inspiration. In *These Crooked Things* I mention a visit that Esmé made to that infamous speakeasy before Repeal, and the fact that after Prohibition many bootleggers were wondering what the heck to do next.

Magazines from the period are a treasure trove of trends, ads, pictures, and stories. *The New Yorker, McCall's, Ladies' Home Journal, Good Housekeeping, Delineator,* and *Pictorial Review* are just a few of the many popular magazines in print at the time. *The New York Times* Archives allowed me to follow the news day-to-day in the time period of this book.

All these sources provide a contemporaneous view of the times, with a sense of the lingo and the styles and attitudes and what was served for dinner. And then there are the amazing movies of the early 1930s, in particular all those wild, funny, sexy, surprising 'pre-Code' films. These were produced before Hollywood's infamous Hays Office and their Production Code finally kicked in, halfway through 1934. A few examples: *The Thin Man, Dinner at Eight,* and *Murder at the Vanities.*

My thanks and appreciation to artist Kate Lamoure, who outdid herself creating the beautiful cover artwork for this book. It was such a pleasure working with her again.

And what else? We always need that one person who keeps us together through all the long nights, the starts and stops, the discussions of plot and character. Not to mention the frustrations of technology. For me that person is Bob Williams, designer and editor extraordinaire, and incidentally, my husband. He is so talented, attentive to detail, and just plain wonderful, he might be a wizard in disguise.

MYSTERY AND THRILLER writer Ellen Byerrum is a former journalist in Washington, D.C., as well as a produced and published playwright. She also received her private investigator's registration in the Commonwealth of Virginia. Her new Art Deco mysteries, *Crook Tales for Two* and *These Crooked Things*, are a departure from her previous books in terms of setting and time (New York City, after Prohibition). Yet they are still what she calls *screwball noir*, melding mystery, comedy, and romance.

Byerrum's Crime of Fashion Mysteries feature D.C. fashion reporter Lacey Smithsonian, whose talent for solving crimes with fashion clues leads her to bodies dyed blue, haunted shawls, and the lost jewel-filled corset of a Romanov princess. Two books, *Killer Hair* and *Hostile Makeover*, were filmed for Lifetime. The *Brief Luminous Flight of the Firefly* is the 1940s prequel to her Crime of Fashion series, and features a very young Mimi Smith, the "Great-aunt Mimi" mentioned throughout the series. *Firefly* takes place during WWII in Washington, D.C.

Beyond the traditional mystery form, Byerrum has written a stand-alone psychological thriller, *The Woman in the Dollhouse*, which Best Thrillers says, "bewitches on page one and continues to mesmerize until its shocking conclusion." She has also penned a middle grade mystery, *The Children Didn't See Anything*. More recently, she published a children's rhyming picture book, *Sherlocktopus Holmes: Eight Arms of the Law*. In addition, two of her plays (under her pen name "Eliot Byerrum") have been published by Samuel French, Inc., and are available through Concord Theatricals.